FAIR
PLAY

Center Point
Large Print

Also by Deeanne Gist and available from Center Point Large Print:

It Happened at the Fair

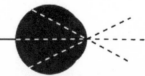

This Large Print Book carries the Seal of Approval of N.A.V.H.

FAIR PLAY

DEEANNE GIST

CENTER POINT LARGE PRINT
THORNDIKE, MAINE

This Center Point Large Print edition is published in the year 2014 by arrangement with Howard Books, a division of Simon & Schuster, Inc.

Copyright © 2014 by Pressing Matters Publishing Company, Inc.

The text of this Large Print edition is unabridged. In other aspects, this book may vary from the original edition. Printed in the United States of America on permanent paper. Set in 16-point Times New Roman type.

ISBN: 978-1-62899-139-0

Library of Congress Cataloging-in-Publication Data

Gist, Deeanne.
Fair play / Deeanne Gist. — Center Point Large Print edition.
pages ; cm
Summary: "In this historical romance, a lady doctor and a Texas Ranger meet at the 1893 Chicago World's Fair. Despite their difference of opinion on the role of women, they fight for the underprivileged children in the Nineteenth Ward"—Provided by publisher.
ISBN 978-1-62899-139-0 (library binding : alk. paper)
1. World's Columbian Exposition (1893–: Chicago, Ill.)—Fiction.
2. Large type books. I. Title.
PS3607.I55F35 2014b
813'.6—dc23
2014011818

In Memory of
Texas Ranger Captain John M. Wood
with whom I had the privilege of visiting
while researching this book.

He was ninety-nine years old and the oldest
living Texas Ranger at the time. He shared
with me stories of his childhood and his days
as a Ranger. You are missed, John.

Special Thanks to my PIT Crew
(Personal Intercessory Team)
Dan & Janie Alexander
Sandy Hickey
Marcia Macey
Debra Larsen Smith

who shored me up while I wrote the first draft
of *Fair Play*. Their words of encouragement and
daily support got me through many long, long
days and late, late nights.

Thank you, my friends,
from the bottom of my heart.

ACKNOWLEDGMENTS

When it was time to find images for the beginnings of many chapters, I wasn't sure where to start. In the past, I've simply used images from my personal library. But I didn't have any photos of Chicago's West Side. So please allow me to take a minute and thank all the folks who helped me find the perfect photographs and who went out of their way to make sure the paperwork went smoothly.

- Lena Reynolds, Research Assistant, Hull House Museum

- Valerie Harris, Special Collections, University of Illinois at Chicago

- Daniel Harper, Special Collections, University of Illinois at Chicago

- Joyce Shaw, Business Development, Chicago Transit Authority

- Bruce Moffat, Author and Manager, Chicago Transit Authority

- Erica Simmons, Author of juvenile book on Playground Movement

- Melanie Emerson, Ryerson & Burnham Libraries, Art Institute of Chicago

All images have been footnoted. Please refer to the Illustration Credits to see where they originated.

I'd also like to thank Meg Moseley, Gayle Evers, Veranne Graham, and Harold Graham for their valuable critiques. J. Mark Bertrand for choreographing my fight scene. Tennessee Gist for drawing a diagram of the Hull House Playground. And Jesse Pareja for giving me a personal tour of Jackson Park and Chicago's West Side. What would I do without y'all? Thanks so much!

MEMORIAL ART PALACE

"Skirting around an enormous bronze lion flanking
the entrance, the woman led Billy onto the grass
and toward the north side of the building."

CHAPTER 1

"Open those doors!" A woman in the new common-sense skirt shook her umbrella at a Chicago World's Fair guard. The motion raised her eye-poppingly short hemline another six inches and revealed a bit of stocking above her navy gaiters.

Blocking the entrance to the International Convention of Woman's Progress, a bearded guard crossed his arms and planted his legs wide. A wave of resentment swept through the wriggling mass of females stretching clear out to the street.

Eve was not the only woman to raise Cain, Billy thought, ducking and dodging her way through the sea of bonnets.

Still, she needed immediate admittance. That guard might not unbolt the doors for an apostle of modern bloomerism, but he'd open them for her. Dr. Billy Jack Tate. She held a seat on the speaking platform and had spent untold hours writing, rewriting, and practicing the address she would present to this Woman's Congress.

"Excuse me, sir." She waved a handkerchief above her head. "I'm Dr. Billy Jack Tate. I'm scheduled to speak in Columbus Hall and I need entrance immediately."

Tall and unmovable in his blue-braided uniform,

he glanced in her direction, then returned his attention to the crowd at large.

She narrowed her eyes. There was no way he could have missed her. Not in this gown. For though the bright spring day offered warmth and a promise of summer, the predominant color of gowns being worn to the Congress was drab brown. Except for hers. She'd allowed the dressmaker to talk her into a startling shade of green with vivid pink accents. A decision she'd second-guessed a thousand times.

Squeezing herself between tightly packed bodies, she pressed her way to the front like a pair of stockings in a wringer. "I say, sir. I need—"

A transom above the guard swung open and a head poked through. A head with mussed salt-and-pepper hair, a harassed-looking expression, and a body cut off from sight.

"The Hall is filled to capacity and more," he shouted, then grabbed the windowsill, his shoulders bobbing. Taking a quick glance inside, he regained his balance on what must have been a ladder, then once again turned to them. "Admission will no longer be granted. I advise you to turn around and go home."

Cries of protest covered Billy's efforts to capture the man's attention.

"Sir!" she called again. "I'm Dr. Billy Ja—"

Retreating like a frightened turtle, he slammed

the transom shut. The guard widened his stance.

Another roar of disapproval rang from the women. Some raised their voices, others raised their fists.

Caught up in outrage, the dress reformer scrambled over the rope, her split skirt parting, before she started up the steps. "Move aside!"

Whipping a short broadsword from its scabbard, the guard held it in front of him.

The woman paused, her right foot on one step, her left on another. Billy tensed. The murmuring of the crowd tapered off.

The sword was supposed to be for ornamentation more than anything else, but it was well polished and, most likely, freshly sharpened.

"I've got a patrol wagon just beyond the copse to cart off the disorderly." His voice was low, even, and full of conviction. "I've a force of guards that can be dispatched the moment I give the signal, and a swarm of the most efficient body of men ever assembled in the world will be here en masse. I strongly suggest you step down."

A sparrow, unaware of the tension, flapped to a stop on the landing and chirped a greeting.

Billy eased her way to the front. Surely it wouldn't come to bloodshed, but just in case . . .

"Come on, Martha," a woman nearby coaxed. "Let's try another entrance."

Though the guard never took his eyes from the threat, Billy sensed he was aware of every movement around him. Chill bumps rushed up her spine. She dipped under the rope.

Crouching into a half squat, he tossed the sword to his other hand, formed a half circle with his arms, and darted his gaze between them.

"I'm Dr. Billy Jack Tate." Her voice carried in the sudden quiet, similar to the way it traveled across the frozen pond at her sister's place. She maintained a calm, reasonable tone. "I'm a surgeon and a speaker here at the Congress. We want no trouble." She turned her attention to the woman called Martha. "I think we'd best do as he says. He's given a pledge to follow orders and the orders are no one goes inside. We are not a bunch of barbaric men, but women. Women much too sensible and creative to resort to brute force."

A long, tense moment crackled between them. Finally, the woman jerked up her chin and spun about. Again, she straddled the rope rather than ducking underneath.

The guard did not relax his posture, did not replace the sword in its scabbard, and did not remove the force of his gaze. "Step down."

Billy offered him a calm smile. "I mean no threat. I really am a speaker and I really do need to slip inside. My address begins in"—she glanced at her watch pin—"thirty-eight minutes."

"You're no more a doctor than I am a house-wife. Now step down."

She bristled. "I most certainly am a doctor. I

earned a medical degree from the University of Michigan, I've practiced in hospitals all across this country for the past seven years, I'm an expert on anatomy, and my speech is about being a woman in a man's profession. Now, *you* step down or I'll let the organizers of this Congress know just exactly who's responsible for keeping me from addressing the thousands who are waiting to hear from me."

With each qualification, his expression became more and more amused until, with her final threat, he emitted a short huff. At least he'd straightened and lowered his sword, though he hadn't put it away. "I'll hand it to you, miss. You're quick on your feet. But you're the one who said women were crafty, not me. Either way, I'm not one to be taken in by a pretty face."

"Creative. I said we were creative, not crafty."

He tucked the sword away. "Same thing. Now, go on. I'm not letting you or anybody else inside."

She glanced at the door. "But I really am who I say I am."

With a heavy sigh, he shooed her with his hands. "I mean it. You can either get yourself back on the other side of that rope or I'll have Willie over there escort you to the patrol wagon. From there, you'll go straight to the city jail. And Chicago's is a particularly nasty one that doesn't do a good job of separating the woman prisoners from the male ones."

With a touch of unease, she glanced to the area he indicated with his head. Amidst millinery of all sizes and shapes, a rather burly man stood only a few steps away. He tipped his hat.

Lips tightening, she flounced back down the steps. She'd have to try another entrance. But the building was huge. By the time she shoved through the crowds and appealed to each guard, the slot for her address would be over and gone.

She should have allowed herself more time. But she hadn't expected so many women, and she certainly never considered a building such as this would fill to capacity.

Before slipping underneath the rope, she looked back over her shoulder. "I'll have your name—so I can tell the officials who barred my way."

He gave a bow. "Peter Stracke. But everybody calls me Pete." He gave her a wink.

She ducked under the rope. The women immediately forged a path for her. Mr. Stracke might not have believed her, but they did and they had the utmost respect for her.

She'd gone no more than ten yards when an old country woman grabbed her hand. "Doc?"

Billy nodded.

"I can get ya in." She looked both ways, then leaned closer. "But it won't be through no doors."

Billy wasn't sure which was more potent, the smell of the woman's breath or the smell of her unwashed body. It wasn't the woman's fault, though. The importance of good hygiene was something those in Billy's profession were in constant argument over. And though she felt she was in the right, she was very much in the minority.

She looked at her watch. Twenty-four minutes left. "Is it fast? Does it involve any guards?"

The woman smiled, more teeth missing than present. "Jus' follow me."

Skirting around an enormous bronze lion flanking the entrance, the woman led her onto the grass and toward the north side of the building. The farther they walked, the less congested it was until finally they reached the fringes of the crowd.

"Quick, over here." Ducking beside a puny bush, the woman dropped to her knees and began to jiggle a cellar window.

Billy glanced behind them. No guards within sight, but several women watched unabashedly. With a growing smile, one of them corralled those around her, then directed them to turn their backs and form a human wall around Billy and her cohort.

The gesture warmed her heart. Women were a wonderful breed. Such a shame they didn't run the country.

"There's a nail loose." The woman grunted, her entire body shaking as she continued to rattle the window.

Dropping down beside her, Billy tried not to think about the moist dirt beneath her knees. Better to arrive with a soiled skirt than not at all. Lining up her fingers along the opposite side of the frame, she pressed as hard as she could.

"That's it." The woman's breath came in huffs. "I clean this place at night. I been tellin' the men-folk about this window for months now, but they can't be bothered with it."

Without warning, the frame swung inward, crashing against the wall. The momentum slammed Billy into the stone wall above the opening. The rim of her hat wrenched its pins to an awkward angle and ripped the hair entwined by them.

Sucking in her breath, she pushed away. At least her hat had protected her face. If the brim hadn't stopped her, she'd have likely broken her nose.

"Go on." The woman waved her arm toward the window.

Ignoring the pain in her scalp, Billy considered her options. There was nothing for it but to lie full out on the ground and shimmy herself in. With a sigh, she flopped down and stretched her arms toward the opening. She was a quarter of the way through when she realized the window was level with the ceiling of the cellar.

She returned her hands to the opening and pulled herself backward. "I'm going to have to go feetfirst. It's a good eight-foot drop to the floor."

Entering feetfirst wasn't nearly as easy as head-first. The old woman grabbed Billy's ankles and guided her feet through.

Raising up on her arms, Billy propelled herself as far toward the window as best she could, then collapsed to her tummy and lifted her hips. Like a worm she inched backward, her body making progress, her skirts and petticoats staying where they'd started.

Without too much effort, her pantalet-clad legs made it inside and dangled against the freezing-cold stone cellar wall. But her skirts were inside out, cocooning her upper body within their folds and inhibiting all progress.

"I'm stuck," she called, sputtering against the fabric of her skirts.

Within seconds, all hands were on deck and bodily lowering her the rest of the way in.

"Wait!" she squeaked. "Slow down! My dress—it's going to tear. And I'm . . . I'm going to fall!"

The women clutched her arms, their grips digging into tender flesh.

Billy lifted her head, the brim of her hat hitting the edge of the window. "Easy. Go as slow as you can."

The rough wooden frame scraped against her midsection, tearing the delicate cotton of her corset cover. Her pantalets traveled up her legs, bunching at her thighs.

In an effort to see how far she was from the floor, she wiggled her feet. Nothing but open air.

They lowered her a bit more. Pain shot through her arms at the awkward angle.

"Wait," she breathed. "Let go of my right arm."

They released it. The pain in her left arm increased tenfold.

She pulled her free arm inside and steadied herself against the wall. "When I count to three. Ready? One . . . two . . . *three.*"

They let go. She hit ground almost immediately, then her knees gave. Between her tangled skirts and the unforgiving floor, it took her a moment to orient herself.

"Doc?" It was the old woman. "You all right?"

She took a mental catalog of all extremities. Other than weak knees and throbbing arms, everything seemed to be in working order. "Yes. Yes! I'm good. Thank you so much."

Instead of a chorus of encouragement, she heard nothing. Complete silence. Eerie silence.

A drop of moisture from the ceiling plopped to the floor. Pushing the hair from her face, she straightened her hat and looked up at her comrades. Four faces peered through the window. All attention was focused on the opposite wall.

The hairs on the back of her neck prickled. Please, don't let it be a rat. She hated rats.

"What is it?" she hissed.

They said nothing, their eyes wide.

Careful not to make any sudden moves, she drew her legs beneath her and straightened, inch by inch by inch.

Finally, she turned, then sucked in a breath.

The silhouette of a man—no, not a man, a guard. A guard with monstrously broad shoulders, a trim waist, a scabbard, and a pair of very muscular legs stood with one shoulder against the doorframe and one ankle crossed in front of the other, exposing a pair of cowpuncher boots.

He cocked his head. "Goin' somewhere?"

COLUMBUS HALL[1]

"I need to go upstairs. I'm scheduled
to speak in Columbus Hall."

CHAPTER 2

The hum of distant electric bulbs explained where the soft glow of light was coming from. Because it was behind him, she couldn't make out more than his outline. And with her large brimmed hat, she felt sure he couldn't see her face. But anything the shade of her hat didn't reach would be easily discernible from his position.

Images flashed through her mind. Her boots breaking the barrier. Her body wriggling as she inchwormed her way inside. Her skirts not following as they should. Her pantalets traveling up her calves. Her pantalets bunching about her thighs. Her back end clearly delineated by her position. Her lower half swinging from the window as her toes sought out a firm foundation.

Heat rushed through her body. She wanted to drop through the floor, to lash out in anger, to shove him with her hands. *Something*. Following that, the urge to flee overwhelmed her.

She managed to resist them all. She'd long since learned how to hold her ground in front of men, regardless of how delicate the situation.

Whispers came from the opening, then a slam as someone wrenched the window closed.

He hadn't moved, hadn't even breathed, that she could tell.

She cast about for something to say. "How long have you been there?"

"Pretty much the whole time."

She kept her arms to her sides, resisting the temptation to fidget. *No weakness,* she reminded herself. *Show no weakness. Make him forget you're a woman.*

She swallowed. Not much chance of that happening.

"I heard the window crash open." His Southern drawl had a gravelly sound to it. "I came right down to investigate."

Investigate. Blood rushed to her cheeks. What would a man say at a time like this? "Why didn't you help me? Surely you could see I needed some assistance."

Lifting his chin, he scratched his jaw. "I wasn't exactly sure what to grab."

She needed to change the subject. Try and erase those images from his mind. But she'd been working with men long enough to know that those images wouldn't easily erase.

"I need to go."

He nodded. "Yes, you do."

"No, I mean, I need to go upstairs. I'm scheduled to speak in Columbus Hall."

"When?"

"Very shortly. I need to hurry."

"Who are you?"

"That's not important." She wasn't about to tell him who she was.

"Clearly it is important, or you wouldn't be one of the speakers."

"I'm nobody famous."

He crossed his arms. "Well, that's disappointing. It would have been a pretty big moment for me if I'd been able to say I'd seen, oh, I don't know, Elizabeth Stanton's trousers?"

"They're pantalets, not trousers." She could have bitten her tongue. Had she become so used to discussing sensitive topics with male colleagues and patients that she'd forgotten how to carry on properly outside of work?

"Pantalets, trousers." He shrugged. "Whatever you want to call them, everyone knows you woman reformers wear them because you not only want to appropriate our clothing, but our power as well." He gave her skirt a quick glance. "And though what you had on were less sturdy than what us men opt for, I can say with complete conviction that they were plenty powerful."

His teasing tone was unmistakable. She was not amused. Her gown bore no resemblance to what a dress reformer would wear. She had no split skirt, no shortened hem, no drab colors. Every single thing she wore was feminine. Just because she was wearing bloomers and working in a man's profession didn't mean she wanted to

24

be male. Usurping their power, however, was a different matter entirely.

Still, she wasn't about to engage in a debate with him. She glanced at her watch pin. She couldn't see it, of course, but maybe he didn't know that. "I'm sorry, but if you'll excuse me?"

She started toward him.

He pulled away from the frame, straightening to his full height. Good heavens. She'd heard one of the criteria for being a World's Fair Columbian Guard was they had to be above a certain height, but this man . . . this man was a veritable giant. His head barely cleared the top of the doorframe.

"I'm afraid I can't let you up there," he said.

"I'm afraid I must insist." She could see him trying to discern her features. She pulled the brim of her hat farther down.

Ordinarily, she'd have told him who she was. She was very proud of her medical degree. She could probably run academic circles around him. After all, how much brainpower could it take to be a guard? Probably not much. Only brawn. And of that, he had plenty.

"I'm quite determined to give my talk." She used her stern voice. One she'd perfected in countless dealings with uncooperative patients. "If you throw me out, I'll turn right around and come back in. You'll spend the entire day traipsing up and down those stairs."

Looking down, he brushed some loose gravel

with the toe of his cowpuncher boot. "Tempting. Very tempting."

She slid her eyes closed. She hadn't meant it like that. "Please, Mr. . . . ?"

He touched the corner of his cap. "Scott. Hunter Scott of Houston, Texas. And you are?"

"Late for my appointment. Please step aside."

"You don't want me to know who you are, do you? Which makes me think that you're either lying or you really are famous."

"I'm not lying and I'm not famous. I'm late. And getting later."

He tapped a finger against his trouser leg. "Columbus Hall, huh?"

"Yes."

"Well, I suppose it won't hurt to walk you over there. If they're expecting you, then all's well. But if they're not, then you'll have to hoof it out of here." He hesitated. "And don't forget, you promised you'd come back in. And you can put money on the fact that I'll be keeping a sharp eye on the cellar for any . . . unusual activity."

Rather than respond, she shooed him back with her hands.

He offered his arm. She sailed past it and took her own self up the stairs.

It didn't feel as good as she thought it would. He followed right behind, and try as she might, there was no way to keep her hips from swaying with each stair-step. She knew what he was

26

thinking, what he was picturing. And he knew she knew.

When they finally made it to the ground floor and stepped into the corridor, the sound of ladies' voices hit her as abruptly as the stone wall had hit her when the window flew open. Chatter and laughter ricocheted throughout the cavernous hallway, bouncing off the high roof and meshing together in a horrendous composition. In order to be heard above the melee, the women simply spoke louder.

The press of bodies was every bit as clogged as the gathering outside. Their combined warmth produced a moisture-laden potpourri of lavender, rose, and jasmine.

The officials were right. There really wasn't room for admitting anyone else.

"Columbus Hall is toward the front." Mr. Scott pointed a finger in a westerly direction.

She stared at the hem of his jacket. Thank goodness he was so tall. Her hat brim easily kept her face concealed from him.

"Come on," he said.

Without giving her a choice, he grabbed hold of her arm. Not her elbow, as a gentleman might do, but her upper arm, as a policeman does when he's hauling off a prisoner. She allowed the rough handling, though. Late as she was, she'd willingly sacrifice her pride as a means to an end.

He knew where Columbus Hall was. She didn't.

And he kept a half step in front of her, clearing a way for them by virtue of his impressive size. When they reached the doorway, however, she began to balk. A person had only one chance to make a first impression. Being dragged to the front like a criminal was not the impression she wanted to create.

"Thank you for your assistance, sir. You can let go now. I can manage on—"

"Scott!" The shout came from several yards down the hallway.

Mr. Scott whipped his head around while keeping a firm grip on her arm. His height allowed him to see over the heads and hats of all the ladies.

"Over here! Quickly!" The voice was decidedly male.

Mr. Scott homed in on the caller. "What is it?"

Though no answer was forthcoming, some type of signal must have been transmitted.

He frowned. "Can it wait? I have a . . ."

She lowered her chin, shielding her face.

"I have a situation here," he said.

She rolled her eyes.

After what must have been another signal, he mumbled something under his breath and spun her toward him, bracketing both her arms. "I'll be back. And when I am, you'd better be on that stage."

She stared at his boots. They were covered with

animal skin of some kind. Not crocodile. Something completely unfamiliar to her. "I'll be there."

"Go on, then."

"Scott!" This summons more urgent than the last.

Without waiting to see if she complied, he released her and made his way through the throng. She'd expected him to plow through with no regard for those in his way. But he excused himself as he lightly took woman after woman by the shoulders and nudged them just enough so he could squeeze by.

She rubbed her arm. He'd not been nearly so gentle with her. Shaking herself, she glanced at her watch pin. Good heavens. Two o'clock exactly.

Pulling open the door, she balked. The auditorium was enormous and full to overflowing. It would take her several minutes to reach the platform. Perhaps she'd been too hasty in letting Mr. Scott get away. She glanced over her shoulder, but he'd already been absorbed by the crowd.

BERTHA PALMER[2]

"As president of the Board of Lady Managers and one of the four chief executives of the Chicago World's Fair, Mrs. Palmer was arguably the most powerful woman in the world."

CHAPTER 3

Hunter slipped into Columbus Hall, his eyes immediately drawn to the stage. Sure enough, there she was. Right at the lectern.

Though he wasn't close enough to discern any features, he'd recognize that gown anywhere. Its lime-green skirt and bright-pink sash were like a tropical garden in the midst of dirt dauber nests. 'Course, what was underneath was mighty delectable, too.

"Men may be gathering at the World's Columbian Exposition to admire one another's innovations," she said, her voice clear and carrying to the rapt crowd. "But since the dawn of history, women were the sources of all early inventions."

He lifted his brows.

"In order to keep herself and her children from harm, she formed homes in the caves of the earth. She was the first to cultivate the soil, produce the crops, grind the grain, raise livestock, and dress the skins. She was the first to exert a healing influence and practice medicine. Man has but supplemented and improved upon woman's original ideas."

What a great bunch of tripe. Hadn't these women ever heard of a fellow named Adam? But her audience absorbed every word. Gave a great cheer of pride. He scanned the room. Not a chair was empty. Not a spot unfilled.

To his left, plaster casts and models had been drafted as favorable perches by the more enterprising maidens. Two had even climbed to sit on each knee of a John Milton statue. That old-time reformer must surely be looking down from heaven with glee. He'd always gone against the current and he'd definitely liked the ladies. The younger, the better.

"Men believe it is unfeminine," she continued, "even monstrous, for women to take a place beside them in their spheres of occupation. They claim we should be lovingly guarded and cherished within the sacred confines of our homes."

No mistake about it, Hunter thought. Chivalry had been around for centuries. It elevated women to the highest pedestal. Why on God's green earth wouldn't they want to stay there?

"But what, I ask you, is to become of the unhappy women who are not living in ideal situations?" Her voice rose with conviction. "Who do not have a manly and loving arm to shield them? Who have been born to poverty? Whose husbands work in the most degrading industrial occupations, laboring as underpaid drudges? Whose men earn far less than what is needed to feed their families? Must these women sit by and watch while they and their children starve?"

Murmuring rumbled through the audience.

Millinery quivered as its wearers shook their heads in denial. Shifting his weight, Hunter perused the packed room. There wasn't enough bass or tenor in the entire place to stock even a country church choir. The only real showing of gentlemen was dignitaries up onstage sitting to the right of Miss Pantalets-Trousers.

They presided in large medieval-like thrones while the female notables sat to the left in modest, plain chairs. The sheep and the goats. Though at this point, he wasn't sure which were which.

"No!" She gripped the edges of the lectern. "We have no desire to be helpless and dependent. We have full use of our faculties and rejoice in exercising them. There is nothing wrong with standing shoulder to shoulder with our men, supplementing and assisting them as true partners. Does this diminish our womanhood? Absolutely not. Nor does it diminish the manliness and strength of our husbands."

Applause softened by gloves accompanied hundreds of waving handkerchiefs. He sure did feel sorry for Mr. Pantalets-Trousers. He couldn't imagine being married to a working woman, no matter how delectable she was.

"Through education and training, we must prepare ourselves to meet whatever fate life may bring until our usefulness is demonstrated, fully understood, and acknowledged. Until we convince the world that ability is not a matter of sex."

More applause and handkerchiefs. This time, even a few whistles.

"*Venimus, vidimus, vicimus*!" she shouted, raising her defiant fist in the air. "We came. We saw. We conquered!"

The women surged to their feet, their applause and whistles unrestrained.

An unsettling sensation in his stomach made it cramp up. *Not again,* he thought.

As he'd done for the past couple of weeks, he held his breath until it passed. Once it eased, he tried to tell himself it wouldn't happen again. Yet each day his discomfort had grown exponentially. He returned his attention to the stage.

Miss Pantalets-Trousers stepped away from the lectern.

Opening the door, he backed out of the room, thanking the stars above that he lived in Texas, where the women were sensible, feminine, and full of Southern charm. He couldn't wait until this six-month stint at the fair was over and he could get back to all he held dear.

Flushed with pleasure, Billy moved toward the wings of the platform. Jennie Lozier, daughter to the woman who'd run for vice president of the United States back in '81, rose and approached the lectern.

Just as Billy reached the steps, Mrs. Bertha Palmer stepped forward and took her elbow, drawing her toward a privacy area behind the stage.

Billy's pulse kicked up. As president of the Board of Lady Managers and one of the four chief executives of the Chicago World's Fair, Mrs. Palmer was arguably the most powerful woman in the world. For the first time ever, women were acting under a commission from Congress and stood equal to men in a great international enterprise. Mrs. Palmer was wealthy beyond imagination, too. All it took for a person —either male or female—to succeed was a nod of endorsement from her, but failure could be attained with the same ease.

Billy gave a surreptitious look at the woman's elegant bonnet, her ribbon collaret, and the large puffed sleeves of her silk gown, all in subdued shades of mingled violet and green. Had Billy's speech been too bold? Too forward? Too controversial? Or perhaps Mrs. Palmer had taken objection to the brightness of Billy's skirt?

That thought led to her unorthodox entrance into the building. She missed a step. Surely Mrs. Palmer hadn't heard? How could word have traveled from outside to inside and all the way up to the platform in such a short time?

She swallowed. She was at the International Convention of Woman's Progress. If there was one thing women excelled at, it was the spreading of titillating tales.

Moisture beaded Billy's hairline. How would she ever explain such shocking behavior?

"Are you feeling well, my dear?" Mrs. Palmer took Billy's gloved hand into hers and gave it a pat. Her wavy blond hair framed a face with the barest hint of age. "You're quite pale all of a sudden."

"Am I?" she breathed. "Must be all the excitement."

Mrs. Palmer patted her again, her brown eyes softening. "You did a fine job out there."

Billy waited for the "But . . ." Yet it wasn't forthcoming.

"Oh." Gently withdrawing her hand, Billy stemmed the impulse to curtsy. "Thank you."

"I have a favor to ask of you."

"Of course." Was this how the privileged couched dismissals? By saying they wanted you to do them a favor? As in, never darken their doorstep again?

"I know you're working on a paper about germ theory for the College of Physicians and Surgeons of Chicago, and you're establishing a private practice, but I was wondering if you could help me with something."

Good heavens. If the woman knew that, then she knew Billy was writing the paper to pass the time as she waited, and waited, and waited for patients to notice her newly painted shingle. Painted on both sides, it was attached like a tail to a string of other doctors' signs hanging at the corner drugstore. It had inspired only one call in five months.

She'd been warned no one would seek out a lady doctor when there were plenty of male ones around. She'd been advised to start up in a city she had connections in. And she'd been told she was crazy to go to Chicago, where she didn't know a soul.

But she'd ignored them all, convinced Chicago was filled with unmarried women who were suffering—perhaps even dying—simply because they couldn't force themselves to submit to an examination by a male doctor. Now, of course, she knew that though some did feel that way, they weren't exactly flocking to her door.

And each day her savings and her optimism had waned a bit more. The only reason she'd been asked to speak today was because the woman doctor who was originally scheduled had become pregnant and suggested Billy take her place.

So here she was. Leading a charge for women to make their way in a man's world when all she'd ever done for the seven years since she'd graduated was to work for men in St. Louis, Boston, Detroit, and Ann Arbor hospitals.

Now the game was up. Somehow the beautiful, smart, and influential Mrs. Palmer had discovered Billy was woefully unqualified to lead a charge of this kind. She wasn't a dress reformer. She wasn't a prohibitionist. She wasn't a crusader.

She was simply a thirty-year-old woman bachelor who'd finally felt as if she had enough experience to step out on her own. To make her own way. To become her own boss. A woman who'd finally accepted what her mother had told her all along. No man would ever marry a hen medic.

"One of the doctors we commissioned for the Woman's Building has typhoid fever," Mrs. Palmer said.

Relief swept through Billy. Now, this she could do. "I'd be happy to take a look at her."

The corners of Mrs. Palmer's mouth lifted slightly. "Actually, what I'd really like you to do is step in and take her place."

Billy's lips parted. "In the Woman's Building? At the fair?"

"That's right. Within our building there is not one single thing made by the hand of man. Everything is by women. The architecture, the exhibits, the frescoes, the sculptures, the paintings, the tomes in the library, all of it. Why should our infirmary be any different?"

"The staff is female only?"

"It is."

Excitement began to bubble up within her. "How often would you need me?"

"Mondays, Wednesdays, and Fridays. From eleven o'clock to seven."

It would mean being away from her "office" three days a week, but she wasn't about to pass up an opportunity to practice. Especially not at the fair, where she was bound to make influential connections.

She held out her hand. "I'd be honored."

Mrs. Palmer blinked, staring at Billy's hand. Billy flushed. Women of Mrs. Palmer's caliber did not shake hands the way men did.

Trying to recover, she moved the offending appendage to Mrs. Palmer's arm and gave it a quick squeeze. "Thank you."

"There is one more thing."

"Yes?" Billy waited.

"I'll need to know your fee."

She suppressed a groan. She hated that question, never knowing what to charge or how to answer. If she charged too little, she ran the risk of devaluing herself and losing the respect of her clientele. If she charged too much, she might dissuade them altogether.

Seeking some neutral ground, she projected as nonchalant an air as she could. "Oh, the usual fee."

Mrs. Palmer smiled. "Excellent. Then five dollars a day will be sufficient?"

Billy's breath caught. Five dollars a *day?* A fortune! "Yes. That's perfect."

Hooking her hand in the crook of Billy's arm, Mrs. Palmer turned them back toward Columbus

Hall. "Wonderful. How quickly can you begin?"

"How soon do you need me?"

"Wednesday is two days away."

Billy nodded. "Then two days it is."

MARSHALL FIELD'S[3]

"Billy placed a hand on her hat, lifted her chin, and squinted in order to see to the very top of Marshall Field's new nine-story terra-cotta building."

CHAPTER 4

Colonel Rice, commandant of the Columbian Guard, leaned his chair back on two legs, his shiny head offset by an impressive handlebar mustache. "You conducted yourself well at the Woman's Congress, Scott."

"Thank you, sir." With feet apart, Hunter placed one hand behind his back, the other tucked his cap beneath his arm. Taking care to avoid eye contact, he stared at a hall tree behind the colonel. On its flattened cactus-like shape hung a gray wool coat and a black umbrella.

"Therefore," Rice continued, "I'm going to pull you from the Administration Building and assign you to the Woman's Building."

Hunter hesitated. "The Woman's Building, sir?"

"Your shift will start at nine o'clock in the morning. You'll work four hours on. Four hours off. Then four hours on again."

This shift was better than the evening one he'd been working, but the *Woman's Building?* "Isn't that just filled with a mess of gewgaws made by women, sir?"

"It doesn't have anything like the model Treasury Building you've been guarding, if that's what you mean."

That's exactly what he meant. He was a Texas

Ranger. A member of the most elite force in not only his state, but in the entire country. When the colonel had recruited him for this six-month stint, Hunter had assumed he'd be protecting foreign kings, queens, princes, and other dignitaries attending the fair. At the very least, he'd expected to guard the most valuable exhibits, such as the African diamonds.

Hunter lowered his gaze to the colonel's. "With respect, sir, are you sure that's where my talents are best served?"

"The place is filled with art, jewels, and frippery on loan from the private collections of queens and princesses. I need a good man on it. Furthermore, the building is overrun with women. Bossy women. Women whom men might decide to put in their place." He dropped his chair legs to the ground with a *thunk*. "I'll not have that. Those women have worked long and hard and they've been sanctioned by Congress. I want it seen to that they are treated with the utmost respect and deference. Exactly the way you treated the ones at the Woman's Convention."

He hadn't treated those women at the convention any differently than normal. Well, except for Miss Pantalets-Trousers. He'd not treated her with deference and respect. He'd thought about it. Thought about turning his back to her when it became apparent what was going to transpire, but he hadn't. The lawman in him knew better.

You never turned your back on a perpetrator. And somebody sneaking into the cellar was definitely a perpetrator. Female or no. Trousers or no.

Maybe he should tell the colonel about that. But he couldn't, of course. Tales of that sort could ruin a woman, particularly when they were true. And as much as he didn't want this assignment, he wasn't willing to sacrifice a woman's reputation over it.

So he held his tongue. The boys in Company A back home sure would have a laugh, though, if they discovered he'd taken leave from chasing desperadoes in Texas in order to guard and protect a bunch of lace and embroidery in Illinois.

At the corner of Washington and Wabash, Billy placed a hand on her hat, lifted her chin, and squinted in order to see to the very top of Marshall Field's new nine-story terra-cotta building. She tarried, letting her anticipation build as the rhythm of the city pulsed about her.

A high-stepping horse and carriage veered around a plodding workhorse and dray. A newsboy in patched-up britches trapped a stack of papers beneath his arm, the smell of fresh ink wafting on the breeze. "Ded'cation of Illinois Buildin' at the Exposition! Time and schedule printed here!"

Steam whistles from the harbor one block over competed with those of the trains pouring in and out of Michigan Avenue's depot. Cable cars and horsecars crisscrossed the roads, making requisite stops as men and women poured from them and headed straight for Marshall Field's red-striped awnings.

Billy cherished every sound, every sight, every smell. Chicago was all the colors of the rainbow and it had been love at first sight. She'd only intended to stop in the city on her way back from a trip to Milwaukee. Instead, she'd taken one look and fallen head over heels. Before the first day was through, she'd rented an apartment and talked the landlady into letting her use the sitting room downstairs for her patients to wait in.

She sighed. One thing was certain, if she ever felt for a man what she felt for this city, she'd do the proposing herself.

Lifting her skirt, she looked in every direction, then darted across the boulevard, avoiding puddles, horse droppings, and moving vehicles. Field's large show windows displayed summer gowns, though it was only May. Tempted as she was to flatten her nose against the plate glass, she contented herself with standing at a proper distance.

With the exorbitant salary she'd be making, she'd decided to celebrate her new position by indulging in the latest craze—shopping. And this time, instead of window gazing only, she could actually afford to go inside and purchase a ready-made gown. Her first ever.

She stepped beneath the ornate stone front of the store and into the five-story atrium. Had she walked into the Sistine Chapel, she couldn't have been more in awe. Up, up, up the walls went, each floor sporting a gallery of shoppers who, if they'd simply taken the time, could have leaned over the balconies and observed all the activity on the ground floor.

The hum of chatter ebbed and flowed. A cash boy hurried across the marble floor, taking change from one counter to the next. An usher in a sharp, double-breasted suit stepped forward. "May I direct you to a particular department, miss?"

"I . . . I'm not sure."

He smiled, though his prolific mustache hid his lips. "Your first time?"

"My first time inside."

"Well, there's a ribbon sale seven counters down, to the left. The carpet sweepers are also at a special price today, though they're at the end of the middle aisle on the third floor."

"I see." Dazed, she glanced at the highly polished tables filled with silks and shoes, hats and handkerchiefs, parasols and gloves. All meticulously arranged, some folded with precision, others fanned out in artful displays.

"And the ready-made clothing?" she asked.

He indicated a section at the south end of the floor. "Right over there. Allow me to show you."

"No, no. I'm fine. Thank you." She spent the

next two hours simply wandering through each department on the ground floor, weaving between the host of clerks and patrons swarming its aisles. The plethora of trinkets, stationery, jewelry, stockings, laces, hair combs, and trimmings overwhelmed her. And she'd yet to make it to the ready-made section, much less to any of the upper floors.

By the time she did, it wasn't the gowns that drew her attention, but the undergarments. They were beautiful. Corset covers and chemisettes of fine cotton and silk teased the senses. Petticoats, combinations, and summer corsets were trimmed with the tiniest of stitches and delicate lace.

But it was a particular pair of pantalets that she studied the most. They were translucent. Were she to slip them on, the outline of her legs would be just discernible through the fabric. They were certainly nothing like the ones in the Montgomery Ward catalog, nor the coarse, cotton ones she'd sewn for herself.

Soft lacy ruffles trimmed the legs. Pastel-pink ribbon woven through crocheted bands separated the ruffles from the leggings.

Rubbing the cloth between her thumb and fingers, she wondered what that Columbian Guard would have thought of these. If he considered drawers scandalous, he'd have had the shock of his life to discover see-through ones.

She stifled a nervous giggle. Still, the pantalets

held her entranced. She'd never gone to the time or expense of adding ribbons and frills to her lingerie. And she'd certainly never considered wearing transparent ones. Didn't even know there was such a thing. What would be the point?

Yet now, her very plain, very ordinary drawers seemed bulky and awkward, chafing the skin beneath her skirts. How delicious it must feel to wear, just once, pantalets so fine and decidedly naughty.

"May I help you?"

Jumping, Billy snatched her hand back.

"They're lovely, aren't they?" The clerk couldn't have been more than nineteen or twenty. Loose red tendrils curled about her temples and nape, while the length of her hair had been gathered and tied through a tortoiseshell ring. A subtle, flowery scent wafted about her. "As you might have guessed from our selection, all the old-time fabrics from the 1830s, when women wore lawns, dimity, and muslin, are again in vogue."

"For undergarments, you mean?"

"For outer and undergarments." Slipping her hands beneath the folded pantalets, the girl lifted them so Billy could again feel of their softness. "Some, like these, are of gossamer thinness, while others are heavier and more durable."

For the next hour the girl took Billy from department to department, floor to floor, outfitting her from the inside out.

By the time Billy left, she'd spent much more money than she should have. Money she'd set aside as savings. Still, she couldn't suppress her excitement. She would start her new job with a new gown, a new hat, new gloves, new stockings, and the most wicked undergarments she'd ever owned.

WOMAN'S BUILDING[4]

"Billy couldn't help but marvel at the size
of the Woman's Building."

CHAPTER 5

Standing on tiptoe, Billy tried to see more of her new gown in the oval mirror above her wash-stand, but she could only glimpse the upper portion of the summery blue-striped bodice. She straightened the perky bow at its collar, then lowered her heels to the floor.

She loved bows. Always had. But she never wore them. Not when she was trying to compete in a man's world.

Yet she'd be working in the Woman's Building. Surely it would be all right to wear something feminine there. At least, that's what she'd told herself yesterday when she'd purchased the gown. Now, she wasn't so sure.

She picked up her watch pin from atop a traveling trunk. She was supposed to leave in ten minutes. After one last glance in the mirror, she yanked free the bow at her neck, pushed buttons through the holes along her back, and shucked off both bodice and skirt.

She wasn't even sure she should wear one of her shirtwaists and skirts. They were so school-marmish. Perhaps she should wear a nursing uniform. A friend had outgrown one and offered it to Billy for when she'd one day have an office and a nurse to give it to.

Lifting the trunk lid, she dug down to the bottom and pulled the uniform out. It was white and feminine without being overly so. Its familiarity would most likely infuse confidence in patients who weren't used to lady doctors.

By the time she'd changed, attached her chatelaine, and dropped her framed diploma into her satchel, she only had time to grab her hat. She'd have to put it on once she arrived.

Threading her arm through the handle of her satchel, Billy couldn't help but marvel at the size of the Woman's Building. Imagine the entire thing being designed and stocked by women.

As she took in its caryatids and a group of sculptured figures standing on the roofline, she absently removed the long pins from her hat's base and stuck them in her mouth. Round arches rested on Doric pilasters. An open balcony with grand Corinthian columns held a collection of visitors.

Finally, she remembered the time and picked up her pace. Balancing her hat atop her head, she hurried up the steps.

"You might want to slow down, miss." The command in the man's voice was unmistakable. So was his accent.

She stubbed her toe but continued toward him as if she hadn't, refusing to accept what her mind was telling her. It couldn't be. It simply couldn't.

Surely that voice belonged to some other person from the South. She kept her chin tucked as she worked on her hat, just in case.

"I'd hate for you to fall with those skewers in your mouth," he continued.

There it was again. The accent. This time she caught a familiar gravelly sound in his voice. Her stomach jumped in revolt.

"I'm late," she mumbled over the remaining pin in her mouth.

"Better late than becoming a patient in the infirmary you're headed to."

A surge of alarm rushed through her until she realized he hadn't recognized her, but had recognized her uniform as one belonging to a nurse. She hoped.

In a bid for time and an excuse to keep her head tucked, she pulled the pin she'd just placed back out and repositioned it. "I'll be careful."

She reached the landing. And the door. And a pair of cowpuncher boots covered in an unidentifiable animal skin blocking her way. *Oh, no. Oh, no. Oh, no.*

She couldn't look up. She simply couldn't.

"All the same," he said, "I insist you finish what you're doing."

"Oh, for heaven's sake." Yanking the last pin from her mouth, she poked the back of her hat as she tried to find a good spot to insert the pin. All she could think of was the new, wicked, gossamer pantalets brushing against her thighs, their delicate lace tickling her calves.

Her cheeks began to tingle. She should have worn her old ones. She'd feel much more fortified with the coarse, stiff, cotton drawers she'd sewn with her own two hands. She'd wear them tomorrow. And the day after that. And the day after that.

Again, those awful moments with him in the cellar sprang fresh in her mind. Though she'd tried not to think about it, tried not to picture what he'd seen as she'd shimmied through that window, she'd relived those moments over and over. The images simply would not be suppressed.

And as a doctor, she'd learned all there was to know about the workings of the human body. The workings of a man's body. And she knew, beyond a shadow of a doubt, that by dint of how he was knit together, those selfsame images were alive and well in his mind, too. And if he'd had a glimpse of her face, then the moment she looked up, those images would revive once again.

The pin was in. There was nothing left to do. It was time to pay the piper.

ENTRANCE TO WOMAN'S BUILDING[5]

"Stepping aside, Mr. Scott reached for the door, but she wasn't about to let him open it for her. Lurching forward, she grabbed the heavy handle, hauled the door open, and sailed through, leaving the door for him to either catch or get knocked in the head with."

CHAPTER 6

Deciding her best defense was offense, Billy tightened her lips and looked up, a challenge in her bearing. "Does that meet with your approval?"

His gaze touched her hair, her newly attached bonnet, and her eyes. His dark brown lingered on her light brown. "Yes, ma'am. It most surely does."

Not a hint of recognition crossed his features.

Her lips parted. She couldn't believe it. Her hat must have shadowed her face after all. And she didn't have an accent, or a catch in her voice, or a pair of cowpuncher boots. Even her pantalets had been ordinary. At least they had been that day. And if he glimpsed the pair she now wore, he definitely wouldn't recognize them. The ones from Marshall Field's were nothing like the ones he'd seen.

Maybe she'd continue wearing them after all.

Lifting a brow, she decided to keep up her offensive in an effort to distract him, if nothing else. "Then make way. I'm needed inside."

He schooled his features, but not quickly enough. She saw the flash of disdain at her directness. A look she'd become all too familiar with. Good. Keep him focused on something else. Anything else.

Stepping aside, he reached for the door, but she wasn't about to let him open it for her. Lurching forward, she grabbed the heavy handle, hauled the door open, and sailed through, leaving the door for him to either catch or get knocked in the head with.

He must have caught it, for a stream of sunshine still splashed across the foyer. She scanned the area, focusing in on a side door with a discreet sign that read BUREAU OF PUBLIC COMFORT. If the infirmary wasn't in there, they'd at least know where to direct her.

She hurried inside, then leaned back against the door, holding it closed. Her breath came in spurts. Her skin flashed hot, then cold. Her pantalets settled against her legs.

Gradually, she began to take in her surroundings. The Exposition had been quite proud of its Bureaus of Comfort. They were located in all the large buildings, in many of the state buildings, and in select spots throughout the grounds.

She'd read they were to be used as retiring rooms, free of charge. Some supposedly had barbershops, bootblacks, parcel rooms, and lunch counters. Others had telegraph offices, messenger services, lavatories, and stands selling necessities.

This one, however, was more of a parlor where families could rest from the fatigue of sight-seeing. An impressive collection of oil paintings dominated the room along with an ornamental fireplace, a lady's writing desk, and a postal box. For the moment no one was taking advantage of those or of the forest-green sofas and balloon-back chairs scattered about in cozy formations.

Directly opposite her was a large wooden door. She could hear no voices coming through the wall and there was no placard to indicate if it was the clinic.

She did not, however, want to go back into that foyer and risk running into Mr. Scott. Thank goodness she hadn't given him her name the other day. Glancing at her watch, she cringed. Almost thirty minutes late.

Pushing herself away from the door, she approached the unmarked one and knocked.

A striking young woman in a nurse's gown immediately answered it. After she glanced at Billy's uniform, two lovely dimples blossomed. "Well, hello. I'm Nurse Findley. I didn't realize I was going to have some help. Please, come in."

Billy stepped across the threshold. "Actually, I'm Dr. Billy Jack Tate. I'm here to replace the doctor who contracted typhoid, I believe."

Miss Findley's cheeks filled with color, setting off her large blue eyes and flaxen hair. "I'm so sorry, doctor. I thought, I mean . . ." Her voice trailed away.

Billy smiled. "It's my fault. I wasn't sure what to wear, so I decided on this. What do the other doctors usually wear?"

"Mostly skirts and shirtwaists. Dr. Ashford's already left for the day, though."

"Yes, I'm terribly late. The cable car took much longer than I expected. I'm so sorry."

"It's all right. We've had a very quiet day."

Billy glanced about her new home away from home. The small room, which was more like an office, led to yet another door. A simple flattop desk had been shoved against the wall to the left. Assorted vials and nursing instruments littered its surface and a cabinet above. In the corner sat a washstand complete with rags and piped-in water. A bar of Brag soap beside it gave off a clean, pleasant odor.

To the right, a grand curtain-top desk with a dozen pigeonholes and drawers drew her with magnetic force. Its upper shelf held Osler's new *Principles and Practice of Medicine*, Avicenna's *Canon of Medicine*, and Meigs's *Obstetrics*. Running her fingers along the desktop, she pushed aside a stethoscope and fanned out Dr. Ashford's notes, which appeared to have been written that morning.

The woman had treated a total of three patients. A young lady for faintness, another for hysterics, and an elderly gentlemen who simply needed a rest. Not much in the way of excitement, but Billy would enjoy it all the same.

"The surgery is right through here." Nurse Findley opened the connecting door.

Entering, Billy inhaled the smell of carbolic acid, barely managing to keep from hugging herself and spinning like a bride in her first home. A long cot and invalid's table sat in the center. Large glass cases lined the north and west walls.

Moving to the one closest to her, she opened one of its doors. An infinite variety of bandages made from gauze and oil silk lined several racks within its shelves. In the next, surgical instruments, cambric needles, syringes, timers, tongue blades, ear scoops, forceps, and every sort of thermometer.

She went from cabinet to cabinet, flinging open door after door. Anthropometric instruments. Enema equipment. Catgut ligatures. Bedpans. Plaster of paris. And knives.

This was what she'd wanted. What she'd dreamed of. A rolltop desk, a nurse for assistance, and an operating room. Except she wanted one all her own.

Propping her satchel on the cabinet, she began to rifle through it. "My diploma's in here somewhere."

When Billy slipped it out, Findley's eyes widened.

"University of Michigan?" the nurse asked. "Why, you must have been the only woman there."

"No, no. There were a scattering of women at UM, but only three of us were in their medical program."

"I think we should hang it up." Findley glanced

about the room. "Right over there. We'll take down the phrenology diagram and replace it with this. That way, the patients can see what a prestigious doctor we have in our clinic."

Undeserved as it was, a flush of pleasure sped through Billy. She wasn't prestigious. At least, not yet.

Covering her reaction, she lifted the lid of a large chest wedged into a corner. Flannel undergarments and an assortment of stockings had been stacked neatly inside. "What are these for?"

"Those are our hygienic clothes." Findley straightened Billy's diploma on the wall.

Billy looked again at the chest's contents. She'd heard of hygienic clothing for children, but not for women. "Who are they for?"

Crossing the room, Findley reached inside the chest while Billy continued to hold the lid. "These ventilated corsets were designed by a Miss Franks of London and worn by British nurses, who then recommended them to their patients. But look at these." She lifted a strange-looking shoe and held it aloft, much like the prince admiring Cinderella's slipper. "They're hygienic shoes."

"I've never heard of hygienic shoes."

"They're brand-new. A Mrs. Fenwick invented them especially for the sickroom."

Lowering the lid, Billy took the shoe and began to examine it.

Findley leaned in and pointed to each feature

as she extolled its virtues. Steel springs over the instep to absorb each footfall. A rubber heel to make it soundless. A contour similar to an actual foot.

"Let me see your feet," Findley said.

"What?"

"Your feet. Let me see the size of your feet."

Lifting a corner of her gown, Billy placed a toe on the floor in front of her and swiveled her foot.

"Yes, yes. I think we might have a pair close to your size. Here, hold this again, will you?" Findley raised the lid.

Billy captured it in her grasp.

"I can't wear any," Findley continued. "On account of my feet being impossibly large. Got them from my father. Very unladylike, but they work marvelously well. Here we are."

She produced another pair and they did, indeed, look close to the length of Billy's foot.

"You must try them. Dr. Ashford wears a pair and says they're just the smoothest things she's ever seen."

Unable to resist, Billy sat on a stool, released a buttonhook from her chatelaine, and began the laborious process of removing her boot. Then she strapped on one of the shoes, held her foot aloft, and admired Mrs. Fenwick's ingenuity.

"How does it feel?" Findley asked.

"Perfect." And sure enough, it did. Perhaps she was Cinderella after all—minus the prince, of course. But who needed him when you had shoes like this?

A bang and a loud shout from the parlor startled them both.

Findley hurried to see what the commotion was about. Billy sprang to her feet. The hygienic shoe was a different height than her boot, throwing her off balance. Nonetheless, she whisked up her discarded boot and the other hygienic shoe, then quickly hobbled to the rolltop desk to deposit them both.

"A little bit more slowly, sir." Findley had left the door open, her voice calm, reassuring. "Take your time."

"It's one of the guards." The man's voice was out of breath, as if he'd been running.

Billy hurried to the parlor. A man in a blue uniform and cap propped himself up on bent knees, his back bowing with each deep breath.

"What's happening?" Billy asked.

"This is our elevator man." Findley crouched beside him, patting his back. "I'm not sure what's wrong."

"He's collapsed," the man said. "A guard collapsed in my elevator."

Two different shoes or not, Billy didn't waste another moment. "You make sure this man's all right. I'll go see about the guard." She started out the door, then stopped. "Where's the elevator?"

COLUMBIAN GUARD[6]

"Carlisle was ex-army, with a craw full of sand and fighting tallow. A year younger than Hunter's twenty-six, he spoke three languages and had pummeled Hunter with questions about life as a Ranger."

CHAPTER 7

What the devil was happening? In the course of his career, Hunter had been bitten by a rattler, thrown off a horse, and shot clean through, but he'd never experienced anything like the pain now searing through his gut and buckling his knees. Something had had his stomach in a noose ever since he'd arrived in this godforsaken city. And though the pain had come and gone and come again, he'd managed to overcome it up to now. Then, just like that, he'd been checking in on some lady doing a cooking demonstration and it had tightened to the point where he could no longer even stand. Somehow he'd managed to make it to the elevator. All he needed now was to get to the front door of the building.

Half-crouched, he stumbled, teetered to the right, and knocked two paintings off the wall in a bid to catch himself. Was God fixing to pull his picket pin? Right here? While he was guarding a bunch of feminine frippery?

Don't You dare, he thought.

His reputation would be ruined. What would they put on his gravestone? *Here lies Hunter Joseph Scott, a fellow capable of grinding the sights off a six-shooter with his teeth. He dropped unceremoniously dead in the Woman's Building.*

The *Woman's* Building. He'd be hanged before he let that happen. Bile rushed up his throat. He pressed a fist to his mouth. His ears began to ring.

The sound of heavy, running footfalls galloped toward him. What had the elevator attendant done, called the fire brigade?

But instead, polished black boots and blue trousers with a familiar red stripe appeared in his vision. Eddie Carlisle. The guard who had the next shift.

Squatting down, Carlisle grabbed Hunter's arm. "What the blazes happened?"

"Get me outta here." He had to push the words through gritted teeth, for the bile still threatened.

"Were you stabbed? Shot? Shoved? Did you break something? Where does it hurt?"

"Stomach."

"Can you walk?"

"Yes." But when he tried to straighten, his legs again turned to jelly.

Carlisle caught him. "Okay, pal. I'm going to carry you. Don't fight me, all right?"

You can't. But even as Hunter thought it, Carlisle grabbed his wrist, slipped an arm between his legs, and hoisted Hunter's torso across his shoulders. Carlisle stood, bearing all two-hundred-plus pounds of Hunter's six-foot-two bulk.

Wheezing, Carlisle staggered for a second. "Die

and be doomed. What'd you eat for breakfast? A grizzly?"

But Hunter wasn't fooled. Carlisle was ex-army, with a craw full of sand and fighting tallow. A year younger than Hunter's twenty-six, he spoke three languages and had pummeled Hunter with questions about life as a Ranger.

"This way," a female voice whispered, dainty heels clipping along in front of them.

The floor rushed by in a blur. He held on to consciousness, refusing to close his eyes, not wanting to chance succumbing to the pain until he was across the threshold and on the gravel walkway.

But instead of emerging into sunshine, he was carried sideways through a doorway and into an apartment of some kind.

No, he thought. *You're going the wrong way. The front door. Go to the front door.*

A cabinet with glass-fronted doors held multitudes of vials, jars, and boxed medicines. He groaned. The infirmary. Carlisle had taken him to the blasted infirmary.

"Get me out of here." His voice held a raspy quality he wasn't accustomed to.

Another door. A female voice. A flash of white.

Carlisle bent his knees, then did a thrust, tossing Hunter up and over. He landed with a *thunk* on a cot.

Oooph. Hunter grabbed a fistful of Carlisle's

jacket. "I don't want to die . . . in an infirmary . . . in the Woman's Building."

Carlisle didn't so much as flinch. "Then get up and walk out."

Hunter tried to rise. Pain sliced across his gut.

Carlisle pushed him down with two fingers.

Why was Carlisle doing this? Doctors were the enemy. They tortured people. Killed them, even.

Still, Hunter didn't say anything. He was a Ranger first, a Columbian Guard second. If he fell into the hands of the enemy, he wouldn't do it with his eyes bulging out like a tromped-on toad.

He looked at his friend. "Go on. Save yourself."

A touch of humor flashed across Carlisle's face. "I'm going to go make the rounds. I'll check on you after a while."

I'll be dead. But before he could voice the thought, the pain in his stomach spread up his back and wrapped around his chest. Much as he wanted to curl up, he didn't move or make a sound.

A nurse with flaxen hair and large blue eyes took Carlisle's place beside the bed and placed a cool hand against Hunter's forehead. "You're burning up."

At least she wasn't the one he'd stopped on the steps. He wouldn't have wanted his insistence on safety to come back and bite him now.

Unscrewing a cylindrical case on her chatelaine, she removed a thermometer and shook down the mercury. "Open up."

"Just call in the doc and let's get this over with."

"The doctor needs to know your temperature."

"Knowing my temperature isn't going to change a thing." He was dying. He knew that, and he was ready to meet his Maker. He might be too incapacitated to do anything about his location, but he could sure do something about what occurred during his final moments on earth. And if it was the last thing he did, he was going to die with a little dignity.

The gas he'd been holding made a fierce, noisy, involuntary exit.

The nurse's eyes widened.

His face went from feverish to scalding. "Get out."

Her expression softened. "Now, there's nothing to be ashamed—"

"Out," he barked.

She stumbled back. "You needn't—"

"Out!"

Whirling about, she fled.

The minute the door closed behind her, he let the rest of it loose. He knew the doc wouldn't mind. Those fellows had seen and smelled a lot worse.

The expulsion offered a tiny bit of relief. Not enough to sit up, but enough to turn his head. His cot stood higher than normal, with an invalid table on his left. A framed diploma on the wall caught his attention. It was from the University of Michigan. That was something, at least. The doc was trained. Didn't make him trustworthy, but it offered a tiny measure of reassurance.

The name had been written in fancy script. *Billy* . . . He squinted. *Billy Jack Tate.*

The door opened. It was the hat-pin lady. A stethoscope curled about her neck like a winter scarf, a tiny megaphone-looking thing on one end, earpieces on the other. If the odor in the room affected her, she gave no indication of it.

"You frightened Nurse Findley." She approached the cot, yet only the swish of her petticoats gave her away.

He looked at her hem. Was she barefoot? Why didn't her boots make any noise?

"I won't stand for that kind of behavior," she said. "Not even from a Columbian Guard."

Easy for her to say now that she had him flat on his back. "Go away."

She removed a thermometer from her chatelaine and began to shake it. "What happened between the time you saw me outside and now?"

"I'll tell the doc when I see him."

"I am the doc. Now, open up." She held the thermometer poised.

Pushing her wrist aside, he gave her an exasperated look. "His diploma's right there on the wall. You tell Billy Jack to come in here and quit sending me his nurses."

"I'm Billy Jack Tate. Now open up, and let's get a read on your temperature."

She couldn't be serious. His stomach began to spasm. "Look, lady," he breathed. "I'm not much longer for this world, so if you'll just get the doc and let him say a few words, I'd be grateful."

Her entire countenance changed. She put the thermometer in its case and reached for his cap.

He caught her wrist.

"Something's happening," she said. "You're experiencing pain somewhere. I can see it in your face. Let's not waste time. I was named after my granddaddies on both sides. I graduated cum laude from the University of Michigan. I've been practicing for seven years. And I can help you. But you have to tell me where it hurts."

"You'd lie to a dying man?"

"Nobody dies on my watch. Not if I can help it. And I'm not lying. I'm Dr. Tate. I really, really am. Now, you need to tell me what's going on while you still can."

His grip on her wrist had weakened to a point where she simply pulled free and removed his cap. From there, she went straight to the brass buttons holding his jacket together. Shoving the jacket open, she started on his shirt. Maybe dying in the Woman's Building wouldn't turn out so bad after all.

"Where does it hurt?" she asked.

"The gut."

"Did something happen? Did you run into anything?"

A sharp pain lanced through him. Sucking in a breath, he gave a quick shake of his head.

"What did you have for breakfast?"

"A grizzly."

"I hope you're joking." She shoved open his shirt, then wrenched his undershirt from his trousers and scrunched it up to his armpits with quick strokes. Lips parting, she swept her gaze from his torso to his eyes.

Jaw clamped against the spasm, he managed a wink. "Not bad for a dying man, huh?"

Her expression was all business. "Point with one finger where it hurts the most."

He drew an upside down *U* from his hip bone up over his belly button and down to the other hip bone. If she wanted to see it, though, she'd have to undo his belt. Instead, she simply pressed her fingers against the indicated area.

He jumped, forgetting about everything but the pain, and shoved her hands away.

"I know it's tender. I'll be as gentle as possible."

This was why he hated doctors. Instead of taking his word, they prodded him to see if they could get a holler. Well, he'd be dad-blamed before he'd give her the satisfaction of a holler.

She finished her exam, then, quicker than he could spit and say howdy, she released his belt, unbuttoned his fly, mumbled an "excuse me," and slipped a hand down to his hip bone. He

72

registered a flash of shock until she pressed down. Agony arched his back.

He gripped the edges of the cot. She continued her inspection, hands kneading the path he'd drawn for her.

"Have you been on any long train trips recently?" she asked.

He opened one eye. Was she trying to distract him? Even without the pain, he'd be hard-pressed to dismiss the fact that she had her hand inside his pants. "Rode up from Houston last month to—" He winced as she pressed a spot just to the right of his belly button.

"Sorry." Still, she didn't let up on the pressure. "What did you do before you became a Columbian Guard?"

He tightened his hold on the cot, but forced his spine to relax. "I'm a Texas Ranger."

"I see. I assume life as a Ranger is quite a bit more active than life as a Columbian Guard?"

"Yes'm."

Head cocked, eyes closed in concentration, she kneaded the area up over his navel, then back underneath along his right side.

"Where are you staying?" she asked.

He rolled his eyes. Diploma or not, she was female, and clearly felt a need to fill the awkwardness with chitchat.

"We stay in some barracks here on the grounds," he answered.

At least her eyes were closed, allowing him to grimace undetected. It also allowed him to study her. He surveyed the tendrils of hair still loose from this morning. The lashes resting against smooth cheeks. The pulse at her throat. The curves so close to brushing him, but not quite making contact.

She must bathe in a basket of apples, peaches, and summer berries. Whatever it was, it smelled mighty good. The boys back home could put whatever they wanted on his tombstone. He couldn't imagine a better way to die.

"When's the last time you defecated?" she asked.

All thoughts went up in a powder. "What?"

She opened her eyes, her caramel brown finding his dark brown without even having to search.

"When's the last time you had a bowel movement?"

Warmth crept from his chest to his neck. "I am not about to discuss that with you."

The eyebrow again. "I'm a doctor, Mr.—" She stopped, as if catching herself. "What's your name?"

That was quite a question, all things considered. "Hunter Scott."

"Well, Mr. Scott. If you want some relief from this pain, you need to answer my question. When's the last time you've defecated?" She removed her hand and began to button him up.

He swatted her away, doing the job himself. "I'm not discussing it with you."

Unwrapping the stethoscope from her neck, she hooked one end into her ears and set the other against his gut.

"My heart's up here, Billy."

"I'm listening to your stomach, and you may call me Dr. Tate."

"Where I come from, we'd definitely be on a first-name basis."

"Where's the commode located in your barracks?"

"For the love of Peter." His nausea began to rumble again. Sweat collected beneath his arms and along his forehead.

Straightening, she took the earpieces from her ears and allowed them to catch against her neck. "Do you have privacy issues, Mr. Scott?"

The nausea peaked, then receded a bit. "I wouldn't want to do what we just did with an audience present, if that's what you mean."

Pink suffusing her cheeks, she wrestled his undershirt back down to his waist. "We didn't *do* anything. I simply examined you the same as any other doctor would. And what I meant was, is the toilet in your barracks in close proximity to the sleeping area? Close enough for others to hear awkward sounds and smells?"

If this wasn't the darndest conversation he ever did have. "It is."

"And have you ever used it?"

"No."

She nodded. "When's the last time you defecated?"

He pinched the bridge of his nose. "Are we back to that?"

"Answer me."

Sighing, he let his arm fall over his eyes. "Coming up on three weeks."

"Good heavens. You must have an extremely high tolerance for pain. I can't believe you haven't sought help before now."

He said nothing.

After a few seconds the door opened. "Nurse Findley, put together a pouch of psyllium tea please."

He glanced toward the door. Billy had her head poked through the opening, causing her white skirt to drape over a curvy backside.

Straightening, she shut the door.

"Are you barefoot?" he asked.

She blinked in surprise. "Of course not."

"Then what's on your feet? You don't make a sound when you move."

A smile lifted her cheeks and brightened her eyes. "It's my hygienic shoes. They have steel springs over the insteps and rubber heels, rendering them noiseless. They were invented by a woman and are marvelously comfortable."

He stared at a line of frilly white trim along the

bottom of her skirt. He figured after all they'd been through he ought to at least be allowed to have a glimpse beneath those hems, but she didn't offer to lift them and he didn't ask.

"A woman's invention, huh?"

"Yes. A woman by the name of Mrs. Fenwick."

The nausea began its ascent once again. He wasn't sure he'd have the strength to keep it down this time. "Get me a dustbin, Billy."

The animation fell from her face as she rushed to accommodate him.

He tried to roll onto his side, but was as helpless as a cow in quicksand.

Digging under his back, she rolled him onto his shoulder, then propped him against her while she reached over and held a bowl beneath his mouth. When he was finished, she eased him back, took the bowl out of the room, then returned with a cool cloth.

Wiping his mouth, she gave him a soft smile. "Better?"

"I'm not dying, am I?"

"No." She folded the rag inside out and ran it across his forehead. "You're constipated."

He slid his eyes closed. "That can't be right. How could something like that knock me so low?"

"It's not something to trifle with. Has it ever happened before?"

"No."

"Well, I can give you some immediate relief today, but until you're defecating at least three times a week, there are a few things you'll need to do."

"Like what?"

"I have a tea I'd like you to drink every morning. And so you know, this came on in part because of the inactivity of your new job, not to mention sitting on that train from Texas to Illinois. I suggest you begin performing calisthenics in your room or in a gymnasium. Chicago has several I can recommend. You'll also need to eat a nutritious diet that is easily digested. Last, you'll need to come in for daily massages."

He studied her. "Massages? As in, the kind of massage you gave me a few minutes ago?"

"No, that was an examination. I was needing to see if I could feel your colon through the abdominal wall, which I could. That's a sure sign it's much too full. Your massage will be in the same area, but it can be done through the fabric of your trousers."

"More's the pity."

Though her expression remained stoic, a blush crept into her cheeks.

"Who gives the massages?" he asked. "You, or a nurse?"

"Me."

He pursed his lips. "What does your husband think about your job?"

"I'm not . . . that's none . . ." She swept a hand up the back of her hair, but the loose tendrils floated down again the minute she lowered her arm. "You also need to quit being shy about attending to your needs. Everyone defecates. It's a perfectly normal thing to do."

A slow smile lifted one corner of his lips. "You're not married, are you?"

"Mr. Scott, you need to be paying attention to my instructions. They are very important."

"Hunter. My name's Hunter."

Spinning about, she whisked up a sheet from a nearby chair and plopped it on his stomach. "Remove everything from the waist down and roll onto your side."

CHAPTER 8

Hunter's jaw slackened.

She opened a glass-fronted cabinet with shelves full of surgical instruments and withdrew a large wooden box. Inside nestled a syringe for the likes of Paul Bunyan, along with tubes and a long ivory pipe.

"If that's what I think it is," he said, "you can just put it right back in that cabinet." But his brief respite had passed, and the pain began to build again. It didn't matter. No way would he sit still for this.

She turned to him, back straight, face set. "You're having an enema, Mr. Scott. It's the only way. Afterward, you'll have immediate relief, and then you can do the three things I've recommended for a period of three months. Otherwise, it will happen again."

"I'm leaving." With a Herculean effort, he pushed himself to a sitting position. The room wobbled, the blood drained from his head. Billy handed him a bowl.

This time she didn't stay by his side. Instead, she wrenched open the door. "Go find the Columbian Guard who brought Mr. Scott in here and bring him to me immediately."

Even as he retched, her words brought relief.

Carlisle would get him out of here. He'd never let this woman do what she planned. By the time he'd finished, his arms trembled, his head spun, and he could hardly remain upright.

She carried off the bowl and returned with Carlisle.

"Get me outta here." Hunter still sat upright, barely.

Carlisle scratched his chin. "The doc says you're giving her some trouble."

"She tell you what she plans to do?"

Carlisle's gaze touched the instruments strewn across the counter. "She did."

"Then let's go."

But his friend did nothing. Just stood there. Finally, he turned to Billy. "Would you give us a minute, doc?"

"Certainly." She left, her woman-invented shoes making no sound.

The door clicked shut. Carlisle rubbed the back of his neck. "Did I ever tell you my dad's a doctor?"

"I don't care. Get over here and help me up."

"I think you ought to do what she says."

"You either help me out of here or I'll knock your ears down so they'll do you for wings." A spasm curled him up like a scorpion's tail, robbing him of his breath.

Carlisle sighed. "Listen, this isn't so bad. Lots of people have had one. And if you don't do it, then I'll have to work all your shifts. Besides, you're acting as scared as a rabbit in a wolf's mouth. It's embarrassing."

Embarrassing? Carlisle wanted to talk to him about *embarrassing?*

Holding Hunter's gaze, Carlisle removed his hat and jacket, then rolled up his shirtsleeves. "I'm going to call her in here. And when she comes, you hunt up something you can use for a backbone, because if you give her any trouble, I'm going to knock you out cold as a meat hook."

This could not be happening. "I've got more backbone in my little finger than you have in your entire spine."

"Then let's get this over with."

But it wasn't Billy who came back in—it was the nurse. Hunter did as he was told, and when all was finished, Carlisle kicked the nurse out while the treatment took effect. Finally, Carlisle led him back to the cot. Hunter collapsed into an exhausted sleep.

When he woke, he was alone, and it took him a moment to get his bearings. Once he did, he threw an arm over his eyes. Death and the deuce, but he hated doctors. Still, he had no pain and he didn't hear any harp music, so the purgative must have worked.

He tapped his ribs, looking for his watch, but his jacket and shirt had been removed, leaving him in nothing but trousers and undershirt. There was no window, so he had no way of gauging the time.

Someone had cleaned the examination room, lit a flowery-smelling candle, and set a fresh bowl within reach on his invalid's table.

The diploma on the wall snagged his attention. Billy Jack. What kind of parents named their daughter Billy Jack? And what kind of woman went to college to take up a man's profession? Miss Pantalets-Trousers came to mind along with the bevy of women who'd clambered through the halls of the Memorial Art Palace. He shook his head. He'd never seen such a bunch of foolishness.

Still, he had to admit, Billy Jack Tate was no quack. She'd managed to diagnose his problem in a matter of minutes and to cure it without sawing, leeching, or administering electric currents. Not that he was happy with the solution she'd come up with—but still, he'd seen an awful lot worse.

As if his thoughts had conjured her up, she opened the door and stuck her head inside. "You're awake."

He didn't reply, not sure whether to thank her or strangle her.

Stepping into the room, she shut the door and leaned against it. "How do you feel?"

"Like I've been riding the rough string with a borrowed saddle."

She pushed away from the door. "What does that mean?"

"Means I've felt better."

"Does your stomach still hurt?" Approaching

the bed, she glanced at the sheet twisted about him and tugged it loose, then brought it up to his chest. "Well? Does it?"

"I'm all right."

She folded the lip of the sheet over and smoothed it across him.

"You tucking me in?"

"You still sleepy?"

"I need to get up. What time is it?"

"Around eight o'clock."

His eyes widened. "At night?"

"Yes."

Throwing off the covers, he pushed himself to a sitting position. "I've got to go. My shift started two hours ago."

She placed a hand against his arm. "Not so fast. Mr. Carlisle said he'd work your shift for you."

"He should have woken me." Swinging his legs over the side, he paused. The room spun for only a few seconds, and his stomach made no objection at all.

"You're too weak to be doing any guarding, Mr. Scott. If something were to happen, you'd be in no shape to take it on. I have some dinner for you. Then my orders are for you to return to your barracks, drink your tea, and head right to bed."

He studied her. "You always work this late?"

"If a patient needs me."

"What's for dinner?"

"Oatmeal with prunes."

He cringed. "Not much of a cook, are you?"

Smiling, she rolled the invalid's table to him. "They're from the Garden Café up on the roof. And your stomach's had a traumatic day, so we're going to feed it something that will help your digestive tract."

The oatmeal was cold and he hated prunes, but he cleaned his bowl all the same.

After he finished, he pushed the table aside and stood. "Where are my clothes?"

"Right over here." She retrieved them from a lower cabinet, then handed them to him.

"Somebody brushed these for me," he said.

Glancing down, she shook out her skirts. The chatelaine no longer hung from her belt.

He shrugged on his shirt and adjusted it against his shoulders, then began buttoning it. "Thank you for brushing them."

"Yes, it was, I only . . ." Looking up, she swallowed. "You're welcome."

Her discomfort surprised him. She'd not so much as hesitated when she'd undressed him. But that had been different. He'd been a patient on a cot in a great deal of pain. Now he was a half-clothed Columbian Guard, and, if he wasn't mistaken, she was an unmarried lady doctor.

She cleared her throat, fiddled with her hair, tugged down her sleeves, and crossed her arms.

He pulled on his jacket. "My boots?"

"Oh!" She shot off to another corner of the room

and came back with them. "So, you're from Texas."

"That's right. Where are you from?"

"I grew up in Boston, but I live here in Chicago now."

"A city girl?"

She smiled. "Through and through."

"But you went to school in Michigan?"

"Yes. They're the first state medical school to formally admit women."

With his jacket gaping open, he pulled on a boot. She reached out to steady him.

"Cum laude, huh?" he asked.

Again, she blushed. "Did I say that?"

"You did." He pulled on his other boot.

The minute he finished, she released him and took a step back. "What about you? Did you go to school?"

"I did." Lifting his chin, he began securing the brass buttons on his jacket. "Only I graduated 'praise the laude.'"

Her laugh changed her entire face. Bright eyes. One dimple. Straight teeth. Rounded cheeks.

"Is your home far from here?" he asked.

Her laugh tapered off, but her smile remained intact. "It's about a ten-mile train ride, but I've been offered a room at a women's dormitory built for the accommodation of the unprotected during the fair. So I'll be staying there on the nights I work. That way, I won't have to go so far."

Nodding, he secured the last button and pulled

down on the hem of his jacket. "How do I look?"

Her smile dissipated. She handed him a pouch of tea. "You look very charming, Mr. Scott."

He tucked the pouch into his pocket. No sounds from outside penetrated their room. Only her breathing, his breathing, and the sudden rushing of his blood.

"May I walk you home?" he asked.

"Under the circumstances, I thought perhaps I should walk you home."

He lifted the corner of his mouth. "Despite what you may think, I never get sick. Most of us boys from Texas have been raised with a gun in one hand and a milk bottle in the other. So, no need to worry. I'll be fine. I feel a hundred times better already. Thank you . . . I think."

Her smile returned. "You're welcome . . . I think."

"Are you ready to go?"

She shook her head. "I have some paperwork yet."

"I thought you closed at seven."

"We do. But I imagine I'll be staying until a little bit after nine on most days."

Nine. Good to know. That's when his second shift of the day ended.

He placed a hand on the doorknob. "I'll see you tomorrow, doc."

"Tomorrow?"

"For my massage." Winking, he stepped through the door and gently pulled it shut behind him.

INTERIOR OF THE WOMAN'S BUILDING[7]

"Hunter nodded. 'I'm going to sweep
through the building.' "

CHAPTER 9

Billy didn't see Mr. Scott the next day, of course, for she worked only three days a week. But she'd seen him the following day and all of her workdays since.

Though his massages took fifteen, twenty minutes at the most, he always managed to draw her into conversation until, eventually, an easy friendship had formed between them.

Today was no different. Stepping into the surgery, he removed his sword, then began unfastening his blue sackcloth jacket. To the right and left of each shiny brass button, black braid radiated out in a straight line, culminating in a cloverleaf design. "Afternoon, Billy."

Though she addressed him as Mr. Scott, he insisted on calling her by her Christian name. The only time he used her proper name was when they were out in the public area.

"Good afternoon, Mr. Scott. How are you feeling?"

"Light as a feather, ma'am."

She held back her smile. That had become his way of letting her know he'd had his tea and taken care of business. Folding a swansdown cloth, she placed it in a stack with other like-sized ones.

"What're you doing?" Sliding his jacket down his arms, he caught it before it dropped, then draped it across the hygienic chest. Thank goodness he'd never asked to see what was inside it.

"I'm separating bandages," she said.

Approaching her, he leaned a hip against the counter and crossed his arms. "What are they for?"

"This stack right here? Bandages for the nose."

"What about that one?" He indicated some muslin with his chin.

"Those are patches for the eyes."

"And these?" He continued to single out each pile until she'd identified the dressings for jaws, knees, abdomens, and chests.

"You ready?" She placed the last piece of flannelette in the knee pile.

"Sure." Moving to the edge of the cot, he grabbed the heel of his boot and worked it off his foot. She'd learned that his cowpuncher boots were made of armadillo—an animal that, according to Mr. Scott, looked like a miniature dinosaur, birthed only quadruplets, tasted like pork, and jumped four feet in the air when startled.

She still wasn't sure she believed him, but he swore he was telling the truth.

Locking his hands behind his head, he stretched out on the cot. "Got a letter from LeRue yesterday."

"Your brother?" Starting at the lower left hip, she began to knead his colon.

"Uh-huh. He's going to a rodeo over in Pecos this week."

She glanced at him. "Have you ever been to a rodeo?"

"Sure. Plenty of times. Matter of fact, back home, us boys used to gather up at whoever's folks had gone to town and have a rodeo of our own with their stock."

"And when would that have been?"

"I don't know. When I was about twelve or so." Tensing, he grimaced.

She immediately stilled. "Is that tender right there?"

"A little."

She backtracked and did it again.

"Do you do that on purpose?" he asked, scowling. "Do you press it again to see if you can get a holler out of me?"

"Of course not. I'm just trying to see if I feel any inflammation."

He rolled his eyes. "Anyway, there were about six of us and we got to be pretty good at riding. We even drew for our stock, just like real rodeo cowboys."

She only had one sister, and Pauline was so much older than she, it was more like having an extra mother. But Mr. Scott and his brother were only a year apart in age. The way they'd whiled away their childhood was a great deal different from the way she had.

"What kind of animal did you draw?" she asked.

"All kinds. One time, though, I drew a wild steer. I got on that thing and, boy, did he pitch. He went right through a brand-new wooden gate and left me on the back side of it."

A smile tugged at her lips. "Were you hurt?"

"I was pretty bummed up and we had to rebuild the gate as best we could before his pa got home."

"Did he notice?"

"His pa? Yeah, he noticed. Whipped his boy pretty good. Said we could've gotten me killed."

Looking up, she paused. "What did your parents do?"

"They never knew. LeRue painted me with iodine and bacon grease."

She nodded. "All that salt in the bacon grease will heal about anything, won't it?"

"Sure enough."

And so it went. Mondays, Wednesdays, and Fridays she worked at the infirmary and had a little peek into the life of Hunter Scott. And upon very rare occasions, she'd give him a peek into hers.

On the other days of the week, she stayed at her apartment on Congress and Forty-third, hoping someone would see her shingle and send for her. But no one ever did.

• • •

With Osler's large tome, *Principles and Practice of Medicine*, sprawled open on her lap, Billy curled her stockinged feet up under her legs on the bureau's couch and read the section on tumors of the intestine. To her relief, Mr. Scott showed none of the symptoms outlined. In fact, she decided it was time to cut back on the frequency of his massages.

Yawning, she checked her timepiece. Almost nine o'clock. More and more she stayed after hours in the parlor of the Bureau of Comfort. It was much more comfortable and spacious than her tiny room at the Women's Dormitory, if a bit cooler, and it gave her a chance to peruse Osler's exciting new medical book.

She glanced out the window to the electric lamps lining the walks outside. She knew she'd regret it if she didn't at least attempt to tour the fair, but so far she hadn't been able to summon up any enthusiasm for wandering through its six hundred acres when she'd been on her feet all day.

And her off days were out of the question. For if she wasn't going to spend any time in her apartment, then she might as well take down her shingle. She wasn't about to do that.

Sliding the tome from her lap, she brushed aside her hems and began to massage her arches. Hygienic shoes or no, her feet were still sore by the end of her shift. The work hadn't been demanding, but it had kept her busy. Most every day she saw someone for fatigue, swollen feet, or dehydration. Her most exciting case by far had been Mr. Sc—.

An insistent pounding on the parlor door caused her to jerk upright.

"Open up!"

She raced to the door.

Mr. Scott barged inside, his eyes spooked like a horse's. Balanced in his large palms, a newborn in nothing more than a diaper kicked its tiny arms and legs giving forth a squall equal to that of a mighty warrior.

Billy touched her throat. "What on earth?"

Mr. Scott stretched his hands toward her. The babe turned red and increased its protest at being handled in such an unmotherly fashion.

"I found it abandoned." His breath came in spurts.

"Abandoned?" she asked. "Where?"

"It was wrapped up in that cloak made of prairie chicken feathers."

"Good heavens." Supporting the child's bald head, she took it into her arms. "I'll examine it immediately."

He nodded. "I'm going to sweep the building. See if I can locate the mother."

Without waiting for a response, he was back out the door, leaving it ajar.

Securing the infant against her chest, she jiggled

and shushed it, gently buffing its back and arms to ward off the goose pimples covering its chilled skin. There was certainly nothing wrong with its lungs.

Though she'd delivered many a baby and had treated that many more, she realized this was the first time she'd ever actually been alone with one. Usually the mother or the nurses were right there. Having this one all to herself touched a chord deep inside.

Temporarily securing the babe in a corner of the couch, she tucked a towel around it, hastened to scrub her hands in the sink, then placed her instruments on the invalid's table. The abandoned babe screamed the entire time.

Newborns had such a distinctive cry. A sound very different from a baby of even two months. Collecting it into her arms, she took it to the cot in surgery.

"Well, hello there"—she unfolded the towel and crude swaddling—"fellow. What were you doing wrapped up in that feather cloak? Didn't you know that was a beaver collar trimming its neck? Why, it took a Dakota woman ten years to make that thing, one feather at a time."

His skin color was good. His chest movements were superb. His umbilical cord had dried up, but the stump had yet to fall off.

Picking up her stethoscope, she listened to his heart and lungs. "It's a very good thing your diaper was dry. It would have been a shame had you decided to christen the cloak."

At the sound of her voice, the babe's cries briefly came down in volume, his blue eyes big and watery. But when she began to examine his skull and fontanelle, his protests rose again. She was glad he was a fighter. With the challenges he was sure to have ahead of him, he'd need to be.

Hunter could find no trace of the mother. No workers or visitors had seen anyone with a baby either. Pushing open the door to what he'd come to think of as Billy's parlor, he stepped inside. The babe was still kicking up a ruckus. Crossing to the examination room, he stopped at the door.

"If Mr. Scott doesn't find your mother," she said, acting as if the tot were listening instead of crying, "I'll do my best to locate a wet nurse. Some people believe being born with a silver spoon in their mouth is most advantageous, but being born with a mammilla in your mouth is a much better state of affairs and the key to excellent health."

He blinked, unsure he'd heard correctly.

"Do you know where I first learned that?" Finishing the one task, she moved her index fingers to each of the baby's fists. It grabbed on tight, then quieted a bit when she lifted it clear off the cot by nothing but the strength of its grasp.

"I learned it from my mother. She was visiting

with the neighbor ladies and one of them was going to have to bottle-feed her newborn. Well, my mother didn't like that. Not one single bit. She firmly told the woman that it would be worth her while to find a wet nurse or the baby might become sick."

The babe quieted completely. Billy eased it down, then gently took hold of its right leg, rotating it at the hip joint. The babe stared at her with the same fascination Hunter felt.

"Wouldn't you know, a few days later, my rag doll became very ill. I just knew it was because I'd been bottle-feeding her."

A smile tugging at his lips, Hunter settled against the frame of the door. He'd discovered she wasn't the type of woman who checked her mirror much. As a result, she often had a mussed look about her. Tonight, the pins holding her dark blond hair had loosened, disheveling the twist at her nape. A single curl fell along her back, leading his eye down to the curves at her waist and those below. The wrinkles resting against her backside gave evidence of her having sat on the couch reading for some time now.

"Even back then I knew I wanted to be a doctor. So I went outside to the pump and soaked myself with water. When my mother discovered what I'd done while wearing my best white pinafore and kidskin boots, I calmly explained my doll was sick and needed a wet doctor."

Hunter burst out laughing.

Billy twisted around, one hand holding the babe securely on the cot, one hand clutching her collar. Red filled every inch of her skin.

"What are you doing here?" she hissed.

Instead of answering, he chuckled and shook his head. He couldn't imagine why any little girl would want to be a doctor when everybody knew girls were supposed to grow up and become mothers.

She turned her back to him, then began to diaper the infant. It was a boy, he noted.

"What's the matter with you, Hunter Scott?" she asked. "What were you doing to sneak in here and eavesdrop on a conversation that wasn't meant for you?"

The tenor of her voice upset the babe and it started to cry again.

Making his way to her side, he cocked a hip against the cot. "I'm sorry, Billy. I really am sorry to have upset the babe, but I wouldn't have missed that tale for the world."

Grabbing a flannel blanket from the invalid's table, she swaddled the babe, then pulled it to her shoulder, rocking it, nuzzling it, cooing to it. Its crying settled into whimpers. He couldn't help but notice how good she was with the little tyke.

"Did you find anything out?" Her voice was soft. Low.

"Not a thing. Nobody saw a mother. A baby. Nothing. How is he?"

"He appears to be just fine. Hungry, I'm sure, but not malnourished."

"How old do you think he is?"

"Judging from the umbilical cord, I'd guess between seven to fourteen days old."

"That young."

"Yes." She rubbed her cheek against its bald head.

"What are we going to do with him?"

"I don't know. I'll take him with me tonight to the Women's Dormitory. See if anyone knows anything."

"And if they don't?"

Their eyes locked. The gravity of the situation sinking in.

He nodded toward the door. "Come on. I'm walking you home."

"No need for—"

"It wasn't a question. I'm not about to let you to take that thing clear over to Fifty-second Street by yourself."

"It's not a thing. It's a he. And it's not that far."

"I'm going with you, Billy."

"What about guard duty?"

"It's after nine. Carlisle's already on the job." He walked to her. "Here, give him to me. You go pack your doctor's bag."

She looked up, her creamy brown eyes accented

with shots of translucent chocolate and outlined with a fine black ring. "Careful. You need to support his neck. Like this."

Taking Hunter's hand, she positioned it. He wasn't sure which was softer, her or the baby.

"I need to go to the café on the roof," she said. "Hopefully they'll have some goat's milk."

"Go on, then. I'll stay here with him."

Biting her lip, she hesitated, then did as she was told.

WISCONSIN BUILDING[8]

"A set of wind chimes hanging above Wisconsin's porch clanked together in a discordant composition."

CHAPTER 10

The nighttime crowd gravitated toward Lake Michigan, where an elaborate fireworks display could be seen to best advantage. Though the show was on the opposite side of the park from Billy and Hunter, the bangs and pops were still plenty loud. She hoped they wouldn't upset the child. His tiny body curled up like a sausage inside the flannel blanket, its round little rump soft against her arm.

"Is this night air going to harm him?" Hunter asked, the sword at his side jostling against the doctor's bag he'd insisted on carrying for her.

"I hope not. I wish I'd have thought to bring an extra blanket, though."

They crossed through the fair's northernmost section, where forty-four states of the union and four territories had erected buildings. Only an occasional couple graced this section, making the park feel eerily abandoned. Still, the electric lights inside the buildings threw off iridescent halos that competed with the moon's silvery glow and reflected a rainbow of colors in the lagoon.

"I'd give you my jacket," he said, "but my superiors frown upon guards walking around in their shirtsleeves."

She hugged the babe closer. "We'll be all right."

A set of wind chimes hanging above Wisconsin's porch clanked together in a discordant composition. A mother and father several yards ahead of them each carried an exhausted, slumbering child against their shoulders.

Billy wondered if some observer straggling behind Hunter and her would assume the three of them were a family. She'd always wondered what it would feel like, being a wife and mother in a unit such as this. Tempting as it was to indulge in the fantasy, she didn't allow herself such a guilty pleasure. She preferred to deal in truths.

And the truth was, if she couldn't locate this child's mother, he, too, would wonder what it was like to be part of a family unit.

Crossing over a bridge, they exited the turn-stiles, leaving the fairyland of the Columbian Exposition and entering Chicago, the Metropolis of the West. Smoke from the trains pulling into South Park Station hovered like rain clouds. Train whistles pierced the air.

The baby began to fidget and fuss, his legs kicking against the swaddling and pressing into Billy's ribs. She shushed and patted him.

Taking her elbow, Hunter helped her across Stony Island Avenue and onto Fifty-seventh Street. "Do you take the train or the cable car?"

"Neither."

He stopped her, the elevated train rumbling past

overhead. "You can't mean to walk all the way to the Women's Dormitory. The cable car's right here. It'll practically take us to your doorstep."

"For five cents."

"I'll get our tickets."

She sighed. "You can ride if you want. The baby and I are walking."

"Why?"

Because she'd squandered a great deal more money than she should have on a gown too feminine to wear and on undergarments no one could see. "Because I enjoy walking," she said.

"You can't mean that you, a lone, unprotected female, have been walking home, in the dark, by yourself, in this city of a million strangers?"

"I have. And haven't had a moment's trouble."

He gave her an incredulous look. "For a brainy woman, you've got no more sense than that little duffer there."

That was exactly why she'd chosen not to marry. So she didn't have to do what men thought she should simply because she was female. Pulling free of his grasp, she continued down Fifty-seventh Street. A few seconds later she could hear his long strides closing the gap between them, the baby bottles inside her doctor's bag clinking.

The farther they walked from the train station, the thinner the crowd, until there was none at all. A distant shout from an open window filtered through the night air. A dog barked. The smell of someone frying up bacon made her stomach growl.

Hunter's eyes continually swept the shadows, the side streets, the rooftops, the nooks, and the alleyways. His diligence began to give her the willie wobbles. It seemed to her that if one expected the bogeyman to jump out at them, he would.

The baby must have picked up on her tension, for he began to cry again and would not be consoled. When they reached Woodlawn Avenue, Hunter collected the child and tucked it into the cradle of his left arm.

"Let me have the bag, then," she said.

"It's too heavy."

"I carry it every day."

"Not with a night's supply of baby bottles in it."

She grabbed the handle, her hand half-covering his. His was rough, warm, and very different from hers. "Let me have it." She gave a gentle tug. "Please."

Finally, he released it to her, then placed himself between her and the street. There was no need, though, for there were no carriages or drays or wagons to shield her from. Simply a few vagrants sitting on the front steps of the First Baptist Church of Hyde Park.

By the time they reached the dormitory, the babe had fallen asleep.

"Cradle your arms," Hunter whispered.

Tightening her hold on the bag, she formed a sling with her arms.

Stepping close, he spread his free hand against her back and pulled her up against him. Every point of contact sent a jolt as if she'd given herself an electric current treatment.

He rolled the babe into her arms.

At the feel of her womanly form, the baby immediately began to root. Her body responded the way Mother Nature intended. Heat rushed up her neck and face.

"Looks like somebody's hungry," he said, stepping back. "You better get inside and give him one of those bottles before he wakes the whole place up."

Her throat quit working. "Yes," she croaked. Swallowing, she tried again. "Thank you for carrying him all this way."

"It was my pleasure." He slid his hands into his pockets.

Chin tucked, she kept her attention on the babe. "I'll let you know what I find out."

"But it's Friday. You won't be back to the infirmary until Monday."

"I need to collect more milk, so I'll be back in tomorrow. That is, if I don't find the mother."

He said nothing, but she could see the crisp crease in his uniform trousers, the cowpuncher boots peeking out from underneath.

Pushing its tiny hand against her, the baby

latched onto the upper curve of her breast through her gown, just above her corset. Gasping, she jerked away from the baby's mouth. The backward momentum threw her off balance.

Hunter caught her elbows. "Whoa, there."

The baby gave a choppy sob at the jarring.

She regained her footing, but Hunter didn't let go. Crickets hummed, their song rising and falling in soft waves.

He brushed a thumb back and forth against her elbow.

She took a shuddering breath. There was no mistaking his action for anything other than a caress and she felt the impact clear down to her toes.

"Billy?"

"I have to go, Hunter." Pulling away, she was inside the building before she realized she'd used his given name. She glanced back over her shoulder.

He stood outside, the door in his grasp, the wind kicking up a corner of his jacket.

Turning back around, she flew to the stairs and the safety of her room.

Hands shaking, she jerked the pins from her hat, peeled off her shirtwaist, stepped out of skirt and petticoat, unhooked her corset, tossed it onto a chair, shucked off her drawers, then pressed her palms against her stomach through her fancy

Marshall Field's chemise. But it did little to calm the storm within.

Don't think about him.

The babe lay on her bed, kicking his arms and legs, his entire body red as he worked himself into a full-blown tantrum. His shrieks filled the room, bleeding through the walls and the crack beneath her door.

Snatching a bottle from her bag, she crawled across the mattress and lifted him against her. "*Shhhhh.* I have your dinner now. Here we go."

The bed had been pushed into the corner, with the wall as its headboard. She propped herself up and placed the bottle in the baby's mouth. He drank lustily, though tears still pooled in his blue eyes, which had yet to change into their permanent color. With his bald head, she had no indication as to whether he would be blond and blue-eyed, brunet and brown-eyed, or some other combination.

He emitted a whimper.

Without warning, her eyes filled, too. "We're quite the pair, you and I. You facing a lifetime with no mother and me facing a lifetime with no baby."

Against her will, the what-could-have-beens and what-should-have-beens broke free from the tightly secured box she'd buried deep inside. Noiseless tears rushed to the surface. Tears she'd denied herself since her college days when she'd entered her first class of medical school in a beautiful gown with pretty bows and tiny pink rosebuds. The male students had whistled and clucked, throwing an equal number of kisses and paper wads.

From that day forward, she'd worn nothing but black, brown, and navy. Until recently. She'd had a pink-and-green gown sewn for her speech at the Woman's Congress. And she'd purchased the blue-and-white-striped ready-made at Marshall Field's. The former she'd worn only once. The latter, not ever.

She wondered if she ever would wear it or if, for the rest of her life, the only pretty things she'd be able to enjoy would be undergarments. Undergarments only she could see.

She closed her eyes, but tears still seeped out.

She hummed to the baby. She rocked the baby. She held him as close to the breast as she could while letting the bottle do what she'd never have the privilege of doing herself.

When he'd finished feeding and burping, she drew up her legs, sat on her heels, and laid him on the mattress in front of her. "Hello, there."

Peeling off the swaddling layer by layer, she examined the baby again. Not as a doctor this time, but as a daughter of Eve. She marveled at his minuscule fingers and toes. Kissed the soles of his feet. And rubbed his tummy. "My name's Billy."

The baby tried to focus, but didn't know how yet.

Unpinning his diaper, she replaced it with a new one. "I know. It's a boy's name. I was supposed to be the much wished-for son. But no matter, I was the apple of my father's eye and I am more grateful to my mother for marrying him than for anything else she ever did."

After swaddling him, she began to pull the pins from her hair. "With such a wonderful example as them, you can understand why I could hardly wait to find my own prince and wed him. Never did it occur to me that I wouldn't marry. But as the years progressed, I discovered that no man wanted a wife who played the same role as he did. He wanted a wife who would sit at home and bake the bread and entertain the neighbors and see to his needs."

Scooping up the pins, she placed them on a bedside table, then tunneled her fingers through her hair and shook out her blond tresses. "Mr. Scott is no different, I'm sure. He's strong. He's capable. And he's quite virile."

After giving her scalp a good scratch, she pulled her hair over one shoulder, broke it into three sections, and deftly braided it. "He would never sit still for a wage-earning wife. So I must not, under any circumstances, start something that I know has no hope of ever coming to its natural conclusion."

The baby yawned, stretching its mouth wide.

She yawned in return and tied off her braid. "Don't you be a man like that, dear one. When you grow up, you be strong and confident enough to let your wife be whoever she is. Even if that 'whoever' is a wage earner."

Getting up, she padded a drawer, placed it on the bed, and tucked him inside. Then, with the sweet smell of baby filling her, she crawled in beside him and fell into a wearied, if not sound, sleep.

OLD TIMES DISTILLERY CO.'s LOG CABIN[9]

"If you're liking Kentucky, ya can go to the other side o' the park over by the windmills and see an old moonshiner's still from there."

CHAPTER 11

With the babe propped against her shoulder, Billy stopped just short of the Woman's Building and bought the day's official schedule from a young boy in blue toggery. Hunter shook his head. She'd purchased one every single day she'd worked even though Hunter knew she never attended any of the events listed. The boy never had to make change, for she came with the exact amount every time.

When she approached the entrance, Hunter reached for her doctor's bag, gently prying it from her. "How did it go this morning?"

Her mouth turned down. "No one at the dormitory knew anything about the baby."

Sighing, he took her elbow and helped her up the steps. "I didn't have any luck either," he said. "I questioned every staff member and scrubwoman in the building. No one saw a thing."

"I was afraid of that."

"So what are you going to do?"

At the landing she paused, resting her cheek against the baby's. "I spoke with the matron in charge of my floor at the dormitory. She said there's a settlement on the West Side run by a couple of women. They do all kinds of services for the poor. She said they take in the sick, prepare the dead for burial, shelter women who have violent husbands, and they save babies from neglect."

Glancing at the infant, he swallowed. "So you're taking him there?"

"I don't know what else to do. I looked for a wet nurse at the dormitory, but the women there are only in town to see the fair. None had the time nor the interest in taking on an extra little one."

He smiled a bit at her mention of a wet nurse. "Where is this settlement, exactly?"

"It's called Hull House and, according to the woman I spoke with, it's at the corner of Halsted and Polk—about a mile west of Marshall Field's."

"Marshall Field's?"

"A department store in the heart of downtown."

"So around seven miles from here." He pulled a timepiece from his pocket. "When are you leaving?"

"What is it now, about twelve?"

"A little after."

She looked to the side. "Well, he's hungry, so I need to feed him again. And I was going to go through a trunk we have in the infirmary. I think I saw some infant clothes in it. Then I need to gather up some more goat's milk to take with me to Hull House."

"So about one-thirty?"

"I was hoping for one o'clock."

He tucked his pocket watch away. "Will you wait until one-thirty?"

"Why?" A slight breeze loosened some wisps of hair and brushed them across her face. Hooking them with her finger, she tucked them back up into her twist.

"Because I want to go with you," he said. "And I need time to talk to Carlisle and to change out of my uniform. Also, unless I miss my guess, this settlement probably isn't in the best part of town." He held up a hand, halting her objection. "Let me say it this way, I'd like to escort the baby."

"I wasn't going to walk. I was going to take the cable car."

"I'd still like to go."

She sighed. "All right. But if you aren't right here at one-thirty on the dot, then I'm leaving without you."

It felt good to be in his denims. He hated wearing that stiff, awkward uniform. And the sword was downright embarrassing. But it was the cap which was the worst. It was about as useless as a four-card flush and provided no shade for the neck or ears. And he absolutely refused to wear the pompon on top. He'd been reprimanded twice and had pulled extra duties because of it.

He couldn't have cared less. Nobody'd ever catch him wearing a bunny tail on his head. He adjusted his Stetson, never so glad to have it right where it belonged.

"Ded'cation of Kentucky State Building t'day!" Billy's little friend thrust a pamphlet in Hunter's direction. "Statue of Daniel Booth to be unveiled, Southern meals in the dinin' room."

Daniel *Booth?* Stopping, Hunter took the schedule and perused it, relieved to see Kentucky, at least, had gotten Boone's name right. "How much?"

"Five cents." The boy's earnest black eyes captured Hunter's.

"Five cents? Why, I can get clear to downtown for that."

The boy stiffened, his face defensive. "It's a fair price. The fellas in the Court of Honor sell 'em for ten cents. But not me. You buy from Derry Molinari and you'll always get a fair price."

"Is that right?"

"It sure is. And what'd ya want to spend five cents goin' downtown for when you can go to the Kentucky Building and see what Daniel Booth looks like?"

"Daniel *Boone.*" Hunter pursed his lips. "And I'll admit, you have me there. I can't imagine why anybody in this town would want to go anywhere but due south." Digging in his pocket, he pulled out a dime and flipped it toward the boy. "Keep the change."

Derry caught it midair, his face lighting, his

116

smile showing some bottom teeth missing. "Thank ya, mister. Since you're a good egg, I'll give ya a little more for your money." Leaning in, the boy lowered his voice. "If you're liking Kentucky, ya can go to the other side o' the park over by the windmills and see an old moonshiner's still from there."

Hunter felt a smile begin to grow. "Well, that is a bonus. And I'm glad you told me. Somehow I think the governor of Kentucky might leave that part out of his dedication speech today."

"He ought not to. It makes real sour mash and was captured by revenue officers."

Grin still lingering, Hunter pushed up the rim of his Stetson. "How old are you, Derry?"

The boy puffed up his shoulders. "Nine and a half."

Hunter lifted his brows. "That old?"

"Yep. And I do my share. Ever' day."

"Your share of what?"

"Bringin' money home. I get one penny for every paper I sell. Papa got to stop by the grocer's last night 'cause of me." Looking left and right, he leaned forward again. "Say, are you a real cow-boy?"

"I'm a Texas Ranger."

"What's that?"

Hunter stared at the boy, aghast. *What's that?* "You've never heard of the Rangers?"

"Nope."

Rubbing his eyes, Hunter tried not to react. The boy was only nine. And most likely Italian, with his coloring and name of Molinari. He obviously came from a poor family who probably didn't know much about the world outside of Chicago. But still, *what's that?*

Billy stepped out onto the landing, capturing Hunter's attention. Holding the babe against her shoulder, she looked around but had yet to notice him. A Chicago breeze whisked through the boulevard picking up the edge of her simple brown skirt and whipping it. Frothy ruffles from her petticoat peeked out from underneath before being covered again when the wind settled.

The image of Miss Pantalets-Trousers backing into the cellar flashed through his mind. He hadn't thought of her for a while now, but still, he didn't think he'd ever forget the sight she'd made hanging from the window with skirts, petticoats, and trousers bunched up while long, shapely, stocking-clad legs reached for the floor. That gal sure did have a nice pair o' legs on her.

He stared at Billy's skirt, wondering what kind of legs she had under there. Pulling his thoughts back where they belonged, he approached the steps. "You ready?"

She turned toward him. Eyes widening, she perused him from hat to hoof and then back up again. "I didn't recognize you with your clothes on."

Tugging the rim of his hat, he winked. "Wish I could say the same, ma'am."

Red rushed into her cheeks.

Die and be blamed, but he liked to see her blush.

She hadn't made any move to come down the steps, so he went on up to help her down.

Lips parting, she took a step back.

"You all right?" he asked.

She didn't answer.

He glanced at the child. "He all right?"

"Who?"

"The baby. Who do you think?"

"Oh!" There was the blush again. "The baby. Yes. Fine. He's fine. Drank a whole bottle. Burped loud as any man. I found him a nice white gown. Has pleats all across the front and fits him just right. How are you?"

He drew his brows together. If he didn't know better, he'd think she'd sampled some of Kentucky's sour mash.

"You're late," she said.

"*I'm* late? I've been over there with Derry for a good ten minutes while he about talked the hide off a cow. The minute you stepped out, I came right over."

She glanced at Derry, but the boy had drawn in another customer.

"Yes, well. Let's go, then." She took off down the stairs.

He grabbed her elbow. "Easy, woman. Slow

down before you get tangled up in your skirts."

Tensing, she allowed him to assist her, then pulled out of his grasp the minute they reached the walkway. What the deuce was the matter with her?

Churning up more dust than could settle in a day, she scurried toward the exit. He had no trouble keeping up. And though he didn't know what kind of bee had gotten into her bonnet, he sure as cockleburs wasn't going to ask.

CABLE CAR[10]

"He thought they only had cable cars in San Francisco, but Chicago had enough grips to supply the whole country, seemed like."

CHAPTER 12

He'd never ridden in a cable car before. Until arriving at the fair, he'd thought they had those only in San Francisco. But Chicago had enough grips to supply the whole country, seemed like.

Taking the babe from Billy, he helped her up onto the car, handed her the infant, then climbed in next to her and waited for the ride to start. Each bench was designed to hold four people, but they were split down the middle like pews in a church. Wooden barriers restricted folks from entering the center aisle reserved for the gripman. The uniformed man walked down its length collecting tickets.

Hunter tucked in his legs, his knees almost as high as his chest, his shoulders and elbows scrunched together. He'd never make it all the way downtown like this.

He laid his right arm behind Billy, stretched out his legs as best he could, and extended his left elbow beyond the armrest. Much better.

The car was completely open, with small columns supporting the roof overhead. Bedraggled children, tired mothers, and weary husbands who'd toured the fair filed into the benches behind them. Bending low, Billy whispered to the infant and tickled his chin, her profile and jawline as fine as any fairy-tale princess's. Everything about her intrigued him. Nothing about her made sense.

She'd taken to the babe like a bear to a honey tree. Clearly, she'd make a good mother. So why would she have intentionally given up the sacred calling of her sex in exchange for the toil and hardship of a man's? Had she feared she'd become a spinster and didn't want to be a burden to her family?

But that didn't make a bit of sense. Not with her curves and face and easy laughter. There had to have been plenty of men willing to guard and protect her within the walls of their homes and the strength of their arms.

A clanging gong and a yell warned passengers to either get on or get off. The babe scrunched up his face at the noise, but Billy tickled him again to keep him from crying.

Though Hunter braced himself for a jerky start, the ride was surprisingly smooth and quiet—almost as if they were gliding over ice. No screeching wheels since everything was controlled by a cable underneath the tracks. And no coal-burning odor since the powerhouse running the car was kept in some building downtown.

At the end of Fifty-fifth Street, the gripman slowed the car to make a ninety-degree turn north onto Cottage Grove Avenue. Several men jumped off. Others jumped on. All the while the grip still moved. But Hunter fastened his attention to an expansive pleasure garden now stretching out on his left as if it had been dropped straight down from heaven.

"That's Washington Park," a woman behind them pointed out to her son.

Hunter wished he could jump off, too. Never had a sight been so welcome. Young boys played a game of baseball not too far from a flock of sheep grazing in an open field. A man in a canoe rowed his best gal down a winding canal. A smattering of couples walked along handsome trails lining the park.

He took a long breath. He missed home. Missed its wide open spaces. The slower pace. The people. His horse. His guns. He'd never been outside of Texas before now. If he'd had any idea how noisy, filthy, smoky, and crowded it was here, he never would have come.

But it was his lifetime dream to be, not just a Ranger, or even a captain of the Rangers, but chief of the entire Rangers outfit. And to do that, he needed to broaden his horizons. Meet and work with men in powerful positions. Learn more about the places some of their outlaws were migrating from. The World's Columbian Exposition offered him a way to do that in six short months.

Never had time passed so slowly.

They left the park behind and reentered the city with building after building looking like overgrown store boxes with holes punched in them.

He looked down at Billy. The subtle motion of the car had put the babe to sleep and she wasn't too far behind. Her head nodded, then jerked up. Nodded, then jerked up. He wondered how much sleep she'd lost last night because of the child. Tempted as he was to wrap his hand around her shoulder and pull her against him, he resisted. He'd given in to temptation last night and would've stolen a kiss if she'd allowed it. But she hadn't, and it was just as well.

Starting something with her might make the five months he had left here a lot more pleasant, but the last thing he needed was to become involved with a woman who worked. Which begged the question—what was he doing arranging to have the rest of the day off so he could spend it with her?

But he already knew. Where he came from, a fellow didn't leave a woman and child to take a seven-mile trek across a booming city and into the slums unescorted. Adjusting his hat, he started paying closer attention to the streets they crossed.

"What stop is ours?" he asked, giving Billy a gentle nudge and trying to keep his voice down, though he didn't know why. If the babe could sleep through all the racket from the city streets, he could sleep through anything.

"Canal and Polk," she answered, her voice groggy.

A few minutes later the car turned onto Twelfth Street and the cosmopolitan face of Chicago turned seedy. One look at the plethora of brothels along with the character of the men on the street and Hunter was glad he'd insisted on accompanying Billy and the babe.

Finally, they made it to Polk. He signaled the gripman, learning that while the men hopped on and off the car, the gripman brought the car to a complete stop for women, children, and old-timers.

He helped Billy off the car. "You want me to carry him?"

"No, we're fine."

"You sure you have the right address?"

"Halsted and Polk. That's what the matron at the dormitory told me."

Tamping down his concern, he appropriated her doctor's bag and took her elbow. Best he could tell, they'd left the brothels behind, but the buildings still weren't the fancy kind they'd passed coming up. They were factories, mills, and warehouses, each emitting its own pungent odor.

The farther they walked, the more the buildings deteriorated until at last they were in a neighborhood the likes of which he'd never seen. And in his line of work, he'd seen plenty. Plenty of hideouts, plenty of hovels.

But these . . . these were worse than hovels.

They were rickety sheds, thrown-together lean-tos, and dirt-encrusted fleapits all snuggled up tighter than books on a shelf with saloons only a spit and a stride apart.

Leaning down, he removed a gun from his boot and tucked it into the back of his trousers.

Billy's eyes widened. "What's that for?"

"I just want to put it where I can get to it a little easier."

"You mean it's loaded?"

"Of course it's loaded."

"And you've had it this whole time?"

He sliced her a glance. "Seeing as you graduated cum laude, I'm figuring that question doesn't really require an answer."

Lifting an eyebrow, she turned her attention to the sidewalk, which with each step, weakened, then split off, then disappeared altogether.

They came to a stop. They could either turn around or step into the mire that masqueraded as a street.

Abandoned wagons rested in gutters. Poles from peddlers' decrepit carts welled up toward the middle of the roadbed. Rotten wooden blocks, which had once served as pavement, lay in patches.

Billy made a move to advance.

Hunter held her in check. "There're probably enough fleas in there to herd like cattle."

"I imagine there are."

His jaw begin to tick. "You'll ruin your skirts."

"There's nothing else for it."

"We could go back," he said. "I'll find a livery. Hire a couple of horses."

She studied him, a challenge in her bearing. "You worried about your armadillo boots?"

"I sure enough am."

"You don't have to come." She extended a hand for her bag.

He held it out of reach.

"Listen, Hunter, you're the one who invited yourself along. The baby and I will be fine. It can't be too much farther."

She was touched in the head if she thought he'd leave her and the babe at this point. Made him mad she even suggested it.

A group of laughing children with stringy hair and rags barely covering their rail-thin bodies tore around the corner, dipping under a makeshift clothesline.

"You're it!" one of them shouted, then they all scattered, leaving the tagged ragamuffin to stand in a river of slime where she covered her eyes and counted to twenty.

As she did, her playmates hid in crates, wagons, and garbage boxes. *Garbage boxes*. A youngster in short pants jumped feetfirst into the refuse. A covey of flies ascended. A huge, black rat scampered out of the offal and onto the edge of a hinged wooden box.

Hunter palmed his gun and aimed.

Billy sucked in her breath.

But the child ignored the rat and it scuttled off.

Uncocking his weapon, Hunter returned it to his waistband. The horrendous smell and filth should by all rights have caused the boy to cast up his accounts. Yet he didn't seem bothered in the least. A couple of other youngsters up the street played leapfrog. The smaller of the two splatted his hands right into the quagmire, only to straighten and put those selfsame, mud-caked hands on the back of the boy who'd just jumped over him.

Billy made a move toward the morass.

Grabbing her arm, Hunter spun her around. "I'm not leaving the babe in this cesspool."

The baby whimpered.

Billy's expression hardened. He figured that as a doc she'd seen all kinds of things in her work. Well, so had he. That didn't mean he had no feelings at all.

"The women at Hull House," she said, "have a reputation of being kind, good, and hardworking. All are college educated. I feel sure they'll see the child is well taken care of."

"So he can what? Live in these disgusting conditions? Is that what you want for him?"

Her face remained stoic. "It's not a matter of what I want. I didn't create this situation."

"But you're willing to drop him right in the middle of it."

Her eyes flickered. "What would you have me do, Hunter?"

He lifted his shoulders. "I don't know. Keep him?"

Her lips parted. "Keep him? You think I can simply keep him? Just like that?"

"Sure."

"And I suppose you think that's possible because I am, after all, a woman?"

"Well, yes." He tried to keep the exasperation from his voice, but didn't quite manage it.

"And just how, exactly, would I do that?" She jerked her arm out of his grasp. "I'd have to quit my job in order to take care of him. And if I did that, I'd have no source of income. Then he and I would both end up living in this mess."

He shook his head. "Not if you got married."

Her eyes widened. "Got *married?* To whom?"

"I don't know. I'm sure I could find you somebody."

She narrowed her eyes. "Well, I don't want a husband, Hunter. Because husbands don't much like it when their wives have ambitions and earn wages."

"But don't you see, that's the whole point." Grabbing a bandanna from his pocket, he swiped it across the back of his neck. "You wouldn't have to earn wages. Once you married, your husband could take care of you, and you, in turn, could take care of the baby." It was the perfect solution.

He didn't know why he hadn't thought of it before. He took the first easy breath he'd had since they'd found the little fellow.

"I see." She held her back straight as a fence post. "And what about my ambitions?"

He gave her a stern look. "Now, Billy, what are ambitions when compared to a child's life?"

"What, indeed? But, as it happens, I have a better idea. One that won't affect my marital status or my occupation."

He eyed her warily. "And what would that be?"

"I think *you* should keep him."

He reared back. "Me? I can't keep him. My assignments take me from the Rio Grande to the Louisiana border to the Gulf of Mexico. I spend half my time chasing gun-toting, fast-shooting men on the run and the other half hauling them in. I can't be towing a little one along. Out of the question."

She shrugged. "So get married."

His jaw dropped. "Married? To who?"

"I don't know. I'm sure I could find somebody for you."

His ire began to rise. "Well, aren't you the one thinking the sun comes up just to hear you crow."

Her lips thinned. "Are you coming or not?"

He stood rigid, facing off with her. By all that's holy, she had tongue enough for ten rows of teeth. And she was crazier than a Bessie bug if she thought he could keep the child. He didn't know the first thing about children.

"You sure you won't keep him?" he asked, his voice tight.

She studied him, those pretty brown eyes delving into his. "I can't. I'm sorry."

After several tense seconds, he blew out a long breath. "Well, I can't leave him here. Not like this. Not without some breathing space, at least."

"I don't know what to tell you, Hunter, but I plan to continue on to Hull House and talk to the women there. Maybe they'll be able to ease our minds some."

With a resigned heart, he nodded. "All right, then. Hold the baby tight." Leaning over, he swooped her up into his arms and slogged his way toward Halsted.

CHICAGO YOUTH FROM THE WEST SIDE[11]

"He gestured toward a young boy smoking across the street. 'Kids who don't have anyplace to go loaf around street corners.' "

CHAPTER 13

Billy sputtered and fussed and sputtered some more. He couldn't have cared less. After a block and a half, the sidewalk improved enough to set her back on her feet.

Shaking out her skirts, she mumbled underneath her breath.

He gave her no never mind, his attention completely on the children. Most all were of foreign descent. Some thigh high to a mule, some with a little fur on their brisket. Some playing catch, some loitering about the saloons. Some sleeping in upstairs windowsills, some running down outside staircases. Their numbers had multiplied and they now paved the streets and alleyways.

He thought of the farm he'd grown up on. He'd had fifty acres of his own and those of his neighbors as his personal play space. From can-see to can't-see he'd explored every inch of it. Rather than returning home for the midday meal, he'd snack on the bounty provided by the fruit and pecan trees, the bushes and brambles, the roots and gums. If he'd longed for playmates, he had dogs, cats, birds, horses, and farm animals at his beck and call. He couldn't imagine being reduced to closed-in streets, a neighborhood divested of any hint of green, and a choice of rats for companions.

The ground floors of the two-story wooden houses along this stretch were either shops or saloons. Coal stores covered in soot stood next to grocers and butchers. Brightly painted wooden Indians announced an abundance of cigar shops. Red-and-white-striped poles identified the occasional barber. And large glass globes filled with colored water designated the drugstores.

He wondered how people living in such squalor could afford what the stores offered. Or how the merchants stayed in business.

A group of older boys spilled out of a saloon, cutting Billy off. Straightening, Hunter stepped between them and her, but the young men never even noticed their blunder and wove across the street on unsteady legs. A handful of youngers scurried out after them.

"You needn't do that," Billy said.

"Do what?"

"Treat me as if I were . . ." She scanned the rooftops. "I don't know . . ."

"Female?" he asked.

"Yes." She smiled up at him. "Exactly."

He rolled his eyes and took her elbow. "How much farther?"

"I don't know. The woman said it was a big brick mansion and I couldn't miss it."

The more children he saw frequenting the beer halls, the more his unease grew. He couldn't possibly leave the babe in this mess. Not when the only places of amusement within walking distance were saloons.

Billy might not understand the implications, but he did. A boy without a place to play was father to the man headed for jail. So if she was going to refuse to keep the babe, then before he left for Texas, he'd see to it the child had a place to run around in. A place free of filth, vermin, and vice. He'd been the one to find the waif, it was his responsibility to see to the child's circumstances. Even abandoned babies had a God-given birthright to wholesome play. And Hunter wouldn't rest without doing something, however little, to make sure this one got at least that much.

"Are there any pleasure grounds nearby?" he asked. "You know, like the one we passed coming up here. Washington Park, I think it was?"

Billy swapped the babe to her other shoulder. "Well, let's see. There are plenty on the north and south sides of town—that's where all the affluent people live. But the closest one to here would be Garfield Park."

"Is it within walking distance?"

"Oh, no. You'd have to take a cable car."

He shook his head. "Well, that won't do."

"Do for what?"

"The little pitcher here. He won't be able to afford a ten-cent round-trip fare. It has to be within walking distance."

"What has to be within walking distance?"

"His breathing space. A place for him to spread his wings and run around in without worrying about getting into any trouble."

"Trouble?"

"Well, yeah." He gestured toward a young boy smoking across the street. "Kids who don't have anyplace to go loaf around street corners. They get into the saloons and pick up bad habits. They bust out windows or lampposts with their sling-shots. They form crowds and bully those who aren't a part of their group. When some lawman comes to break things up, the boys resent it and end up getting arrested. And that, I'm afraid, is the first step in pushing them into the criminal class. What they need is a park."

"You're certainly assuming a lot. You don't know the babe here will fall into habits such as those."

"And you don't know he won't."

Sighing, she stepped around some debris. "There's no room here for a park, Hunter. And even if there was, the taxpayers wouldn't spend their dimes on beautifying this part of town."

"I'm not talking about beautifying it. A park with STAY OFF THE GRASS signs would defeat the purpose. I'm talking about a place they can run in, play games in. Someplace where they can work off all their energy."

She bit her lip in thought. "Hull House has a

gymnasium. And it's within walking distance."

He shook his head. "No walls. It needs to be outdoors."

"Are you talking about a playground, then?"

He gave her a sharp glance. "I've heard of those, but I've never seen one. Have you?"

She nodded. "They have them in Boston. It's basically just a plot of land with equipment the children play on. They have swings, seesaws, and hammocks. Once I even saw one where they'd stacked up a mound of street pavers the children climbed on."

His shoulders settled with relief. "That would be perfect. Do they have one of those around here?"

"I guess we're about to find out. Look."

And there it was. Just up a ways, a two-story redbrick manor that, by all rights, should be situated on a grand boulevard in an affluent neighborhood. The clatter of horses' hooves caught his attention. That sound only came from a paved road.

Reaching the corner of Halsted and Polk, he looked north, then south. Not only paved, but lit with street lamps. A steady stream of wagons and drays rumbled past. A cable car slid to a quiet stop in front of them, then continued on after picking up its passenger.

He looked at Billy. "Did you have us walk the last leg on purpose, knowing all the while that if we'd stayed on the cable car, it would turn on

Halsted and bring us right to the front door of Hull House?"

She tightened her mouth. "How was I supposed to know it was going to turn on Halsted? Are you trying to pick a fight?"

"Maybe."

"Why?"

"Because this area is full of dissipation and refuse and disease," he said. "And, like it or not, you're a female and he's a babe. The cable car provides protection and the both of you should stay on it for as long as possible."

Tightening her hold on the infant, she stepped into the street and wove between traffic. "Ah, but we have with us a big Texas Ranger and his ominous-looking gun."

He narrowed his eyes. "Are you baiting me?"

"Maybe."

"Why?"

"Because, like it or not, you're an overbearing male who thinks I'm made out of porcelain." Reaching the boardwalk on the other side, she squared up to him. "Well, I'm not made of porcelain or crystal or any other fragile material."

She had no idea how vulnerable she was. Things weren't like they used to be when they were kids. Tycoons were losing their businesses. Farmers were losing their land. Laborers were losing their jobs.

And desperate times gave birth to desperate men

who preyed upon the weak. It made no difference whether a woman considered herself to be tough or fragile. If she was of the fair sex, she was susceptible. Perhaps it was time she was reminded of just how female she was.

He leaned in toward her, not stopping until they shared the shade of his Stetson. "Never fear, Dr. Tate. Fragile or not, there's one thing I'm clear on. You are made of very real, very soft, very delectable womanly flesh. And you can be assured, I'm not likely to forget about it anytime soon."

Lips parting, she stumbled back a step. If she wasn't holding the baby, he'd have let her fall on that pretty little backside of hers. That would also accomplish his purpose and she'd see he was right.

But he didn't let her fall. This time. Once he'd steadied her, she regained her footing and headed toward the front landing of Hull House. Right before she reached it, she stopped and looked over her shoulder. "What's your middle name?"

He blinked. Had she not been listening at all? How in all that was holy did that brain of hers go from womanly flesh to middle names? "Joseph. What's yours?"

She lifted a brow. "Jack."

Ah, yes. How could he have forgotten? The woman who was named after both her grandpas and who was determined to live up to those namesakes.

JANE ADDAMS[12]

"A young woman in a high-collared, big-sleeved burgundy dress with delicate lace trim entered the room, her step sedate, her bearing straight."

CHAPTER 14

Don't show any emotion. Don't show any weakness. Don't show your softer side.

Billy had repeated her mantra over and over in order to conceal her horror at the intensely pungent odors of rotting food, animal carcasses, spilled beer, and human waste they'd passed. With each step deeper into the Nineteenth Ward, her dismay had escalated.

But had she shown any of her alarm, Hunter would have turned them around and then what?

As she stood in front of the fine old redbrick mansion, a spark of hope flickered within her. It was as if an orchid had taken bloom amidst a field of thistles. She strode beneath a broad piazza supported by white Corinthian pillars, stepped up to the door, then lifted the knocker. Hunter raked the soles of his boots against a boot scraper.

A tiny young woman with a demure collar answered, her smile broad, her eyes lit from within. She invited them inside even before Billy had explained their purpose.

"Thank you for having us. I'm Dr. Billy Jack Tate. I work as a physician at the Columbian Exposition, and Mr. Scott here is a Columbian Guard."

"How delightful." She waved them past a

lush mahogany staircase and into an oversized drawing room. "I'm Miss Frances Weibel. I live here at Hull House. And who might this be?" She indicated the child.

"This is Joseph," Billy said. "But we call him Joey."

Removing his hat, Hunter gave her a sharp glance.

"He's why we're here," she continued. "Mr. Scott found him abandoned at the Woman's Building while he was making his rounds. We've made every attempt to locate the mother, but haven't had any luck."

"Oh, no. The poor thing." Delicate brows furrowed as she glanced again at the babe. "Please have a seat here in the reception room and I'll go collect Miss Addams. She's the owner of Hull House and will be better able to advise you."

The young woman retraced her steps, swept past the staircase, then disappeared into an adjacent parlor.

Billy and Hunter settled onto a claw-footed, mauve brocade sofa. If the home's exterior had been stately, its interior was all that and more. White and gold trim complemented floral wallpaper gracing the long room that ran the entire length of the home's north side. Tall, elegant windows welcomed in sunshine from its north and east ends. Two marble fireplaces offered yet another source of warmth.

Retrieving a bottle from her bag, Billy shook it, then began to feed Joey.

Joey. She was glad he had a name now. On the stoop outside, she'd realized it would be one of the first questions asked. She couldn't bear to say she didn't know. He was such a good baby. He ate heartily, slept soundly, and never fussed. She'd heard of babies like that, but in all of her practice, she'd never run across one. Of course, babies coming to see her were either sick or injured.

Still, he was a fine boy and deserved a name. A name that meant something.

A woman in a high-collared, big-sleeved burgundy dress with delicate lace trim entered the room, her step sedate, her bearing straight. "Good afternoon. I'm Miss Jane Addams. Miss Weibel tells me you've a foundling from the fair."

Hunter rose. "Yes, ma'am. I'm Hunter Scott, the one who discovered him. And this is Dr. Tate."

Billy had been expecting a dowdy spinster, but Miss Addams couldn't be any older than she was herself. The woman's skin was clear and smooth, her figure youthful. Her eyes, however, were not those of a sparkly, idealistic maiden like Miss Weibel. They were old before their time, as if they'd seen much, experienced much, and lost much.

"So tell me about this young man. Joey, I believe Miss Weibel said?" Smoothing her skirt, she nodded at Billy in greeting, then sat in a Windsor chair at a right angle to them.

"Yes, ma'am." Hunter resumed his seat. "I was making my rounds in the northwest corner of the Woman's Building when I heard a baby crying somewhere around the dressmakers' exhibit. I made a search with my lantern and discovered this little pitcher wrapped in a fancy feather cloak."

While he talked, Billy looked around the room. The arched doorways, Turkish rugs, glass-enclosed bookcases, potted ferns, plaster busts, and beautiful paintings were every bit as fine as any which might be found on Boston's Commonwealth Avenue. How in the world did Miss Addams help her neighbors when they couldn't come inside without dragging in all the filth and odors with them? Where would they sit without soiling the furniture? Where would they walk without ruining the floors?

Yet even as she had the thought, a ragamuffin of about ten skipped through the drawing room, her hands and face clean, her dress and boots still quite dirty. "I'm all finished, Miss Addams. Now I get to go to the Butler Building!"

"Excuse me for a moment," Miss Addams said to them, then she rose from her chair and crossed the foyer to open massive pocket doors on the opposite side of the stairs. "And what are you reading today, Miss Hilda?"

"*A Midsummer Night's Dream*. Puck has just spread a love potion on Lysander, who has woken up to see Helena. I don't know what Hermia's going to do when she finds out." The girl gave Miss Addams a rather panicked look, then slipped through the pocket doors.

Smiling, Miss Addams returned to the drawing room, her eyes filled with warmth and animation. "Forgive me. I believe you were telling me about Joey?"

"That's about all there is to it," Hunter said.

Billy nodded. "I'm afraid neither I nor Mr. Scott can take care of the child, what with our work and all. I was hoping you might know of a wet nurse or someone who could take him in?"

"Of course. How old is he?" Miss Addams asked.

"Only a couple of weeks."

The woman tut-tutted, the matronly gesture highlighting the timeworn soul within her youthful body. "The poor little tot. We have a nursery right here at Hull House. Ordinarily we only keep the children during the day while their mothers are at work, but we do, upon occasion, take in foundlings."

Billy pictured the hundreds of unsupervised children on the streets outside. "Is there room in your crèche? With as many families as we passed on our way here, I can't imagine how you'd have an extra crib."

"We have to charge the mothers five cents per

day to cover our expenses. That keeps several of them from participating." She shook her head. "I wish we could do it for free, but we simply can't afford it. Still, between our nursery and kindergarten, we average about fifty children per day."

Fifty? *Fifty?* How on earth would Joey receive any attention when there would be fifty others to watch, feed, and diaper? And how would he sleep amidst all that commotion?

Kicking his legs, the babe loosened his swaddling, causing it to cut across his neck. Hunter immediately placed an arm behind her on the sofa back, and reached over to tuck the blanket back out of the way.

"Fifty," she breathed. "That's quite a handful."

Setting the bottle down, she lifted the babe to her shoulder and patted his back.

Hunter straightened, a smile hovering as he made eye contact with Joey.

"They're no trouble," Miss Addams said, her face softening. "And we have an experienced kindergarten teacher in charge who has the constant assistance of two women."

Joey belched, a bit of milk dribbling from his mouth.

Pulling his handkerchief free, Hunter wiped the babe's lips and grinned as if he were the one responsible for such a hearty burp.

"Would you like to see the nursery?" Miss Addams asked.

"I would," Billy replied. "But, if it's all right, may I finish feeding Joey?"

"Certainly."

Billy switched arms and again gave Joey his bottle.

"While we're waiting," Hunter said, leaning forward and resting his elbows on his knees. "Can you tell me if there are any playgrounds in the area?"

Miss Addams's shoulders wilted a bit. "I'm afraid there aren't."

"But all these children," he said. "They're everywhere. Are you saying they have no place to play at all?"

"We provide what entertainment we can here. We have a Fairy Story Club, a Jolly Boys' Club, the Pansy Club, the Young Heroes Club, and the Story Telling Club."

As Miss Addams continued to list the astounding number of activities and centers they'd made available to the neighborhood, Billy's pleasure grew. She knew they had a gymnasium, a coffeehouse, and a reading room, but she had no idea they'd organized so many literary, cultural, and social clubs.

Hunter, she could see, was not impressed. Over the last few weeks of massages, she'd come to know him quite well. He was an outdoorsman. A man who'd rather hunt and fish than read a book, study a painting, or attend a concert. When they'd discussed the special programs and performances held at the fair, he'd conceded there was some inherent value in the arts, but he didn't consider them a necessity. Not like fresh air and the bounty provided by God's green earth.

Still, her conscience eased considerably. If they left Joey here, he'd have a place to go to kindergarten and to learn about the arts and life outside the Nineteenth Ward. He'd have a community of friends who'd share the use of this house with him. She'd be able to visit him as often as she liked. Perhaps she could even offer her services once a week. Heaven knew, these people needed a physician in their midst.

Joey finished his bottle.

Miss Addams stood. "Shall we head to the nursery?"

"Of course." Billy propped Joey against her shoulder and accepted Hunter's assistance to her feet. Their eyes connected, hers filled with relief, his filled with misgivings.

HULL HOUSE NURSERY[13]

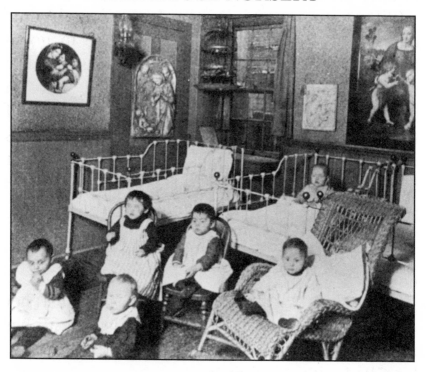

"Brass cribs lined the walls. Some of the tots slept,
others stood at the railings. Some cried,
and yet others crawled along the floor."

CHAPTER 15

They passed beneath an arched doorway, then through a kitchen full of light. Its yeasty fragrance filled the back part of the house. Three girls with miniature aprons stood on stools, flour up to their elbows as they kneaded bread. With an expressive voice, Miss Weibel read a book about a happy-go-lucky dog of an uncertain breed.

Hunter held the back door. Following Miss Addams, they left the little cooks behind, then crossed an alley free of filth, walked down another, passed a water pump, and arrived at a tiny brick cottage.

Sounds of children laughing and chattering poured from its windows. Inside, the kindergarten gathered in a main drawing room. Miniature Italians, Hebrews, French, Irish, Africans, and Germans filled every available space. One little girl with bright red braids stood on the seat of a chair, talking to a baby figure in a painting. As Billy and Hunter wove past, the girl leaned over and kissed her newly found friend.

"The nursery's upstairs." Miss Addams led them to the second floor and two rooms of babies. Brass cribs lined the walls. Some of the tots slept, others stood at the railings. Some cried, and yet others crawled along the floor.

151

"Miss Chaffee, we have a foundling for you. He's come all the way from the World's Fair."

Miss Chaffee touched her toe to the floor and set her wicker rocking chair into motion. A hint of fine facial hair dusted her upper lip. The baby in her arms looked doubly small against her large girth. "The fair?"

Miss Addams crossed to a crib and lifted a crying baby from it, then repeated the story Hunter had told her.

"My stars and garters. The poor little tyke." With a sideways nod, Miss Chaffee indicated the beds lining the walls. "Well, set him down in one of those and I'll get to him as soon as I can."

Billy glanced at the cribs. There were so many. How long would it be before Joey was picked up again? With him not being of a fussy nature, she feared he might be overlooked while the other babies received all the attention.

"Did you say you had two nursemaids?" Billy asked.

"Yes." Miss Addams returned the child she held and picked up a different one. "Miss Rorabaugh works across the hall. She's all full up today, too."

"I see." There were only two vacant beds. With slow, heavy steps, she headed toward the one closest to a window so Joey could enjoy the sunshine. When she reached it, she stood beside the crib, her arms about the baby, his heartbeat next to hers.

She thought of his sweet presence beside her throughout the night. Maybe she could keep him, after all. Perhaps if she rearranged her schedule? Her habits? Her work? But she knew better. There was no possible way. She was having enough trouble attracting patients. Adding a baby to the mix would be impossible.

She had no one to watch him. And if her practice ever did start to flourish, she'd need to be able to work at any time of the day or night.

A baby in the crib beside them pulled itself up into a standing position, then bounced in excitement, hoping to be picked up.

Billy gave it a smile. "Hello. This is Joey. He's going to be your neighbor."

On a shelf above the tot, a neat stack of diaper cloths caught her eye. Perhaps she should change Joey before she left.

She retrieved a cloth, then laid him in his crib.

"I want you to know," she said, lowering her voice so only Joey could hear, "there isn't a shadow of a doubt in my mind that your mother wanted you." She unwrapped his swaddling. "But the world is full of tragedy, and nothing short of that would have parted her from you."

Kicking his legs and waving his arms, he gurgled.

She unfastened the pins holding the old diaper on. "I've delivered many a baby to mothers out of wedlock. Some had been violated by unconscionable men. Some had been forced to sell themselves in order to survive. Some had simply anticipated their wedding night, only to discover there wasn't going to be any wedding after all."

His flailing fist landed on his mouth. He immediately began to suckle it.

"But in every case, Joey, every single case, those mothers were racked with grief. Inconsolable. And the only reason they gave their babies up was because they knew in their heart of hearts someone else could provide their precious child with a better, healthier, happier home than the one they faced on the street."

Of a sudden, she wondered if Joey's mother lived in the Nineteenth Ward. Would she hear of the child who'd been abandoned at the fair? For surely his story would be told among the workers of the house and the people of the neighborhood. Would she come to see him? Claim him? Or would she only have a peek without revealing her secret?

But, of course, she might not be here at all. She might be one of the women from the brothels they'd passed earlier today. Or she might be a woman from the country who'd come to the city, fallen into trouble, and couldn't return home with a child or she'd be disowned by her family. Whatever the case, Billy knew his mother was thinking of him and mourning her loss and his.

She secured the new diaper. "So you see, you

were loved the most because your mother was willing to make the ultimate sacrifice and give up the one thing she wanted more than anything else on earth . . . you." Pulling his gown over his legs, she tapped him on the nose. "And don't you ever forget it."

He looked at her then, his bright blue eyes holding hers.

Her throat closed. She couldn't leave him. She couldn't. She turned to look for Hunter, but he was right there. Right behind her. His dark eyes as troubled as hers.

"It's not too late," he said. "You can pick him up, walk straight out of here, and take him home with you."

Moisture rushed to her eyes. "I can't."

"You can."

Biting her lip, she turned back to Joey and ran a hand across his soft, bald head. "I'm sorry, my sweet. I'm so, so sorry."

With careful, tender motions, she swaddled him one last time, then leaned over and kissed his forehead. "Good-bye," she whispered.

Then she turned and walked from the room.

NEWSBOYS, CHICAGO[14]

"He saw a group of children huddled under an outside stairwell, two young boys hawking newspapers, and a fruit stand selling apples for ten cents a peck."

CHAPTER 16

Hunter caught up to her at the cable stop. "He needs a playground."

"He needs a mother."

He barely caught her words over the noise of the street, she'd spoken them so softly. But catch them he did.

Leaving the babe had been hard. For both of them. And much as she tried to hide it, her eyes still held a telltale sheen.

Sighing, he settled his hat back onto his head. "Miss Addams said she's a member of several women's clubs here in town. She thinks she might be able to find a good family to take him."

Billy raised her gaze to his. "She does?"

"She does."

"How soon?"

"I didn't ask. And until then, I want to make preparations for the other eventuality. The one where no one rescues him from here. And if that's what happens, then I want him to have a playground."

He glanced down the street. No evidence of a cable car yet. "Whoever abandoned him knew a guard would find him." He looked at the toes of his boots. "It's a tremendous responsibility. One I take very seriously. I'd never be able to live with myself if I didn't do something to ensure he had a place to play other than a saloon and a reading circle."

She crinkled her brows. "But you can't just leave him a bunch of five-cent pieces for the cable fare to Garfield Park. What if he decides to spend the money in a saloon instead?"

"I agree. That's why I'm going to make him a playground."

Her lips parted. "Make him a playground? How? Where?"

"Here in the neighborhood. Someplace within walking distance."

"Where would you get the land? Every square inch is filled with these hovels."

"We haven't seen the whole neighborhood. There's bound to be a lot somewhere."

"What about the equipment? The sand? The builders?"

He rubbed the back of his neck. "I don't know. But I need to figure out something. I'm heading back to Texas as soon as the fair's over. That leaves me five months."

"Hunter, you work six days a week. You don't have time to build a whole playground by yourself."

"I'll manage."

"How?"

He scowled. "I just said I'd figure out a way. Which means I'll figure out a way."

He swept his gaze about the street, pinpointing spots where undesirables might be lurking. But he only saw a group of children huddled under an outside stairwell, two young boys hawking newspapers, and a fruit stand selling apples for ten cents a peck.

"Let's assume," she said, "you somehow find some land. Who, then, is going to pay for the equipment?"

"I'll make it."

"Who's going to pay for the materials?"

He drummed his thumb against his trouser leg. "You could wear the horns off a billy goat, you know that? Are you purposely trying to make me mad?"

"No, I'm trying to be realistic. I'm not saying it's a bad idea. It's not. It's a wonderful idea. Not just for Joey, but for all the children. It would be a great boon to both their physical and mental well-being. But there's a lot to consider. There's the financial side—which is no small part—but there's also the little things. Things like making sure the swings aren't too high off the ground. And the poles are stabilized and firmly planted. You'd need to be certain the surface isn't too hard, that there's a fence between them and the street, that the equipment is spaced so it doesn't endanger—"

"Enough!" He held up his hand. "I haven't asked for your help. I haven't even asked for your opinion. I simply stated I was building a playground and that is that."

She propped her hands on her hips. "Well, you can't do it by yourself. You can't. You need some help. My help."

"Your help?"

"Yes. I'd have a much easier time raising the funds."

"How do you figure that? Didn't you just move here from Boston? Do you even know anybody in Chicago?"

She hesitated. "Well, not really. I have many, many connections in Boston. And I'll admit to having next to none in Chicago. But I could still join the Chicago Women's Club. I could see if Miss Addams would give me an introduction to some of her benefactors. I could ask Mrs. Palmer at the Woman's Building for suggestions. And I could help you with all the little things you might have overlooked. Besides, I only work three days a week. I have much more time than you."

"What about that shingle you have hanging on the corner of Congress and Forty-third? I thought you spent your off days there?"

She paused. "I do."

"What about those patients?"

Shifting her weight, she tracked a tired swayback horse clomping up the road. Its wagon held a mound of odds and ends and a peddler at the reins.

"Any rags?" the man shouted. "Any bottles? Any junk today?"

Hunter scowled, wondering when the poor old horse had last been groomed, then he forced himself back to the matter at hand. "How many patients do you see per day out there?"

She hesitated. "Not as many as I'd like."

"What's the number?"

She tugged at her gloves. "It varies."

"Approximately, then. Twenty a day?"

She gave her head a negative shake.

"More or less?"

"Less."

"Ten patients a day?"

Another negative shake.

He raised a brow. "Five?"

She pressed her lips together.

"Three?"

She brushed a nonexistent speck from her skirt.

"Any?"

A nod.

"What then?"

She lifted her chin. "One, if you must know."

He studied her, then gentled his voice. "Per day or in all?"

She bit her lip. This time she watched a rickety frame house being rolled away by a horse and two men, most likely to make room for some factory.

Swiping a hand across his mouth, he grappled

for something to say. It didn't take much to figure out what had happened. She'd received one call, then word had spread that Billy Jack Tate was not a man.

Indignation on her behalf welled within him. They should at least have given her a chance. He'd seen plenty of doctors a lot worse than her. A lot. She might not be a man, but she wasn't half bad as far as doctoring went.

Still, if she couldn't even muster up two patients, how in blue blazes did she expect to find donors for him? "Why haven't you called on all those women to help establish your practice?"

She shrugged. "I didn't have access to Mrs. Palmer until I started at the Woman's Building. I didn't even know about Miss Addams. And I hadn't gotten around to joining the Chicago Women's Club. I'd started instead by getting to know the leading surgeons in the city, then I'd simply assumed my credentials would speak for—"

"Run, sheep! Run!" a young boy down the street screamed.

Whirling around, Hunter had his gun out and feet spread before he realized it was just a game.

The group of huddling children darted out from underneath the stairwell, squealing as they tried to reach their designated "sheep pen" before the "foxes" beat them to it.

Sighing, he eased his gun back into his waistband. "If you're offering your help, Billy, I certainly won't turn it away. I know you care about the babe as much as I do. But I'm figuring you'd have to to take down your shingle in order to do what you're proposing and I don't want you blaming me for that."

She swallowed. "It would just be for as long as it takes to build a playground. I think Joey's worth it. Don't you?"

Joey. Joseph. That had been a shock, her naming him that. But it hadn't taken him long to warm up to the idea. The fella needed a name. Might as well be one of his. And by all that was holy, he'd see to it that the boy didn't grow up someplace without a tree or play spot free of dung and vermin.

Still, he could do it on his own. He didn't want her help if it meant she'd have a knot in her tail the whole time.

"You want to think about it before you decide?" he asked. "Just to be absolutely sure?"

Sighing, she nodded. "Yes. All right. Let me think about it."

A cable car approached. Raising his hand, he gave a whistle. She settled in and he kept his arms at his sides, but he couldn't help notice hers looked awfully empty without Joey in them.

CHAPTER 17

Billy lay on the unforgiving, putrid yellow sofa of her little hall bedroom on Congress Street. The couch boxed her in on three sides by back and arms of equal height and served as her Procrustean bed—six inches too short. Fortunately, Procrustes wasn't there to lop off her redundant parts.

Still, her cramped legs kept her from sleeping well on the best of evenings. Tonight there had been no sleeping at all. She stared at the plank ceiling. Minute cracks between the boards allowed her to have fleeting glimpses of the tenants in the room above and, when she was standing, in the room below. They, too, had glimpses of her. A disconcerting thought.

But there was no movement upstairs now. No movement below. No movement outside. Nothing but stillness and darkness.

She pulled her braid from underneath her and plopped it over her shoulder. It had only been one day since they'd taken Joey to Hull House. One day since she'd offered to remove her shingle from the corner drugstore. What in the world had she been thinking?

She hadn't. Clearly. Hunter said he'd build the playground. She should've simply left it at that.

But even now she couldn't imagine how he'd do it. Not by himself. And if he was going to do something for Joey, she wanted to be a part of it, too. But did she really need to take down her shingle?

She maneuvered onto her side, her cambric Mother Hubbard nightgown twisting about her legs. Lifting up her hips, she wrenched the fabric free, then settled back into her crouched position.

Though only a quarter moon was out, she had no trouble seeing the room's outlines, for her eyes had long since adjusted to the darkness. The Morris chair, which she could convert into an examining table, took a place of honor in the middle of the floor. She'd hung a curtain across a small bookcase to cover her books on one side and her instruments and medications on the other.

Her washbowl and slop bucket remained hidden in the closet while two cane seat chairs sat against the opposite wall. An oversized sign she'd made to fill the window of her second-story room rested beneath the sill, allowing for a cool nighttime breeze.

No one but she had ever seen her carefully prepared office. She'd had only one person come for help and he'd made it no farther than the front door of the building. When she'd followed the boy to his home, his mother's ailment had been nothing more than a bunion.

The clock downstairs gave two gongs. She sighed. The three hundred dollars she'd saved for starting her practice had dwindled down to half that amount. Then, when the position at the Woman's Building had presented itself, she'd foolishly spent a month's wages on a new gown and undergarments. She couldn't afford to take down her shingle. She couldn't.

Rolling to her other side, she faced the back of the couch and again untwisted her nightdress. Neither could she afford to pay thirty dollars a month for an apartment when no one came to call and she had free lodging at the Women's Dormitory.

Last week she'd thought to bribe God into gracing her with patients by committing the Book of James to memory. She'd chosen it because it only had five chapters.

Now she wished she hadn't. For today she'd memorized the last verse of chapter 1.

Religion that God our Father accepts as pure and faultless is this: to look after orphans and widows in their distress and to keep oneself from being polluted by the world.

She covered her head with her arm. She'd looked after Joey in his distress. She'd taken him in and fed him and clothed him and kept him warm. She'd taken him to Hull House, where he'd be looked after by loving women with a passion for the poor.

So why was she feeling so unsettled? But she knew why. Joey wasn't the only orphan on the West Side. There were hundreds of them. If not orphans in the strictest sense, then at least orphans during the days while both parents worked. And Hunter had presented her with an opportunity to help. An opportunity to make their lives a little bit brighter. An opportunity to look after them in their distress.

She curled herself up tighter. Did it have to be either-or? Couldn't she do both? Start a practice and build a playground?

She closed her eyes. She didn't see how. She was already away from her apartment three days a week. Building a playground would require even more time away. It wasn't something she could do from home.

Maybe she should just let Hunter do it. It wasn't as if she was the only person who could get the job done. Yet every time she thought of him working on a playground while she sat in this apartment twiddling her thumbs, her insides clenched. Already she'd thought of a hundred things he needed to do and a hundred more he could do.

Lying around in this apartment doing nothing reminded her of dropping money in the offering basket. Making an offering was good. Important, even. But getting out there and doing the actual labor was also required.

She closed her eyes. Forced her muscles to relax. And at some point, she fell asleep.

It wasn't until much later that morning, when she stood in front of the Woman's Building buying a catalog from the newsboy, Derry, that she came to a decision. She would temporarily remove her shingle, move out of her hall apartment, stay full-time in the Women's Dormitory, and help Hunter build a playground.

It might not be the smartest business decision, but it was the right thing to do. And it would give her a chance to save a few pennies in the process.

CHAPTER 18

Hunter checked his pocket watch. Billy should be out any minute. He still couldn't believe she'd removed her shingle. He only hoped she didn't come to regret it. Meanwhile, he'd take all the help he could get.

Since it was her day off from the infirmary, they were to meet outside the Women's Dormitory once his morning shift had ended. This time he'd stopped by a livery and picked up a couple of horses for them. He was through with cable cars, and if he had to leave early in order to get back to work, he'd feel more comfortable leaving her on the West Side if she were on a horse.

The doors opened and all thoughts took a powder. Miss Pantalets-Trousers stood with one hand on the door, her face turned as she spoke with someone inside. She might not have on her bright-pink sash and wide-rimmed hat, but he'd only ever seen one lime-green skirt in his entire life. And it was that day in the cellar of the Memorial Art Palace on a woman of her height and form.

With the sun at the top of noon, he'd finally be able to get a look at her face. Straightening, he kept her right between his sights.

The longer she stood there, the faster his heart

pumped. A few seconds later she turned around and his insides stacked up against his throat.

It couldn't be. His skin flashed hot, then cold. His blood gushed throughout his body. All sounds receded. *Billy.*

Giving him a little wave, she crossed the landing to the steps. He continued to stare, unable to reconcile what his mind was telling him. Dr. Billy Jack Tate was Miss Pantalets-Trousers. *Dr. Billy Jack Tate was Miss Pantalets-Trousers?*

His gaze drifted to her skirt. In his mind's eye, he recalled the utilitarian bloomers. No trim, no rickrack. Just a pair of trousers and a simple petticoat. Something so bland only a dress reformer would wear them.

But there was nothing bland about those stocking-clad legs.

He swallowed, images shuffling through his mind like a series of risqué stereoscopic cards. Those long, gorgeous, stocking-clad legs belonged to Billy. Those tiny feet and ankles belonged to Billy. That curvy backside belonged to Billy.

She stopped in front of him. "Sorry I'm late."

He searched her eyes. Eyes he'd come to admire way too much. "You're her."

She blinked. "What?"

"You're her. The woman in the cellar. Miss Pantalets-Trousers."

She blanched. "What cellar?"

"You know."

She immediately masked her expression, giving nothing away. She was cool as a skunk in the moonlight. And that was her undoing. For if she'd not been Miss Pantalets-Trousers, she'd have a look of confusion. Instead, she'd donned her doctor's face.

Other details from that morning began to flood his memory. Before, most of his recollections had centered on what he'd seen. Now he began to think about what he'd heard. What she'd said. What he'd said.

And unlike her, he'd introduced himself that day. Which meant she'd known who he was from the very first day she'd walked up the steps of the Woman's Building with two hat pins stuck in her mouth.

"You've known." He grappled with his new-found knowledge, still trying to make sense of it. "You've known who I was this whole time, haven't you?"

She didn't answer. But then, she didn't have to.

His eyes began to widen. "Did you . . .?" Pointing in the direction of the fair, he felt himself bowing up. "Did you order that, that *procedure* in retaliation for—"

"No!" Shock broke through the barrier. She pulled back. "Of course not. I'd never, ever . . ."

He narrowed his eyes. "So help me, Billy, if I find out that treatment was all for nothing, I'm gonna snatch you baldheaded."

"It wasn't. I promise, Hunter. I promise." She stared at him straight on. No shifty eyes. No fidgeting.

He studied her. "Then why didn't you tell me?"

"Tell you? Tell you what?"

"That you're Miss Pantalets-Trousers."

"Miss Who?"

A woman exiting the building gave them a sideways glance. Another made no effort to hide her curiosity as she openly listened to the exchange. Hunter waited for them to pass.

He was a lawman. Trained to ferret out those who had something to hide. Yet this entire time, he hadn't suspected a thing. Nothing.

But she'd known all along who he was. He didn't think she'd use her power as a doctor to retaliate, but then, he'd never have thought she'd have lied to him, either.

"Why didn't you tell me?" he asked again, struggling to mask his anger and confusion.

Pulling her lips down, she crossed her arms and lowered her voice to a near whisper. "What exactly is it you expected me to say? 'Nice to meet you, Mr. Scott. I'm the woman you caught breaking into the cellar of the Memorial Art Palace.' "

"Yes. That would have been plenty sufficient."

Her lips parted. "You must be jesting. What happened down there is one of the most mortifying moments of my life. Why on earth would I point it out to you if you'd forgotten all about it?"

His eyes widened. "Forgotten about it? *Forgotten about it?* Sweetheart, I have replayed those moments in my mind a hundred times, at least."

Red flooded her face.

His warmed as well. He hadn't meant to say that. Reveal that. But it was true. It couldn't come as a surprise to her. Maybe if she were some young, innocent miss. But not Billy. Not with her being a doctor. She might be unmarried, but she was no innocent. At least, not in her knowledge.

And that bothered him. She should be an innocent. A woman should learn from a man about the mysteries that occur between members of the opposite sex. Not by some tome she'd read and been lectured on by a dried up old professor.

"Have you ever been kissed?" he asked.

Arms coming uncrossed, she stepped back. "What?"

"Have you ever been kissed?"

"That's, that's none of your business."

She hadn't. Grabbing her hand, he hauled her around the corner and into the quiet alley tucked between the dormitory and the furniture building beside it. He propped her against the wall and flattened a hand on either side of her.

Her eyes wide, she stared at him, her chest rising

and falling. Teasing him with each breath she took.

He said nothing, just tried to lasso the thoughts, the images, the needs, the wants rushing through him. "I'm fixing to kiss you now, Billy. It's well past time."

Trying to press herself farther into the wall, she shook her head. "I don't think that's a good idea."

"Why not?"

"Because . . . because . . ." She searched the alley as if it would provide her with an answer to whatever doubts she was tussling with. "Because I'm not attracted to you?"

Even if he hadn't already known she was lying, the very fact that she ended her sentence with a question confirmed it. "That dog don't hunt, Billy girl."

She spread her hands against the wall. "What does that mean?"

"Means you're lying and we both know it."

"I still don't think it's a good idea."

"Why not?"

"Because nothing can come of it."

"Why not?"

"Because you're going back to Texas and I'm not."

"I'm not asking you to marry me. I'm asking for a kiss. Nothing too involved. Just a little one."

She said nothing.

He was inches away. Inches away from something he realized he wanted very, very much. But he didn't make a move. Wouldn't make a move. Not until he had permission.

"I think we'd better go." Her breath fluttered the folds along the front of her bodice. A subtle scent of summer berries teased his nose.

"Aren't you the least bit curious?"

"Yes," she whispered.

Bending his elbows, he leaned down.

She placed her fingers against his lips. "I think we'd better go."

Stopping his descent, he took the end of her finger into his mouth and grazed it with his teeth, then kissed it.

She sucked in a breath, watching as he treated each finger with equal consideration. Finally, she lowered her hand, running it from his mouth to his chin to his neck, then stopping at his collar.

"Billy?"

She looked at him, her eyes liquid, her lashes long.

"You sure got some pretty legs."

Her lips parted. "You mustn't say things like that."

"I know. I just thought I'd tell you in case you were wondering."

She pressed her hand against her stomach. "I wish you'd forget all about that."

"I'll never forget those moments. Especially now. Now that I know it's you." He curled his hands against the brick. "Die and be blamed but I want to kiss you."

With a stuttering breath, she looked down, then ducked under his arm and made her way toward the horses.

As disappointment and desire warred for dominance, he watched her progress, no longer needing his imagination to fill in the blanks.

WEST SIDE CHICAGO[15]

"When they turned onto Canal Street,
conditions rapidly deteriorated."

CHAPTER 19

They stayed off the busier streets, establishing a leisurely pace and a less noisy route. She gave Hunter a sideways glance. Seeing him in his denims and cowpuncher hat always made her breath catch. But seeing him in his denims and cowpuncher hat while astride a horse was spellbinding. The horse responded to his slightest touch as if the two of them had been riding together for years.

And though she'd ridden occasionally in Boston, she still had to work to make the animal do her bidding. Not so Hunter. His ease on the horse mesmerized her.

After their episode in the alley, she'd acted as if nothing had happened. As if she weren't the woman from the cellar and as if she hadn't almost let him kiss her. But it was taking every bit of self-control she had.

A teener hauling a load of flour sacks in his wagon rumbled by.

Hunter smiled. "I know just how he feels."

"You used to haul flour sacks?" she asked, forcing herself to look at something other than him.

"I used to haul our cotton. The mill was about six miles from our place."

He scooted his horse to the right, giving the boy a bit more room to pass. "Took all day to be ginned off. Then about midnight, I'd head home with my two-horse team. I'd tie the reins around the brake, lie down on the cottonseed in the back, and go to sleep."

"But if you were in the back, who was driving?"

"Nobody. Didn't need to. Those horses knew where home was. I could always tell when we were getting close, though, because they'd start to run." He adjusted his hat. "Unfortunately, I'd only have a couple of handfuls of seed left because it would've all sifted out through the cracks in the bottom of the wagon." He chuckled. "Come the next summer, there'd be this nice stand of healthy-looking cotton right down the middle of the road. Everybody'd say, 'Wonder how come cotton's growing in the middle of the road?' "

Smiling, she perused the tiny bit of shade his cowpuncher hat cast onto his forehead. The broad shoulders that swayed with each step of his horse. The leather reins he held above the saddle horn with one masculine, sun-kissed hand. The denim-encased thighs that only lacked a pair of chaps to fill out the picture. She wondered if he wore spurs over his pewter-colored armadillo boots when he was home.

She allowed her gaze to retrace its route and admitted she'd come far too close to letting him kiss her. And not just because he was ruggedly handsome. But because he was solicitous. He took his guard duties extremely seriously. He had a tender spot for those in need. And he had the most wonderful accent she'd ever heard.

But she'd managed to remind herself he was also domineering. And had definite opinions of what women should and shouldn't do. Opinions that were polar opposite to her own. Still, maybe a kiss would be okay. Just a little one, like he'd said.

She guided her horse onto Twelfth Street. If she did decide to allow him one, she probably ought to wait until she knew for certain his thoughts about a woman having a profession after marriage. He'd made it clear in the alley that he wasn't proposing. That didn't mean kisses were to be given—or taken—lightly. Whether he admitted it or not, a kiss was a commitment of sorts. At least for her it would be.

It was a way of saying she'd be interested in entering into a deeper level of friendship. One that, in its completion, would lead to marriage. And she wouldn't walk blindly into it. Better to establish where things stood before crossing that line.

But how was she to find out what his thoughts were? She couldn't simply ask him. What would she say? *So, Hunter, how would you feel about your wife being the wage earner?*

No, there was no graceful way to ask the

question without insinuating there was more to their relationship than there actually was. So she'd continue to say no to the kisses and remove herself from his immediate vicinity when temptation reared its head.

They crossed the river, then passed a series of bakery shops, the sweet doughy aroma of rye bread and poppy seed wafting through the air.

You sure got some pretty legs, Billy.

Willing away a blush, she twisted the fabric of her green skirt around her finger. She shouldn't have worn it. But she loved it and didn't have many chances to wear it since it was too colorful for work. Still, she never thought he'd recognize it, especially since she'd left off the pink sash and hat. After all, who ever heard of a man remembering what a woman wore?

She sighed. It had been foolhardy in the extreme and she'd paid the ultimate price. He now knew who she was and he thought he knew what she wore underneath her skirts. But she drew a grim satisfaction from knowing her current undergarments were vastly different from the ones he'd seen her in.

Ice cream parlors, Chinese laundries, and stores that sold steamship tickets ushered them into the Nineteenth Ward. When they turned onto Canal Street, conditions rapidly deteriorated. Distant factories vomited up dense clouds of coal smoke, making the air a danger to breathe. The pleasant fragrance of bread vanished, overpowered by the stench of rotting food and sewage. Their horses' hooves ground newspapers, garbage, and filthy rags into the street while she and Hunter searched for vacant lots.

Children ran behind them and cheered as if they were the lord and lady of a castle riding through their modest village. But these children had no flowers to throw, for there wasn't a single bloom in the entire neighborhood.

Hunter nudged his horse into an alley. Following, she breathed through her mouth. The lower floors of these rear houses served as untended stables and dilapidated outhouses, as well as an open depository for slop buckets. She only prayed no one from an upper story decided to empty one while they passed through.

Broken sewer pipes added to the diseased odors. Yet children still followed behind them, undeterred by the filth and foul smell. Eventually, their devotees tired of the game and dropped off one by one.

When they finally reached Hull House, discouragement had set in. There hadn't been a single empty lot, no open breathing space, no possible candidate for their playground.

He reined in, his eyes bleak. "I didn't see anything, did you?"

She shook her head.

"What should we do?" he asked.

Her gaze drifted past the settlement and to the cottage behind it. "Go see Joey?"

His expression softened. "Why not?"

They tied up their horses, then headed toward the kindergarten and nursery.

WEST SIDE CHICAGO[16]

"He'd not realized the tumbledown shed was
a brothel or he would have turned right
instead of left when they reached the street."

CHAPTER 20

Hunter couldn't believe how much the little fella had grown in just a few short days.

"Let's take him outside for a stroll," Billy suggested.

"To get fresh air?" He raised a brow. "There is none."

She glanced at the window. "It can't be any worse than what's coming through now, and at least Miss Addams keeps her alleyways free of filth."

They walked out of the alley and onto Polk. She cradled the babe, talking to him as if he could understand every word she said. "Her Royal Highness, the Princess of Spain, came to the fair yesterday and was given a reception in the Woman's Building. You should have seen how they'd decorated the place. I'd hoped to be able to sneak in to see her, but Mr. Scott refused to let me in—simply because I wasn't on the approved list."

Placing a hand at her back, he ignored the pique in her voice and moved a bit closer. Hopefully Joey would keep her from catching sight of the scantily dressed woman on an upper windowsill blowing Hunter kisses and giving him come-hither motions with her fingers. He'd not realized the tumbledown shed was a brothel or he would have turned right instead of left when they'd reached the street. The only thing to do now was brazen it out.

"It wasn't as if I was asking for an introduction," Billy continued. "I merely wanted to see the princess, is all. But he didn't allow me to put so much as my big toe into the room."

Hunter didn't bother to make excuses. He'd had a job to do and that was that.

She continued to voice her displeasure while Joey stared at her, captivated by the sound of her voice and by her undivided attention.

A dissipated group of young men stumbled out of the rickety brothel, elbowing one another, straightening their ties, and snorting with ribald laughter. Their shirts were yellowed and stained, their trousers baggy. Only one wore a jacket over his youthful frame, the rest made do with mismatched vests.

Billy looked up.

The tallest one gave her a thorough perusal. "Well, hello. Are you, um, moving in here?"

His friends sniggered and coughed into their hands.

Stepping in front of her, Hunter bowed up. "You keep a civil tongue in your head when you speak to this lady."

The boy looked him up and down. "Or what?"

Hunter grabbed the young man's collar and yanked him forward.

Billy sucked in a breath. "Hunter! What in the world?"

One of the friends stretched his arms to the side, blocking the forward motion of the remaining two fellows.

Hunter leaned in close to the one he held. The boy's alcohol-riddled breath and unwashed body odor enveloped him. "Or I'll knock you six ways from Sunday."

"Now!" the friend behind them hollered.

Hunter pitched the one he had aside, preparing to take on the ones coming at him. But before they advanced, the boy he'd tossed skidded into the building. The walls of the rickety structure wobbled and creaked, threatening to crash to the ground.

The woman in the window gripped the frame as if she'd done so many a time before. Tenants on the lower floors poured out like ants from a disturbed anthill. But it wasn't women of ill repute who evacuated, it was families with children of all ages and in deplorable condition. Hunter swooped Billy and the babe into his arms and raced across the street, plopped them down, then hurried back to help those he could.

By the time he reached the threshold, the building had only a slight sway to it. The woman in the window bent out, shaking her fist and cursing with no regard for the young, sensitive ears within hearing distance. If he'd been in

Texas, he'd have gone up and arrested her. But he wasn't in Texas. And the men, women, and children outside didn't seem affected by her crudeness. They simply returned the way they'd come.

The young man who'd first offended Hunter allowed his comrades to help him to his feet.

"Come on, Kruse," one of them said. "Let's get out of here."

Kruse struggled to stay upright, whether from alcohol or from his flight across the boardwalk, Hunter wasn't sure.

Still, the youth straightened his hat and sneered. "You touch me again, cowboy, and I'll—"

Hunter grabbed him by the arm and swung him around so he faced his friends. This time Hunter spoke to all of them. "I'm a Texas Rang—" He took a breath. "I'm a lawman from Texas, and where I come from hot words lead to cold slabs. We live a life down there that would make your pulp fiction novels look like a New Testament. So unless you're in a hurry to get to heaven, I suggest you keep your thoughts to yourself, you treat a lady like a lady no matter what her occupation, and you steer clear of me and mine. You got that?"

"Or what?" one of them asked, pulling a smoke from his pocket.

Hunter gave him a steely stare. "Or I'll draw quicker than you can spit and say howdy."

The boy widened his eyes, his gaze sluicing down Hunter's body. "You have a gun?"

"Of course I have a gun." What was the matter with folks up here?

They remained still and quiet.

"So, do we have an understanding?" Hunter asked.

The three in front of him nodded.

"What about you, Kruse?" He raised his captive's arm a mite.

"I heard you."

"And?"

"I'll leave you and your lady be."

Hunter slowly released the boy.

He scrambled away. His friends caught and stabilized him. He couldn't have been more than twenty, if that. His vest was too big, his jacket too small and frayed at the sleeves. Turning back toward Hunter, he curled his lip, showing a set of brown, crooked teeth, the front two a good deal longer than the rest. "Come on."

They pushed past Hunter.

He watched until they'd turned the corner and disappeared.

"Hey, there, cowboy." A new feminine voice floated down from the window. "If you're looking for someone to tussle with, I'm a regular Annie Oakley."

He glanced up. A gaggle of newcomers leaned out like chicks in a nest begging for food and showing off their plumage. The one who'd spoken gave him a wink, a smoke dangling from her berry-stained lips.

Tugging on his hat, he gave a slight nod. "Y'all have a nice day, now. Sorry for the fright I caused you."

"Well, I know just how you can make it up to—"

A woman beside her gave her an elbow, then indicated something in the road with a nod of her head.

The group of them glanced into the street, then began to retreat.

Hunter whirled around, his hand already reaching for his gun. But it was just Billy and the babe picking their way across.

"What in heaven's name was that all about?" she asked.

"Nothing. Let's go." He placed a hand at her back and propelled her toward the kindergarten cottage.

"Well, it was certainly something."

"I didn't like that boy's tone."

"You didn't like his tone. So you picked him up and tossed him into the next county? Hunter, you can't do that. Things are different here."

"Not that different. A lady is a lady and a fellow ought to respect that no matter where he hails from."

She sighed. "Was he hurt?"

"Just shaken up."

"Well, did you see the shape that building was

in? It looks like it will tumble down the next time a stiff breeze comes in off the lake. And they had women and children in there."

"I saw."

"Well, I think we ought to find out who owns it and issue a complaint. People's lives are at stake."

"Why don't you just write an editorial for the newspaper?" he asked, his tone a touch sarcastic.

Her eyes brightened. "That's a wonderful idea."

Her response shouldn't have surprised him, but even so, the fact that she took him seriously fouled his mood even more.

They made it to the alley. He guided her down it and to the door of the cottage. "Go put Joey to bed and let's go. I have to be back at work by five."

"You go on. I think I'm going to stay a bit—"

"No. You're going with me."

"No, I'm not. I'm staying right here with Joey and we're—"

"Do you know what that place was?" He pointed in the direction of the bawdy house.

She blinked. "You mean that tenement?"

"It wasn't a tenement." He hesitated. "Well, maybe it was. But part of it was being used as a house of ill repute. And you had no idea. You just walked blindly down that street giving no regard for your surroundings."

She propped a fist against her waist. "I've been in plenty of brothels, Hunter, tending to the sick. I've nothing to fear from them."

Rearing back, he looked at her aghast. "During working hours?"

"Their working hours? Well, no, but I would if I were needed."

"The devil you would. No telling what'd happen."

Her exasperation gave way to irritation. "There were children and their mothers living in that building. If they have nothing to worry about, neither do I."

He ground his teeth. "You have no idea. And we're wasting daylight. Take Joey upstairs, say your good-byes, and let's go."

"I'm not—"

"You either take him up there or I will. Now, *move*."

Joey's lip began to quiver.

"Look what you did." She hugged the babe to her, kissing his forehead and whispering soothing words. Turning toward the door, she stopped at its threshold. "I'm taking him up and I'm staying for as long as I like. You're welcome to stay or go. But I'll not be bullied by you any more than I'd be bullied by those other boys."

"Don't you dare compare me to them."

"Then quit telling me what to do." With that, she stepped inside, the click of the door loud in the ensuing silence.

He had no choice but to wait. Fortunately, she didn't linger long.

SITTING ROOM IN THE WOMAN'S BUILDING[17]

"Hunter grabbed one end of the sofa, pulled it up to the fire, then went to the other side and evened it up."

CHAPTER 21

He had no ears to hear. Billy's horse whinnied, then sidestepped away from his. She pointed out that women ran Hull House. He pointed out that men lived there, too. She told him she'd been a doctor in an asylum at Kalamazoo State Hospital. He grilled her, then gave a satisfied I-told-you-so when she revealed she'd worked with seven other doctors—all of whom were male.

"Never mind," she said, sighing. "It doesn't matter. I'm not going to debate the issue with you. You are not my father. Not my brother. Not my keeper. And certainly not my husband. I can and will do whatever I want, when I want, how I want, and where I want."

"The devil you will."

She looked him square in the eye. "Watch me."

He blustered and harangued. Threatened and lectured. She gave no response. Her mind was made up.

Furthermore, she'd told the women in the nursery that she'd start coming out to Hull House—without escort—a couple of times a week to see to any who needed a doctor's attention.

And that's exactly what she did. She no longer waited for Hunter's afternoons off. She rose the mornings she wasn't working in the infirmary and started her day. Sometimes she went to the Nineteenth Ward, sometimes she attended women's charity clubs. Sometimes she wrote editorials for the *Tribune* as Hunter had suggested, and sometimes she worked on plans for the playground.

On the days she did work, though, Hunter met her for lunch and waited for her after hours until she'd finished all her paperwork.

Turning off the infirmary's electric lights, she stepped into the frigid parlor.

He sat on the couch, reading the *Chicago Tribune*. "You kept the clinic open awfully late."

"I know."

He didn't look up from his paper, but continued to read. His jacket lay folded over the end of the sofa. His white shirt, stretched across his chest, highlighted the golden color of his neck and face.

"We had several cases of dehydration, upset tummies, and fatigue," she said. "What they lacked in seriousness, they made up for in quantity. I simply didn't have the heart to turn any away. We're closed now, though."

"I see your editorial about the condition of the tenements on Polk ran in today's paper. It's very good." His tone held a hint of surprise.

"Thank you." She, too, had been surprised to see its inclusion in the back. Pleasantly so. No one had notified her. They'd simply printed it exactly as she'd written it.

She hadn't mentioned the brothel in her article, of course. Only the danger the building posed to those who were living inside it. "The owner of the house read it, too, evidently."

He lowered a corner of the paper. "He did?"

"Yes. I received a message from him. We're going to meet out there tomorrow to have a look at it."

"What time?"

"Two o'clock."

Folding the paper, he drew his brows together. "How do you know he's the real owner?"

She rolled her eyes. "I'm sure he is. Why else would he have contacted me?"

"I can think of a lot of reasons—none of them good."

The extra chill in the room signaled a temporary drop in temperature outside even though it was only July. She still hadn't quite adjusted to the severe fluctuation of the city's weather. Miss Weibel over at Hull House had laughingly said a person in Chicago could experience all four seasons in a single day. Billy was beginning to believe that it might be true. Perhaps she'd grab a blanket before sitting down.

"If you don't believe the owner is legitimate," she said, "you're welcome to come with me."

"I think I will. This whole thing was my idea, after all."

"I don't want you to feel obligated."

"I don't."

"You're sure?" she asked.

"I'm sure."

She acted as if she didn't care, but the truth was, she'd be glad to have him along. Now that they took horses instead of the cable car, they had more time for quiet talks. Like this one. Where no one bothered them and no one overheard.

Turning back around, she reentered the infirmary and flipped on the switch.

"Where you goin'?" he asked.

"I'm getting some blankets."

"Um." The rumble came from low in his throat. "I like the sound of that."

Thrilling sensations tumbled about in her abdomen. He probably hadn't meant anything by his statement. He probably just thought having a blanket tucked around him sounded good after sitting out there in the nippy room. But that's not what her body heard. It heard something elemental and enticing.

They weren't a spooning couple the way Nurse Findley and Guard Carlisle had become. Billy had worked hard to keep her relationship with Hunter platonic, maintaining they were friends who temporarily shared a mission. A vision. Yet the more time she spent with him, the less inclined she was to keep things impersonal.

Whipping up two blankets, she returned to the parlor.

He knelt before the fireplace and began arranging logs.

"Are we allowed to light that?" she asked.

"The chimney goes all the way up and is bricked. I checked with the architect a few days ago." He placed kindling in strategic spots. "Did you know she was only twenty-one?"

"Who?"

"The architect."

She blinked. "Of this building?"

"Yes. The Board of Lady Managers had a contest and took submissions from women all over. Miss Hayden's plan won. She'd just graduated from MIT." He took a match out of the hopper, then struck it on the bottom of his boot. "This was her first project."

"Good heavens."

Lighting the kindling, he fanned the flames, then used a poker to shift a log. "She was here the other day, so I got to meet her. I still can't quite fathom that she did all this."

Standing, he grabbed one end of the sofa, pulled it up to the fire, then went to the other side and evened it up. It now blocked the entire hearth. "There. That'll help trap the warmth some."

Flames consumed the kindling and encroached upon the logs, then reached for the chimney. Handing him the blankets, she lowered herself into the middle of the sofa, careful not to crush his jacket on the cushion beside her.

He draped the coverlet over her knees and feet, then switched off the lights. "I hate those electric things. Would you mind if we just used natural light like I have at home?"

"Of course not." She felt the same way. The electric ones were nice, but natural was so much more soothing, somehow.

Darkness shrouded the room outside the cocoon of their firelight, though the lamps outside still cast a bit of artificial light through the windows. Sinking down beside her, he whipped his blanket like a tablecloth, then let it settle over his out-stretched legs.

Neither spoke for several minutes, but words weren't necessary. Just being together was enough, and the fire filled the room with comforting warmth and sound. A constant crackle provided a bass for the sudden snaps and bursts of sparks.

"So tell me what you did yesterday." He kept his gaze on the fire, its constant movement throwing highlights onto his tousled hair. "Start from the beginning."

At the beginning of the day, she'd put on her beautiful undergarments. The more she wore them, the more pleasure she derived from them. She'd never imagined how much of a difference they would make. They allowed her to enjoy her femininity without sacrificing her hard-won facade. "I'm starting to make some influential contacts at the Chicago Women's Club."

"Do you think any of them would be willing to help fund the playground?"

"I don't know." She tucked the blanket around her skirt. "I've casually mentioned it to a few of the women, but their responses weren't overly enthusiastic."

"What'd they say?"

"That we already have parks."

"But they're too far away to be practical." Drawing up his legs, he grabbed the poker and overturned one of the logs. A flurry of sparks shot out.

"I told them that, but they shook their heads and in very patronizing tones told me parks were for the affluent, not the poor. That the slums weren't worthy."

Mouth thinning, he settled back against the sofa. "That's ridiculous."

"I know, but that's what they said. What about you? What did you do in between shifts yesterday?"

"Visited the city jail."

"The jail?" She blinked. "How in the world will that help us with a playground?"

"I wanted to find out how many boy delinquents were in there and where they were from."

She tilted her head. "And what did you discover?"

"Every single one of them was from the slums."

Her shoulders wilted. "Do you think it's because

they have no supervision during the day?"

"That's certainly a factor, but I also think it's because those boys have no place to exercise their growing bodies. I can't imagine what I'd have done with all my energy if I'd been pent up the way those children are. The only way the boys can show their prowess is by stealing, drinking, or picking pockets."

"They could show their prowess at Hull House's gymnasium."

"They need to be outdoors, Billy. They need to be playing, not just lifting weights and throwing Indian clubs."

The snap of the fire drew her gaze. Smoke swirled off each end of the stack, its woodsy smell intoxicating.

He drew a deep breath, then released it. "Do you think the women of your club might be more inclined to have their husbands help if they realized a playground in the tenements would reduce the number of delinquents in the city?"

She considered his question, impressed not only by the investigating he'd done, but by the connection he'd made. She'd never even thought to map the locations of the delinquents' homes and establish a correlation between them and a playground.

"I'll ask," she said. "I'll definitely ask."

When he didn't respond, she turned to look at him. His head still rested against the sofa, but his attention was on her. He surveyed her hair, her cheeks, her chin, her lips, her eyes.

She stilled. Of a sudden, it hurt to breathe.

Seconds ticked by on the mantle clock. With slow deliberation, he reached over, encircled her waist, and slid her toward him until they sat side to side, thigh to thigh.

He smoothed her hair from her face. "How come you hardly ever wear a hat?"

Because a hat might give people the impression I'm a frivolous female. "They get in the way of my work."

He turned his index finger over and brushed her cheek. The heat from the spots he touched came from a completely different source than the heat of the fire.

Tracing her jawline with the tip of his finger, he reached her chin, then gently lifted.

Her pulse hammered. Her insides squeezed. If she looked away, the moment would pass. But if she didn't . . . Head back, she tilted her face up toward his.

He hesitated, giving her plenty of opportunity to retreat, then brought his lips to hers.

Sweet heaven above. Euphoria sang through her veins. She wanted to throw her arms about his neck. Press herself against him. Curl up her knees. Instead, she did nothing.

Bringing both hands to her jaw, he cupped her face as if he were drinking from a golden chalice.

"So sweet." His lips began to explore her cheeks, her nose, her eyes, her brows. He hugged her closer and kissed her again. This kiss less gentle than the one before.

She meant only to rest her hands against his shoulders, but the moment she made contact her fingers spread and pressed into him. She gloried in the feel of his sinewy chest and massive arms.

He broke the kiss, his eyes picking up the tumultuous light from the fire.

"You have very nice clavicles," she whispered.

With a half smile, he grazed her lower lip with his thumb. "What's a clavicle?"

"This." She ran her fingers along his collarbones. "And your sternocleidomastoideus is nice, too." She stroked his neck.

His grin widened.

From there, she spread out her fingers, tunneled them into his hair, and brought his lips back to hers. All traces of humor fled from his face.

Wrapping her in a giant hug, he kissed her again. He turned his head one way and then the other. Until finally, he deepened the kiss. Her body grew limp.

How long they kissed, she wasn't sure, but he finally pulled back, then pressed her head against his shoulder. His heart hammered against her ear.

"Billy . . ." His voice was ragged, almost tortured.

He pressed his mouth to her hair, his oversized

hands running up and down her back, her sides, and up underneath her arms.

It felt heavenly. It felt wanton. It felt right. She slid her eyes shut, allowing the sensations to inundate her.

About the time she began to regain equilibrium, he cupped her chin and started all over again. Nothing she'd read, nothing she'd heard, nothing she'd studied came close to the actual experience. And she wanted more. Much more.

The fire dwindled to a mere glow. Her blanket twisted and bound her.

He rested his forehead against hers. "The fair's shutting down. We have to go."

"I don't want to."

Kissing the tip of her nose, he placed his hands on her shoulders, then propped her up. "Tidy up your hair."

Yet he didn't release her and she made no move to do his bidding.

Reaching up, she laid her fingers against his mouth, familiarizing herself with its texture and contour and nuances. "Do you think you could ever be with a woman who was a wage earner?"

The infinitesimal stilling of his body lasted only a second, but she felt it.

He offered no response.

The haze she'd been in began to dissipate. She let her hand drop. Perhaps now wasn't the time to talk about it.

Grasping that hand, he pulled her palm to his lips and kissed its very center, then brought it against his cheek. "It's not something I'd ever considered. Or even imagined."

"Then why did you kiss me?"

He lifted one shoulder. "Because I wanted to. Do I have to have a reason?"

Withdrawing her hand from his grasp, she masked her disappointment and forced herself to speak in gentle tones. "You will if you ever want to do it again."

She rose, then returned to the infirmary to repair her hair. The brightness of the bulbs cast a sordid light onto what moments before had been a thing of beauty.

DAVY CROCKETT'S CABIN[18]

"The dirt yard, thick scrub, and backwoods hut
couldn't have been more antipodal to
the ostentatious White City."

CHAPTER 22

Hunter couldn't sleep. Leaving the barracks that housed the guards, he made his way through Government Plaza, past the Manufactures Building, across the North Canal, and then to a Paris-like bridge that led to the Wooded Island.

The designers of the fair had included the island for the sole purpose of offering an escape from the humongous buildings and plethora of attractions bombarding the visitors. Many took advantage of the rose garden and quiet walkways through the lush pleasure grounds—particularly lovers who wanted a bit of privacy once the sun had set.

But Hunter's destination was even more secluded. It was a Wooded Island Key known, appropriately enough, as Hunter's Island.

The fair had long since closed, leaving blessed silence in its wake. The street lamps lighting the pathways still cast off a gentle glow, but it was the moon and stars that reigned in full glory.

He gave a wave of acknowledgment to a guard on night duty, then crossed a rustic bridge and headed toward a replica of Davy Crockett's cabin. Instead of luxurious gardens and landscaping, the Boone and Crockett Foundation had opted for more primitive surroundings. The dirt yard, thick scrub, and backwoods hut couldn't have been more antipodal to the ostentatious White City. And with it being on its own tiny little island apart from all the others, it was as if they'd honored those men from the Alamo with a pseudocountry like the one they'd paid the ultimate sacrifice for, the great Republic of Texas.

It was the only place on the grounds, or even in the entire city of Chicago, in which Hunter could completely relax. It was his cleft in the rock and he often came at night to simply absorb the hints of home.

The logs that made up the one-room house still had their bark on them. The clay floor and stick chimney spoke of eras gone by, but he'd seen plenty of cabins just like it still being used in secluded parts of Texas.

Tiny hints of moonlight crept through the cutout windows, illuminating Crockett's flintlock rifle, beaver traps, and hunting gear. Grabbing a cowhide off the floor, Hunter dragged it outside, then stretched out on it. With hands interlocked behind his head, he immediately located the North Star at the tip of the Little Dipper, then sighted the Little Bear, the Big Dipper, and the Great Bear.

These friends had greeted him countless nights on the trail. And though they rotated in the sky depending on the season, they were always there. Strange to think Billy might have been looking at the very same stars at the very same time he had, even though she'd have been clear on the other side of the country.

Do you think you could ever be with a woman who was a wage earner?

Covering his face with his hands, he rubbed his forehead. She might as well ask him if he'd like a bear in his hog pen. No, he didn't want to be with a woman who was a wage earner. What man would?

He knew things were changing. He knew some women in special circumstances needed to earn their own living. Maybe they'd married a lazy man. Or a drunkard. Or a man who beat them and they had to get away. Maybe their man was locked up in the pokey, or perhaps he didn't earn enough money to make ends meet, like those families in the Ward. He'd even be willing to concede some widows or old maids might find themselves in need of work.

But that's not what she was asking about. She was asking about being a wage earner after she was married. Married to a man fully capable of taking care of his own.

He slid his eyes closed. He may have been a long way from making any declarations, but he was honest enough with himself to admit her question was justified. There was something different between them and had been for some time now. And both of them knew it.

Still, a wage earner? *After* marriage? When she'd soon have little ones to look after?

Resting his arms up beside his head, he surveyed the night sky. The stars weren't as bright here as they were out on the trail. Nothing, in fact, was as bright here as it was back home.

Back home. He didn't even want to think about what his family's reaction would be if he brought home not only a woman who earned wages, but a woman who earned wages as a doctor. It was all fine and dandy for the occasional gal to be a schoolteacher or a typewriter girl, but Billy was crossing a line. She was stepping into a man's shoes.

He could just see his brother shaking his head. *That makes about as much sense as horns on a mule.*

And with Pa gone, Ma would have no one to temper her tongue. *You gonna let her be alone with other men? Put her hands on 'em, all in the name of an examination? It ain't proper. It just ain't. Why, next thing you know, she'll be wanting to wear your trousers.*

At least he didn't have to worry about that. She already had her own pantalets-trousers. But he sure didn't like the idea of her doctoring other men. Not one single bit.

He thought about that first examination she'd given him. How she'd unbuttoned him and slipped a hand right down to his hip bone without a by-your-leave. She was a bun short of a dozen if she thought he'd tolerate her doing that to other men.

Which left him where?

Why did you kiss me?

Because I wanted to. Do I have to have a reason?

You will if you ever want to do it again.

But he didn't have a reason. He didn't want to marry her. No, that wasn't quite right. He didn't want to marry a wage-earning lady doctor. But he wanted to kiss her. He definitely wanted to kiss her.

And she wanted to kiss him. Her response tonight had proved that ten times over. Shoot fire, but she'd been something else. He couldn't even think about those moments in the parlor without his body responding in kind.

But she was a stubborn woman. She didn't do anything without a definite purpose in mind. Not even kissing.

So if he wanted any more—which he did—then he'd have to come up with a reason. A good reason.

There was only one reason Billy would find acceptable, though, and that would be if he stated flat out that he wanted to court her. And the goal of every courting man was to bring his gal to the altar.

Would he be interested in courting Billy?

Courting her with the intention of marrying?

The breeze from the lake ruffled his trousers. Crickets sang their lullabies. Footfalls of a guard crossing the bridge echoed across the lagoon.

For the first time in his life, the answer to that question was yes. He could actually picture himself growing old with Billy. He liked her smarts, her drive, her sense of adventure. All the things that made her a lady doctor. He simply didn't like that she *was* a lady doctor. If he could pluck that piece out of the puzzle, he'd have no hesitation whatsoever.

But her question tonight clearly insinuated she had no intention of giving up her doctoring after marriage. In all good conscience, could he court her knowing that?

The answer was no. Maybe not an absolute no. Just a not-until-you-answer-some-questions no. Questions like, What about the children? Who'd raise them? A nanny? Well, what if he didn't want a nanny raising his kids? What if he wanted his wife to raise them? Was that too much to ask?

What would happen if she were called out in the middle of the night to treat some patient? He couldn't let her go by herself. And what if she got summoned while he was out on a call from the Ranger Station?

Even worse, what about her men patients? Did she plan on treating men after she was married?

He flung his arm over his eyes. There were

simply too many what-ifs. So for now, there'd be no more kissing. At least, not until she'd answered some questions and he was sure, absolutely sure, he was willing to go whole hog.

SWEATSHOP[19]

"A mother and her children sat in a semicircle of chairs sewing buttons and pulling threads."

CHAPTER 23

The unwitting landlord of the brothel rolled to the front of Hull House in a black and purple Coupe Rockaway edged with gold. Hunter didn't know a whole lot about carriages, but the man's horseflesh was of superior quality.

A uniformed driver jumped down and opened the door.

A tall, lanky man with heavy eyelids and a fancy frock emerged. He tucked a cane beneath his arm, tipped his hat at Billy, then turned to Hunter. "Are you Dr. Tate?"

"I'm Dr. Tate," Billy replied.

"You're Dr. Tate?" He looked her up and down. "You wrote that article in the paper?"

"That's correct."

He glanced at Hunter for clarification.

"And this is Mr. Scott," she said, once again cutting off Hunter's response. "He's a Columbian Guard at the fair."

Eyes brightening, the man offered his hand to Hunter. "Warren Green. What do you think of the fair?"

Hunter accepted his hand. And though the man's flagrant dismissal of Billy raised Hunter's hackles a bit, he'd learned through his work that honey attracted more flies than vinegar. "I've been to two goat ropings and a county fair, and I've never seen anything like it."

Mr. Green chuckled. "Where are you from?"

"Houston, Texas."

"Well, welcome to our 'fair' city." He laughed at his own joke, then looked up and down the street. "Now where's this property that has Miss Tate in such an uproar?"

"Dr. Tate," Hunter corrected. "She graduated cum laude from the University of Michigan and has been practicing medicine for seven years."

"Is that so?" He gave Billy an assessing look. "Where's your practice located?"

Her cheeks filled with a spot of pink. "I've taken my shingle down temporarily in order to work in an infirmary at the fair."

He gave Hunter a smug look, for only a doctor struggling to make ends meet would have closed down his practice and all of them knew it. Still, the man's presumption irritated Hunter.

"You don't know where your own property is?" Hunter asked, giving up any pretense of being diplomatic.

But Mr. Green merely waved his hand in dismissal. "I've much more important properties in other parts of town that require my attention. The rents from these here are more trouble than they're worth. I'd never seen much reason to inspect them until I saw Miss Tate's article."

"I see." Hunter gave Billy a slight bow. "Dr.

Tate, why don't you show Mr. Green the way to his property."

Rather than taking him through Hull House, she led him down slimy streets and horrific alleyways. The man picked his way through the filth, pressing a handkerchief to his nose and hopping over refuse. When they reached the brothel, the ladies were all atwitter over seeing a man of such obvious wealth.

His face flamed at their attentions.

Placing a hand on the building, Hunter gave it a good shove. "This is your property, sir."

It gave a fairly decent wobble, but not like it had before. The women didn't grab the window-sill. None of the occupants evacuated.

"Why don't I take you on a tour?" Billy stepped up to the door.

"No!" the man shouted, right as Hunter barked the same.

Raising an eyebrow, she placed her hands on her hips. "Families with women and children are living inside."

"Yes, come on in," one of the women cooed. "Come see Marquita. I'll give you a fine tour."

A young man upstairs threw his arms around the necks of two girls and stuck his head out the window, bringing the women with him. "Thaz right. Come up and we'll have us a grand time."

Hunter narrowed his eyes. It was the same young man who'd spoken disrespectfully to Billy the last time they were here. A fellow by the name of Kruse, if he wasn't mistaken. So the boy was either associated with the business going on upstairs or a frequent visitor.

Hunter glanced at Mr. Green, glad for once Billy was a doc. The man's mottled face had turned so red, Hunter worried he might collapse in shock from the prospect of being shown around a brothel by a proper lady.

"Maybe I better be the one to take you in," Hunter offered.

"No, no," Kruse shouted. "We want *her* to come up here."

Startled, Billy glanced at the drunken boy. Hunter stiffened.

"Hey, I remember you." Releasing one woman, Kruse pointed at Billy. "You and him were here before." He looked to the ladies beside him. "She's that lady doctor who goes to Hull House."

Hunter snapped his attention to Billy. She was doctoring at Hull House?

The young man grabbed himself and made a lewd gesture. "Quick. I'm in awful pain. I—"

The women howled, covering whatever it was Kruse said. It was all Hunter could do to keep from racing up the stairs and knocking the boy into next week. But if Billy insisted on walking these streets, she'd best learn what to expect from them.

She didn't blush or seem the least bit affected.

But he knew her well enough now to recognize when she'd retreated behind her armor.

"I don't need to see inside." Mr. Green wiped his forehead with a handkerchief. "I've seen enough."

"You'll do something about the condition of the building, then?" Billy asked.

"I'll do better than that. I'll knock it down."

Up in the window, Kruse released one of the women he'd been hanging on to. "Now wait a minute!"

Billy ignored him, and her eyes brightened. "You're going to build a new one?"

"Certainly not," Mr. Green answered. "The rents don't even cover the property taxes. I'll just leave the lot vacant."

"You can't do that." Kruse shook his finger at Mr. Green. "Wait right there."

Hunter held out a hand for Billy. "Dr. Tate, would you mind showing Mr. Green the way back to Hull House? I have a few things I need to say to Mr. Kruse."

Mr. Green nodded. "Come, let's get away from here. I've no interest in staying any longer."

She placed her hand on Green's arm. "So tell me, what do you plan to do with the property?"

Hunter watched them head down the street just as Kruse sailed out the door.

Hunter jumped into his path. "Go back inside, son."

The boy shoved Hunter's chest.

Hunter had him on the ground in two shakes, his knee in the boy's back, his hands pinning the boy's wrists. "You're getting on my last nerve, Kruse. When I tell you to go back inside, you go back inside. I don't cotton to anybody disrespecting the ladies. I've told you that before and I don't like repeating myself."

"He wants to tear down the building," the boy snarled.

"It's a hovel and going to collapse any minute now."

"It's our home."

"You live with those women?" Hunter asked.

"No, I live with my family on the lower floor toward the back."

A sawmill whirred in the distance. A cable car bell on Halsted clanged. Hunter glanced behind him. There was no sign of Billy and Mr. Green on the sidewalk.

He eased up on the pressure. "If I let you up, will you keep a civil tongue in your head?"

The boy said nothing.

Hunter again pressed his knee a little more firmly. "Will you?"

"Yes."

Hunter released him.

The boy jumped to his feet, his scrawny body bowed up defensively. "Where'd they go?"

"They've left."

"I've got to find him." He started to brush by Hunter.

Hunter grabbed his arm. "Slow down there. We'll walk together."

"He's not really going to do that, is he? Knock it down, I mean?" The alcohol clogging Kruse's brain had cleared some, but his steps were still uncertain.

"I imagine he is."

"But what about the girls? What about my family? Where will we go?"

Hunter rubbed the back of his neck. "Why don't we ask Miss Addams at Hull House? She'll probably have some suggestions. But I expect you to be respectful."

Kruse pulled to a stop. "I don't want to talk to her. I want to talk to that gent."

"You'll speak and act like you should?"

He nodded.

"Well, come on, then. I'll show you where he is."

By the time they arrived at Hull House, the carriage was nowhere in sight. Only the horses he and Billy had ridden, their tails swatting flies.

Billy stepped out from underneath the portico and hurried toward him, her eyes filled with excitement. "He's going to donate the land for our playground!"

Much as Hunter wanted to share her enthusiasm,

he first needed to take care of the boy's concerns. "Dr. Tate, you remember Mr. Kruse?"

She looked at him, as if just now noticing him.

Hunter held back a sigh. That was why she had no business going on calls alone at night or in neighborhoods like this. She simply didn't pay attention to her surroundings.

Her armor fell into place. "How do you do, Mr. Kruse."

"Where's the gent you were with?" Kruse asked.

"I'm afraid he's left."

"Left?" The boy looked up and down the street. "Which way did he go?"

"He left by carriage," she answered.

"But, but . . ." The boy's face turned red.

Hunter indicated Hull House with his arm. "Why don't we go inside and see what Miss Addams has to say. I'm sure she—"

Without another word, the boy spun around and ran in the opposite direction of his home, disappearing down one of the alleys.

"What was that about?" Billy asked.

"His family lives in that building. He's worried about where they'll go if the building's torn down." He lifted a brow. "And he's worried about where the women upstairs will go as well."

"They should be able to find another place. At least, that's what I've heard Miss Addams say upon occasion." She approached her mount and freed the reins from the post. "According to her, the residents are very nomadic, moving to more comfortable apartments when they can afford it and resorting to poorer quarters during times of illness or hard luck."

Hunter clasped her waist with the intent of lifting her into the sidesaddle, but the moment he touched her, all the desire and turmoil from the night before flooded him.

She must have felt it, too, for their eyes locked.

It would have been the most natural thing in the world to lean down and kiss her. Instead, he scratched his thumbnail against her shirtwaist. "We have some talking we need to do."

She swallowed, but said nothing.

He kneaded her waist while caressing her ribs with his thumbs. "I want to kiss you."

Her gaze dropped briefly to his mouth. "Why?"

A reason. He needed to give her a reason. "That's what we need to talk about."

A movement behind her caught his attention. A little newsboy barreled toward them. Wait, was that . . . ?

"Derry?" Releasing Billy, Hunter snagged the little shaver by the back of his collar. "Hold up there a second. What are you doing here?"

Derry struggled until he realized who it was. "Oh, hello, Mr. Scott. I can't talk right now. I've got to get home and release my sister, then get back to the fair before somebody realizes I'm gone."

Billy stepped around Hunter, her hand resting on his back as she gave Derry a look of confusion. Hunter wondered if she even realized she was touching him.

"Release?" she asked the boy. "What do you mean, 'release' your sister?"

Derry strained at the bit. "I hafta go. I can't lose my job."

Hunter nodded toward his horse. "How 'bout a ride? You tell me where home is and I'll take you there."

Derry's eyes widened. "You will?"

"Sure enough." Grabbing his buckskin's reins, he swung up into the saddle, then leaned over. "Give me your arm."

Derry quickly complied and Hunter settled the boy in front of him.

"Hold onto the saddle horn and tell me which way." He started to tell Billy to wait for him, but she was already mounted and arranging her skirts.

"I'm over on Jefferson." Derry pointed east.

Whirling his buckskin around, Hunter wrapped an arm around Derry's waist. "If you can't keep up, Billy, come back and wait for me here."

He dug his heels into the horse's flanks, spurring the horse toward Jefferson while being careful of the children in the streets. In minutes they arrived in the poorest section of the ward, the houses veritable shells.

"That one."

Hunter pulled to a stop, swung down, and reached up for Derry. The boy's eyes were big, his smile wide. "That was fun!"

Chuckling, Hunter plopped him on his feet just as Billy arrived and joined them. Without waiting for an invitation, they followed Derry into one of the most vile grocery stores Hunter had ever seen. Bugs crawled in and out of burlap bags filled with grain and other staples. Slimy egg whites seeped from cracked eggs, spreading to the foodstuffs beside them. Fruit rotting with age swarmed with flies.

Weaving past the bags, buckets, and tables, Derry pushed through a door to a tiny stairwell. Upon reaching the upper floor, he led them through a labyrinth of flats swarming with Russian, Hebrew, and Italian families. In order to enter one room, they had to pass through others. A mother and her children bent over uniforms of the Chicago police, or maybe the Illinois militia. Hunter couldn't really tell. They sat in a semicircle of chairs sewing buttons and pulling threads. On a cot beside them lay an elderly woman with a sickly pallor, her withered skin stretching over her skeletal structure.

He couldn't help but wonder if youngsters such as these had made his uniform. The thought brought pangs of guilt, though he had nothing to do with the acquisition of it.

He sidestepped chicken droppings left behind by one of the many clucking chickens strutting about the apartment. Muttering an "Excuse me," he held a door on the opposite wall for Billy. They advanced into a dark, damp kitchen. A black stove dominated the west corner of the room. The stark walls held no ornamentation and gave no other indication this was a home where families shared warmth and laughter.

A stoop-shouldered Italian woman sat beside a table piled with cloth petals in every color of the rainbow. At her feet, a basket of green cloth leaves with stamped designs were anchored by coils of thin wire.

Five stair-step children of tender years helped her make decorative flowers similar to the ones Hunter had seen on ladies' hats. The youngest ones wrapped green paper around wire stems. A girl of about six looked at him, her haunting black eyes set in a face that hadn't been blessed by the sun's rays for a good long while. Of a sudden, he was glad Billy didn't wear hats. Very glad.

Every room held a tale of poverty and wretchedness. The farther they progressed into the interior, the more stifling it became. The tenants had no running water and poor ventilation. The stench coming from unwashed bodies and the outhouses in the alley made the rooms even more intolerable.

Finally, they reached Derry's flat. The moment the boy opened the door, the smell of human excrement overwhelmed Hunter's senses. He immediately found its source.

Hunched over in a puddle of her own making, a moppet with a filthy face and matted hair was chained to the leg of a kitchen table.

HULL HOUSE[20]

"Billy stepped out from beneath the portico
and hurried toward him."

CHAPTER 24

Billy sucked in her breath. The child couldn't have been more than three.

The girl smiled at her brother and held up a long spike wrapped in a grubby rag.

"Put your doll down, Alcee," he said. "I've come to give you your lunch."

Doll? That stick was her *doll?*

Billy could see from here the child's spine was curved. She looked around for something to clean the mess up with, but there were no pails of water. Only a heap of stiff, soiled rags that had dried and turned yellow.

She couldn't even confiscate the bedclothes, for whoever slept on the wooden frame in the corner covered themselves with newspapers.

She moved closer. No, not newspapers. Flyers from the fair. Old flyers Derry hadn't been able to sell.

"Do you have any more catalogs, Derry?" she asked.

Freeing his sister from the chain, he nodded. "They're under the bed."

Before she could look, Hunter knelt down and reached for them.

"How many do you need?" he asked.

"Several."

Though Derry had released his sister, she stayed right where she was. Billy tossed the papers onto the floor surrounding Alcee, watching as the fluid changed the newsprint to a dark gray.

"Where's your mother, Derry?" Hunter asked.

"She works in the pickle factory." He removed a muffin from his pocket.

Billy assumed he'd collected it from the Agriculture Building where exhibitors distributed free food for advertising purposes. The airy confection had fallen apart, so he packed it like a snowball, then handed it to Alcee.

After one bite, her eyes lit and she stuffed the entire thing into her mouth. "More."

Derry shook his head. "Chew it up good. I only have one more, then you'll have to wait until suppertime."

"Where's a change of clothes for her?" Billy asked.

"She don't have none. She just wears those till they dry. She don't mind."

Billy flattened her lips, but forced herself to use a moderate tone. None of this was Derry's fault. "How long has she been chained up like this?"

Derry gave her a strange look. "All day."

"No, I mean, how old was she when your parents started chaining her?"

"Since afore she could walk."

Hunter rubbed his eyes.

Billy gripped her hands in front of her. That explained the curvature of the spine. A growing child who'd been hunched over and chained to a table for three years would not be able to grow properly. She wondered if the girl could even walk. "Where's your father?"

"I don't know. He's a ragpicker. He could be anywhere."

Grasping the chain, Derry began to wrap it around Alcee's ankle.

"What are you doing?" Billy asked.

"I hafta go back to the fair. The only reason I came home today was 'cause Nefan couldn't let her loose."

Billy placed her hand on the chain, stopping Derry. "Who's Nefan?"

"My brother. It's usually his job to feed Alcee, but he can't no more 'cause he's in jail."

"In jail?" She glanced at Hunter, then back at Derry. "What did he do?"

"Stole some coal from a freight car."

Her heart squeezed. More than likely the boy just wanted a bit of coal for his mother's stove. "How old is he?"

Derry scrunched up his face and counted softly under his breath. "Eight, I think."

"Eight?"

Derry shifted his weight, the chain in his hand clinking. "Listen, doc, I hafta go. I can't lose my job."

"Well, you're not restraining her. You go on. I'll take her to the nursery at Hull House."

Shaking his head, Derry again wrapped the chain about Alcee's ankle. "That costs five cents."

"I'll pay for it."

"Mamma won't like that."

"I'll talk to her. Now, you go on. I'll see to your sister."

The boy hesitated.

Squatting down beside them, Hunter rested his arms on his knees. "How 'bout I give you a ride back to the fair on my horse? I can get you there quicker 'n a wink."

Billy could see the boy was torn between wanting to ride on a horse and not wanting to leave his sister with her.

Hunter placed a hand on the boy's shoulder. "Come on, Derry. Alcee will be in good hands."

"What about my mamma? She's gonna get mad when she gets home and Alcee's gone."

"I'll make sure the neighbors let her know where Alcee is." Billy gently pulled the chain from his hand. "Now, you go on with Mr. Scott. But hold on to that saddle horn, all right? I don't want to be called in to work because you need patching up."

The boy's eyes lit at the hint of a wild ride.

Hunter stood, then touched Billy's chin, raising it so he had her full attention. "I won't have time to come back and get you. Will you come to the park and let me know you made it home safely?"

Instead of being irritated, she was starting to warm up to the way he hovered. It was rather nice to be fussed over once in a while. "I'll be fine."

"If you aren't back by the time I get off tonight, I'll be coming to look for you."

She offered him a small smile. "I'll come find you, then."

Billy bathed Alcee, washed her hair, dressed her in a sack dress Miss Addams had on hand, then left her in their care. But she knew once five o'clock arrived, Mrs. Molinari would go to get her, then chain her up again in the morning. And there was absolutely nothing Billy could do about it.

She could, however, do something about Derry's brother. Imagine, an eight-year-old in jail. With that in mind, she only had time to pop in and see baby Joey for a few short minutes. He'd begun to recognize her voice now. His little hands and feet waved in recognition.

"Hello, there." She tickled his tummy. "How's my boy today?"

Kicking his legs, he cooed and bestowed upon her his very first smile.

Her breath caught. A smile spread across her own face. "Why, Joey. You have a dimple. Right here." She touched a spot just beside the corner of his mouth. "Can you show it to me again? Can you?"

Pushing his tongue out as if he were trying to swallow molasses, he made a little baby sound, then smiled again.

Joy filled her and she laughed. Scooping him up, she kissed his neck, then breathed in his sweet, sweet scent. She loved him. When she wasn't looking, he'd sneaked into her heart and stolen it from her.

For the first time in her life, she wished she were simply a wife and mother. Someone who didn't have to worry about putting food on the table or paying the bills. Someone who could bring little Joey home and keep him forever.

But she wasn't a wife and mother. And, Joey aside, she didn't want to be one. Her mother had spent every last minute cooking for Papa, cleaning for Papa, looking nice for Papa, entertaining for Papa, producing babies for Papa. The measuring stick she used to judge herself was based on how pleased or displeased Papa was with her, their home, and her ability to raise their children properly.

The very thought of being measured by that same stick horrified Billy. She couldn't think of anything worse. As far as she was concerned, domesticity was nothing more than a glorified jail sentence.

She sighed. "Speaking of jails, little one, I have

to go." Giving him a kiss, she returned him to his crib. "You be good, though, and I'll see you day after tomorrow. Maybe I'll take you out for a walk. How about that?"

But she wasn't able to coax another smile. In fact, his face scrunched up and he started to whimper. He was probably tired of being in that crib.

She bit her lip. "*Shhhhh*. All right. Maybe I can get up early and come see you tomorrow before work. Would you like that?"

A teardrop fell from the corner of his eye and onto the sheet. Dabbing it with her handkerchief, she gave him one last kiss, then hurried out before she abandoned her decision to go and rescue Derry's brother.

CHAPTER 25

No expense had been spared for the new criminal court building on Hubbard Street. The lofty seven-story stone building that housed the state attorney's office and criminal courts boasted tall glass windows, heavily waxed floors, and high ceilings. Billy quickly discovered, however, the jail was not part of the new complex. Not so much as a dime of the taxpayers' four-hundred-fifty-thousand dollars had been allotted to it.

Exiting the rear of the grandiose building, she followed a long corridor to Chicago's city jail. Opening its front door, she was greeted by a dingy vestibule and vacant table desk. The slight swaying of the revolving chair indicated the owner of the desk had recently left the room.

A small scale, an inkstand, and a smattering of papers littered the table's surface. Behind it, cobwebs and filth accumulated on WANTED posters pinned to the wall along with a framed piece of parchment listing the jailhouse's regulations. Clearly the dust brush had not been used in quite some time.

Moving closer, she perused the rules. *Prisoners are forbidden from using loud, boisterous, or profane language. A kangaroo court is absolutely prohibited. Suitable meals—*

A police officer in a uniform not unlike Hunter's entered from the back. He had a large brown mustache that carpeted the entire expanse of skin beneath his nose, then curved down in an over-sized, upside-down U.

"What can I do for you, miss?"

She stepped away from the desk. "I'm here to see Nefan Molinari, please."

"You a relation?"

"I'm his doctor."

The officer's brows shot up. "Doctor?"

"Yes, I'm Dr. Billy Jack Tate."

"You're a doctor?"

"That's right."

"A midwife, you mean?"

She looked him square on. "No. A doctor. The kind who cuts people open and saws off limbs."

Chuckling, he plopped into his chair and swiveled around to the front. "Now I've heard it all. Have a seat in that chair along the wall, miss."

She eyed the dusty, unraveling cane-bottom chair he'd offered. "I'll stand, thank you."

"It's going to be a while." He dipped a pen into the inkwell.

"And why is that?"

"Because I don't feel like going down there and figuring out who this Nefan character is and which cell he's in."

She tapped her finger against her skirt. "Perhaps this will help. He's eight years old."

The man placed an index finger on one piece of paper, then copied the figures onto a tablet in front of him. "We have lots of kids down there."

Her lips parted. "Surely not of such a tender age."

He harrumphed. "You keep watch over that bunch and you'll not be using the word 'tender' to describe them."

"I see. I'm sorry, but I didn't catch your name, Mr. . . . ?"

"Irwin."

"Mr. Ir—"

"*Officer* Irwin."

She took a breath. "Officer Irwin, I'd like to speak to my patient, please. If you don't want to go get him, just point me in the right direction and I'll find him myself."

Looking up, he narrowed his eyes and again indicated the cane-seat with his pen. "I'm pointing you in a direction, and it's right in that chair. Now sit down and be quiet or leave."

Discretion being the better part of valor, she brushed off the chair with a handkerchief, then sat along the edge. The scratching of his pen kept time with the ticking of a wall clock. She wondered where the prisoners were. Certainly not anywhere close or she'd have heard them.

He opened a tin of tobacco and stuffed a wad behind his lower lip. A few minutes later, he spit into a cuspidor, brown juice dribbling along his lip.

After thirty minutes she couldn't stand it anymore and rose. "I'm ready to see my patient. I can wait in the infirmary, if you'd prefer."

"We don't have an infirmary."

"A pharmacy room, then?"

"I'm not letting you in there. I don't even know who you are or why you're here."

She drew in a calming breath. "I'm Dr. Billy Jack Tate. I'm here to see—"

"Oh, I know who you claim to be. I just don't believe you."

"I assure you, officer, I'm—"

"Where's your doctor's bag?"

She hesitated. She'd come straight from Hull House. She hadn't even thought to claim Nefan as a patient until she was standing in this vestibule. "I don't have it with me."

"I don't know too many doctors who do examinations without bringing their bag along."

"I was at Hull House when I found out about Nefan. I didn't have time to go get my bag."

"Uh-hum." Looking her up and down, he leaned back in his chair and linked his fingers across his rounded belly. "Maybe you could give me an examination first. Show me what you know. We have a nice private room in the back. If you're good at what you do, then I just might be inclined to let you see your boy."

The clock continued its steady click while his offer and all its implications hung in the air.

Finally, she drew a breath. "I'm sorry, but I can't give you an examination because I'm not a doctor for the insane."

After a slight widening of his eyes, he chuckled, then scooted back up to his desk. "Suit yourself."

She returned to her seat. At some point, he'd have to leave that desk. All she had to do was outwait him. It took about an hour and a half. Finally, he stepped into the back portion of the jailhouse and turned right.

She waited a couple of minutes, tiptoed toward the opening, then peeked around the corner. A long empty corridor led to rooms on the right. No sign of the officer. To the left, a set of stairs. The prisoners had to be in the basement.

Dashing to the stairwell, she hurried down. A young guard sat at the bottom, his chair leaned against the wall, his eyes closed. He was of a muscular build, and from the looks of it, fairly tall. Probably a prerequisite for prison guards. Still, he was young. That should work in her favor.

"Open up," she snapped.

He startled awake, his chair slamming back onto four legs.

"Officer Irwin sent me." She looked at her watch pin. "I'm a midwife and have an eight-year-old patient by the name of Nefan Molinari. I'm here to check on him and I don't have much time."

Standing, the young man eyed her dubiously. "What's a midwife need with a little boy?"

"Midwives deliver babies. And we help mothers and their children. Nefan is a child. Now, I have other calls I'm to make, so if you please?" She whirled her hand toward the door.

He glanced up the stairs. "I don't know."

She raised a brow. "You're twice as tall as I am and twice as strong. Do I look like I pose a threat to you?"

"Well, no."

"That's because I don't." She softened her tone. "And I really am in a hurry."

Hesitating, he took a step toward the door. "Have you ever been here before?"

"Not this particular jail, no."

"It's not much of a place for ladies."

"I'm not a lady. I'm a midwife."

He stood in indecision. She held her breath, convincing herself her untruths were justified. Nefan was eight years old. She'd do whatever it took to get him out. Well, almost.

Finally, he inserted a key and opened the door.

Only years of schooling her features and checking her reflexes kept her from gagging. Two long rows of dark, cave-like cells stood on the east and west sides of the basement. A small trough ran the length of each row, serving as the prisoners' outhouse and flushed by running water. Whatever entered the trough in one cell passed through all the cells downstream.

The cages had been meant for two, three men at

the most. Yet close to ten were stuffed into each, leaving no room to sit or lie down. Did they stand all day and all night?

No effort had been made to separate the different classes of prisoners. The children were thrown in with the men. Respectable-looking inmates—most likely witnesses being held for their testimony—were shoulder to shoulder with hardened criminals. The women, though not in the same cell as the men, were adjacent to them and had no barrier for privacy or protection from verbal barbs. She knew many were not convicted criminals, but were waiting to be tried and were therefore presumed innocent. Vermin and rats played chase between their feet.

"Nefan?" she called. "Nefan Molinari?"

An inmate looked at her with a vacant, dull expression. Others shook the cage doors, whistled, and made kissing noises.

The guard rapped his club against the bars. "None of that."

"Nefan?" she called again.

A shuffling in a cell farther down captured her attention.

"Mamma?"

She hurried to the cage. A boy in filthy short pants and a collarless, ruined shirt squeezed past bodies and grabbed the bars. His face was drawn and pale, his eye sockets hollow.

"Are you Nefan Molinari?" she asked.

He nodded. "Do you know my mamma?"

"I'm Dr. Tate. I know your brother, Derry, and your sister, Alcee. What happened? Why are you here?"

"I took some coal off a freight car." His voice held a note pleading for understanding. "But it was just sittin' on a siding. Nobody was usin' it."

"But why? Why did you take it in the first place?"

"The boys at the saloon dared me. Said their grandmother was cold and needed some coal." Tears began to fill his eyes. "I didn't take it all. Only a little bit. There's lots more on the train still."

A fit of coughing seized him.

She swept him with her gaze. His pallor was gray. His cough made a faint gurgling noise. "How long have you had that cough?"

He ignored the question. "Are you takin' me home?"

Straightening, she turned to the young guard, who'd followed her in. "Release him at once."

"I can't do that, miss."

"You can and you will."

"I'll lose my job."

"Then give me the keys and I'll do it."

"I'm sorry."

Her ire began to rise along with her voice. "He's eight years old. This boy is in poor health and needs medical care. I'm a doctor. It is within your power to release him to me for medical supervision."

"I thought you were a midwife."

"I've delivered plenty of babies, but I'm also a surgeon with a medical degree from the University of Michigan. Now open this cell."

"I'd have to ask my superior."

"Then go ask him."

He shifted his weight. "I can't leave you here. Not unless I lock you up with the others."

Turning to Nefan, she stooped down so she'd be level with him. "Let me talk to the officer in charge. I'll be back."

Tears poured down his face. "Don't go."

"I'll be back."

"Please. I gave the coal to the copper. I won't do it again."

She drilled the guard with her gaze. "Have you no heart?"

"Not with this job. Not anymore."

Straightening, she swept past him and toward the exit. "Take me to your superior."

Instead, the young man took her no farther than his post, refusing to leave it.

Furious, she stormed up the stairs and into the vestibule.

Officer Irwin vaulted to his feet. "What are you doing back there? I thought you left."

"I went to see my patient. I told you that's what I was here for and that's what I did." She pointed toward the dungeon. "That is the most vile excuse for a prison I've ever seen. It's unspeakably filthy. There's no light or air. The seepage is revolting. And my patient is being exposed to the most loathsome diseases. His cough and pallor indicate he's suffering from pneumonia, at the very least, and he's caged in like an animal. I demand he be released into my care this instant."

Irwin narrowed his eyes. "Lady, I went to see what we had on your little Italian and found that urchin went before the judge on a burglary charge. But he was bawling so hard we couldn't understand a word he was saying. So the judge decided to continue with the hearing after the boy got used to things and could talk normally."

She gaped at him. "So you took him down to that dark den with its foul odors and filthy vermin to soothe his fears?" Anger heightening, she took a step toward him. "You think locking an infant behind iron bars, charging him with burglary, and throwing him into a cell with hardened criminals will train him in the way he should go?"

"You'd better get ahold of yourself, missy, or you'll be right down there with him."

"*Me* get a hold of myself? You, sir, *you* are the one who'd best get ahold of the situation here." She shook her finger at him. "For when the officials of our city put eight-year-olds in jail, they become the ones guilty of the most heinous of crimes. They are the ones contributing to the downfall of our future citizens." She curled her lip. "You sicken me."

"That's it." He reached for her.

She jumped back. "Don't you *dare* touch me."

He whipped out his handcuffs. "You're under arrest, lady."

Without another thought, she whirled around, flung the door open, and raced out. The fact that no one would know she was down there in that filth was enough to make her all but fly down the corridor and out the first exit she reached.

With trembling hands she released her horse and had it on the move before she'd fully secured her knee around the sidesaddle's horn.

VIEW OF MIDWAY PLAISANCE
FROM FERRIS WHEEL[21]

"Straight ahead, crowds poured into and out
of the mile-long strip that made up
the Midway Plaisance."

CHAPTER 26

Chills of alarm raced through Hunter as he caught sight of Billy hurrying toward the Woman's Building. Her pace was so quick, she stepped on her skirts, stumbled, then caught herself and started all over again.

Galloping down the steps, he left his post and jogged toward her. Her hair looked like one of last year's bird's nests. Her shirtwaist was twisted about her waist. Her eyes were swollen and red.

Sweet Mackinaw, had she been crying?

His heart jumped to his throat. Had something happened to Joey? His jog turned into giant lopes, then he was there.

She grabbed his upper sleeves, her eyes filling with moisture. "Those awful police put Nefan in a cage with so many men he can't even sit down, much less lie down. And if he did lie down, he'd be covered in sewage because when the trough overflows, it floods the floor. And rats are everywhere. The men are diseased. The officer in charge propositioned me, then threatened to arrest me and I had to race out—"

"What?" He freed himself from her grip, only to grasp her shoulders. She was babbling so fast, he had no idea what she was even talking about. "Who propositioned you?"

"The officer in charge. Officer Irwin. But that's not what I'm upset about. I'm upset because—"

"Officer Irwin?" Of a sudden her words began to make sense. "Did you go to the city jail?"

She rolled her eyes. "Yes. What do you think I've been talking about? I went to get Nefan out—"

Fury rushed to the surface, but he suppressed it, refusing to let his imagination take hold of him. Irwin wouldn't have let her down in that cesspool. He simply wouldn't have.

Hunter had met him when he'd visited the jail to talk to the children about where they lived. He'd wanted to see how many of the delinquents were from the slums.

The conditions of Chicago's lockup were the foulest of any he'd ever seen. There were laws on the books that punished those who overcrowded their cattle in cowsheds, but there was nothing—other than common decency—to prevent humans from being herded into a cage ten times too small for them.

One of the boys he'd spoken with shared a cell with a man whose mouth and tongue were half eaten away by syphilis. Yet the inmates had to share the same tub, the same towel, and the same drinking cup with him and everybody else.

Not only that, but the women had no privacy. Not in their cells or in their baths. The tub at each end of the long corridor had an open steel grating with no curtain or protection.

"—and I promised him I'd go back and get him out," she continued. "But Officer Irwin threatened to arrest me and I—"

Her words began to register again. "You talked to Derry's brother?"

"Yes." She frowned. "Haven't you been listening?"

"I missed the part where you told me just exactly where you were when you spoke with, what was his name? Nefan?"

"Yes. Nefan. And we were in this horrid dungeon downstairs. And he was frightened and upset and—"

His mercury went straight to the top. "Billy Jack Tate, what the Sam Hill were you doing down there?"

She placed a hand against her chest. "Don't you yell at me, Hunter Scott. What was I supposed to do? Leave him down there?"

"Yes! I would have gone and gotten him. I'd planned to go just as soon as my shift today was over." Whipping off his cap, he dragged a hand through his hair. "Death and the deuce, but I've a mind to paint your back porch red. That's no place for a lady. I can't believe Irwin even let you—"

She shoved him. With both hands and plenty of force. It was so unexpected, he stumbled back.

"I am sick and tired," she began, following her shove with a step forward, "of you telling me what I can and can't do simply because I have functioning mammary glands and you don't."

His jaw dropped in shock.

"If I want to visit a jail, I'm visiting a jail. If I want to walk every street in Chicago at night, I'm going to walk every street in Chicago at night. If I want to earn wages after I'm married, I'll earn wages after I'm married. So if you tell me one more time I can't do something, I'm going to . . . to . . ."

"Solve it with fisticuffs?" His jaw began to tick. "Because that's what those of us with superfluous mammary glands do. We roll up our sleeves, curl up our fists, and settle things once and for all."

Her eyes burned with fury. "With the way I'm feeling, I just might try it. It sounds wonderfully refreshing."

"Easy for you to say. I wouldn't be allowed to hit back. If you'd ever taken a solid punch in the face or gut, you'd be a bit more particular before you started something you couldn't finish."

"Who says I couldn't finish?"

"*I* say you couldn't finish. You think you're so—"

"Children, children." Carlisle appeared beside them and placed a hand on each of their shoulders. "You're creating a bit of a scene."

The sounds of the fair rushed back. Gondoliers singing in Italian. A bell in one of the towers ringing. The hum of the crowd's conversation.

Hunter swept his gaze across the area. Though

most were making a wide circle around them, no one was actually gawking.

He gave Carlisle a hard look. "What do you want?"

Carlisle raised his hands to either side. "That newsboy outside came to get me. Said he wasn't sure who he was worried about more. Her or you."

His anger, still perilously close to the surface, bubbled over again. "That boy was worried about *me?* He didn't think I could handle her?"

With hands still in the air, Carlisle took a step back. "I'm just repeating what he said to me."

"Quit bullying Mr. Carlisle," Billy said. "He's simply trying to help."

Hunter made a slicing action with his hand. "Not another word, Billy."

Narrowing her eyes, she leaned right up to him. "I'll talk if I want to, when I want to, and how I want to. *Lalalalalalalalalala.*"

Sweet mother of all that is good and holy, but he wanted to wring her neck.

Carlisle bit the insides of his cheeks.

Spinning around, Hunter stormed back to the Woman's Building. He wanted to hit something. Kick something. Rip something up and throw it across the lagoon.

Instead, he stomped up the steps and charged into the building. But it wasn't big enough to hold his anger. So he simply walked straight from the front door to the back door and out the other side.

He still couldn't believe she went down into that jail. He didn't care how tough she thought she was, she had no business down there whatsoever. None.

Straight ahead, crowds poured into and out of the mile-long strip that made up the Midway Plaisance. Two-thirds of the way down, the giant Ferris wheel took its occupants on a ride into the sky. Everyone having a wonderful time—while Billy nearly got herself thrown into jail.

He locked his jaw. If she had wanted that boy out of the pokey, she should have come to him. Like it or not, there were some things in this world that a man had to do. But instead, she'd run headlong into the lion's den.

The very thought of her being held in that vile lockup frightened him like nothing before. And that made him mad all over again. Nothing was supposed to frighten him.

Back home he had the reputation of being the toughest man west of anyplace east. People said he chewed up nails and spit out tacks. That he ate a man for breakfast every morning. That when he bellowed, everybody ran for cover.

But it was as if Billy had given herself some sort of inoculation against him. She was no more scared of him than the man on the moon. Dad-blamed if that girl didn't defy his every word—and right to his face, no less.

He worked himself back up into a dirt-pawing,

horn-tossing mood. And, boy, did it feel good. Maybe he'd go over to Hull House's gymnasium and give that punching bag a good workout. He needed to do something.

The back door opened. He didn't bother turning around. Just stood at the bottom of the steps in a wide stance. Feminine footfalls descended so slowly, he figured it was an elderly woman. Well, he didn't want to help any women right now. He didn't want anything but to be left alone.

Still, his Southern breeding refused to be suppressed. Turning, he started to ask if he could be of assistance, then stopped cold.

Billy stood a few steps up, her hand on the railing, her lower lip clamped beneath her teeth. She'd tidied herself up, smoothed her hair, fixed her shirtwaist, and washed her face.

He couldn't have cared less. He was still mad as a rained-on rooster, and if she didn't like it, she could jolly well leave. "What do you want?"

"I'm sorry I shoved you."

He turned back around. She was apologizing for the wrong thing.

"I'm sorry I yelled."

Still the wrong thing.

"I'm sorry I made you mad."

He opened and closed his fists. "How sorry?"

A few beats of silence. "Very sorry?"

He looked at her over his shoulder. "Sorry enough not to do stupid things like go to the city jail and almost get yourself thrown in when I had no idea you might end up in there? Sorry for all the anxiety you'd have caused me if you hadn't returned here before my shift was over, which would have then forced me to go out looking for you? Sorry about the apprehension I'd have had when I couldn't find you? That sorry?"

With each question her eyes softened a bit more. For several seconds her answer weighed in the balance.

"I think I'm falling in love with you," she said.

It was the last thing he expected to hear and, at the moment, the last thing he wanted to hear. "Well, you're wasting your time. I could never love a woman who was so delusional she thought she could be a man."

A look of sympathy crossed her features. "I think it's too late, Hunter. If you weren't falling in love with me, you wouldn't be experiencing so much distress over the prospect of not being able to find me. Or over the thought of me visiting the jail. And you wouldn't kiss me until I was senseless."

Despite his valiant effort to hang onto his anger, that last bit loosened his moorings a bit. His kisses did that to her? "It's not hard to kiss you senseless when you don't have any sense to begin with."

With a slight hint of amusement, she took another step down.

"Stay away from me." But he didn't turn his back on her. Instead, he held those eyes. Those incredible, beautiful, creamy brown eyes.

Another step.

"I'm warning you," he said. "I'm in no mood to be tangled with right now."

"I don't think I'm a man."

"No? Then what was all that 'I'll do this and I'll do that' about?"

"It was about me trying to explain I'm not some debutante venturing out for the first time. I've been on my own for my entire adult life and I'm used to doing whatever I want without answering to anyone. I've fed myself, clothed myself, provided myself with shelter, and put myself through school. All without the help or protection of any man."

What kind of parents allowed their daughter to do that? Had she been thrown out of the house? "What about your father? Didn't he help you along the way?"

"He told me my mother cried whenever my medical studies were mentioned and he couldn't in all good conscience furnish me with money for something that upset her so much. So I did it on my own."

"How?" The question was out before he could stop himself. He couldn't imagine how a young miss could make enough money to pay for schooling, books, room, board, and everything else.

"I waited on tables during the school year," she said. "In the summers I peddled scales to farmers' wives and picked berries, then sold them for two cents a quart."

He didn't want to like her. And he definitely didn't want to respect her. But he knew what it was like to put yourself through school, then set out on your own. He just never imagined a girl having to do so.

And even if he had, he wouldn't have imagined being drawn to her. But he was more than drawn to her. And it seemed like she knew it. "I'll admit to being attracted to you. And even liking you some. But I could never settle down with a woman who thought she could act like a man simply because she'd put herself through school and earned a man's degree."

"I don't act like a man. Men belch and swear and scratch their armpits."

"Don't split hairs with me. You know what I mean."

Looking down, she rubbed the railing with her finger. "So what exactly is it you expect? For me to come running to ask permission for every little thing?"

"Descending into the depths of that jail is no 'little' thing."

"I didn't know that at the time."

"Well, I did. And if you'd discussed it with me, I would have told you. I also would have told you I'd planned to go retrieve the boy myself. And as an officer of the law, I have a much better chance than some female who goes in there with a chip on her shoulder because she isn't taken seriously."

She stiffened a bit. "How do you know whether or not I went in there with a chip on my shoulder?"

He crossed his arms, but said nothing.

Her posture wilted. "All right, I might have been a tad presumptuous."

He could just imagine. It really was a miracle they hadn't thrown her in.

"Are you still going to go get Nefan?" She peeked up at him, her expression contrite.

"Yes."

"Can I come?"

"No."

"What if I wait outside?"

"No."

She drew her eyebrows together. "I'll stay by the horses the whole time. But I'm the one who told Nefan I'd go back for him and I want to be there when he gets out. I . . . I'm afraid I'm going to have to insist."

He studied her. "Are we setting a precedent here? Because what I hear is you asking permission, then telling me you're going to do what you want to anyway."

"What I hear is that I compromised by asking

258

permission—a huge concession on my part—and you withheld it for no good reason."

"It'll be late. You'll be outside by yourself. You have no way to protect yourself."

"So, give me your gun."

"Not likely."

With a deep breath, she scanned the rooftops of the Midway's buildings. The sun had long since started its descent, splashing the sky with oranges and yellows.

"In the course of my practice," she said, "I've crossed dangerous viaducts after dark. I've had a drunken man land at my feet after he hurtled out a saloon door. And I've seen a man held up by a ruffian at two in the morning. I think I'm perfectly capable of standing by a couple of horses beside a building swarming with police officers."

No wonder she had such a false sense of security. But all it took was one time. Just one.

"As long as we're setting precedents," he said, "let's just make this clear. Any woman I court—doctor or no doctor—will not *ever* be out at night on her own without me or someone else for protection."

Her fingers drummed the rail. "So you expect me to quit making night calls? To ignore my patients who have emergencies at inconvenient hours?"

"That's not what I said. I said I expect you not to go anywhere without me at night."

"That's not practical. What if you aren't around? What if you're out chasing bad guys?"

"Then we'll hire a driver. But I'm not budging on this point. Take it or leave it."

The elevated train rumbled past, then added to the confusion of the Midway by tooting its whistle. She pulled her lips down. She shifted her weight. "I don't like it."

"Not near as much as I dislike the thought of you being out alone at night."

Placing two fingers on her forehead, she closed her eyes. When she finally came to a decision, he hadn't realized how much he'd banked on her making one in his favor.

"All right," she sighed.

His spirits buoyed up.

"But if I get a call," she continued with a frown, "and you aren't at my place and saddled up the minute I'm ready to—"

He took the remaining two steps between them, grabbed her shoulders, and pressed a quick, hard kiss on her lips. "I think I'm falling in love with you, too."

Then he released her and jogged back inside to make his rounds.

SALOON, CHICAGO[22]

"Behind a roomy oak bar a man in a tidy waistcoat
and thin tie poured a beer, his gaze taking
Hunter's measure."

CHAPTER 27

Keeping his horse at a slow pace, Hunter tried to ignore the foul odor coming from the boy in the saddle with him. Last night Officer Irwin had refused to release Nefan without talking to the judge, and the judge had been home in bed.

"There was a woman in here earlier asking about this same boy," Irwin had said. "She tried to palm herself off as a doctor, then a midwife. I had to threaten to throw her in the lockup to get rid of her. And if she ever sets foot in here again, I will. She goes by the name of Tate. You know her?"

Slipping his hands in his pockets, Hunter nodded. "Yeah, I know her. She works in the building I guard at the fair."

Irwin hitched up his trousers. "What is she, the scrubwoman?"

Hunter rubbed his neck. "She's the doc. Works in their infirmary."

The officer stared at him. "A nurse, you mean?"

He shook his head. "The doc. She's been practicing for seven years. Has a diploma on the wall and everything."

At least Hunter hadn't let on he was courting her or he'd have never gotten the boy out.

Courting her. How had that happened, exactly?

He wasn't sure. And he still didn't have all his answers—like what she was going to do about her male patients. He took a deep breath. Stepping out with her would be like tying a bobcat with a piece of string. He'd need to go slowly and tread lightly. Very lightly.

In the meanwhile, her parting kiss last night when he'd escorted her home had been ardent and passionate. He'd make do with that and her promise to not go traipsing around alone at night.

Nefan shifted in the saddle, but didn't wake up. Hunter had returned to the jail to fetch him between shifts today and since Billy was working, he'd done so without her.

The boy had cried in fear when he'd stood before the judge, then in relief when the man had dismissed him and, finally, he'd cried himself to sleep on Hunter's lap once they'd started home.

Hunter hadn't had much interaction with children before now. Had no idea how to talk to them or what to say. With Derry it was easy. He'd give Hunter a fifty-cent answer for a nickel question. But Nefan hadn't put two words together since standing before the judge.

'Course, he'd never even seen Hunter before today and Hunter's size had been known to intimidate grown men. It'd do a lot more to a kid who'd been through everything this one had. Still, the boy had gotten on the horse without any fight.

When they made it to the West Side, instead of

taking Nefan home, Hunter took him to Hull House. He knew those women would see to it the boy was scrubbed with soap and doused in kerosene.

"We'll take care of him, then let his parents know he's here." The young woman who answered the door was Miss Weibel, the effervescent gal who'd first welcomed him, Billy, and Joey into Hull House. She smiled at Nefan, her kind blue eyes wrinkling at the corners, before returning her attention to Hunter. "Thank you for getting him, Mr. Scott. It's awful the way the children are thrown in those cells."

She didn't know the half of it. Hunter tugged on the rim of his hat. "Thank you, miss. I'll leave you to it, then."

He'd barely taken a step back when Nefan launched himself at Hunter.

"No!" the boy cried. "Don't leave me! Please!"

It was the most he'd said since they left the judge's office.

Reaching down, Hunter patted his knobby back. "It's okay, son. Miss Weibel will take good care of you. And then you'll be home in your own—" He started to say "in your own bed" then remembered the state of the boy's home and wasn't sure he even had a bed. "You'll be home with your parents before nightfall."

Instead of being reassured, Nefan locked his arms and ankles around Hunter's leg and slid down until Hunter's boot served as a seat cushion.

Reaching behind his calf, Hunter unfurled the boy's hands. "Come on, now. It'll be—"

"No!" He started crying and pressed himself against Hunter's leg even tighter.

Hunter took a step, then tried to gently shake the boy off. For such a puny tyke, he sure had a death grip. The more Hunter and Miss Weibel tried to untangle him, the worse his cries became until they turned into full-blown bellows.

Sighing, Hunter looked at the woman. "I guess you'd best show me where the washtub is. Looks like I'll be doing the honors."

It ended up taking Hunter, Miss Weibel, and two more women to bathe him. The boy had never been submerged in water before and didn't cotton to it at all. To get rid of the lice and any other livestock he might have picked up, they had to drench his hair in kerosene.

By the time they were done, Hunter's hands were raw and he was wet enough to bog a snipe. But the boy was clean. Drying Nefan's light brown hair with a towel, Hunter marveled at its color. It had been black when they'd started.

Placing a hand on the boy's back, he propped up the bony little body and patted moisture from it. The kid was so skinny he'd have to stand up twice just to make a shadow.

His eyelids began to droop and his head bobbed

like a neck-wrung rooster's. Wrapping the towel around the boy, Hunter pulled him against his shoulder and stood. "You have anyplace he can get a little shut-eye?"

He followed Miss Weibel to a room upstairs. The smell of lye soap, the lingering remnants of kerosene, and the weight of the boy all brought a warmth to Hunter's breast. He wondered if this was what it was like to be a father.

If he married Billy, would bathing their sons be a task they shared? Or was it one he'd do alone while she was out doctoring?

The thought didn't set well. He simply did not like the idea of his woman being away from home. What was the point of being married if she was always gone?

On the heels of that thought came the demands of his own job. A job that had him on the trail a majority of the time. Would she feel resentment over it?

He tried to tell himself it was different. He was the man. If his job took him away, that was simply the cross they'd have to bear. But it gave him pause. More pause than he cared to admit.

Miss Weibel opened a door off the hall and led him into a dark bedroom. Without bothering to light a lantern, she pulled back some covers.

Hunter laid the boy down, then tucked the blanket about him. "Night, little fella. You stay away from the boys in those saloons now, you hear? 'Cause you can't touch pitch and figure not to get dirty."

But the boy was already asleep and unable to hear Hunter's warning.

He took his time leaving the neighborhood, letting the aftermath of caring for the boy linger. It was the first time he'd done something like that. He had a little brother, but they were close in age, so Hunter had never been expected to help LeRue in those kinds of ways. Nor would he anyway. Only the womenfolk did stuff like that.

After a bit, he began to pay particular attention to the saloons and wondered which boys had dared Nefan to steal that coal. They'd better hope he never found out.

He'd just passed the O'Leary place on De Koven Street—famous for having the cow that started the Great Fire of '71—when he caught sight of Derry trailing behind a group of older boys. They pushed through a door to a two-story shanty with the words TAVERNA ITALIANA painted on a rickety sign. Anger whooshed through Hunter. Yanking his horse to a stop, he swung out of the saddle and charged into the saloon.

Behind a roomy oak bar a man in a tidy waistcoat, thin tie, and trimmed goatee poured a beer, his gaze taking Hunter's measure. A bearded man straightened, removing his boot from the brass foot railing and onto the floor. The easy conversation between the men at the tables wound down like a toy whose key needed to be cranked. In silence, they turned toward him.

In what little time Hunter had spent on the West Side, he'd discovered each ethnicity had staked out a certain section of the Ward, making it nothing more than a mini-European continent right in the middle of Chicago. And nobody crossed the lines.

The Irish served Irish. The Scandinavians served Scandinavians. The Germans served Germans. The Italians served Italians. The Jews served Jews. Nobody served Texans.

He scanned the occupants, zeroing in on Derry. A teener handed him a smoke. The bartender slid him a beer.

"What the devil do you think you're doing?" Hunter barked.

Jerking in surprise, Derry turned, then flushed at the rebuke. "I—"

"Leave that beer alone, snuff that thing out, and go wait for me by my horse."

An older man stood up. He might have been soft around the middle, but his eyes were hard as whetstone. "You are not Italian. You leave our saloon and you leave our Italian boy alone."

Hunter took stock of the fellows around him, identifying the threats in the room. Half a dozen likely comers, and big men, too, hard-eyed drinkers with hands rough from labor. They had the advantage, but he was used to being outnumbered.

"Are you Derry's father?" Hunter asked.

The man nodded. "We are all his father. We look after all our boys as if they were our own."

Hunter pointed at the group of teeners. "You call that looking after them? Where were you when Derry's brother was arrested because boys just like those dared him to steal some coal? I didn't see you going to get the boy out of jail."

Two more men stood. They sized Hunter up, then exchanged a glance between them, as if looking forward to teaching the interloper a lesson.

He couldn't have cared less. "You know how I know that? Because *I* went to get him. And he was being treated worse than an animal. So I suggest you and your friends sit down and stay out of this." He impaled Derry with his gaze. "Get out and wait for me."

Derry scrambled to do his bidding.

The older man grabbed the boy by the back of the collar. "Not so fast, *figlio*. You don't have to do what this *americano* says."

"Yes, I do," Derry said, his voice earnest.

"No, you don't."

"Yes, he does," Hunter growled.

With an impatient curse, one of the larger men swept a chair aside and launched himself at Hunter. Instead of shrinking back, Hunter caught the man short, knocking him sideways with a haymaker. The man stumbled, then pitched against the bar. The impact knocked loose a mug of beer balancing on the bar's edge, drenching the fallen man in suds before thudding against the floorboards.

The others stared at Hunter with wide-eyed surprise. A second later they moved in.

Rather than retreat, he charged forward, dodging a punch from the first man, then sinking a fist in his kidney. With a shout of outrage, a thick, powerful man drove a meaty fist toward Hunter's jaw. He slipped the impact, then flattened the fellow's nose. The man buckled to his knees.

Hunter knew his business. They didn't. He was fresh for the fight. They were in their cups. As long as he could bob and weave, ducking their blows and surging back to land punches, he could keep them at bay.

After the initial fury, they regrouped, forming a semicircle around him as they touched their busted noses and lips. They shared a look among themselves. A look that didn't bode well.

"Rush him all at once," the older man said. "Come on now, get him!"

Nobody moved.

Hunter could see half the posse had had enough. His chest lifted and lowered from exertion. "I don't want any trouble. All I want is the boy. In the meanwhile, the rest of you get on out of here and don't let me catch you serving youngsters again."

Still, no one moved. Still, the ringleader held Derry. Hunter snatched a chair and charged forward, menacing the old man with the chair's pockmarked wooden legs. The old-timer stumbled back on his heels, and that show of weakness was enough to convince the undecided they wanted no more of what Hunter was handing out.

Focusing on the door so as not to catch the eye of those they were leaving behind, the bulk of them scurried out.

Only three remained. Releasing Derry, the ringleader stood warily on his toes, dodging the points of the chair legs. One of the others—Hunter couldn't tell which out of the corner of his eye—took a bottle off the bar and smashed the base off. He came at Hunter, the sharp glass glistening in the dim light.

Derry screamed a warning. Hunter pretended to ignore it until the last possible moment. When the shattered bottle was nearly at his throat, he whirled and broke the chair across the man's outstretched arm.

"Run to the door, Derry," Hunter barked. He used one of the legs of the chair sword-like to jab at the man with the bottle, opening up a gash on the man's cheek. Then he circled the others, keeping them at bay with a few reckless swings.

Once he'd gotten his back to the door and seen Derry safely outside, he hovered at the exit. "I'll leave you fellas to your drinking."

"That's right!" the old man shot back. "You get out and stay out."

Hunter cast the chair leg away and pulled the bridge of his hat in a wry gesture of leave-taking. Let the old man claim his hollow victory. Hunter had what he'd come for, and he was leaving the bar unscathed. There would be no need to patronize the punching bag at Hull House. He'd gotten his practice in after all.

Outside, he threw Derry up into the saddle, mounted behind him, then yanked the horse to the left. "If I *ever* catch you inside a saloon again, I'll slap a knot on your head, then slap it off before it has time to rise. You understand me?"

"Yes."

"Yes, *sir.*"

"Yes, sir." His voice held a note of awe.

"What were you even doing in there? Why aren't you at work?"

"I came home to feed Alcee, and on my way back to the fair, those fellas offered to buy me a beer. I hadn't had one in a long time and I suddenly had a mighty big thirst."

"Well, I don't want to see you anywhere near those boys again. I've seen too many times what happens to their kind when they grow up, and it's a life you don't want."

"Yes, sir."

"If you lie down with the dogs, Derry, you're going to get up with fleas. You just ask Nefan."

"You got Nefan?"

"Yeah, I got him. And that cell he was in was worse than anything you've ever imagined."

Hunter's breathing was still faster than it should be. His arms shook with anger. His knuckles bled where his skin had split. Clearly Derry was no stranger to the saloon, the drinking, or the smoking. Of a sudden, he realized just how desperate the boy's situation was. He had no home to speak of. No place to play. No place to expend the innate energy residing in all youth.

They had to get that playground. Had to. Mr. Green had agreed to knock down the buildings on his property and donate the land for it. Hunter needed to find out when demolition was set to occur, for it couldn't be soon enough.

"I should've helped ya," Derry said. "But I forgot I had a knife until just now." He held up a pine-handled pocketknife.

Hunter forced his anger and concern to the side and made a deliberate effort to temper his voice. "That's a mighty fine-looking one. Where'd you get it?"

The boy stiffened. "I didn't steal it."

"I never thought you had."

After a slight hesitation, Derry flicked it open. "Dr. Tate gave it to me. Somebody gave it to her for doctorin' 'em, but she told me she already had one."

"Well, a knife like that's a big responsibility.

You be sure to keep it clean and sharp. But remember, it's for whittling or cutting twine or cleaning your fingernails—not for fighting. You hear?"

"What if it's a 'mergency?"

Hunter considered the teeners in the saloon. "If you need it to defend yourself or a lady, that's okay. Just don't kill anybody. All right?"

"All right."

"Yes, sir," Hunter prompted.

"Yes, sir," the boy repeated. Closing the knife, he slipped it into his pocket, then leaned back against Hunter's bulk. A few minutes later he fell into the dreamless slumber of the innocent.

COLONEL RICE, COMMANDER OF COLUMBIAN GUARDS[23]

"After a tense moment of silence, Rice blew out a breath and rubbed a hand over his bald head."

CHAPTER 28

Colonel Rice threw a report down onto his desk. "What is this I hear about you removing a delinquent from the city jail?"

Hunter kept his eyes on the same cactus-shaped hall tree he'd stared at every time he was in this office. "He wasn't a delinquent, sir. He was an eight-year-old boy who'd performed a dare."

"Did he or did he not steal coal from the Illinois Central?"

"Yes, sir. The boy had grabbed a handful of it from an unused freight train left on a siding. Just enough to keep somebody's grandmother warm."

Whipping off his glasses, Rice tossed them on top of the report. "I don't care if it was for Saint Peter himself. My guards are not to interfere with anything the city of Chicago is doing. Our jurisdiction is over the World's Columbian Exposition only. Is that clear, Scott?"

"Yes, sir."

"Well, it had better be. Because the reputation of my regiment is to be pristine. Anyone who even looks like he might make so much as a speck on our record will find himself packed on a train and headed back from whence he came."

"Yes, sir."

"I'm putting you back on night duty. You'll keep

watch over the Woman's and Children's Buildings from ten at night to six in the morning."

Hunter let his gaze drop to the colonel's.

The man's eyes blazed in anger. "You have a problem with that assignment?"

Die and be blamed. He focused again on the hall tree. "No, sir."

"Good. Get out of my sight before I change my mind and assign you to the toilets in the Public Comfort Building."

"Yes, sir." He knew better than to move before being officially released.

After a tense moment of silence, Rice blew out a breath and rubbed a hand over his bald head. "You're a good soldier, Scott. Let's not forget your purpose here."

"Yes, sir."

He hooked his glasses back on. "Dismissed."

Billy approached Mr. Green's lot on Polk where the tenement and brothel had once stood. The structure now lay in a heap, along with several other heaps. Many more than she'd expected. He must have decided to demolish all of his buildings, for about three-quarters of an acre had been leveled.

Crawling like ants over each mound, children and teeners of all sizes and shapes cleared the land. Some pulled planks from the piles and dragged them to a boy of about sixteen who sorted the keepers from the throwaways. Others carried stones to another section and stacked them according to sizes. Others corralled rags for the ragpickers. And yet others threw trash into a wagon parked on the street. The youngsters were of all different nationalities, yet their voices rose together in excited chatter and laughter.

In the center, organizing the madness, stood Hunter. His shirt was drenched in sweat, revealing the sculpted muscles of his chest and the flatness of his stomach. Instead of suspenders, his denims sported the biggest silver belt buckle she'd ever seen, easily the size of her fist. The sun glinted off its shiny surface. She shielded her eyes with her hand.

In front of him, one of the young women from Hull House offered him a drink from a large wooden bucket she hugged against her torso. Tipping his hat back, he lifted the dipper to his lips, then drank deeply. Rivulets of water ran across his jaw, down his neck, and into the open collar of his shirt.

Swiping his mouth with his sleeve, he caught sight of Billy and smiled. Her breath hitched. How could a man covered in grime and sweat be so appealing?

Adjusting his hat, he thanked the woman, then made his way to Billy. He stepped over obstacles, circumvented piles, and ruffled a boy's hair—all without taking his eyes off her.

The closer he came, the more her stomach bounced and flip-flopped. He'd escorted her home every night she'd worked and kissed her with such fervor she fairly floated inside afterward.

"What are you doing here?" He looked her up and down. "I've not seen that dress before."

She glanced at her calico. The pink baby roses against their ecru background had faded from many washings. "It's my work dress."

"Work dress?" He frowned. "Doesn't look like anything you've worn to work before."

"No, I mean, my outdoor work dress. The one I wear when I help my mother with her flower garden."

He inspected her again, this time lingering on the sheer cream blouse beneath her scoop-necked bodice. The way the bodice hugged her torso from just below the breasts on down to her waist. The flare of her skirt. Her pushed-up sleeves.

"I like your work dress." His voice had dropped to an intimate level. "Reminds me of the dresses the gals at home wear. Simple. No poufy stuff at the top of the sleeves. But plenty for a man to admire."

Her cheeks warmed. "It's just a work dress."

He dragged his gaze to hers. "Can I kiss you?"

She glanced behind him. The children had all lined up for a drink, but the woman was watching Hunter.

"Um, I don't think this is a good time."

"I do."

"Yes, well." She wound her skirt with her finger. "What I meant was, I don't think this is a private enough place."

His eyes darkened. "You're probably right. The way I want to kiss you would definitely require some privacy."

Several parts of her body reacted to his words. She pressed a hand to her stomach. Such a strange phenomenon. None of these physiological responses had been written about in her medical books. Did they happen to him, too? She didn't have the nerve to ask.

"You keep looking at me like that, Billy girl, and I'm gonna have to find us someplace private."

"Oh!" Jumping back, she clapped her hands once. "Sorry. So, where would you like me to start?"

His look intensified.

Oh, no. He was still thinking about kisses. She waved a hand toward the lot. "With the cleanup, I mean. Where would you like me to start with the cleanup?"

After a second, he shook his head, the fog clearing from his eyes. "It's Sunday, Miss Tate. Don't you know folks can get arrested for working on a Sunday?"

She smiled. "I went to church, as you well know. Besides, I'm fairly confident you won't let anyone take me to that awful jail. And seeing as you're up all night at the fair and here all afternoon working, I thought you might like some help."

"Me and the boys have it under control."

"But I came all the way out here to help."

"I appreciate that."

She tapped a finger against her skirt. "Is this a male-female thing?"

"No. It's an all-male thing."

She nodded. "I see. Did I mention I was supposed to be a boy?"

"Once or twice." With an indulgent smile, he interlocked his fingers with hers, brought her hand to his lips, and kissed it. "I better get back to work."

"You do that. And don't mind me."

He gave her a sideways look. "Billy . . ."

She shook him loose. "I'm not asking permission. If seven-year-old boys can help, so can I."

After a few seconds his grin returned. "Then get to it, woman. Daylight's burning."

Three hours later, her chemise, corset, bodice, and petticoats were wet with sweat and clinging to her body like butter-soaked cheesecloth. Thank goodness she'd had enough sense to wear her old undergarments. She just wished she'd thought to bring her battered straw hat.

Balancing a bent iron headboard against her body, she wove across the lot like a man who'd been imbibing. She'd almost made it to the sorting-out section, when the headboard became much lighter.

"I've got it." Hunter stood behind her, his hands above hers, his voice holding a mixture of teasing and exasperation.

She looked at him over her shoulder. "I can do it."

"Let go."

"I can *do* it."

"Let go."

She let go.

"Thank you." In a few quick strides, he handed it over to the sorter, then returned to her and tucked a piece of hair behind her ear. "Your cheeks are getting burned. Maybe you ought to call it a day."

"I'm fine."

"You want to borrow my hat, then?"

"You'd let me wear your hat?"

"I would. I'm not sure it would fit, and the inside band's all sweaty, but it's yours if you want it." He reached up.

Placing a hand on his arm, she stalled him. "That's okay. I really am all right."

"You sure?"

"Yes, thank you."

Dirt coated his face, making the white grooves beside his eyes and mouth look as if they'd been painted on. A drop of sweat ran over the stubble on his cheek. He wiped it off with his shoulder. "I want to touch you. I'm not sure how much longer I can hold out."

She gave a self-deprecating huff. "I'm a total mess."

"Not to me." He looked at her sweat-plastered bodice. "You're looking mighty good. You sure you're holding up all right?"

"I am."

"Think you could do me a favor, then?"

"Of course."

"Could you go and fetch the fellas and me a bucket of water? Our water gal quit coming for some reason."

She bit her lip. "That's strange. Wonder why."

"I don't know."

She smiled. He really had no idea.

"I'll be glad to get some water." Turning toward Hull House, she could feel him watching her and became aware of the way her hips swayed when she walked. She'd never noticed it before and could do nothing about it. She hoped he didn't think she was doing it on purpose.

Instead of going through the house, she went down an alley behind it and started working a pump. Bending over the handle, she pushed the lever over and over. Finally, water began coming up. Grabbing a bucket, she held it under the spout.

"Well, look what we have here."

Squeaking, she dropped the bucket and whirled

around. Water splashed onto her skirt, then saturated the bottom of her boots.

It was Kruse, the boy from the brothel, and three of his friends.

He sashayed toward her. "Look, boys. It's the petticoat who had our houses razed."

She wanted to look around for something she could use to defend herself, but was afraid to break eye contact.

"Don't mind us, doc." He spun his finger in a circle. "Turn back around and finish what you were doing. We won't bother you."

With slow movements, she squatted down, picked up the bucket, then put the pump between her and them. "What do you want?"

"To watch." Removing a thin scrap of paper from his pocket, he balanced it between his fingers. "We like to watch. Don't we, boys?"

Their laughter was low and suggestive.

"I'm sorry about your home," she said. "But that building should have been condemned. Having it knocked down probably saved your lives and those of your family and . . . friends."

One of the boys held an open pouch of tobacco toward Kruse. But he kept his eyes on her and the vicinity of her bodice.

Willie wobbles sent gooseflesh up her arms. She forced her facial features into a neutral position, and straightened her spine. *Show no weakness. Make them forget you're a woman.*

But these boys were not doctors competing for status in a hospital. These boys were ne'er-do-wells looking for someone to blame their troubles on.

Sprinkling tobacco onto his paper, Kruse rolled his smoke, then locked eyes with her and licked the edge of the paper.

Her stomach soured.

"We're waiting, lady." He stuck the smoke in his mouth. "Bend over that pump for us."

She needed a stick. And she needed to put her back against a wall so none of them could sneak up behind her.

"You boys go on home," she said, her voice surprisingly steady. "Before you find yourselves in a good deal of trouble."

"Boys?" Striking a match on the seat of his pants, he waited for it to flare, then held it to his smoke, puffing until it was lit. "I'm afraid you're mistaken, lady. We're no boys. We're full-grown men. Would you like us to prove it?"

"That's enough." She infused her voice with authority. "I said go home and I meant it."

He took a long pull on his roll-up. A few seconds later, smoke poured out his nostrils. "I'm afraid we can't do that anymore. We no longer have a home. Remember?"

She hadn't. She hadn't thought at all.

The next moment he threw down his smoke and they charged her.

Screaming, she backed against a brick wall and swung the bucket. She made a solid connection with one of them, but there were too many and they were too strong. Wrenching the bucket from her grasp, they threw it aside.

She shouted and kicked.

One grabbed her hair and yanked, banging her head into the brick. Pain shot through her skull, cutting off her scream. Another covered her mouth and nose, making it impossible to breathe.

Their hands were everywhere, but it was air she wanted. Air she fought for now. She slammed a knee into the one pressed against her. He howled and stumbled back.

She sucked in air, but before she could scream again, a fist slammed into her jaw. Pain exploded in her head. Her assailant caught her by the arms and flung her toward the other two. Still, she struggled.

"Hold her," Kruse hissed, shrugging off his vest and yanking down his suspenders.

The next moment he was flying backward through the air and Hunter stood in his place. He started toward the ones holding her, his lip curled, his eyes narrowed, his intent clear.

They dropped her and ran. She slammed onto the ground, her tailbone taking the fall. Pain ricocheted up her spine.

Footfalls receded. She curled up on the wet dirt, fighting a sudden bout of nausea.

"Billy." Hunter went down on one knee. "Death and the deuce, are you all right?" His hands hovered over her as if he didn't know what to touch and what not to. "Where does it hurt?"

Everywhere. "Give me . . . a minute."

"Would you rather me go get them? I'm happy to go get 'em. More than happy."

Closing her eyes, she grabbed a fistful of his trouser leg. "Don't go." Tears shot from her eyes. "Don't go."

"Okay, honey. Okay. I'm here. I'm right here. I'm not seeing any blood, but your jaw's swelling up something awful. Can I pick you up? Carry you inside?"

"I think . . . I'm going to . . . cast up . . ."

"That's fine, Billy girl. That's fine." Jumping over to her other side, he grabbed the bucket and slid his hands underneath her. "Here, let me hold you, then you—"

She emptied the contents of her stomach into the bucket.

"Hey, this is like when we first met, except I was the one casting up my accounts. Remember?"

She continued until there was nothing left.

"That's it, darlin'. Okay, now. I'm going to scoop you up and carry you over to Hull House. They didn't break any arms or anything, did they?"

"No," she whispered.

"All right, then. That's good. You don't need to hold on. I'll do all the work. Here we go."

The change in elevation made her stomach roll. She moaned.

"Easy, girl. We'll be there in two shakes."

It was the last thing she remembered before all went black.

UPSTAIRS BEDROOM[24]

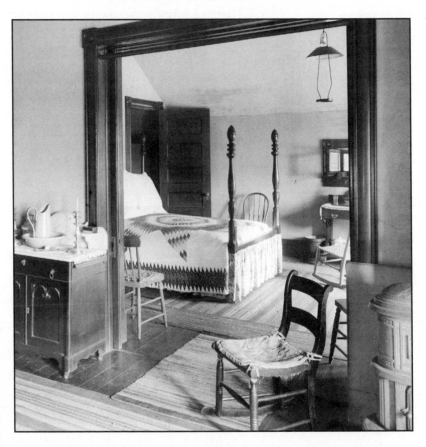

"The Hull House women had him carry her
upstairs and lay her in one of their beds."

CHAPTER 29

He was going to kill them. First, he was going to hunt them down. Then he was going to lay them out cold, tie them up, and haul them in. Only he couldn't haul them in. He only had jurisdiction over the World's Columbian Exposition.

Frustration gnawed at his gut. Rangers had jurisdiction over every county in Texas, and sometimes more, depending on whom they were pursuing. But the colonel had made it clear. Hunter didn't have any authority in Chicago.

Crossing his arms, he stood over Billy. The Hull House women had had him carry her upstairs and lay her in one of their beds. They hadn't said a word about how filthy her gown was. Those kinds of things didn't seem to matter to them.

He shook his head. He'd never met any women like them. But now that he had, he couldn't help but hold them up as a standard.

Billy's eyes slowly opened. She'd woken up from her faint the first time within minutes and started telling everybody what she needed—though each word had taken its toll. She now had her head wrapped and she held a block of cloth-wrapped ice against her jaw.

"How you feeling?" he asked, keeping his voice low.

Instead of answering, she gave him a half smile, then grimaced at the pain and let her eyes close again. Yep, some heads were going to roll. Just as soon as she was strong enough, he'd have her tell the police what had happened. Then he'd lead them to the perpetrators.

When he thought about what those fellows had planned, he trembled with rage. That rank jail was too good for the likes of them.

A motherly type stepped into the room, her bearing confident, her dark hair streaked with gray, her figure thick about the waist. "You can go now, Mr. Scott. We'll all take turns sitting with her."

He rubbed the back of his neck. "Is she going to be all right?"

"She says nothing's broken and that she'll mend. Since she's the doctor, I guess we'll have to take her at her word."

"I thought I'd still sit a spell, if that's okay. Just to make sure."

She crossed to a ewer in the corner and poured water into a bowl. "She's wet, dirty, and uncomfortable. I can't remedy that until you're gone."

Sighing, he scooped up his hat from a wall peg, then leaned over Billy. "I'm going to leave you with this gal, now. If you need me, you just tell her and I'll be here lickety-split."

Though she didn't open her eyes, she offered him the barest of smiles—this time without a grimace.

Straightening, he watched the woman wring out a washcloth.

"I'll be over in the lot on Polk catawampus to the nursery," he said. "We're cleaning up some debris. If she calls for me or takes a turn for the worse, you come fetch me, you hear?"

"We'll come get you if anything changes."

Tapping his hat against his leg, he took one last look at Billy, then left the room.

She felt like she'd aged a hundred years.

"You're going to scare all the patients with the bruises on your cheek." Nurse Findley handed Billy a hot cup of tea. "I had the cook put in some ginger for the swelling."

Hunter had been none too happy to find Billy working today, but lying in bed wasn't going to make her heal any faster. And she couldn't sleep anyway.

She took a sip of the tea. "Thank you. Hopefully it will be a slow day."

It was anything but. With the summer heat intensifying, several patients came in with fatigue, dehydration, and overexposure to the sun. Some pretended not to notice her bruised face, others stared with open curiosity. And though she'd escaped her ordeal with fairly minor injuries, her movements were slow and her jaw hurt like the very devil.

By the end of the day, her entire head felt as if it

were a giant bell being struck by a clacker. Sinking into her desk chair, she toyed with the idea of ignoring the daily log, but the other doctors relied on it. They all did. For if a patient returned, they each needed to know what had been done the first time around.

The concentration required for the task magnified her headache. Finally, she folded her arms on the desk and rested her head in them. The next thing she knew, she awoke to Hunter squatting down beside her, his hand rubbing her neck.

"You all right, Billy girl?"

She kept her head hidden, allowing his ministrations to loosen the tension. "That feels wonderful."

Standing, he moved his hands to her shoulders and massaged those as well. Heaven. He continued down her back, then skimmed her scapula with his thumbs. "My grandma used to call these angel's wings."

"Ummmm." She'd like to meet his grandmother. His entire family, actually. He spoke of them with great affection. "Is she still alive?"

He rubbed her lower back, stopping just above the point where her waist curved into her buttocks. "Unfortunately, no. But she was a great old gal."

Placing his thumbs on her spine, he kneaded his way back up one vertebra at a time. She couldn't believe the soothing effect it had. She'd have to remember that the next time she had a patient with a severe headache.

With a slight lift of her head, she pulled her arms from the desk and let them hang beside her, then rested her good cheek on the patient log.

He moved his hands to her arms. "If you'll go lie on your examination table in there, I could do a better job."

"I don't think that would be very appropriate," she mumbled.

"You massaged me."

"That was different. I'm a doctor. I was providing you with a treatment."

"I'm providing you with a treatment."

"Yes, but you're not a doctor."

He didn't answer.

"How is all that, by the way?" she asked. "Your constipation, I mean."

"Billy . . ." His voice held a warning.

"I'm just asking."

"I'm fully recovered and we're never discussing it again."

She sighed, her eyes still closed. He'd long since quit taking his tea and once she'd transferred his massages to Nurse Findley, he'd quit coming in for them. So she'd have to take his word for it, she supposed.

By degrees his hands slowed, his "treatment" becoming less of a massage and more of an exploration. A caress. Splaying his hands, he stroked her arms, shoulders, neck, and back until he'd worked his way to her waist.

Her body stirred. And much as she'd like to indulge in the pleasure of his touch, she braced her palms against the desk and pushed herself up.

Behind her, he moved his hands to her shoulders.

She leaned her head back and looked up his tall frame.

His eyes were full of heat and something more. Something deeper. Love? Perhaps. Perhaps.

He stroked her arched neck, then moved his hands to the yoke of her bodice.

"No further," she whispered.

He nodded, his thumb dipping into the indention at the base of her neck. "Your jaw looks like it hurts."

"It does."

He smoothed her hair from her face. "We need to talk about what we're going to do about the men who did this to you."

She crossed her arms, rubbing them. "I don't want to talk about them. I don't want to think about it."

"The police need to be told."

She pulled away from him and scooted back her chair. "I'm not telling them."

Squatting beside her, he braced his hands on the desk and armrest. "You've nothing to be ashamed of. You did nothing to bring it on."

"Oh, but I did."

He frowned. "Like what?"

"Like having their homes demolished."

"You saved their lives. Those buildings were a death trap."

"All of them?" Reaching out, she smoothed a stray lock of hair away from his forehead. "I had only meant for Mr. Green to tear down the one building. Not all of them. No telling how many parents and children are without a home because of me."

"I was part of it, too. And they'll find a place, if they haven't already."

"You really think so?" She traced his eyebrow with her fingertip, then rubbed his cheek with her knuckles. Tiny whiskers abraded her.

Turning his face, he kissed her hand. "I really do. But even if they haven't yet, it doesn't excuse what those men did to you."

She let her hand drop. "I'm not sending them to that jail, Hunter. If I do, they'll be forced to associate with the most depraved criminals, who will have nothing better to do than instruct them even further in the criminal arts."

"No, Billy. They need to—"

She placed her hand on his mouth. "Please, let's not argue. I'm too—" She was going to say fragile, but the thought so stunned her, it never passed her lips.

He looked away, his jaw ticking.

She touched the place that vibrated, wondering what physiological phenomenon occurred to trigger it.

He swallowed, his Adam's apple jumping. "As long as they're out there, you're in danger."

Touching his chin, she brought his face back around. "With the way you looked when you came after me, I feel sure they'd not dare to come near me again."

"Then you'll wait for me?" he asked. "You won't go back to the ward unless I'm with you?"

She brushed a piece of lint from the shoulder of his jacket. "Let's not argue. Please."

He dragged a hand down his face. "You tell me when you feel good enough to argue. Because we're not done with this."

Cupping his face, she leaned in. "Hold very, very still."

As close as she was, she could see tiny specks of black in the browns of his eyes, making them appear darker than they really were.

She grazed her lips against his. The barest of touches, but all her bruised jaw could manage. "Walk me home?" she whispered against his lips.

"Yes." Helping her to her feet, he tried to mask his distress.

Of a sudden, she realized she'd never said anything to him about what he'd done. "Thank you for saving me yesterday."

"It's what I do."

She could tell from his tone he wasn't being boastful. Simply matter-of-fact. Protecting the weak was second nature to him.

Was she weak, then? Yesterday morning she'd have staunchly denied it. Now she wasn't so sure.

LOG MOUNTAIN ON
HULL HOUSE PLAYGROUND[25]

"Older boys sliced logs in the shape of sausage patties.
Others handed them to Hunter, who then arranged and
nailed them into a giant, climbable mound."

CHAPTER 30

What Billy's appeals for playground support hadn't done, her battered face had. The Chicago Women's Club devoted a full thirty minutes to her in its program. She spoke of the conditions of the streets and the children who played there, the sweatshops conducted around kitchen tables in dilapidated buildings, the tragedies occurring because mothers couldn't be home to supervise their little ones, the young innocents being arrested, and the horrid conditions of the jailhouse.

"Crime on the West Side is really a matter of athletics." She wore the same green and pink outfit she had when she'd spoken at the Woman's Congress. It was feminine and fashionable, yet in a bold way. "Every young person has a natural, God-given animalistic spirit that needs an outlet. If we don't provide one, they will turn to criminal activity, for it offers a convenient and adventurous way to exercise it."

The women muttered and shook their heads. They could hardly refute the point when Billy herself stood before them as visible evidence.

"A playground will provide them with light and air," she continued. "A place to enjoy themselves and to learn the importance of courtesy and citizenship. If boys are given space to expend their energy and show off their prowess, they'll no longer need to frequent saloons or loiter in the streets where their activities will lead to arrest."

No one moved. Not a sound was made. They all knew what had happened to her because of the "activities" of loitering young men.

"The most expensive part has been done," she reminded them. "The land has been acquired. All that's left now is the comparatively small cost of preparing it. I believe two hundred dollars is all that is required." She placed both hands on the lectern. "This is not only a matter of necessity, ladies, it is a matter of civic pride. We can cut down on disease, clean out our jails, and restore our city's reputation. So what do you think? Shall we provide a playground or enlarge the jail?"

An immediate response came from the group, their voices rising until gloved hands came together in enthusiastic applause.

I came. I saw. I conquered. She didn't shake her fist or chant her battle cry, but the words echoed in every fiber of her being.

She didn't raise two hundred dollars, but did manage one hundred, which allowed them to buy the tools and materials they needed to start on the equipment. Miss Addams introduced her to a wealth of other possible donors. After an untold number of hours calling on them, explaining the conditions of the streets, the danger the children were in, and the absolute necessity for a playground, she finally managed to scrape together the last hundred dollars, thus ensuring she and Hunter would have the fence they needed, materials for the rest of the equipment, and even an awning for the sandbox.

Hunter recruited the help of boys and teeners to grade the land, haul sand, chop logs, and prepare planks. Billy enlisted girls and Hull House volunteers to make skipping ropes, toy brooms, sewing cards, rope ladders, and flags. Miss Addams's coffeehouse became her home away from home and a place where she formed friendships with women her own age and children of all races.

During her time there, she often retrieved Joey from the nursery and set him on a blanket where he could see and hear all the commotion. In between tasks, she held him, fed him, rocked him, and told stories to the children.

Swaddling him in a light cotton cloth, she made her way to the playground with five girls between the ages of seven and ten. They'd finished measuring out ropes for the swings and wanted to show the boys. They skipped ahead of her, braids bouncing and hems fluttering as they dodged trash and jumped over puddles. When they passed the alleyway with the water pump, Billy glanced down it. No one was there.

She'd made herself walk through it on several occasions, but instead of building her confidence, it shook her to the core. So, she stayed on the bigger streets and kept her eyes open, constantly sweeping the alcoves and doorways for possible threats.

Kruse and his cohorts kept well out of sight when Hunter was in the neighborhood, but they often showed themselves to her when he wasn't. Never too close. Always from a distance. But enough to keep her on edge.

She hadn't mentioned it to Hunter. He was unhappy as it was about her spending so much time in the ward. His graveyard shift, however, allowed him to be out there almost as much as she. Still, she usually arrived in the mornings and he didn't make it until after he'd had a few hours' sleep.

At least her face had returned to normal, leaving only a bit of yellow to show for her ordeal. She was lucky. And she knew it.

The sounds of saws, hammering, and children's laughter lifted her spirits. Green's property was the antithesis of its name, for not a tree, shrub, or blade of grass graced the L-shaped lot. But neither did any trash, debris, waste, or mud. And as each phase of construction concluded, the boys helping felt a sense of ownership and pride.

She smiled. The playground was already achieving its goal and it hadn't even opened yet.

A flurry of activity congregated on the western side of the lot. Older boys sliced logs in the shape of sausage patties. Others handed them to Hunter, who then arranged and nailed them into a giant, climbable mound.

"Look, Dr. Tate! It's so tall!" The girls raced toward the structure, squealing in excitement.

One of the boys working a saw scowled. "Get on out of here. This isn't anyplace for you to be. There's dangerous work going on."

Four of the girls immediately stopped and cowered. But Elspeth, a young Irish girl who'd been unfailing in her effort to help Billy, didn't so much as slow, her thick orange braid lying over her shoulder. "This playground is as much ours as it is yours, Terence McIntosh. And if you don't let us see what you're doin', I'll be telling our ma you've been stealing kisses from Kristin Hannigan."

Flushing, the boy threw down his saw. Though he didn't have orange hair, he too was of Irish descent. "You take that back, or you'll be sorry, you will."

Boots planted wide, Elspeth flipped her braid over her shoulder and prepared to deal with her brother. Hunter leaped the ten feet to the ground, landing in front of her, then turned and faced Terence.

Billy couldn't see Hunter's face or hear what he said, but whatever it was, it gave Terence pause.

Still, when Hunter wasn't looking, the boy's green eyes promised his sister retribution.

Billy joined the girls still holding back. "Come on, now. Let's show these boys what we've been working on."

Hunter snagged her gaze, gave her a private hello with his eyes, then waved the children over.

They laid the ropes on the ground, showing how they'd been cut to just the right length with large knots tied on one end.

"This one won't work." Terence held up an extra-long one with knots on both ends.

"That's our jump rope, ya giddy goat." Elspeth rolled her eyes.

Dropping the rope, Terence leaped toward his sister.

Hunter snagged the boy's arm, his reflexes fast and unwavering. Billy wondered if he was as quick as those sharpshooters the Wild West Show advertised.

Stepping forward, she bounced Joey at her shoulder. "Who'd like to try the jump rope out?"

All were willing, yet only the girls and a couple of the boys knew how. Appalled, Billy propped Joey farther up on her shoulder, then picked up one end of the rope and directed one of the boys to the other end.

"Now, swing it back and forth like this," she said. "Like a hammock."

They rocked the rope.

"That's right." She searched the group. "Elspeth, why don't you start. And once you're jumping we'll all say 'Bluebells, cockleshells, easy, ivy, over.' On the word 'over' "—she looked at the boy at the other end of the rope—"you and I will start swinging the rope up and over. Are you ready?"

Biting his tongue, he nodded.

"Anytime, Elspeth," she said.

The girl jumped over the swaying rope with ease, her braid lifting and falling.

"All right," Billy glanced at the others. "Here we go. Bluebells, cockleshells, easy, ivy, *over*."

They swung the rope over the girl's head with plenty of clearance. After a few jumps, Elspeth began to recite a skipping rhyme, her Irish lilt bringing it to life.

My ma's man's a miner.
He works at Abbeyhill.
He gets his pay on Sa-tur-day,
And buys a half a gill.

He goes to church on Sunday,
A half an hour late.
He pulls his buttons off his shirt,
And puts them in the plate.
One . . . two . . . three . . . four . . .

The rest of them joined in with the counting until Elspeth's feet missed a step and stopped the rope. Laughing, the girl ran to relieve the boy at the other end of the rope.

Next, a blond girl of about seven jumped over the swaying rope.

"Bluebells, cockleshells, easy, ivy, *over*."

To Billy's surprise, the girl recited her rhyme in German, though she could speak English without any trouble. When she finished, she relieved Billy.

The next jumper was new to the game, so Terence recited a rhyme for him.

Eaver Weaver, chimney sweeper,
Had a wife and couldn't keep her,
Had another, didn't love her,
Up the chimney did he shove her.
One . . . two . . . three . . . four . . .

They continued until everyone had a turn. When Elspeth reached the front of the line again, she waved Billy over. "It's your turn, Dr. Tate."

"Oh, no." She patted Joey's back. "I have the baby."

"I'll take him." Orli, a Jewish girl from the back of the line, ran forward, arms open.

Biting her lip, Billy looked at Hunter standing on the other side of the children. "I haven't jumped in years."

He winked. "You'll be fine."

Relinquishing the babe, she caught the timing of the rope, then lifted her skirts, and began to jump.

"Bluebells, cockleshells, easy, ivy, *over*."

She held her breath, but found that the rhythm came back to her immediately—as did a skipping rhyme.

Mrs. White had a fright,
In the middle of the night.
She saw a ghost eating toast,
Halfway up the lamppost.
One . . . two . . . three . . . four . . .

From the corner of her eye, she saw Hunter hand one of the boys his hat, then step up to the front. After watching the rope for a second, he ran in and began jumping with her.

The children squealed in delight.

Facing her, he held her gaze and called his chant in a loud, clear voice.

Will I marry? Tell me so.
Is the answer yes or no?
Yes, no, may-be so.
Yes, no, may-be so.

The children immediately took up the chant. "Yes, no, may-be so. Yes, no, may-be so. Yes, no—"

Her foot missed a beat. The rope struck her ankle.

"Oh!" She put her arms out to steady herself.

Hooking her around the waist, he pulled her against him and dropped his voice. "Maybe so."

Her chest rose and fell with deep breaths. Her heart pounded from more than the exertion.

He kept his voice soft and her body against his. "How's your jaw, Dr. Tate?"

She knew what he was asking. "I'm much better, Mr. Scott."

He drew up one side of his mouth. "Fully recovered?"

"Yes, I believe so."

The girls began to giggle. The boys looked on with disappointment, their hero sliding a bit in their estimation. Terence wore a knowing smirk.

She stepped away, hoping they would credit her red face to the rigors of jumping. "Well, girls, we'd best let these gentlemen get to work."

Thanking Orli, she took Joey, then stepped backward and encountered Hunter's bulk.

He stopped her with one hand on her waist and cupped the babe's head with his other, then gave it a peck. "See you in a bit, fella."

She looked at Hunter over her shoulder.

Leaning down, he gave her a quick kiss, flush on the lips, right there in front of everyone.

The boys groaned.

He smiled. "I'll see you in a bit, too, Billy girl. I'm glad you're feeling better."

Clearing her throat, she had the girls gather up the ropes, then head back to Hull House.

"He's watching ya, Dr. Tate," Elspeth whispered, looking over her shoulder. "Aren't ya gonna turn around and wave?"

"A man enjoys the chase, Elspeth. It's how God made them. We mustn't spoil all his fun by making it too easy." They were words Billy's mother had passed down to her. She took a surprising amount of pleasure in passing them along to others.

The girl took on a contemplative look and Billy almost pitied the boys who'd one day catch the young girl's eye.

The words of Hunter's skipping rhyme repeated themselves in her mind. Had she found him? Had she finally found a man whom she was wildly attracted to, whom she had deep feelings for, and who would stay home with their children while she worked?

She hugged Joey close and whispered in his ear. "I hope so, little one. I really hope so."

NEW ENGLAND
CLAM BAKE BUILDING[26]

"The two-story structure just beyond the
Fisheries Building held thousands of
restaurant goers all talking over one another."

CHAPTER 31

Texas Ranger Captain Heywood sat across from Hunter, his silver-gray Stetson on the chair beside him, his expression none too happy. He'd arrived at the Columbian Exposition without any forewarning and found his top Ranger still abed. Or what appeared to be still abed. When, in fact, Hunter had only just fallen asleep.

"So you're telling me Rice has you on night duty?" Though the captain had recently turned sixty and now spent his time checking on his Rangers rather than chasing desperadoes, he still had eyes that could chill a side of beef.

"Yes, sir."

The staff-covered facades, arches, and pilasters of the New England Clam Bake Building were festooned with fishnets, lobsters, clams, and other crustaceans. The two-story structure just beyond the Fisheries Building held thousands of restaurant goers all talking over one another. Hunter never expected to be one of them. It would mark his first—and most likely last—fancy meal at the fair.

The captain leaned back in his chair. "Your letter back in May said Rice moved you to the day shift."

"He had."

"You never said in what capacity." Despite its gray color, the man's hair was thick enough to supply two others half his age.

"I was assigned to control the crowd at the Woman's Congress, then, once that was over, I was stationed at the Woman's Building."

The captain stared at him. "The Woman's Building."

"Yes, sir. They have priceless art there, along with jewels, gowns, and valuables on loan from queens and other royalty from all over the world." He hesitated. "Much of it is rather impressive, sir."

A waiter in a blue-and-white-striped nautical shirt and red bandanna brought them a platter of clams and two plates.

The captain made no move toward his food. "Did you do something to make Rice angry?"

"No, sir. He said he was impressed with how well I handled the women at the Congress. They were, um, challenging for many of the other guards."

"But not for you."

He thought of Billy coming through the cellar window. "No, sir. I had no problems with them at all."

With a deep breath, the captain tucked his napkin into his collar and scooped some clams onto his plate. "What about that big fire they had in one of the other buildings? Did you do anything to distinguish yourself there?"

Sorrow settled on his shoulders. "There wasn't anything, sir. Everything that could be done was being done."

The fire had been of unprecedented proportions and had occurred on one of Billy's days off. He was glad, for once, she'd been on the West Side and out of reach. He hated to think about her having to deal with the victims of that tragedy.

"So what's this about night duty?" the captain asked.

Hunter jabbed some clams with his fork. "Rice put me on it a few weeks back."

"What do you guard?"

"The same building."

The captain stared at him. Waiting.

Hunter put the clams in his mouth.

"That's it?" the captain said. "You've done nothing but guard the Woman's Building this entire time?"

"I'm to keep my eye on a much smaller building right next to it, but nothing worth mentioning."

Setting down his fork, Heywood sat back in his chair. "Why did he take you off the day duty? Were they having a problem at the Woman's Building during the night?"

"No, sir."

"Then why did he move you?"

Hunter swallowed his bite. "He got wind of something I did."

"And what was that?"

"I had an eight-year-old boy released from the pokey."

"An eight-year-old? What the blazes did he do?"

"Some older boys dared him to steal a handful of coal out of an inoperative train."

The captain pulled on his ear. "And instead of taking him home and telling his parents, the officer arrested him?"

"The boy was from the wrong side of the river."

"Ah." The captain served himself a second helping. "And Rice didn't like you seeing to the boy's release?"

"No, sir. Our jurisdiction is over the fair. He doesn't want us interfering with the city."

"I can appreciate that." He took a swig of coffee, then looked at the watery brew. "That's awfully weak."

"I know. They've nothing but stump water up here."

Heywood set down his cup. "I'm assuming you've done as Rice has told you, then? And kept yourself away from the jail?"

"Yes, sir."

"That's good. Because things are kinda tense back home. With the frontier beginning to disappear—and the outlaws with it—there's talk of curtailing the Rangers. Even dissolving us."

Hunter's stomach dropped. All his plans, all his dreams, all his future were tied up with the Rangers. They couldn't shut them down. They couldn't. "Dissolve us? But, we . . . they can't . . . don't they realize . . ."

"I know. We're fighting it tooth and nail, but in the meantime, it's mighty important you do well up here. This fair is getting attention from the top down. If you could do something, anything, that would distinguish yourself, well, I'm just saying it would help."

Hunter shook his head. "Nothing happens here at night. The most excitement I have is a duckling from the lagoon venturing too far from its mama."

Gravity pulled at the captain's features, making him look every bit his age. "I have to say I'm disappointed, Scott. I thought you'd do us proud. But women's buildings and night shifts aren't much to go home and crow about."

Shame flooded him. He was one of the best Rangers in their company, if not the best. That's why he'd been sent to the fair in the first place. But everything was different up here. They didn't ride horses. They didn't wear guns. They didn't do ambushes. He had no power to speak of. And nobody needed him to track any outlaws.

Still, he wasn't going to make excuses. "What do you reckon I should do, sir?"

"Your job. You can't play with the big dogs unless you get off the porch. So make sure you do what you have to to get yourself promoted to a higher-profile position." Throwing some bills onto the table, he shoved back his chair. "And in the meantime, stay clear of anything going on outside the boundaries of this fair. You're representing our entire organization. What you do—or don't do—could very well influence how we weather this thing." Rising, he placed his Stetson on his head. "I'm counting on you, Scott. We all are."

Hunter rose. "I won't disappoint you, sir."

"See that you don't." The captain walked out of the restaurant. He was set to meet with the governor in just under an hour. He'd not volunteered what it was they'd be discussing.

Hunter sat on a bench in Crockett's island, elbows on his knees, face in his hands. The early morning dew seeped through the seat of his trousers, but his shift was over, so he'd be taking the uniform off anyway.

After his meeting with the governor, the captain had left for Washington, D.C. The jeopardy of the Rangers shook Hunter to the very core. He wasn't worried about obtaining another job. With his background, any sheriff's office in Texas would take him on right quick.

But he didn't want any other job. The Rangers had been around since before the Alamo, though nothing was official until '35. Still, through hard work and discipline and sheer willpower, they'd

317

become a force to be reckoned with. A legend of their own making.

They'd investigated murders, caught bank robbers, tracked down outlaws, put out riots, out-drawn gunslingers, protected their borders, and guarded presidents. They inspired pulp fiction novels and many a campfire story. Only the best of the best were allowed into their companies.

And he was one of them. He liked his silver badge with its five-pointed star. He liked the awe it inspired. And he liked the danger. The risk. The wide-open spaces. A Ranger was all he'd ever wanted to be.

Most sheriffs were only responsible for one county. But he didn't have to be cooped up like that. He and his fellow Rangers watched over all of Texas. And because of it, there were things he could do, criminals he could track, that other lawmen couldn't. The thought of a bunch of soft, paunchy politicians signing them out of existence just about frosted his ankles. Couldn't they see they were driving their ducks toward a mighty poor pond?

What you do—or don't do—could very well influence how we weather this thing.

He rubbed his eyes with the balls of his hands. He'd been working this fair for almost three months. There'd been no murders. No shoot-outs. No mobs. No hangings. Nothing. If something like that were to happen, he'd be the one for the job. But if there wasn't—and he didn't expect there to be—just what was he was supposed to do to set himself apart from the rest? Every single one of the Columbian Guards was tougher than a basket of snakes.

They were army men and navy men. They were tall and they were strong. A blue million of them could converse in a dozen different tongues. Some were even experts with their swords. Their intelligence, discipline, and zeal would give the Rangers back home a run for their money.

So just where did that leave him? On the night shift.

Stay clear of anything going on outside the boundaries of this fair.

He didn't even want to think about what the captain would say if he found out Hunter was building a playground in the heart of the city. Playgrounds weren't exactly the kind of thing a Ranger used to inspire fear and awe.

Still, he couldn't simply walk away from it. Not now. It was set to open this Sunday after church. He only had a few details left. The fence around the perimeter was finished, the sand bin full, the maypole sunk, the frame for the swings erected. He still needed to seat the seesaw and fit the ropes Billy had made onto the swings. Other than that, all that was left was opening the gates.

Once Sunday was over, however, he wouldn't be going to the West Side anymore. He needed to stay on the premises and do what he could to help save the Rangers. Maybe he could pick up a few shifts from some of the other fellas. Particularly those who were guarding priceless artifacts. If he did that, and did a better than good job, perhaps the colonel would hear about it and move him back to days—hopefully to something more prestigious than the Woman's Building.

MAYPOLE ON
HULL HOUSE PLAYGROUND[27]

"Billy had been teaching girls the steps to the
maypole dance, but today would be their dress
rehearsal and the first time they'd practiced
with actual ribbons."

CHAPTER 32

Billy shaded her eyes and watched as Hunter secured the last colorful ribbon to the maypole. Someone from the Chicago Women's Club had spread the word about tomorrow's grand opening of the playground and a groundswell of support had resulted. Various schools and individuals had been dropping off baskets full of flowers for winners of tomorrow's competitions. A volunteer brass band offered to provide music during the maypole dance. And a reporter from the *Chicago Tribune* was set to attend.

Billy was as excited as the children. She'd been teaching a dozen girls—all of different nationalities—the steps to the maypole dance, but today would be their dress rehearsal and the first time they'd practiced with actual ribbons.

The girls raced to grab their favorite color, then held the streamers aloft while Hunter slid down the pole. As soon as he ducked out from under them, Billy clapped out a beat. The girls wove and unwove, tied and untied, all in choreographed formations. They had many starts and stops as some jumped ahead and others fell behind, until finally, the girls caught the rhythm and plaited the streamers in an intricate and colorful pattern.

The boys hanging swings stopped to watch.

Children outside the wire fence sat cross-legged and clapped in time. Hunter pushed back the rim of his hat and tapped his booted toe.

When they completed the dance, Billy lifted her arms in the air like a pugilist and jumped up and down. "Yes! That's it! Look, girls! It's beautiful."

Their impromptu audience cheered. Hunter whistled.

Terence grabbed his sister by the neck and rubbed his knuckles along her scalp. "That was a pretty fair dance you did, Elspeth."

She gave him a playful shove and broke free. "Can we untangle them now, Dr. Tate?"

And so they began again, except reversing their steps.

Mr. Carlisle arrived and gave a shout of greeting.

Opening the gate, Hunter held out his hand. "Eddie, thanks for coming."

Billy had never seen Mr. Carlisle in anything but the Columbian Guard uniform he wore at the Woman's Building and almost didn't recognize him in regular clothes. He, like Hunter, was tall and broad, but where Hunter exuded a virile, rugged, cowboy masculinity, Mr. Carlisle had more of a little brother, devil-may-care way about him. His winsome ways and quick smile caused not a few sighs from the girls.

The eighteen boys who were to be part of tomorrow's military drill were let inside the area and Carlisle began teaching them their steps.

Leaving them to it, Billy corralled the girls and headed back to Hull House, a rush of joy filling her. The sullen, downtrodden girls of before were now chattering and laughing. Skipping and holding hands. Racing and singing. The more they spoke in English and learned American customs, the more they began to forget they were of different skin tones and from different countries.

At the kindergarten cottage, Billy paused at the door. "You girls go on to the coffeehouse and start sorting out the sacks, potatoes, and ropes for tomorrow's races. I'm going to get Joey, then I'll be right there."

She stepped into the noisy cottage of youngsters and gave a small wave to the teachers, but instead of smiling back, they looked at one another, then avoided eye contact. Perhaps the children had been unusually fussy.

Lifting her skirts, she jogged up the steps, humming under her breath. The familiar smells of soiled diapers, malted milk, and borated talcum powder added to her happiness. They were scents she would forever associate with Joey.

"Good afternoon, Miss Chaffee," she said.

Again, no smile was forthcoming from the stout, middle-aged nursemaid. Instead, she put down the baby bottle in her hand, placed the infant she'd been feeding against her shoulder, and set her rocker in motion.

Walking across the room, Billy approached Joey's crib. Only, it was empty. "Where's Joey?"

She looked in the other cribs, but he wasn't there.

Miss Chaffee said nothing.

A tingle of alarm raced up her spine. She looked again at Joey's crib. The bed linens were not mussed but pristine, as if he hadn't been in the bed all day.

She'd been a doctor long enough to know infants often died in their cribs for no apparent reason, but she'd just seen him yesterday and he'd been fine. More than fine. He'd learned to laugh and giggle. Smile and babble. He was healthy, round, and pudgy. He was . . . perfect. "Miss Chaffee?"

The woman lifted her gaze, her blue eyes dull.

"Where is he?"

"He's not here."

"I can see that. Where is he?"

Miss Chaffee swallowed. "A fancy lady came to deliver some flowers for tomorrow."

Her arms began to tremble. "Please don't change the subject. Just tell me where he is."

"That's what I'm trying to do. He's, he's with that lady."

Billy frowned. "The one who brought the flowers?"

"Yes."

Letting out a *whoosh* of breath, she laid a hand on her chest. "Oh, Miss Chaffee. Don't do that. You scared me to death. I thought something had happened to him."

"No, doc. Nothing's happened. He's right as rain."

"Thank goodness." The vise around her heart began to loosen. "Are the two of them at the coffeehouse, then?"

Miss Chaffee pulled her chin down, causing it to fold into two. "No, child. I meant she took him with her."

Billy shook her head. "I don't understand."

"She and her mister. They don't have any children. And Joey, well, everyone's heard his story, about being abandoned at the fair. So this lady, she came to peek in on him after dropping off the flowers, took one look, and, well, she spoke to Miss Addams. The woman's husband came right down and it was all arranged."

Her heart started hammering again. "Are you saying she took him home with her? To *keep*? Just like that? Just took one look and said, 'He's mine'?"

The baby Miss Chaffee held began to fuss. She returned him to her arms and gave him the bottle. He rooted, missing the rubber nipple in his desperate search before latching on. A look of contentment immediately followed.

Emotion rushed up Billy's throat. Joey used to

do that. She grabbed onto the edge of his crib. "Who was she? What's her name?"

Miss Chaffee gave her a sympathetic look. "I don't know. Only Miss Addams knows. But she's not going to be able to—"

Billy rushed out of the room, down the stairs, and out the door. With skirt hiked up, she ran to Hull House, in the back door, through the kitchen, and into the drawing room.

No one there.

Crossing the entryway, she passed through the first and second parlors until she reached the door of Miss Addams's octagonal office.

She rapped on the door. "Miss Addams?"

"Come in."

Billy flung open the door, her chest rising and falling. "They said you gave Joey away."

Miss Addams quickly rose and rounded her desk. "Come in, doctor."

Billy shook her head. "You didn't really, did you? He's coming back, right?"

Miss Addams reached for Billy. "Please, come—"

"No." Her throat began to work. "No. How could you? You knew how I felt. I . . . he's . . . how *could* you?"

Miss Addams clasped her hands in front of her. "They are a very well-to-do couple and have been unable to have children. They will be able to give him a life of privilege and love. You are like me. A working woman. You're not married and would not be able to keep him. If you had, he wouldn't have been here."

"I've helped." Tears filled her eyes. "I've helped as much and as often as I could."

"You have. You've been a wonderful boon. Not just to Joey, but to Hull House and the children of the West Side. But we're not an orphanage. We're not equipped to take children in permanently. We were only keeping Joey temporarily with the hopes we could find a loving home for him. We're extremely lucky to have found someone. And someone who doesn't need him as an extra laborer or farmhand. In another month, we'd have had to take him to an orphanage."

Billy's nostrils distended as she tried to hold back her emotions. "But I might get married. I would have taken him then."

She lifted her brows. "You're planning to give up your practice when you marry?"

"No, no. My . . . the man I'm going to marry. He's agreed to let me work after marriage."

"Then who will take care of Joey?"

"He will."

Miss Addams stared at her. "He's going to be the . . . wife?"

"Yes."

"Are you sure you haven't misunderstood?"

"I'm sure. Very sure. What if we get married right away? Today? Can we have Joey back?"

Stepping forward, Miss Addams took her by the hand and led her to a pair of chairs. They sat, facing each other.

"I cannot get Joey back, Dr. Tate. It wouldn't be right. Not after they've already welcomed him into their home."

Her lips became dry, sticking slightly when she opened them. "But what about me? I've had him since birth almost. She's had him for less than a day. Please, Miss Addams."

"I'm sorry. I cannot." She took a deep breath. "I will not."

"Who took him?"

"I can't say."

"You can't even tell me who they are?"

"That was part of our agreement."

Clamping her lips with her teeth, she hugged herself. This couldn't be happening. How would she ever find him? Chicago was huge. Filled with over a million people. He could be anywhere. For all she knew, he might have been given to a couple passing through to see the fair.

She had no idea what to do. Where to even start. But Hunter would know. And he wouldn't allow this. He'd get Joey back.

"Excuse me, but I have to go." Shooting to her feet, she rushed out of the office, burst into the alley, and ran pell-mell for the playground. He saw her the minute she rounded Polk Street and dropped the ropes in his hands. Knocking open the gate, he never slowed until he reached her.

She launched herself into his arms, sobbing, trying to tell him, but she was too upset, too distraught.

"Are you hurt?"

She shook her head.

"Did those boys come back?"

She shook her head again.

"Then what?"

"Jooooey."

He held her then, shushing her, stroking her hair, pressing his mouth against her neck in an effort to still her shakes.

"We have to get married right away," she finally managed.

"Why? What's happened?" He stiffened, then held her at arm's length, searching her eyes. "Did those boys last month do more than—"

"No, no. Nothing like that. It's Joey." She swiped her cheeks.

"What's happened?"

"They gave him away."

"What? Who?"

The tears started afresh. "Miss Addams. She gave him away. He's gone. *Gone.* Some rich couple took one look at our precious Joey and just whisked him away like he was theirs. But he's ours. *Ours.* Only, we have to be married if we want to keep him."

He looked toward the kindergarten cottage as if

trying to sort it out. "Slow down, slow down. Let me make sure I understand. Someone has taken Joey in. Someone rich. Is that right?"

"Yes."

He cursed. "All right. And you're saying that if we get married, we can have him back?"

"Yes."

"When do we need to get married?"

"Right now."

His eyebrows shot up. "Today?"

She bit her lip. "Well, tomorrow might be okay."

He frowned. "Billy, if they've already taken him in, are you sure they'll give him back?"

Her eyes filled. "Of course they won't. Who'd give up that sweet, sweet boy? But you'll get him for me, won't you?"

His eyes became troubled.

"Won't you?" Her voice rose.

"Who has him?"

"I don't know. Miss Addams won't tell me. But you find people all the time. That's what you do, right? Find people who are hiding?"

"Are they hiding?"

"Well, sort of. They won't let Miss Addams give me their names, so they may as well be hiding."

Tucking her into his side, he steered her toward Hull House. "Let's start with Miss Addams, then."

Billy sniffed. "She said we can't have him back. Even if we were married. But I know you'll get him. You're not going to let anyone take our Joey off like that."

They reached the back section of Hull House.

Setting Billy down on the outdoor steps leading to the kitchen, he joined her and took both her hands. "You know, he's not really ours."

"We found him. We've been watching after him."

"That's not exactly true. We found him, but the women at Hull House have been watching after him."

"Maybe technically. But not like I do. I'm up here with him every chance I get. Of course, we'll have to start paying five cents a day for them to watch him while we work. At least until the fair is over."

He looked at her hands, then ran a thumb over her knuckles. "Billy, if this couple really has taken him as their own, and they're of the wealthy set, then they'll have the resources to keep us from taking him back. And it won't matter who found him."

She yanked her hands out of his. "Are you saying you won't go after him?"

"Not until I talk with Miss Addams and get all the facts."

She crossed her arms. "Then go. Go talk to her. I'll wait right here."

He looked up and down the alley. "Maybe you better wait in the kitchen."

"I don't want to go in there. I'll be okay. Go on."

Blowing out a breath, he stood. "I'll be right back."

He stepped through the door. She hugged her legs, put her head down on her knees, and let the tears come. For she knew what was going to happen. What Miss Addams was going to say. And she was no longer sure Hunter would go after whoever it was who took Joey. And if he didn't, all would be lost. For Joey could be anywhere. Anywhere.

When the back door finally opened again, the tears had slowed to droplets.

Sitting beside her, he scooped her up, pulled her into his lap, and hugged her tight. "I'm sorry, Billy girl."

"No." She clutched his shirt with her fists.

"I'm sorry. There's nothing we can do. He belongs to that other family, love."

Pressing her face into his neck, she found she wasn't out of tears after all. She sobbed. She wailed. She bawled.

He rocked her. Kissed the top of her head. Patted her back. Shushed her.

After she was spent, he still held her. The sun began its descent before she finally lifted her face. "I want to go home."

It was then she saw that he'd been crying, too.

GIANT STRIDE[28]

"Hunter shimmied up the maypole and
replaced the ribbons with ropes, loosened
a spinning mechanism, and turned the
maypole into a giant stride."

CHAPTER 33

Billy sat on the edge of her bed and ran a hand across her dress from Marshall Field's. The blue-and-eyelet candy-striped gown was bright and summery and feminine. She'd been planning to wear it to the playground's opening for quite some time. She just hadn't expected a cold lump to be where her heart had once been.

Wiping her tears, she took a deep breath, then stuffed her handkerchief into her lacy sleeves and walked to the little oval mirror in her room. Beneath her swollen eyes and splotchy cheeks, a bright, pretty blue bow accented her collar, while another set off the lace ruffle running across her chest. She reached behind her, adjusting a third bow at the back of her skirt.

She needed to put aside her grief for a few hours. On a rational level, she knew Joey wasn't hers. Never had been. But it didn't make her love him less, nor did it mend her heart. Still, the children had worked hard to prepare for today's festivities. It was their big moment. She needed to be gay and cheerful.

So, she'd lock her feelings inside for now and try her best to make it through the day without thinking of the tremendous loss Joey's absence had caused.

Picking up her hat, she placed it on her head and ran a long pin through its crown. She'd assumed Joey would always be there. Even if things didn't work out with her and Hunter, she'd thought she could carry on her practice and stop in to see Joey whenever she wanted. On her terms, her time line, and Hull House's pocketbook. How naive and selfish she'd been.

She fingered the flowers decorating her hat's rim. The pitiful sight made by the children who'd been creating cloth flowers in Derry's building jumped into her mind. What if they came to the playground today? What would they think if they saw her wearing this hat?

Removing the pin, she placed the hat back into its box, wondering if she'd ever be able to wear it or any other hat ever again. At least Joey wouldn't be working in a sweatshop like that or on the street like Derry.

With a deep breath, she locked her feelings away and headed downstairs where Hunter was waiting.

Hunter couldn't believe the line. It wrapped clear around the playground and was two and three children deep.

Miss Addams had arranged for two police officers to be present in case there was trouble, but Hunter hoped their mere presence would curtail any mischief. He certainly didn't want any of these youngsters to end up in that godawful jail.

Billy rushed around, setting up an area for the sack races, giving instructions to the five-man brass band, following behind an old sea dog from the neighborhood who'd taught Hunter and the boys how to make sailors' ladders and hammocks and who now inspected their work.

She was just about the prettiest thing he'd ever seen in her seaside-looking gown. Its vertical stripes drew his eye to all the dips and swells, while a bow on her tail swished this way and that.

He'd expected her to bring up Joey again, but she hadn't. Had instead chosen to grieve in private. He'd wanted to reassure her, comfort her, make the pain go away. But he could hardly think about it himself without his throat swelling up.

The only good thing was, he knew she'd be willing to marry him. She'd all but proposed to him right there on the street. Of course, it was merely a means to an end, but he knew she had feelings for him. Strong feelings. And he sure had feelings for her. He just hadn't been all that confident she'd be willing to follow him to Texas. He didn't think giving up her male patients would be much of a hurdle. There were more than enough women who needed doctoring.

But a city girl moving clear across the States to become a country gal, well, that was something else altogether. Still, maybe she'd figured out she could doctor anywhere, while he could only Ranger in one place.

She smiled at something the old sea dog said and Hunter found himself smiling merely because she was. He slipped his hands into his pockets. He'd sent a wire to his mother asking for Grandma's ring. The request would surprise her, but she'd do as he asked. He wondered how long it would be before it arrived.

A dark cloud rolled in offering welcome relief from the treeless playground. He glanced at the awning Billy had had him construct in the L of the lot for the babies and the little ones who'd play in the sand bin. For today, at least, it looked like they wouldn't be the only ones in the shade. He only hoped that cloud didn't get too heavy.

Some women from Hull House approached carrying baskets brimming with flowers of every color. They tried to get past the throng and to the gate, but the faces peeping through the net wiring with hungry impatience had yet to see them.

Hunter headed in that direction. "Make way for the ladies, kids."

When the children saw the blooms, excited squeals and pointing fingers swept through the ranks. Opening the gates for the women, he shook his head. The children lived but ten blocks from a florist's window. With the way they were carrying on, though, he figured they hadn't been inside the shop. Made him wonder just how long it had been since they'd had their hands on flowers of any kind.

A handful of boys couldn't stand the wait any longer and began to scale the fence. Jogging to them, Hunter scooped one up and corralled the others. "It won't be too long yet, boys, but everybody's got to wait in line."

He deposited them outside the gate, only to discover a rascal on the other end of the grounds had dug a hole under the fence and by dint of squeezing shimmied under. Half a dozen more followed and headed straight for the swings.

The other children reacted with fervor, whistling, jostling the fence, and once again scaling it.

Instead of capturing them, he headed toward Billy. "We're going to have a riot on our hands, Billy girl, if we don't open that gate in a hurry."

Biting her lip, she glanced at her watch. "It's still early."

He adjusted his hat. "I'm telling you. I've quelled a lot of uprisings and this one's just about to erupt."

"You think it's okay to open early, then?"

"It'll be the first time I've ever given in to a mob, but seeing as it's children we're dealing with, there's not a lot I can do." He held out his elbow. "Would you like to do the honors?"

Taking his arm, she smiled. "I would."

Maybe today would be good for her, he thought. He sure hoped so.

The two of them threw open the gates and the scrambling mass rushed in. Swings were tackled. Rope ladders ascended. Seesaws mounted. Log heaps climbed.

The brass band struck up an enthusiastic, if not harmonious tune. Those who didn't reach the equipment first picked up balls and jump ropes. Mothers with mud-coated carriages came in and quickly overflowed the three benches he'd built.

A few minutes after the initial rush, Carlisle and Nurse Findley arrived to assist with the races.

"I confess I thought you'd exaggerated when you described the conditions here," Nurse Findley whispered to them. The hem of her yellow gown held evidence of the sludge in the streets. "It's even worse than I imagined. The death rate must be horrific."

"There are no official figures, of course," Billy answered, her voice quiet. "But I see coffins leaving the shanties most every day."

Carlisle, never without a smile for too long, clapped Hunter's shoulder. "You ready to organize this group of ragamuffins?"

"I'm ready." Blowing his whistle, he gathered the children and introduced the contests. Large boys kicked off their shoes and raced barefoot. Small boys emulated their example, and in the midst of them were Derry and Nefan.

Hunter tied the brothers' ankles together and helped them get to the starting line for the three-legged race, offering tips on how to stay in sync. When Carlisle gave the signal, they took off. Derry counted "*Uno, due, uno, due,*" and Hunter shouted his encouragement.

A pair of boys to their right lifted their tied legs completely off the ground and simply hopped their way down. Not to be outdone, Derry sped up the count.

Nefan couldn't keep up and they tumbled to the ground, but those flowers were powerful motivators and they scrambled back to their feet. The fall had cost them, though, and other pairs passed them, leaving the Molinari boys to come in seventh. Flowers were only given to the first six.

Jogging over to untie them, Hunter was stunned to see Derry choking back his disappointment.

"Don't give up, now." Hunter squatted down and loosened the knot. "There's still the sack races, potato races, footraces, and younger boys' races."

But they didn't place in any of them, and Hunter felt their disappointment as keenly as if it were his own. Every instinct he had made him want to sneak them a bloom. But that wouldn't be the same as winning one. And it wouldn't be fair to all the other children.

One thing was for certain, though. He'd never again take for granted the bounty that surrounded his cabin back home. He wouldn't even curse the blackbirds, for at least they came. The Nineteenth Ward had no birds at all—of any variety. Only rats and maggots.

When the flowers were gone, the military drill was marched, and the maypole dance was completed, Billy joined Hunter along the periphery.

"Did you see the Molinaris?" he asked.

"I did." She scanned the area. "Where are they now?"

"Derry's on the seesaw. Nefan's in a hammock."

She looked at him. "You've been keeping up with them today, haven't you?"

Shrugging a shoulder, he rested against the fence behind him. "Did their sister, Alcee, come? The one who was chained?"

She nodded. "Yes, thank goodness. She's been in the sand bin the whole afternoon."

An impromptu tug-of-war began with the jump rope. When the team to the south started to tie the rope to a fence post for better advantage, Hunter pushed himself off the fence. "I'll be right back."

"Hunter?"

He turned to her.

"The boys on the other end are stacking their team."

Shaking his head, he jogged toward them. He and Carlisle sorted it out, then officiated until they had a winner.

A brisk breeze kicked up a swirl of dust, followed by a crack of thunder.

Mothers began to stir and rounded up their tired and dusty but content children. He'd bet this was one of the happiest days they'd had since arriving on the shores of Lake Michigan. He was proud to have been a part of it.

Miss Addams called everyone to attention and invited all to the coffeehouse for free refreshments. Those who'd been reluctant to heed the call of their mothers found they couldn't resist the lure of whatever sweet confection awaited them at Hull House.

In a few minutes, the playground was devoid of little ones. Carlisle, Nurse Findley, and the two policemen helped gather up sacks, ropes, potatoes, and balls.

"Miss Addams has agreed to store all the equipment that can't be left out here," Billy said. "If you'll drop the things you've collected by the house, I'm going to have Hunter remove those ribbons."

Carlisle glanced at the streamers fluttering in the breeze, his hands full. "You need any help?"

"No, I think it's a one-person job." Hunter squeezed his friend's shoulder. "Thanks for coming and for teaching the boys that drill. They sure were proud of it."

Carlisle smiled. "They're good boys."

Billy held the gate open and thanked them again.

Hunter shimmied up the maypole and replaced

the ribbons with ropes, loosened a spinning mechanism, and turned the maypole into a giant stride.

Rolling the ribbons into one big ball, Billy looked around. "Well, I think it was a wonderful success."

The breeze took on the smell of rain and a cooling edge. A tendril curling down her back lifted and swirled.

"The girls did great," he said. "I don't know how you taught them to tie the ribbons like that, but they sure turned out pretty."

"They did, didn't they?"

He took the streamers from her arms and wrapped them about the bottom of the pole. "I don't know about you, Miss Tate, but I haven't been on a swing in a mighty long time." He held out his hand. "What do you say?"

Eyes brightening, she took his hand. "I've been secretly wanting to all day."

As soon as she settled in, he began to push her, generating a welcome breeze in the late afternoon air. The scent of freshly cut wood still clung to the swings. The creak of the rope kept time like a slow-ticking clock.

"You don't have to push." She pumped her legs. "I can do it."

Shoot fire, but that woman was independent. Still, he ignored her protests and continued to push.

Finally, she gave herself over to it, her head back, her feet out, laughter trickling over her shoulder. The wind whipped her skirts, teasing him with glimpses of petticoat and booted ankles. Visions of her crawling through the cellar came flooding back. He couldn't help but imagine what the view must be like on the other side of that swing.

When he had her going pretty good, he grabbed the ropes and jumped on, his feet straddling her hips.

She squealed, then laughed, then pumped her feet. He swiveled the seat with the force of his legs, propelling it higher. When they'd gone as high as they dared, they both stopped driving and simply enjoyed the momentum. She rested her head against his legs. He gloried in the feel of her and the freedom of flying through the air.

At last they slowed. She dragged her feet on the ground. When the swing came to a stop, she slid off and turned to look at him. "That was fun. I haven't ridden double since I was a child."

A jagged streak of lightning tore across the sky behind her, followed by a distant bark of thunder. Her hair had been mussed before, but their ride had loosened the moorings even further, leaving locks of dark blond hair trailing over her shoulder and down her back.

He slid down to the seat, then planted his feet on the ground. "Come here."

She eyed him. "I don't know how to swing on somebody's lap."

"Neither do I." Widening his knees, he patted his leg.

Looking around, she took a hesitant step toward him.

He snagged her hand and gave a gentle tug.

She sat.

"The day was perfect," he said. "One those kids will remember the rest of their lives."

Folding her hands in her lap, she looked down. "Yes, I believe they will."

He picked up a curl and held it to his nose. Apples, peaches, and summer berries.

"I'd thought you wouldn't be able to do the playground without me." She looked up. "But the truth is, I couldn't have done it without you. Thank you."

Putting a hand behind her neck, he kissed her. It had been the first time since they'd found out about Joey. The first time since she'd proposed to him. The first time since he'd sent the wire to his mother asking for the ring.

Scooping up her legs, he draped her over both of his and slid her closer. She hooked her arms around his neck. He tightened his around her waist. Sweet Mackinaw, but she tasted good.

He wrapped his arms even farther so they completely encircled her back. He wanted her like nothing he'd ever wanted before. He should have said yes when she'd asked him. If he had, he'd have her in his bed by now.

A droplet of rain fell on his shirt, penetrating the fabric.

He ignored it and ran a hand down her hip to the bend in her knees, then drew her close. She tucked herself around him, the rope of the swing anchoring her bent legs.

He wanted to ask her. He wanted to ask her right now, but he didn't have the ring. He needed to wait for the ring.

His hand began to wander. She reached around and brought it to safer ground. He pulled back from the kiss and buried his face in her neck, nibbling, tasting, imbibing. Her fingers drove into the hair at his nape, knocking his hat askew.

Marry me. Marry me. But he didn't say it out loud. Not yet.

Another raindrop. And another.

She rocked back, straightening her legs. "It's starting to—"

"I know. I don't care." He captured her lips again.

A flash of light, immediately followed by a shattering clap.

She pushed away and jumped to her feet. The skies opened up. Plucking his Stetson from his head, he jammed it onto hers, grabbed her hand, and they ran from the playground.

"The ribbons!" she shouted.

"Leave them!"

They continued to run, his feet splattering mud with each footfall. When they reached the back steps to Hull House, they were soaked, muddy, laughing, and out of breath.

Tipping her head back, he bracketed her face. "Death and the deuce, but I love you, Billy girl."

He kissed her again. She pressed herself against him. Neither noticed the rain, only the storm that brewed inside them.

ELECTRICITY BUILDING[29]

"The guard sought Hunter out in the
Electricity Building where he'd
picked up an extra shift."

Snyder County Libraries, Inc.
1 N. High St.
Selinsgrove, PA 17870
(570) 374-7163

CHAPTER 34

Within a fortnight, delinquents had taken over the playground. The very area she and Hunter had carved out was now providing a setting for precisely the sort of behavior they'd been hoping to decrease.

Derry handed her the day's catalog. "They drink up their grog by the sand pit and make you pay a penny to get in the gate, then another penny to play on anything."

Outrage filled her. She glanced at the Woman's Building, wishing Hunter were there, but another guard had long since taken his place.

"Have you told Mr. Scott?" she asked.

"I tried to stop him this morning, but he was in a big hurry. I told him it was about the playground. He just kept walking, and over his shoulder said he wouldn't be able to do nothin' about the playground no more."

She nodded. He'd probably thought something needed repairing. He'd told her he was going to try and pick up some extra shifts in hopes of earning his way back onto the day shift. And with his captain's assignment to distinguish himself and Colonel Rice's order to not be involved with anything other than the fair, the last thing he needed to do was become involved with whatever was going on with these delinquents. She'd simply have to take care of it herself.

"How many of them are there?" she asked.

He shrugged. "Four, eight, ten. Depends on when ya go."

"And no one gets in without paying?"

"Nobody but the girls. The girls get in without pennies. All they have to do is play a game."

"What game?"

"I don't really know. The girl gets in the middle and the fellows form a circle around her. That's all I know. My sister did it once. She don't go back no more, though. I don't know why. I'd go if all I had to do was play some game."

Chill bumps raced up her arms. "I didn't know you had a sister other than Alcee."

He gave a huff. "I got two more sisters. Brothers, too. I'm the only one who's not in a factory, though." He straightened, his chest jutting out in pride.

She wondered what would happen to him once the fair ended. "Were your brothers and sisters at the playground opening?"

"Most of them, I think. I don't really know."

She paid him a nickel for the catalog. "You stay away from there, all right? At least until I figure out what to do. You tell your brothers and sisters to do the same."

He scratched his side. "Don't worry. Pa would give us a whupping if we spent any of our pennies."

His nonchalance saddened her. She couldn't imagine how dismal it must be to never have a childhood. To never buy a licorice drop at the mercantile. To never go to school. To only have Sundays off. And to work every day from the time you were six until the time you died.

She took a deep breath. "Thank you for the paper, Derry."

"You're welcome, doc."

With a heavy heart, she headed to the infirmary.

"Dr. Tate asked me to show her how to protect herself if she were attacked."

Hunter gave Carlisle a sharp look. The guard had sought Hunter out in the Electricity Building, where he'd picked up an extra shift.

Waving a line of people toward the entrance to Alexander Graham Bell's theatorium, he scowled. "She what?"

Carlisle shrugged. "I asked her who was bothering her and she said nobody, she just wanted to learn how."

"That dog don't hunt."

"I know."

"So what'd you tell her?"

"To kick him in the shin, hit him in nose, knee him in the groin, then run."

Hunter blew out a breath. "When did all this happen?"

"Just before she left today. I asked Imogene if

the doc had said anything to her, but she hadn't."

It took Hunter a minute to realize Carlisle was referring to Nurse Findley. He glanced at his pocket watch. "Between Billy's schedule and the way I've been working, I've not seen her but in tiny snatches. My first instinct is her trouble is with somebody on the West Side, but with Joey being gone, she hasn't been over there since the playground opened. Said she's been too busy working on some paper about a germ theory or something. You sure she didn't say anything else?"

Carlisle nodded. "Nothing. Though Imogene told me the doc's going to the West Side tomorrow."

Hunter swore under his breath. Tomorrow was her day off and he was working another double shift. He stopped the line. "I'm afraid that's all for this show, folks. But you'll be first in line for the next one."

Good-natured grumbling skittered between those who'd just missed the cutoff. Before closing the doors, he glanced inside. The crowd found their seats below a mammoth telephone receiver built into the roof of the theatorium. In a few minutes an orchestra in New York would begin playing. Yet everyone in the room would be able to hear it as if they were right there beside it instead of a thousand miles away.

Making eye contact with a guard on the inside,

Hunter nodded, then backed out and pulled the doors shut. "Thanks for letting me know, Eddie. I'll try and catch her in the morning in between my night shift and the shift I'm picking up for Pete Stracke."

Carlisle nodded. "I'd pick up Pete's shift for you, but I'm due to be at the Woman's Building."

Hunter shook his hand. "Thanks anyway, buddy. Maybe she was asking on someone else's behalf. Either way, I'll find out tomorrow."

But the next morning, the matron at the front desk of the Women's Dormitory refused to wake Billy up. He glanced at his watch. He didn't have time to wait on the front steps for her. So he left a message with the matron, then headed back to the fair.

ALLEY, WEST SIDE CHICAGO[30]

"Instead of taking Halsted, he kept
to the alleys and their shadows."

CHAPTER 35

Derry chained his sister to the table. He hated doing it, but last week one of the babies next door fell out of a window because it had been locked in a room, but not chained up. There was still a stain on the street where she'd fallen. He shuddered. He didn't want that to happen to Alcee.

He squatted down in front of her. "Ma will be home before you know it. So you be good. Okay?"

He didn't get an answer, nor did he expect one. Making his way through the other rooms of the apartment building, he hurried toward the stairwell, then waved to the grocer on his way out. He'd just made it to Halsted Street when he saw the doc sail past Hull House and round the corner at Polk.

She must be going to the playground. And she was walking like she was mad. He'd only been there on Sundays. But the other kids told him those boys were there all the time.

He looked up and down the street for Mr. Scott but didn't see him. Derry was going to be a Texas Ranger like Mr. Scott when he grew up. And he knew Mr. Scott wouldn't let the doc go over to that playground by herself, even if they did let the girls in for free.

Turning around, he raced back inside, grabbed

his slingshot and a handful of rocks, then hurried toward the playground. Instead of taking Halsted, he kept to the alleys and their shadows. Once he reached Polk, he collected several more rocks, then ducked into an apartment one of his friends lived in.

Nobody was home, but he went in anyway and opened the window that looked out over the playground. He couldn't hear what they were saying, but those fellows didn't like whatever the doc was telling them. He pressed a rock into his slingshot, took aim, then held it taut, waiting.

The bigger fellow grabbed her arm.

She kicked him. Hard.

Derry let his rock fly. He missed, but the fellow heard it whiz by. He jerked his head toward the street.

Derry shot another. And another. The fellows held up their arms, shielding themselves.

The doc ran through the gate.

The leader spotted Derry and shouted.

But Derry continued to shoot until the doc had a good lead. Then he made his own escape. Texas Rangers may not run, but those fellows on the playground were really big and really mean. Especially when they'd been drinking. The last thing he wanted was to be caught alone by them.

Hunter paced the landing in front of Billy's dormitory waiting for her to respond to his summons. The minute he'd gotten off work, he'd come over only to find she wasn't home and his message had never been delivered.

He'd immediately ridden to the West Side. But she'd already come and gone.

So he'd ridden back dog tired and fit to be tied. He'd not shaved nor bathed nor slept nor eaten.

Finally, she stepped through the doors, her smile wilting the moment she saw him. "You look awful. Are you running a fever?" She lifted a hand as if she were going to feel his forehead.

He dodged it. "Who's threatening you?"

She frowned. "When's the last time you've had a full night's rest?"

"Don't answer my question with a question."

"Then don't bark at me."

Opening and closing his fists, he moderated his tone. "Who's threatening you?"

"Nobody."

"You want to lick that calf over?"

She scrunched her brows. "What does that mean?"

"You want to try answering that one more time?"

Rubbing her temples, she let out a *whoosh* of air. "Fredrick Kruse and his friends have seized the playground. They're charging the boys a penny to gain entrance and another penny to play on the equipment. Any who don't pay the toll are beaten." She gave him a pointed stare. "The payment required of the girls is of a more personal nature."

Anger surged through him. "How do you know?"

"Derry told me."

His jaw began to tick. "And I suppose you went down there today to see for yourself?"

"I did."

"Tell me you didn't confront them, Billy."

She held up her hands in a shrug. "I didn't know it was going to be them. By the time I did, I was already through the gate."

Whipping off his hat, he squeezed the rim. "Didn't you learn big wood from the brush the last time?"

She tightened her lips. "I said I didn't know it was going to be them."

"For the love of Peter, woman, who else did you think it would be?"

She stiffened. "Derry said there were anywhere from four to ten boys. So, I assumed it wasn't them."

"Ten? *Ten?* And you went anyway?"

"I'm not going to let them control me or the children, Hunter. Not with fear or anything else." She crossed her arms, her chest rising and falling.

"That doesn't mean you go driving your horse like you're in a hurry to get to heaven. You need a plan. A strategy." Sighing, he gentled his tone. "You know what I'd really like?"

"I have no idea."

He captured her gaze. "I'd like you to come to me first before you go off half-cocked. Just once, would you give me a chance? I know you're smart. I know you've got a fancy education. I know there's a lot of things you can do just as well—if not better—than some men. But there are also a few things us men can do that you can't. And dealing with bullies is one of them."

She looked down.

"Will you concede that point, at least?"

"You're stronger," she said. "I'll give you that."

Not the full endorsement he was hoping for, but it was a start. "Then you'll let me deal with them?"

"It's already been taken care of."

He lifted his brows. "How?"

"After visiting the playground, I went to Hull House. We decided the playground needs to be supervised. Miss Addams agreed to provide volunteer staff as soon as she can work out a schedule. It will mean the playground will only be open certain hours, but it was the only solution we could come up with."

He nodded. "It's a good solution, except how are you going to keep the interlopers out in the meantime?"

"We're going to put a lock on the gate."

"And if they decide to invade the playground while it's being supervised?"

"Miss Addams is going to ask a police officer to help until things settle down."

"One of the ones who was there on opening day?"

"I'm assuming so. She didn't say."

He put his hat back on. "What about today? Did Kruse do anything to you?" He didn't see any bruises, but that didn't mean they weren't there.

"He tried, but I kicked him, then ran."

He waited a couple of beats, forcing himself to keep calm. "They didn't chase you?"

"No." She gave him a confused look. "I'm not sure what happened exactly. Just that he let go and I ran."

He could take care of Kruse. The boy and his gang had kept well out of sight, but Hunter knew he could flush them out. The problem was what to do once he had them.

He couldn't arrest them because he had no jurisdiction. He couldn't report them to the police, or Rice would hear and so would his captain. He supposed he could give the boys a pretty good scare, but if word got back to Rice, he'd once again be putting his job and the Rangers in jeopardy. And for what? For four ne'er-do-wells the officers on the playground could handle without any trouble?

No, he needed to stay out of it. He needed to let the Chicago police handle it.

He slipped his hand into Billy's, entwining their fingers. "Kruse is dangerous. I don't want you near him. So, no more confrontations with him or any of his ilk. All right?"

Biting her lip, she nodded. "All right."

Pulling out his watch, he flicked it open. "Listen, I'm going to try and get a little shut-eye before my shift starts tonight. I'll be free for lunch tomorrow, though. You want to go to the Agriculture Building? Have some of that free food the exhibitors are giving out? I've heard Quaker Oats is making fresh muffins and cakes."

"I'd like that."

He pressed his lips to the palm of her hand. "You doing okay?"

Her eyes misted. "I miss him."

Sighing, he nodded. "Me, too, Billy girl. Me, too."

"Thirty pieces of Italian lace went missing
yesterday while you were on the West Side."

CHAPTER 36

August turned into September and with it came a bit of relief from the heat. Rice had heard about the extra stints Hunter was working and acknowledged them by not only reinstating him to the day shift, but by assigning him to guard priceless paintings in the Art Palace. And now he'd received even better news. It had come just this morning in the form of a cable and lay tucked inside his jacket pocket.

He was up for the position of captain. Old Captain Dunwoody from Company B had decided to retire come the new year and Heywood would be submitting Hunter's name as a possible successor.

Between his excitement and the hushed atmosphere of the Art Palace, the hours dragged by. He found himself constantly checking his pocket watch in anticipation of his shift ending so he could head to the Woman's Building and lunch with Billy. Tell her his news.

He'd finally made it over there only to find she was running behind. If she didn't finish up with her patient soon, they'd miss lunch altogether. Out of habit, he made a circuit of the ground floor. Upon his return, a tall fellow who'd been pacing the entryway earlier was still there. His face was drawn, his brilliantined hair mussed.

"Is everything all right, sir?" Hunter asked.

The man gave him a blank look.

"You've been circling this foyer like a squirrel in a cage." He studied the man. "Is there something I can help you with?"

"No, I'm sorry. I have a . . ." He looked at the door leading to the Bureau of Public Comfort, then back at Hunter, his face perplexed. "The lady I'm with is in the infirmary."

Hunter smiled. "Is that right? Well, don't you worry about a thing. The doc in there's the best of the best."

"He is? He's trained, then?"

"Graduated cum laude from the University of Michigan." Hunter paused. "And it's a she, not a he."

The man frowned. "Who's a she?"

"The doc."

Jaw slackening, he took a step back. "He's a *she?*"

Hunter nodded.

"Do you mean to tell me my lady isn't seeing a real doctor?" The man's voice rose.

Hunter narrowed his eyes. "She's real. And before you say anything else, you probably ought to know she's my woman."

The man had enough sense not to make any further comment. Instead, he took up his pacing again. Shaking his head, Hunter made a second sweep of the downstairs for lack of anything better to do. He paused in front of a series of dolls dressed up in costumes from Puritan days to present time. A slow smile crawled onto his face. Some mischief maker had spruced up the dried-up Puritan woman with a fancy hat that belonged to the Civil War gal and the New York lady's fox stole.

Looking in all directions to make sure no one would see him "playing dolls," he repaired the Puritan to her former glory and returned the other pieces of clothing to their proper owners before the Board of Lady Managers got their knickers in a twist. He wouldn't put it past Carlisle to be the culprit, but the only way to know for certain would be to confess he'd re-dressed the dolls. And he wasn't about to admit that to anyone.

By the time Billy had finished with her patient, Hunter had discovered the man in the foyer was showcasing a fire sprinkler system he'd invented over in Machinery Hall and his lady was a teacher of the deaf in the Children's Building.

As soon as the couple left, Hunter opened the door to the parlor and had to jump out of the way to keep from being run over by Nurse Findley.

"Excuse me, Mr. Scott. I'm sorry. I was on my way to lunch and not watching where I was going."

Smiling, he held the door. "You enjoy your lunch, then."

"You, too." She scurried out.

"Billy?" He stepped into the parlor. "You ready to go eat?"

"We're going to eat in here." She came in balancing two bowls. "Last week I treated a woman who works in the Louisiana State Pavilion and today she brought me some gumbo from their kitchen." She set the bowls on a side table. "I've never had any, have you?"

"Not here, but I've sure had some back home. Gumbo's one of my favorites."

They settled in to eat, her on the sofa, him in an armchair. Just thinking about all that had happened and what it could mean for the Rangers made him want to spit in the fire and call the dogs. He could hardly decide where to start. "Thirty pieces of Italian lace went missing yesterday while you were on the West Side."

She looked up, her spoon halfway to her mouth. "From here? In the Woman's Building?"

He nodded. "And the U.S. government had a bond of a hundred thousand dollars guaranteeing their safe return to Italy. Rice called me in to find them."

"I thought you were working at the Art Palace?"

"I was. I am. It only took me a few hours to figure out what had happened."

Her brows lifted. "Who took them?"

"I don't know. The first place I looked was at

the shipping records. The laces had arrived under the escort of customs inspectors and two private detectives. A countess who'd been detailed by Italy's queen had taken each piece of lace from its wrappings and recorded it in a log. The ones she logged in are still over there in the Italian exhibit—you know, in that alcove on the opposite end from where I found Joey?"

Dabbing her mouth, she nodded. "So what did you do?"

He shrugged. "I told Rice it had happened either before the laces ever left Italy's shores, at some point on the boat, or somewhere between New York's docks and the Woman's Building. I offered to find out which, but Rice said the Exposition's bond didn't cover the safety of exhibits in transit. So the fair's been cleared of all responsibility."

"You saved the government and the fair a hundred thousand dollars, then." It was a statement more than a question and pride rang in her voice.

"I did." He placed his finished bowl of gumbo on the side table. "Queen Margherita still lost some priceless laces, though. Kind of leaves a bittersweet taste in my mouth. I'd a lot rather have caught the person responsible."

"Well, don't tell Queen Margherita that. She's likely to hire you and then off you'd go to Italy, leaving me here by myself."

His gaze captured hers. "I've no plans to leave you, Billy girl. Not ever."

Her breath hitched.

He took the bowl from her hands and set it next to his. A flurry of nerves kicked up a ruckus in his stomach. "I've been thinking about asking you this a long time now, but it just never seems the right time. Either I'm working or you're on the West Side or we're both exhausted."

Her eyes zigzagged as she looked at both of his. Hope, a spark of excitement, and love shone within their pretty caramel depths. A surge of the same filled his chest.

Pushing himself off the chair, he knelt before her on one knee and took her hand. "I love you, Billy girl. And I'd be right proud to have you as my wife. Will you do me the honor?"

Tears sprang to her eyes and a tiny laugh escaped from her throat. "Yes. Yes!"

Smiling, he leaned forward and captured her lips in a show of celebration. It quickly transformed into something more.

Breaking free, he rested his forehead against hers, his chest rising and falling as if he'd run clear across Texas. She'd said yes. She'd said yes. "I have a ring for you. I just don't have it on me right this second. It's over at my barrack. I'll fetch it for you, if you'd like."

"I'd like that very much." Her voice was husky, her lashes fluttered.

He started to rise.

She grabbed him. "Not now. Not right this second. I'd rather . . . I mean, by the time you get there and back . . ." Her cheeks filled with color.

Kicking up a corner of his mouth, he cupped her face and kissed her again. She tugged him up next to her on the sofa. When his passion began to outpace his good sense, he pulled back and tucked her head beneath his chin.

A distant whistle from the elevated train announced its arrival at a platform. Muffled cries from a hawker outside crystallized in his brain as belonging to Derry. A bell from one of the buildings heralded in the half hour, warning them lunchtime would soon be over.

Her breathing settled. His heart slowed. And he found simply holding her was a pleasure all its own.

Settling his lips against her hair, he breathed in her scent. "My captain sent me a wire. He said I'm up for the position of captain of Company B. Nothing's been decided, but it's something I've been wanting for a while now."

Instead of congratulating him, she remained silent.

He looked down, but she wasn't asleep. "Did you hear me?"

She nodded, her hair sending a shock of static electricity to his neck. "I thought . . ." She pushed herself up, widening the space between them.

"What?" he asked. "You thought what?"

Scooting out of his arms, she studied him. "What exactly are your plans for us after the fair's over?"

He held up a hand. "I know. You want to keep doctoring after we're married. I'm willing to let you do that."

"I'm confused, then."

"About what?"

"A minute ago you were talking as if you were still planning to be a Ranger."

He blinked. "I'm not planning to be a Ranger. I am a Ranger."

"But I thought we agreed I'd be the wage earner."

He widened his eyes. "*The* wage earner? Don't you mean *a* wage earner?"

"No, I mean *the* wage earner."

Her statement was so outlandish, so incomprehensible, he didn't even know what to say. "Are you fooling me?"

"We've talked about this, Hunter."

He shook his head. "We talked about you continuing to work after we married. We never, ever, not once talked about me quitting my job and living off my wife's income. Because I can tell you one thing for certain, that will never happen. Never."

"Why not?"

"Because it won't." He couldn't even believe

she'd suggested it. Thought it. What did she expect him to do? Stay home and cook? Polish floors? Change diapers?

She picked at her fingernail. "And if we have children? Who will raise them?"

"I guess we both will."

"How? How will we do that if we're both working?"

"We'll hire a nanny. With two incomes, we'll certainly be able to afford it. And then, when you get tired of doctoring, you can quit and we'll get rid of the nanny."

Sadness etched her features. "I'm not ever going to give up my doctoring."

"Not even for our children?"

"It's what I'm called to do."

"Well, I'm called to be a Ranger."

She drew in a disjointed breath. "But you can only do that if you live in Texas."

Dread began to crawl up his insides. "That's right. It's always been my intention for us to live in Texas."

"It's always been my intention to live in Chicago."

"Chicago?" He balked. "But I thought . . . I mean, why would you live in this filthy, smelly, crowded, ugly city when you could live in the wide, green, open spaces of Texas?"

"Because Chicago is where the future is. Where the people are. Where hospitals are developing new lifesaving procedures and using the latest equipment. And it's not ugly. Other than the West Side, it's one of the most beautiful cities I've ever been in. But, Texas. Texas is . . ."

He stiffened. "What? Texas is what?"

"Well, it's not exactly cosmopolitan, Hunter. And the people there are, um, very traditional. I'm not sure they'd ever agree to being treated by a woman doctor."

"The men wouldn't. You're right about that. But once the gals got used to the idea, I'm figuring they'd jump on the wagon. But that's as it should be anyway. It wouldn't be proper for you to be examining men."

"Wouldn't be proper?"

"Well, no." He looked at her, wondering if he'd been wrong about her all this time. "You can't mean to tell me you were planning to examine any ol' man the way you did me that first day. Is that what you were planning to do, Billy? Were you planning to put your hands on other men?"

"Not in a sensual way, Hunter. In a strictly clinical way."

"You're more naive than I thought if you think there's anything clinical about those types of exams. Maybe it's clinical from your perspective. But I can guarantee it's not that way for the man. And I would have some mighty big issues with you conducting yourself in that manner with the fellows I see at church every Sunday."

She swallowed, her lips quivering. "What you're asking isn't possible. It would be like me saying I didn't mind you being a Ranger, so long as you didn't use any guns. But I do mind you being a Ranger. I also mind us living in Texas. And I most assuredly mind giving up my male patients."

His chest tightened. "Billy—"

"I'm sorry, Hunter." Her eyes welled up, then spilled a tear over her cheek. "I'm willing to compromise about you working, but I'm not going to Texas. And I'm definitely not giving up my male patients."

He stared at her, dumbstruck.

She swiped her cheek with her hand. "I'm sorry. More than you know."

Rising, she crossed the room, opened the parlor door, and left. He let her go, still reeling from her being "willing to compromise" about him working. What a great bunch of tripe.

Hurt and anger warred for dominance. But in the end, hurt won out.

He buried his face in his hands, and his throat filled. He loved her. He loved her more than life itself. But he couldn't, wouldn't take on a female's role in his marriage. Not only would she eventu-ally lose respect for him, but he'd lose respect for himself.

SWING ON HULL HOUSE PLAYGROUND[32]

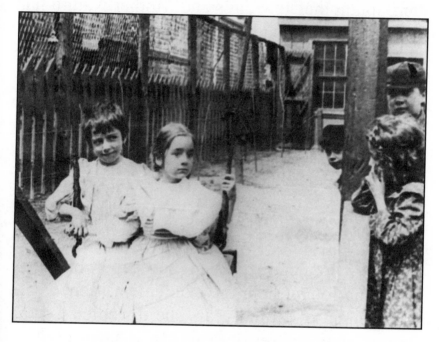

" 'They've had forty!' Nick Gryparis,
a young Greek boy, pointed to two
Italian girls sharing a wide swing."

CHAPTER 37

Flipping up her collar, Billy tucked her hands into the pockets of her jacket. October would be with them in another few days and Mother Nature had decided to foreshadow what was to come. A breeze whipped across the playground, tossing up dust. But the children didn't seem to mind.

They played jump rope, jackstones, faba-gaba, and, of course, on all the equipment. Today she'd taught a group to play Drop the Handkerchief, and a heated game had ensued for the last half hour.

It had been almost a month since she'd seen Hunter and her days had become mundane. Routine. Predictable. Even her paper on germ theory no longer held the excitement it once had. She thought of all the years she'd studied to be a doctor. Then the seven years she'd spent perfecting her skills until she was finally confident enough to branch out on her own. Only to discover no one would come.

But this next time they would. She'd built up quite a clientele since offering her services at Hull House twice a week. Miss Addams and her boarders had been duly impressed. The group of them had many influential contacts, as did the Lady Managers at the Woman's Building.

Between them and the money she'd earned at the fair, she'd be much more successful the next time she hung out her shingle.

She took in a deep breath. Achieving her dream was well within her grasp. So why did it feel so hollow? So empty?

But she knew why. She'd willingly exchanged a man she loved for her shingle. No, that wasn't exactly true. He'd said she could keep her shingle. But on his terms. It's just she didn't like his terms. Not even a little.

She pressed her face into her collar as another harsh breeze kicked up the dust. Still, she missed sitting in the parlor with him after a long day's work. She missed their conversations, their laughs, their kisses. Even their arguments.

But Texas? It was so far away. And so backward. And he'd be gone so much of the time that she'd be returning to an empty house anyway.

No, she didn't want to go to Texas. She didn't want to be married to a man who was never home. And she definitely didn't want to quit seeing her male patients. He was being completely unreasonable about that. Ridiculous, even. Bullheaded.

"They've had forty!" Nick Gryparis, a young Greek boy, pointed to two Italian girls sharing a wide swing.

"We've had no such thing."

Considering who was on the swing, Billy was inclined to believe them. Nella was sweet and very conscientious. And Antonietta wouldn't dream of breaking a rule.

"Course you have," Nick shouted. "More'n forty."

As much as Billy wanted to interfere, it was the survival of the fittest out here. The sooner the girls learned how to stand up for themselves, the better equipped they'd be to face a world run by men. Men who made the rules. Rules that favored them and incapacitated women. Still, she'd pull Nella and Antonietta aside later and give them suggestions on how to handle the boys when they threw their weight around like that.

The children in line, including Derry, decided forty had indeed been reached. They pulled the swing to a stop, shooed the girls off, then engaged in a heated debate over who was next. Derry thought it was his turn. Nick thought it was his.

When it appeared as if fisticuffs were imminent, Miss Weibel, Billy's partner in supervising, headed in their direction. Billy couldn't help but smile. She had no doubt Miss Weibel would find a creative solution to the dispute, one in which all those involved would feel as if they'd won.

Affection for the young woman filled her. She knew she shouldn't have favorites, but anyone who'd worked with Miss Weibel couldn't help but love her. And Billy worked with her this time every Sunday.

Things had been quiet in the neighborhood and on the playground for weeks now. With no more signs of any miscreants, the police officers had quit coming, leaving the supervision of the grounds to Hull House volunteers who taught the immigrant children games and American customs. As an extra precaution, though, Miss Addams had insisted two supervisors be on the grounds at all times during operating hours.

With it being Sunday and the only day off for most families, Billy saw patients after church, then took her turn at the playground with Miss Weibel just before dusk. She'd welcomed her men patients with a good deal of satisfaction. They appreciated her services and never once hinted at any impropriety on her part.

Still, Hunter's words rang in her head.

Maybe it's clinical from your perspective, but I can guarantee it's not that way for the man.

Perhaps it had been different with him because of his attraction to her. Nevertheless, she didn't want any patients misconstruing her actions. So she now requested that the wives or mothers stay during all exams she had with the men. She couldn't help but resent it, though. Her male counterparts had no such limitations.

A child in one of the baby carriages lining the fence whimpered. Mothers had parked them all along the perimeter, then disappeared. But they always came back to fetch them before feeding time.

She walked alongside them, looking for the one who'd fussed. She tucked in blankets and brushed dust from around their eyes. With each face, she couldn't help but hope one would be Joey's. But, of course, they never were.

An ebony-skinned tot of perhaps four sat beside the carriages, hugging a sibling a few inches shorter than herself. The girl was perfectly content to hold the little cherub and watch the others.

"Would you like me to take him for a bit so you can play?" Billy asked.

Her eyes lighting, she nodded.

Billy tucked the baby close. "Run on, now. I'll take good care of him."

Scrambling to her feet, the child headed straight to the area with cedar building blocks, her chubby little legs pumping. Billy smiled. Perhaps she'd grow up to be an architect like the one who'd designed the Woman's Building.

Bouncing the babe in her arms, she tickled his chin. "How do you do? I'm Dr. Tate."

Gurgling, he smiled in return, a drop of drool escaping his lips. Chuckling, she lifted a corner of his dress and dabbed his mouth.

"Doctor!" A woman down the street hurried toward the playground. "Doctor!" she screamed. "Come quick!"

The children quieted. Billy turned. The little black girl appeared at her side, her arms upraised. Giving the girl an apologetic look, Billy handed her brother back to her.

The hysterical woman, her brown hair wild,

clasped a threadbare shawl about her arms and burst through the gate. "My husband. He's collapsed. Come quick!"

Oskar Zimmerman's wife. She recognized the woman now. Billy had treated her husband last week for coughing up blood. It had been a very small amount, and Billy had attributed it to a swallowed nosebleed or forceful coughing. But if he'd collapsed, she needed to see to him immediately. She looked at Miss Weibel.

"Go on," she said. "I'll be fine."

But Billy couldn't leave her. Not alone. "Miss Addams has been adamant about two of us being here at all times."

"This is different. This is an emergency."

Billy scanned the area surrounding the playground, then sucked in a breath. Down the street Kruse and his friends lounged in the shadows of a closed cigar shop.

Her pulse increased. She turned to Mrs. Zimmerman. "Perhaps you should go see if Dr. Young is home."

"What?" The woman's face registered shock. "There's no time. *You* must come. Now."

"She's right." Miss Weibel shooed her. "Don't worry. I'll explain it all to Miss Addams."

"There's some young men down the street." Billy lowered her voice so the children couldn't hear. "They're the ones who held the playground hostage."

Miss Weibel glanced at them, then swatted the air with her hand. "We'll be fine."

"I'll stay with her, doc."

Billy turned to see Derry behind her. His eyes narrowed as he watched Kruse and the other boys. She looked again toward the cigar shop. Kruse took a long draw on his smoke, an orange glow lighting its end. Then he threw it on the ground, mashing it with his toe.

She shook her head. "I'm sorry Mrs. Zimmerman, but I can't leave."

Miss Weibel pushed Billy toward the gate. "Nonsense. Mrs. Zimmerman's husband is the one who needs your attention, not us. We'll be fine. If it will make you feel better, I'll close the playground."

"I'm not sure that's a good idea, either. Besides, the babies won't be picked up for another thirty minutes."

Miss Weibel clucked. "I won't leave them. And the older children will alert their mothers."

Mrs. Zimmerman locked an arm through Billy's and hauled her through the gate. "Come!"

Billy could either go with her or be dragged.

Miss Weibel clapped her hands for attention, then held the gate open. "We have to close early, children."

After a few moans of disappointment, the children began to head to the gate.

"That's it. No pushing now. Everyone file out

peacefully. Be sure to tell your mothers to come fetch their babies, though."

With one last glance at Kruse, Billy lifted her skirts and concentrated on keeping up with Mrs. Zimmerman.

Sensing Billy's cooperation, the woman finally released her. They wove down two alleys, then across a street.

"He's in the Brass Rail." Mrs. Zimmerman pointed to a saloon toward the middle of the block, but headed toward another alley.

"Where are you going?" Billy asked.

"We need to go round to the back."

Women were strictly forbidden to enter through the front door. Even those who lived above stairs had to enter from the alley.

"Nonsense." Billy forged ahead and went right through the front door.

Cries of outrage came from the men inside. Taking advantage of their momentary shock, she pushed them aside, then knelt by Mr. Zimmerman. He lay on the floor, still wearing his Sunday suit. She knew without even touching him that he was dead. Still, she took his pulse, then placed her mouth against his bearded one and blew her own breath into him.

Mrs. Zimmerman rushed through the back door and sank down beside her.

After several minutes the bartender touched Billy's shoulder. "He's dead, doc. Anyone can see that. Come on now and let me and the boys get him back home so he can be laid out proper."

Pausing, Billy checked again for a pulse. As she suspected, there was none. With a heavy heart, she asked for a small glass of whiskey.

The bartender lifted his brows, but did as requested.

"No!" Mrs. Zimmerman cried. "He was fine this afternoon."

The bartender handed Billy the whiskey. Suppressing a shudder, she rinsed her mouth with it, then spit it back into the cup.

Mrs. Zimmerman knocked the glass from Billy's hand, sending it and the dark liquid across the dusty floor. "I've seven mouths to feed and only two dollars. He can't be gone. He can't."

Billy sat back on her feet, her shoulders sagging. She hated losing a patient. Not only for the pain it caused the family, but because of the helplessness she felt. The reminder that she was not God, but only a mortal like everyone else. Feelings of inferiority quickly followed a tremendous dose of guilt.

She shouldn't have hesitated. She should have come immediately. Would he still be alive if she had?

"I'm so sorry, Mrs. Zimmerman," she said. "I'm so—"

"This is your fault!" The woman pulled at her own hair. "You should have come when I called.

What good is a doctor who refuses to come when a husband is dying? You'd never see a man doctor watching over a playground. You'd never see a man doctor refuse to come when called."

"I didn't refuse, I—"

"You did!" she screeched. "I had to drag you. You were more concerned about a bunch of children playing than—"

Four loud bangs reverberated from outside.

Eyes widening, Billy looked to the bartender.

"Gunshots!" he shouted.

She was on her feet and out the door before anyone could hold her back. Saloons up and down the block emptied and men raced toward Polk Street, where the sound had originated, Billy right behind them.

A crowd of yelling men on the playground closed their ranks around Fredrick Kruse, his three friends, and Derry. A red-bearded man jerked Derry by the arm.

"Derry!" she screamed.

"Doc Tate! I didn't do nothin'." He struggled, but his fierce captor refused to let him go.

"I didn't do nothin'," Derry yelled. "It was them who—"

"Doc! Over here!" someone shouted.

The men parted for her. Derry's voice faded into the noisy commotion. Billy's stomach dropped. Miss Weibel, her dark curly hair spread out behind her, lay dead in a pool of blood.

POLICE PADDY WAGON[33]

"The officer locked the cage,
his square jaw set, his eyes hard."

CHAPTER 38

"He didn't do anything!" Billy screeched.

"I'm sorry, miss." The police officer lifted Derry into the wagon with Kruse and the others, then shut the cage. "You weren't here. You don't know what happened any more than the rest of us. So the boy goes with me."

"He was trying to protect her." She gripped the man's arm, her hands and fingernails stained with Miss Weibel's blood.

He narrowed his eyes. "Get your hand off me."

She snatched it back. "He's only nine. You can't take him to that horrid jail. You can't."

He locked the cage, his square jaw set, his eyes hard. Then he circled round toward the front.

"I'll lose my job." Derry grabbed the bars, his panic palpable. "Help me, doc."

She nodded, keeping her emotions in check so as not to scare him further. "I'll speak to the fair officials."

"No! You can't tell 'em I'm in the pokey. I'll never get a job again."

She touched his hands, the blood on hers mingling with the blood on his.

"Try not to worry," she said. "I'll take care of it."

"What about my papa? He needs my pennies. He'll give me a whupping, for sure."

"I'll make sure they know it wasn't your fault." She made no promises about getting him out, though. For she knew she had no power there. But the thought of where they were taking him sickened her.

The officer climbed into the driver's seat and snapped the reins. The wagon gave a jerk, then pulled away, breaking their contact.

Derry pressed his face against the bars. "Don't let 'em take me, doc. Don't let 'em take me."

She swallowed. "Stay strong, Derry. I'll do everything I can."

"Sit down and quit your sniveling." Kruse cursed the boy and called him deplorable names.

She gasped at the crude slurs, at once incensed and distressed. She prayed Derry wouldn't be in a cell with those four.

The undertaker's wagon pulled out behind them. Nothing more than a glorified delivery wagon, it held the remains of Miss Weibel. Tears rushed to Billy's eyes. She shouldn't have left the girl alone. She knew Kruse was there, watching the playground like a wolf, just waiting for a lamb to be separated from the flock.

And now, a life had been snuffed out. The life of a bubbly young woman whose only ambition had been to elevate the poor and help the unfortunate. A young woman whom Billy had come to care a great deal for. Miss Weibel was a favorite of Derry's, too, and other boys who were members of her Young Heroes Club.

Billy pressed a handkerchief to her mouth. What would the reaction of the neighborhood's elderly men be? For Miss Weibel had organized a club especially for them as well, dedicated to the study of Plato.

Extinguishing any innocent's life was unfathomable. But when that innocent was Miss Weibel, it was beyond all comprehension. And Billy was to blame. If she'd stayed, none of this would have ever happened.

The tired clip-clop of the undertaker's horse reverberated inside her. Who would be the one to knock on the door of Miss Weibel's home back East and tell her father, a passionate abolitionist, and her mother, a founding member of a women's seminary, that their beloved daughter was gone? Senselessly killed by boys who carried a grudge against those who'd destroyed their home, pitiful though it had been.

And though she'd explained Derry had been attempting to protect Miss Weibel, there'd been no convincing the men who'd first arrived, nor the police officer.

Miss Addams wrapped a chain around the gate of the playground, then locked it. "I think it best if we close it. Indefinitely. Until we can find out what happened and why."

The lump in her throat grew. "Of course. I'm—I don't know what to say. I'm so sorry."

Miss Addams nodded, a watery sheen filling her eyes.

Billy sucked in a choppy breath. If she could only go back. But she couldn't. She couldn't do anything.

Miss Addams reached over and squeezed her arm. "Perhaps you should stay with us tonight."

Billy's lips parted. The offer was so unexpected and of such a forgiving nature, emotion rushed up her throat. "Thank you, but I think I'll go speak to Derry's parents, then go home. I . . . I need to be alone."

"I understand, dear." Supporting Billy's elbow, Miss Addams turned them toward Halsted. "You needn't worry about Derry's parents. I sent Miss Starr to speak with them. She'll tell them what you told us and that he's not to blame."

Miss Starr had been alongside Miss Addams from Hull House's very inception, when it was nothing more than an idea, and Billy trusted her implicitly. "Are you sure?"

"Quite sure."

But by the time Billy made it home, instead of offering solace, the dormitory hemmed her in. Its walls threw accusations. Remonstrating with her for abandoning Miss Weibel. There were other physicians Mrs. Zimmerman could have called.

Maybe not quite as close, but certainly within reach.

Billy could have, and should have, either waited to leave the playground until someone from Hull House came to replace her or sent Mrs. Zimmerman to another doctor. But the man had collapsed. The time it would have taken for a replacement or another doctor could mean the difference between life and death. How was she to have known he'd be dead before she arrived?

She covered her ears, trying to stop the voices. Why did she think she was the one who always knew best? The one who could solve all the problems? The one who could do all things better than anyone else?

And what about Derry? Was she to simply sit by and take no action? She'd done that with Joey and look what had happened.

Just once, I'd like you to come to me first before you go off half-cocked.

She stopped in the middle of the floor and hugged herself. Hunter wasn't hers to go to any-more.

There are a few things us men can do that you can't.

She thought of the tangle she'd gotten into with Nefan's jailer. Yet when Hunter went, he'd been able to get the boy out. Could he do the same for Derry?

Grabbing her jacket and muff, she headed out the door. It was well past dark and she had no idea where Hunter was, but if she had to storm the guards' barracks, so be it. Better that than leaving Derry in jail.

Feminine boot heels clipped across the bridge leading to Crockett's island. Hunter rolled up off the animal skin he'd appropriated, unbuttoned his trousers, and tucked in his shirt. He figured he'd only been asleep a couple of hours.

The footfalls slowed once they reached the section of the island without lampposts. He quickly redid his buttons.

"Hunter?" she whispered.

"Billy?"

She stepped into the clearing, moonlight throwing shadows against her face. A short, dark jacket masked her figure, but it didn't keep his exhilaration at bay. Just the sheer pleasure of seeing her again brought a moment of complete euphoria, chased down with a quelling shot of sorrow.

"The night guard at the Woman's Building said I might find you here."

She didn't move and he didn't invite her closer.

"What's the matter?" he asked. "Is everything all right?"

"Miss Weibel's been murdered."

He sucked in his breath. He knew it had to

have been dire for her to seek him out, let alone in the middle of the night, but he'd never expected this. "When? What happened?"

"This evening. On the playground." Her voice wobbled as she tried to choke back tears. "There's more. Derry's been arrested for it, along with Kruse and his cohort."

"Derry? *Derry?* Why?"

She told him of the shooting, the events leading up to it, her heartbreak over the loss of Miss Weibel's life, and her anguish over Derry's arrest. He wanted to go to her. To hold her, comfort her. To take her pain onto himself.

But that was no longer his privilege, so he stayed where he was. "Did anybody witness it?"

"I don't know." She swiped her eyes, her tone rising in distress. "It was chaotic and I had to see to Miss Weibel. By the time I was done with that and the undertaker arrived, the men who'd first arrived at the playground had already convinced the police Derry was involved."

"What was Derry's demeanor like?"

"Frantic. Distraught. Panicked. He cried, begging me to help him. Telling me he hadn't done anything, that it had been the others. Which, of course, I already knew. But I wasn't able to talk with him privately, and the men who'd accused him are not very fond of Italians. They wouldn't have it any other way than to have Derry arrested along with the rest of them." She swallowed.

"Me being a doctor meant nothing to them. At that moment, I was no more than a woman. A woman easily ignored."

He dragged a hand through his hair. "When exactly did all this happen?"

"Around dusk. By the time the police wagon left, it was dark."

He knew what she wanted. She wanted him to go get Derry, just as he did with Nefan. But things were a lot more complicated now. And if Rice was upset about Hunter interfering with a boy who'd snatched a handful of coal, he didn't even want to think what the colonel's reaction would be if he interfered in a murder investigation.

"Can you get him out?" she asked.

"What did they say when you went to the jailhouse?"

She looked down, tucking her hands inside a dark, furry muff. "I didn't go to the jailhouse. I, um, didn't want to go off half-cocked."

He let that sink in. "That's good, Billy girl. That's real good."

"So, can you get him out?"

He couldn't see the tears, but he could hear evidence of them.

He slid fisted hands into his pockets. "I don't know. Murder's a pretty serious charge."

"But you'll try?"

He'd just been assigned to guard the duke and

duchess of Veragua, lineal descendants of Christopher Columbus who were coming to see the fair. If he saw to it successfully, he'd not only be awarded a spot on Rice's secret service, but also receive another commendation he could forward to his captain. His captain could then present it to the politicians in Austin.

He'd already sent his captain one commendation he'd received for bringing the Italian lace mystery to a swift conclusion. If he were then to receive another and be placed in Rice's secret service, it would be indisputable evidence that Hunter had skills atypical of regular lawmen. And the evidence wouldn't be coming from just anyone, it would be coming from the head of the most exclusive force ever assembled in the country's history. It would, without question, validate the special skills Rangers had to offer.

The duke and duchess were to arrive this morning. Hunter's duty would entail a night-and-day commitment for the duration of their stay. "I'm not sure when I'll be able to get over to the jail."

She gave him a look of confusion. "What?"

"I said, I'm not going to be able to get over there for a while."

"Why not?"

"I've been put on special assignment and I'll be working without breaks."

"What about Derry?"

"He'll have to wait until I'm free."

Her breath came out in a huff, making a cloud of condensation. "Did you hear what I said? Derry. Nine-year-old *Derry*. He's in that unspeakable jail."

"I heard you."

"And you're not going to do anything."

"Not right away."

"Because you have a special assignment."

"That's right."

"What on this blessed earth is so important that you can't take a couple of hours to go down to the jailhouse and get him out?"

She wasn't his woman. He wasn't her man. He didn't have to answer any of these questions. But he loved her. And he cared a great deal for Derry. "It's going to take a lot more than a couple of hours to get him out, if I even can. And if it were just me who was affected, I'd go right away. But it's not."

"Who else would be affected?"

"The Rangers."

A low rumble came from her throat. "The Rangers this. The Rangers that. I'm so sick and tired of your precious Rangers taking precedence over everything else. It was one thing when it was me. It's quite another when its an innocent nine-year-old." Whirling around, she began to stalk off. "Good night, Hunter. I hope your conscience keeps you awake for many a night to come."

"Billy?"

Pausing, she looked over her shoulder.

"If you get yourself thrown in the pokey, I'm not coming for you, either, until I've finished this assignment."

Black shadows were where her eyes should be, but he knew they were shooting holes in him. "At least I've been reminded that nothing and no one is more important than your job. And honestly, it'll make getting over you much easier." With a toss of her head, she sailed back across the bridge.

He pulled his hands from his pockets. "Well, if that's not the pot calling the kettle black, I don't know what is!" His shout echoed around the clearing, across the lagoon, and, he felt sure, within Miss Doctor Cum Laude's ears.

JANE ADDAMS[34]

"Where Colonel Rice and his captain
demanded respect, Miss Addams inspired it."

CHAPTER 39

Hunter hooked a thumb in the pocket of his denims, removed his Stetson, then looked Colonel Rice straight in the eye. "I'm not going to be able to start guard duty with the duke until tomorrow, sir."

Setting his pen down, the commandant swept him with his gaze. "What are you talking about, Scott?"

"There's a nine-year-old in the city jail I need to see to."

Rice smoothed the mustache hairs beneath his nose. "Haven't we been through this?"

"Yes, sir. But this is different. I know this boy."

"And you didn't know the last one?"

"No, sir."

"What did this one do?"

"That's what I'm going to find out."

"What's he been accused of?"

"Murder."

A lively march tune from the bandstand outside filtered through the window. The incandescent bulb above them hissed.

"No." Rice picked up his pen and began writing.

"I'm sorry, sir. I'll report for duty first thing tomorrow. I'd like to say I'll be back tonight, but I'm not sure how long everything's going to take."

The colonel lifted his gaze. "You'll pick up the duke and his duchess at the terminal at ten fifty-three this morning and you'll stick to their side until they leave next week."

"I'm sorry, sir. I won't be available until first thing tomorrow."

"I'm the commandant. You're the soldier. I say where you'll be today. You say, 'Yes, sir.' "

"Actually, sir, I'm not a soldier. I'm a Texas Ranger. And an innocent boy has been put in the most detestable jail I've ever seen in all my days. I've not only a legal obligation to do something about that, I've a moral one."

He put down his pen. "Under whose authority?"

"Under the authority of the gun tucked into my waistband, the rifle in my saddle boot, and the badge on my vest."

Rice's gaze dropped to Hunter's waistband, but the gun and the badge were concealed beneath his jacket.

"You are not on the frontier, son. You are in the city of Chicago."

"That doesn't make me any less of a lawman. He's nine, sir. Nine. He didn't murder anybody. I just need to talk to the judge."

Rice hardened his expression. "You either be at the terminal at ten fifty-three this morning or you're discharged from the Columbian Guards."

Hunter's lungs quit working. He'd expected to lose his chance at the secret service position, but he'd not expected to be dismissed completely. "Sir, I understand you're unhappy at having to find someone else today on such short notice, but I—"

"I've said what I have to say, Scott. The choice is yours."

"Does it have to be all or nothing? Can't you demote me to night shift again?"

The man's face soured. "That would be a total waste of exceptional talent."

"So would firing me, sir."

A flush rose up Rice's neck and spread to his bald head. "You're perilously close to having no choice whatsoever, Scott."

What the man didn't understand was Hunter already didn't have a choice. He'd wrestled with his conscience all night and if he had to help either Derry or the Rangers, he knew the Rangers were much better equipped to help themselves. Derry, however, had no man to step into the gap for him.

Looking at the shiny polished floor, Hunter tapped his hat against his leg. "I can't leave the boy to wallow around in that cesspool, sir. Every minute he's in there, he's exposed to the worst kind of diseases and the worst kind of men."

Rice said nothing.

Lifting his chin, Hunter drew a deep breath. "It's been one of the greatest honors of my career to serve in your corps, sir. I'd like nothing more than to continue serving you, but that boy needs me. I'm sorry. I really am."

"And your captain? What's he going to have to say about this?"

"Plenty." Hunter swallowed. "He's going to have plenty to say. None of it good. He thinks you're finer than frog hair and I'm going to get a good chewin' about all this."

After a slight hesitation, the colonel nodded. "I wish you luck then, son. And you'll be missed. Soldier or no, you were an asset to the squad."

He gave a nod. "Thank you, sir."

After a tense moment, Rice picked up his pen. "Dismissed."

Miss Weibel's murder made the front page of Chicago's newspapers. The citizens' outrage was strong and vocal, many crying for the delinquents to be hanged. Derry's age received a great deal of comment.

Children up to seven years old weren't recognized by the law, but those eight and over were fully responsible for their actions and were treated just like any other criminal. As a result, many youths were at this very moment housed in adult prisons and many more had been sentenced to death.

Had it only been the teeners, the age of the boys might not have drawn much attention. But a nine-year-old was something different. And many were beginning to question the wisdom of holding Derry to the same standards as those of a fully grown man.

Owing to all the brouhaha, the jailer and the judge both refused to let Hunter see, much less question, Derry, Kruse, or any of the other boys. And since their crime could be punishable by death, there would be no bail.

"Can you at least separate him so he's not sharing a cell with grown men and hardened criminals?" Hunter asked the judge.

The man, who looked like a short version of Abraham Lincoln, shook his head. "We don't have the room, Scott. The cells are so crowded, the men have to take turns sleeping on the planks laid out for them."

"When's the last time you've been down there, sir? Have you seen the conditions?"

"I've seen them."

"And you can, in all good conscience, leave a nine-year-old down there?"

"I have no choice. He was arrested for the murder of Miss Weibel. He'll stay down there just like everybody else who's awaiting trial."

Hunter's jaw began to tick. "Can you at least move the docket up so the trial starts right away?"

The judge tapped his pen on the desktop. "I'll see what I can do. But I'm not making any promises."

After leaving the courthouse, Hunter sent word

to his captain about what was happening. The man would be displeased. Very displeased—on a lot of different levels. It would mean he'd have to use some other means to persuade the Texas politicians. And it could very well mean the difference in Hunter making captain.

As much as he coveted the position, he knew another one would come along. And he knew the Rangers wouldn't go down without a fight. Their enemies were usually of a different stripe, but whatever form they took, the Rangers faced them head-on and came out on top.

He had to believe this time would be no different. He must. The alternative was too horrendous to even contemplate.

And once they'd quelled this enemy, maybe Hunter would still have a chance at promotion. Rangers were trained to make decisions without consulting their superiors. Heywood trusted Hunter's judgment. The captain wouldn't like Hunter's current decision, but he wouldn't make him return home until all had been resolved here to Hunter's satisfaction.

Still, he wasn't off to a good start. Not being able to talk to the accused would definitely hobble his horns. Never in his career had he been denied access to the suspects. It wouldn't keep him from investigating, but it was going to limit his effectiveness and put him at a great disadvantage.

Before he could start to think about that, though, he needed to see if Miss Addams would let him have a room in a cottage on Polk that lodged Hull House's male residents. For he was now homeless, and Chicago didn't have a single place where a fellow could roll out his pack and use his saddle as a pillow.

Hunter sat up straight in his chair. Where Colonel Rice and his captain demanded respect, Miss Addams inspired it. The woman had celebrated her thirty-third birthday a few weeks earlier, and although her skin and figure were still plenty youthful, her demeanor was of a woman much older. One who'd seen a lot, experienced a lot, and garnered wisdom from it.

Moving a stack of mail to the side, she linked her hands and set them atop her desk. "Typically, those who want to live here must make a formal application and, if accepted, commit to staying on at least six months."

"I'm afraid I won't be here near that long. Only until Derry's trial is over."

Diplomas and a gallery of photographs graced the dark paneling that covered the walls of her octagonal office. Windows made from glass-bottle bottoms restricted the view while letting light filter in.

"Can you pay for your room?" she asked.

"For a while, yes, ma'am." He knew those who

couldn't afford rent were supported by fellow-ships from wealthy donors. But he should be able to cover expenses until the trial had come and gone.

"One of the requirements for living here is devoting your spare time, including weekends, to working on Hull House programs and projects. For our male residents, we ask that your work be consistent with your profession." She sat almost as erect as he did, her desk smack-dab in the middle of the room. "What would your offering be, Mr. Scott?"

He thought about the things he was good at. Shooting. Fast-drawing. Fighting. Riding. Hunting. Tracking. Investigating. He was also good at intercepting cattle rustlers, contending with marauders, and protecting unpopular fellows from lynch mobs. He rubbed his hands against his trousers. "I don't rightly know, ma'am. Did you have any suggestions?"

The barest of sparks touched her eyes. "There is a most successful club that Miss Weibel formed for our boys called the Young Heroes Club. She read, in a most dramatic way, old chivalric tales, which taught the boys courage, valor, and loyalty. Can you read, Mr. Scott?"

"Yes, ma'am, though I'm not sure I've ever tried doing it in a 'most dramatic' way." He couldn't imagine sweet little Miss Weibel reading about bloodthirsty champions and gory battles, but he'd learned not to underestimate women of any sort.

"I see. And what grade did you make it to in school?"

"All of them, ma'am. I graduated from the Agricultural and Mechanical College of Texas."

Picking up her pen, she began to make some notes. "And how did you do there?"

"I stayed on the north side of the grass, for the most part."

She glanced up at him. "Where were you in the order of graduates?"

He shifted in his chair. "In the top ten percent."

Nodding, she continued to write. "You graduated cum laude, then. Excellent. What number were you exactly?"

"One."

Her pen stopped. She looked up again. "One? You were the top graduate of your class?"

"Yes, ma'am."

She leaned back, humor lighting her eyes. "Does Dr. Tate know about this?"

The question was so unexpected, it took him a moment to absorb it. Then he realized Miss Addams didn't miss much. She was clearly just as aware as he was of the pride Billy girl felt over graduating cum laude. "I've led her to believe otherwise, ma'am, and I'd like to keep it that way, if it's all the same to you."

As she tapped a finger against her notes, a tiny grin began to form. "Out of respect for the other residents, I need to receive their approval. But I think it safe to say you will be welcome to a room in the men's cottage. It will include meals in the dining room and full use of the bathhouse."

He let out a breath of relief. "Thank you, ma'am. I really appreciate it."

"You're most welcome, Mr. Scott. Come back later this evening and we'll finalize all the details."

He was heading out the front door just as Billy was approaching it. They both stopped and simply stood. Taking a moment to drink in the unexpected sight.

He recovered first and tugged on his hat, then began to pass.

She followed him with her gaze. "I thought you were on an assignment."

He kept moving.

"Hunter?"

Taking a deep breath, he turned back around.

"What are you doing here?" she asked.

"Applying for residency."

"Applying for residency? Here? Why?"

"I lost my job."

Her lips parted. "At the fair?"

"Yes."

"Why? What happened?"

"I refused to show up for work this morning. I had someplace else I needed to be."

She placed a fist against her stomach. "You went to get Derry."

"Yes."

Her eyes lit. "Oh, Hunter. Thank you. He's out, then?"

"No. There's too much attention about the case in the papers. They won't release or even segregate him. I've asked the judge to speed up the docket."

"What did he say?"

"That he wouldn't make any promises."

She fingered the belt at her waist. "How was Derry?"

"They wouldn't let me see him."

"Oh, no. I hate to think of him in there. And without any reassurance from one of us."

"Same here."

"And you were let go because of it?"

"Yes."

She bit her lip. "Are you sure Colonel Rice won't take you back?"

"Yes."

She took a step forward. "I'm so sorry, Hunter. What are you going to do?"

"Live over there in the men's cottage, investigate the crime, and help out around Hull House."

"For how long?"

"Until Derry's trial is over."

"I see." She brushed something off her skirt. "Where are you off to now?"

"The playground."

She looked up. "The playground?"

He held up a key he'd been given by Miss Addams. "A photographer is supposed to come out today and take pictures of where the crime took place. I wanted to inspect it first."

"Do you need any help?"

"No."

She clasped her hands. "May I come anyway?"

"Why?"

She took her time answering. "In case you have any questions?"

"You want to lick that calf over?"

A hint of a smile touched her lips. "The truth is, I'd like to help. I feel so . . . powerless. And guilty. May I? Please?"

He wanted to say no and he wanted to say yes. Instead, he said neither. "Suit yourself."

Then he headed to Polk Street leaving her to follow or not.

TENEMENT APARTMENT, WEST SIDE CHICAGO[35]

"The Molinaris' apartment was noisy, crowded, and chaotic. Children of all sizes and ages came and went."

CHAPTER 40

Billy shadowed him to the playground, trying not to notice the sight he made in his jacket, denims, boots, and hat. She'd never had an opportunity to walk behind him before. He was usually extremely solicitous, keeping her beside him or before him. She had to confess, he looked rather nice from this angle.

But pleasant as it was, it wasn't just the view that had her in danger of succumbing to tender feelings. It was the fact that he'd gone after Derry.

Last night she'd spoken out of hurt and anger and fear. She'd purposely made jabs about his Rangers. But he wasn't one to be manipulated. He only did what he thought best. And he'd evidently thought going after Derry was best.

His parting comment from last night rang in her ears. She had been the pot calling the kettle black. If the existence of all doctors hung in the balance, would she have chosen Derry over them?

It was an impossible comparison, for nothing would ever jeopardize the existence of doctors. But still, if they were at risk, she couldn't imagine being made to choose. Yet Hunter had chosen. And he'd sacrificed his job, his income, his room, and his board to do so. Most of all, he'd sacrificed his reputation. In the end, he had nothing to show for it. And no matter how hard she tried to resist, she couldn't quell the new level of admiration, respect, and love for him building inside her.

The sun splashed warmth onto her skin as she watched him squat in different parts of the playground, staring at the dirt as if it held hieroglyphics only he could decipher. He moved from spot to spot, ending at the place where Miss Weibel had fallen. He looked at it from every angle, the dirt still stained with remnants of blood.

She supposed some would find his detachment callous or insensitive. But she understood what it meant to put personal feelings aside in order to do your job, no matter how unpleasant the task. If she'd thought about who she'd been treating or what Miss Weibel had endured, Billy never would have been able to check for signs of life or try to stem the flow of blood seeping from the gunshot and knife wounds. Empathy was not an emotion she could indulge in and still maintain her equilibrium.

Certainly, she mourned the loss of Miss Weibel. Very much. But when she had a job to do, she had to consider the details of her friend's murder as clinical. Not horrific actions taken toward a lovely, engaging young woman.

She drew a deep breath. She and Hunter were very much alike. More than she'd realized.

A breeze nudged the swings, drawing her attention. She pictured him pushing her. Riding double. Gathering her to him and kissing her until she wished she could throw caution to the wind and consummate their love.

Pulling her gaze away from the swings, she returned it to him. But he was no longer looking at the dirt. He was looking at her. Remembering, same as she.

"Did you find what you were looking for?" she asked.

He held her gaze. "I thought I had."

She swallowed. He wasn't talking about the hieroglyphics.

Just a few steps. Just a few steps and she'd be in his arms. But then, what? Texas? Women patients only? She needed to keep from impulsively reacting to his most recent actions. There was no hurry. No hurry to do anything rash.

"So what's next?" She tried to project a sense of normalcy in her tone.

"You tell me." He was having none of it. He wanted to talk. About them. About her. About her decision.

But she wasn't ready. It was too soon. She was too confused. "I don't know what's next, Hunter. I simply don't know."

He looked off to the side. "Well then, I guess the next thing for me is to visit the families of each boy. See what I can find out there."

She nodded. "When are you going to do that?"

"I'll start tonight, as soon as they get off work."

She waited for him to invite her, but no offer was forthcoming. "May I tag along?"

"Why?"

"Because the people around here know me. Trust me. They might tell me things they wouldn't tell you."

He shrugged one shoulder. "If you want. I'm starting with Derry's family. I plan to head over there around seven."

She wrapped her arms around her torso. "What are you going to do until then?"

"Read about chivalry." Tugging his hat, he opened the gate and waited for her to pass through. "Good afternoon, Dr. Tate."

With such a clear dismissal, she didn't ask any more questions or linger as he locked the gate, but headed toward Hull House without him. She couldn't help but wonder, though, if she presented as favorable a view as he had.

The Molinaris' apartment was noisy, crowded, and chaotic. Children of all sizes and ages came and went. Alcee crawled on the floor, her curved spine making her movements slow and awkward. Finally, she parked herself by the stove, where flies buzzed about a plate of cheese, oil, and bread. When the other children helped themselves, Alcee partook of the crumbs that fell.

Crossing the room, Billy broke off some cheese and bread, then handed it to the child. Mrs.

Molinari sat unaware at the kitchen table. In a horrid state of intoxication, she ripped a bite of wine-soaked bread from a loaf she held, then stuffed it into her mouth. Billy didn't know if this was a regular state of affairs or if her inebriation was due to grief.

The woman's shoulders hunched, her eyes drooped, and her face appeared to be that of a person in her sixties. Yet Billy felt sure the woman was no more than forty.

Tearing off another piece of bread, she offered it to Billy, wine dripping across the table.

"Oh, no. Thank you. But, tell me, have you had some cheese yet? Would you like me to slice some onto a plate for you?"

"It's for the *bambini*."

"Yes, well, you need to have something other than wine and bread. And I saw there was still some left."

"You don't like thiz wine? I have different." Scraping her chair back, she wove to a cupboard, then plopped two new bottles onto the table. "How 'bout one o' these?"

Billy glanced at Hunter, but he was watching the other activity in the room. Taking note of who came. Who went. Asking a few questions about where they worked and how Derry spent his evenings. If they'd had any contact with Kruse and his friends. If Derry had ever made mention of the gang.

Holding up her hands, Billy shook her head. "No, really. Thank you, but I don't care for any. And as a doctor, I have to be frank, Mrs. Molinari. Drinking will only make things worse, not better."

Squinting her eyes, the woman studied Billy, then waved her finger in the air. "Just a moment, *per favore*." She stumbled out of the room, then came back with a small glass of amber liquid. Pushing it toward Billy, the woman gave her a wink. "See, I have brought you the true American drink."

Billy lifted the glass to her nose, then quickly set it down. Whiskey. Good heavens.

Mr. Molinari walked in, a sack across his back like an Italian version of Santa Claus. Unlike his wife, he was full of life and quick to smile. Did he not know of Derry's circumstance? Or was it that he simply didn't care?

He gave Billy a nod. "*Ciao, medico.*"

Turning to Hunter, he held out his dirt-encrusted hand. Hunter didn't so much as hesitate, grasping it in a firm shake. The two of them struck up a conversation as the man dumped out his treasure of rags, cigar stumps, bones, and other filthy scraps he'd gathered in the alleyways and garbage boxes.

Billy recalled Derry saying his father was a ragpicker. It was one of the lowest jobs for the unskilled laborers. She didn't understand why these Italians, who had such an aptitude for farming, didn't leave Chicago and go south where they could till the soil, gather fruit, and plant olive groves.

But they did not. And so they were employed in the filthiest of jobs, from excavation to rag picking.

"Derry works hard," the man said. "Brings home good money. He would never do what they say he did." He lowered his dark brows. "They took him because he is *italiano*, not because he is guilty."

"Has he ever mentioned Fredrick Kruse and the other boys who were arrested?"

"Many times." He nodded. "He keeps a close watch on them to make sure they leave the *medico* alone."

"The *medico*?" Hunter asked.

Mr. Molinari indicated Billy with his head. "The doctor. Dr. Tate."

Billy sucked in a breath.

"They've been bothering Dr. Tate?" Though his tone was casual, Billy saw the tensing of his muscles.

"No, they usually stay out of sight." Mr. Molinari began to separate the items he'd dumped out. "Except the one time Derry had to use his slingshot so the *medico* could get away."

Hunter looked at her. Lifting her hands, she shrugged.

"When was that?" Reaching over, Hunter began to help the man sort.

She cringed. She'd have to take him to Hull House and clean his hands with ammonia the moment they left.

"Before there were *polizia* on the playground, Dr. Tate tried to run Kruse off." He gave Hunter a knowing look. "But, of course, he refused. So my Derry went to the Abertellis', opened a window, and *pop-pop-pop-pop.*" He imitated shooting rocks with a slingshot.

They stayed for another thirty minutes, then thanked Mr. Molinari for his time.

The man sighed, showing the first bit of remorse she'd seen. "If my boy swings, Nefan will have to get some extra jobs. We need the money Derry brings home every Saturday."

She gave no visible response to his callous remark and complete disregard for Derry's well-being, though she did glance to see Mrs. Molinari's reaction. But the woman lay slumped on the table snoring.

As soon as they were outside, she pointed in the direction of Hull House. "That way. We need to clean your hands. Don't touch any of your orifices."

He did as he was told. "For such a friendly fellow, his only concern for his son seemed to be monetary."

"I got the same impression. Very disheartening. But at least he was sober."

He nodded. "The slingshot episode must have been the time you kicked Kruse in the shin."

"Yes. I had no idea. But I do remember something happened, I just didn't pay attention because I was concentrating on getting away."

"I wonder if Kruse knew it was Derry and if he knew Derry had been watching him."

She bit her lip. "I hope not."

Crossing the street, she saw him start to reach for her elbow. She jumped away. "No touching until your hands are clean."

"Sorry."

"Are you going to talk to the other families as well?" she asked.

"I am. But not tonight."

"May I go with you when you do?"

"If you're here and not at work, then I have no objection."

They walked in silence for several minutes, then approached the entrance to Hull House.

"Hunter?"

"Hmmm?"

"Thank you. Thank you for doing this."

"It's what I do."

And this time, she'd seen for herself just how good he was at this Ranger business. Scurrying ahead of him, she opened the door, cautioning him again not to touch anything.

TENEMENTS, WEST SIDE CHICAGO[36]

"Throughout the following week Hunter
visited the homes of all the accused."

CHAPTER 41

Throughout the following week Hunter visited the homes of all the accused. He kept his badge out of sight and made sure to wait until Billy could accompany him. He found her presence gave the parents a sense of security that loosened their tongues. The families hadn't been hard to track down. The papers had filled their columns with the names of the boys along with exclamations of shock that teeners would commit such a violent crime.

No one seemed to comprehend that children aged more rapidly in the slums. The boys might have been adolescents in a chronological sense, but they'd put in a decade of man labor by the time they'd reached puberty.

The mother of eighteen-year-old Rody Lonborg stood in her kitchen, her belly swelled with child, her body unwashed, and her children swarming about her. "I have fourteen little ones and no life outside this apartment. How could I know where my boy was going? What he was doing?"

Her husband came in late every night and left early every morning, spending his days earning food and shelter for his growing family. He hadn't asked his son where he went during his free time. Only, "How much money on Saturday?"

Olsen Shiblawski had turned seventeen the day he'd been arrested. His mother sobbed as she bent over a washtub, scrubbing the family's clothing. "He was a good boy at home. I always asked where he was going at night. He'd say 'by the fence' over there or 'at the corner' of some street. I thought that's where he was."

Fredrick Kruse was the only one who'd reached twenty. At some point along the way, he'd made his eighteen-year-old brother a partner in his escapades. Their father stared at Hunter with cold brown eyes. "I don't care what they do with them. They can hang them, shoot them, or cut them to pieces. It is nothing to me."

Billy shook her head. "You don't mean that."

He shrugged. "Neither of those boys ever brought home a penny."

Sitting in the drawing room at Hull House, Hunter spread out his notes. All the boys had pleaded guilty except for Derry. Hunter hoped the boy stuck to that like hair in a biscuit. For he knew of plenty of jailers who'd beat, kick, sandbag, and bully the inmates until they received the guilty plea they were looking for.

Curled up in a chair, Billy folded the newspaper she'd been reading. "They're making quite an issue about the age of the boys—particularly Derry—and whether or not they should be kept in jail at all, much less with the men."

Over the past month he'd tried to occupy his mind with other things, but whether they were together or apart, his thoughts always circled 'round to Billy. Quiet moments like these were the toughest. Usually the house was full of activity, dispelling any chance for intimacy. But it was Chicago Day at the fair. Miss Addams and the other residents had joined hundreds of thousands of people in Jackson Park for a day of floats, concerts, parades, and fireworks honoring the twenty-second anniversary of the great Chicago fire.

He tossed down his pencil. "With half the world passing through town, maybe the city will speed up the process and set a court date. Did it say anything else?"

She handed him the paper. "The other boys are implicating Derry. I think we need to find him a lawyer."

"I'd thought the same thing." He unfolded the newspaper. "But the courts have already appointed a young untried attorney to serve as counsel."

"But he didn't want the case. I'm worried he won't put forth much effort."

Hunter scanned the article. "The problem is, the boys are being tried together. To hire an attorney for Derry would require hiring an attorney for all of them."

"I still want to find someone. I'll pay the lawyer's fee."

He looked up. "Lawyers cost a lot of money, Billy. It would eat up the cushion you need to start your practice."

"Well then, I guess I'll just have to go back to working in hospitals."

Lowering the paper, he searched her eyes. "It'll take years to save up that money again."

She picked at her fingernails. "You think a lawyer will cost that much?"

"About five hundred dollars. For a good one anyway."

Her shoulders drooped. "I don't have that kind of money."

He didn't either.

"I know." Her eyes brightened. "Maybe I could find a woman lawyer. I bet she'd do it for a reasonable amount."

"Don't joke, Billy. Derry's life is in the balance. We can't take the chance of offending the jury over something like that. I have no doubt a woman could do the job. It's not her I'm worried about. It's the prejudices of the men on the jury that concern me."

"You think Derry's chances are worse with a woman lawyer than with this appointed one who'll put forth no effort?"

"I do. I talked to him as soon as I found out who he was. This will be the biggest case he's ever been assigned. I suggested he use the opportunity to show what he can do."

"Do you think he will?"

"I sure hope so."

She sighed. "And you're sure a lawyer would cost that much?"

"I'm sure." He'd had the same concerns she did, but it didn't take long to find out no one wanted the case. Not without charging an exorbitant fee.

Fingering another piece of paper, she passed it to him. "I've been called as a witness for the prosecution."

"The prosecution?" He looked over the official summons and noted it had been delivered to her early last week.

She crossed her arms, hugging herself. "I can only assume they have some questions concerning the condition of the body when I first arrived on the scene."

He nodded, but he didn't like it. Didn't like it at all. "Just make sure you answer the questions succinctly and don't elaborate. All right?"

"All right." She returned the paper to her satchel. "Anything new with your investigation? Anything you can give to Derry's attorney?"

Leaning back against the downy cushion of his armchair, he gave her a bleak look. "Not a thing. Besides not being allowed to question the boys, I haven't had access to the murder weapons or any other evidence they might have. I've spent days and days going door-to-door throughout the ward, but everyone has suddenly become blind and deaf. They didn't hear anything, see anything, or remember anything. Not one single eyewitness. The arresting officer isn't talking. The coroner isn't talking. Even the children in the streets aren't talking. I've gleaned more information from you than anyone else."

"What about that day you examined the playground?"

He shook his head. "It didn't offer up anything other than the facts we already know—there was a scuffle. It involved four to five people. A gun was used. And a knife was used."

They stared at each other. The trial was looming and there was not one thing they could do to help Derry or his case.

Her face began to crumble. "I can't bear the thought of him being found guilty. Of him being penned up for the rest of his life. Of not ever being able to see him without bars between us. Or worse, of them sentencing him to death. Not after Joey. I know Derry has a family, but I . . . they don't . . ."

Swallowing, he rubbed his hands along his trousers. He hadn't planned to say anything until after the trial, but maybe he should. Maybe his news would bring her some tiny bit of comfort. "Miss Weibel's murder isn't the only thing I've been investigating. I've also been, um, looking into Joey's whereabouts."

Her sniffling stopped, her eyes widened. "Did you find him?"

"I did."

Her lips parted. "When? Where is he?"

"He was taken in by a real estate millionaire by the name of Robert York. York helped rebuild the city after the Great Fire and now lives in a three-story graystone with his wife. Right next door to them is the son of the late millionaire Cyrus McCormick."

"Cyrus McCormick? The man who invented the mechanical reaper?"

"One and the same."

"And Joey lives next door to them?"

He nodded. "Though they don't call him Joey anymore. They call him Robert, Jr."

"Robert, Jr." She let that sink in for a moment. "What's Mrs. York like?"

"Young. About fifteen years younger than her husband, who's forty. It seems to be a love match, though. The two of them dote on each other and are beside themselves over Joey."

"You've seen Joey?" Her spine slowly straightened.

"Once I'd narrowed my search down, I began watching their house. I wanted verification that Joey really was there. I'd expected to follow a nursemaid to the pleasure grounds, but to my surprise it was the mister and missus who pushed the baby carriage to Lincoln Park."

She jumped to her feet and began pacing. "Lincoln Park. They're within walking distance of Lincoln Park. Joey will love that. It's a beautiful pleasure garden and it has an animal house with bears, tigers, elephants, and panthers."

"When I was there, they lingered around an electric fountain. That's where I approached them and struck up a conversation."

She stopped. "How did he look?"

"Huge. I can't believe how much he's grown."

"Did he recognize your voice?"

Emotion stacked up against his throat. The best he could do was lift one shoulder in a half shrug.

"Did you get to touch him? Hold him?"

He looked down. "I'd told myself I wouldn't. I was just going to compliment them on their handsome baby, and look inside the carriage to make sure it was him, but at the sound of my voice he waved his arms and legs, then laughed." Their eyes connected. "He's learned to laugh, Billy. The sound of it . . ."

Tears filled her eyes.

"It was more than I could resist." His nostrils distended in an effort to hold back his feelings. "So I reached over and slipped a finger into his hand. He, he grabbed it and squeezed it in that tiny fist of his." He pinched the bridge of his nose, but moisture still sprang to his eyes, refusing to be contained.

Suddenly she was on the cushion beside him, her hand on his back.

"Oh, God." He grabbed her and held her close. "Walking away from him was one of the hardest things I've ever done in my entire life."

They clung. They cried. They mourned.

"I want him back," she whispered. "I want him back so badly."

"I know. But we can't. We can't."

"I want to see him. Will you take me?"

"No, Billy. It's too hard. Please don't ask me. Please. I simply can't go through . . . I . . ."

She swayed from side to side taking him with her as if she were rocking him. "*Shhhh. Shhhh. Okay. Okay.*" Her tears seeped through his shirt. "What was she like? Mrs. York, I mean."

"Wonderful. Poised. Happy. And she loves Joey. It was so obvious. Her husband, too."

After a while, the pain began to diminish. He kept his eyes closed, relishing for just one more moment the privilege of having her in his arms again. But as good as it felt, as healing as it was, he knew it was an indulgence that would lead to even more heartache if he didn't put a stop to it. And between the loss of Joey, her, and possibly Derry, he didn't think he could handle one more thing.

Kissing the top of her head, he untangled himself and began to gather up his papers. "It's getting late. I'd better see you home."

She scooted over, dabbed her eyes, swooped a hand up the back of her hair, and cleared her throat. "No need for that. Miss Addams knew traffic would be in a tangle with thousands upon thousands trying to leave the fair, so she's letting me use one of the rooms upstairs tonight."

"Oh." He glanced at the rich mahogany staircase. Having her so close suddenly made it that much harder. There was safety, somehow, in having her stay clear over in the Women's Dormitory. Picking up his papers, he rose. "I guess I'll leave you to it, then. Have a nice evening, Billy."

"Thank you. You, too."

They stared at each other, their words belying the raw, tumultuous, heart-wrenching feelings crashing beneath the surface. Still, he gave a polite nod and found his way to the door wondering why, out of all the women in the world, he had to fall in love with the one who preferred the city over the country, working over domesticity, duty over love.

"Pauline sent four outfits she'd outgrown
since having her baby. Billy's favorite
was a green wool with finely
pleated collar and cuffs."

CHAPTER 42

Billy sat beside Hunter in the courtroom of the brand-new criminal court building. Tall windows provided both warmth from the sun and cooling breezes from the lake. The smell of beeswax competed with a bouquet of ladies' toilet waters and men's shaving soaps. Hushed conversations buzzed like the fanning of a thousand hummingbird wings.

She'd wanted to wear something somber yet sophisticated for her court appearance. For if her testimony was to affect the outcome of Derry's sentence, she wanted to make sure she did everything she could to promote a positive verdict for him.

But all she had were schoolmarmish skirts and shirtwaists, along with the two feminine dresses she hardly ever wore. So she'd written her sister asking if she could borrow one of her suits. Pauline sent four outfits she'd outgrown since having her baby. Billy's favorite was a green wool with finely pleated collar and cuffs. She'd removed the flowers from the matching hat and replaced them with loops of velvet ribbon.

She wondered if Hunter's suit was new. The four-button cassimere ensemble was the exact shade of his hair and had replaced his denims, though his Texas heritage was still evident in the Stetson on his lap and the freshly polished armadillo boots on his feet. But it was the five-pointed star encircled by a band of silver that jumped out the most. He'd pinned it to the lapel of his jacket. The word TEXAS had been engraved along the top, RANGER along the bottom.

Clerk, sketch artist, stenographer, and lawyers filed in, each taking their respective places. The hum of conversation dipped. The men sitting in the press seats began making notes.

She and Hunter sat directly behind the defense counsel. An attractive man not much older than the defendants placed his satchel on the table in front of them. His suit was of the latest fashion, his cravat expertly tied, his blond hair styled in a pompadour. He faced the assembly like a young prince viewing his subjects, his bearing proud, his condescension unmistakable.

At the opposite table, the district attorney didn't make eye contact with anyone. His hair had yet to gray, but his hairline had receded significantly. His suit was tight around the stomach, pulling the fabric so it strained the buttons on his double-breasted jacket and caused its tail to flare out. His jerky, rapid movements reminded her of a toy that had been wound too tight.

The tipstaff opened the door the prisoners would come through. Billy's stomach fluttered. The crowd quieted.

Unshackled, the Kruse brothers entered first, looking almost handsome in fresh clothes, combed hair, and clean bodies. Their defiant expressions, however, quickly spoiled the effect.

Lonborg and Shiblawski followed, their eyes downcast, their feet shuffling. Finally, Derry entered. His exposition uniform had been exchanged for a little boy's suit, short pants, and scuffed-up boots. A rush of murmuring swept the courtroom.

He'd easily lost half his weight. The roundness of his cheeks was gone and his little legs looked as if the officers had put stockings on a rooster. Eyes wide, he took in the vast ceilings and richly polished wood gracing the walls and furniture. No church in Chicago had been more finely adorned then the new courtroom.

His gaze moved to the gallery filled with spectators. He stopped and searched the crowd.

Billy held her breath wondering if he was looking for his parents, for if he was, he wouldn't find them. Nor would any of the other boys. None of the parents could afford a day off work or the ride to and from town.

His eyes lit when he spotted them. "Mr. Scott! Doc Tate! The copper gave us a potato pie this mornin', but I had to take a bath 'fore I could eat any."

His words echoed in the silence of the room. Her heart soared at the normalcy of his voice.

Perhaps nothing untoward had happened to him while he was down there, after all.

The tipstaff put a finger to his mouth, shushing him.

Derry clapped a hand over his mouth, then turned again to Hunter and spread three fingers. "I forgot." His whisper easily carried throughout the room. "I'm not supposed to talk to nobody."

The reaction of the crowd varied. Some, who believed Derry to be guilty, were stern-faced with disapproval. Others could not help but have a doubt raised in their mind as to how a young boy of his demeanor could have ever committed such a heinous offense.

The tipstaff flicked him on the head.

Derry jumped back and rubbed the spot, but kept his mouth shut. He followed the other boys to the prisoners' dock and crawled up into a black Windsor chair. Instead of sitting down, he remained on his knees, gripped the back of the chair, and faced the crowd.

But he only had eyes for Hunter. "I made some friends in the pokey, but *pu-wee* it stinks in there." He held his nose.

The man beside them covered his amusement with coughs. But Billy was more distressed than amused. He'd made friends? With criminals?

Humor filling his eyes, Hunter made a locking motion over his lips.

The tipstaff leaned down toward Derry. "If you can't keep quiet, I'll have to take you back and there'll be no more potato pies for you."

Derry immediately plopped into his seat and made no further attempts to converse.

She and Hunter looked at each other, their affection and concern for Derry somehow channeling itself between them. Hunter surreptitiously reached over and gave her gloved hand a quick squeeze.

Love for him swelled within her. She began to fear she just might love him more than the profession she'd devoted the last eleven years of her life to. A quelling thought.

He must have sensed something in her expression, for he gave her the barest of winks.

"All rise for the Honorable Justice Cecil H. Phinney." The court crier stood before the gallery, his uniform crisp, his voice strong.

A rustle of movement ensued, reaching a crescendo, then slowing as all eyes turned to the judge.

He wore the traditional black robe, yet his bearing was anything but regal. He used a cane to hoist his portly body up the steps leading to his elevated station. His progress was slow and painful. When he finally reached the summit, the crowd gave a collective sigh of relief.

He situated himself in his chair, his clean-shaven face and center-parted gray hair restoring a bit of his dignity. The crier gave permission for all to be seated and the judge called the court to order.

One by one the boys stood and entered their pleas.

"Guilty."

"Guilty."

"Guilty."

"Guilty."

"I didn't do nothin'."

Billy bit her lip.

The judge lifted his chin and looked at Derry through his round spectacles. "Your choices are guilty or not guilty, Mister . . ." He fanned out some papers on his desk. "Molinari. Which is it?"

Derry turned to Hunter.

His young attorney rose. "I think the prisoner wishes to plead not guilty."

The judge looked again at Derry. "Do you wish to enter a not guilty plea, Mr. Molinari?"

"My dad's not here, mister. My name's Derry."

"We'll be addressing you as Mr. Molinari during these proceedings and you'll be addressing me as Honorable Judge Phinney. Now, do you wish to enter a not guilty plea?"

Derry turned again to Hunter. Hunter gave a nod.

"Yes, Ornery Judge Funny. Not guilty."

Looking down, Billy pressed a fist against her mouth.

The young attorney gave Derry an impatient look. "Just call the judge Your Honor."

The judge squinted at Derry, as if to ascertain whether the boy's mispronunciation was on purpose or not. After a minute, Phinney moved his attention to the other boys. "Your guilty pleas cannot be accepted in this court. The clerk will enter a plea of not guilty."

Billy and Hunter exchanged another glance. They knew guilty pleas were not allowed in cases where capital punishment was a possibility, but it was a sobering reminder the boys were to be tried as adults.

DIAGRAM OF
HULL HOUSE PLAYGROUND[38]

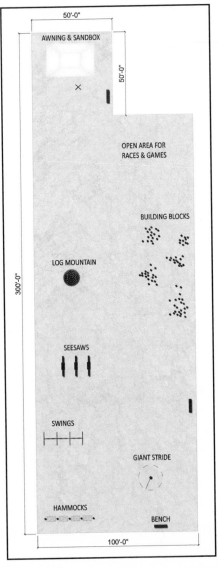

"The engineer handed over a diagram which
illustrated the layout and positioning
of the playground equipment."

CHAPTER 43

District Attorney Urban Hood called a civil engineer as the first witness. The man presented photographs of the playground from several different angles. One by one Hood propped images of the log mountain, the seesaw, the giant stride, the swings, and the sandbox onto easels.

Derry tugged on the sleeve of his attorney. "That's our playground," he whispered loudly. "I helped build that. You can ask anybody."

Scowling, the attorney tapped his lips with his finger.

Derry twisted around and looked at Hunter through the balusters of his chair.

Hunter shook his head, bringing a finger to his mouth, but it was too late.

"They forgot the hammocks."

The judge banged on the gavel. "Quiet."

Sticking a finger in his ear, Derry gave it a wiggle, but remained quiet.

Hunter looked at her, commiserating with her over their frustration that any nine-year-old would be expected to comport himself like an adult—especially when that nine-year-old was as effervescent as Derry.

The engineer handed over a diagram that illustrated the layout and the positioning of the equipment.

"What is this mark here?" Hood pointed to an X just beyond the sand pit.

"That's where Miss Weibel's blood had seeped into the earth." A horseshoe of iron-gray hair framed the engineer's shiny bald spot.

During the rest of the man's testimony, Derry swung his legs, his little body already growing tired of being in the chair. Having no idea the fate of his life hung in the balance. She wished she could sit in the chair with him. Hold him on her lap. Comfort him. Pull his head against her shoulder so he could sleep.

"The court calls Dr. Billy Jack Tate."

Her stomach jumping, she rose and shuffled past the men beside her on the pew-like bench, then entered the arena of the court.

The tipstaff sprang forward. "I'm sorry, miss. You can't come up here."

District Attorney Hood gripped the tipstaff's shoulder. "It's all right, Johnny. This is Dr. Billy Jack Tate."

A shock of surprise rippled throughout the room. After a glance at the judge, the clerk stepped forward and swore her, then escorted her to the witness box.

Hood smoothed what little hair he had left across the top of his head. All the nervous energy he'd had at the beginning of the morning had vanished. "Miss Doctor Tate, you are a physician and surgeon, is that correct?"

Another burst of murmurs. The judge gave his gavel a whack.

"Yes, I am."

"Are you connected with any institution?"

"I'm one of the doctors in the Woman's Building at the World's Columbian Exposition."

"And prior to that?"

"I was connected with the New England Hospital for Women and Children in Boston." The view from the witness box was much different from the view from the gallery. She was higher up than all but the judge, and the five boys were in her direct line of vision.

Kruse curled his lip. His brother gave her a wink. She quickly moved her focus to the attorney, determined not to look their way again. But in her periphery, she could see the two brothers smirk.

"In what capacity was your work at the hospital?" Hood asked.

"I saw every patient in the hospital at least once a day. I did a third of the surgical operations and assisted in the others. I conducted all abnormal baby deliveries. I kept their daybook. I attended their private clinic two times per week. And I was responsible for the teaching and deportment of six medical students."

Complete stillness fell onto the room. The judge, attorneys, jury, and gallery stared at her in shock—Hunter not the least of them.

Hood gave a startled chuckle, his long teeth giving him an equine look. "That's quite a list of duties you had there. Now tell me, were you the first doctor to reach Miss Weibel after her brutal attack?"

"I was."

"And what did you find?"

"There was no pulse and no sign of life." She described the amount of blood loss, the gunshot wounds, and the lacerations.

"Would you say the lacerations were caused by a fist?"

"No. Those were definitely caused by something sharp."

"Like a knife?"

"That would certainly be my guess."

"What kind of knife?"

"It's hard to say. I imagine the doctor who performed the autopsy would be able to give you a better indication of that."

"But in your best opinion, could a pocketknife make that kind of laceration?"

Her breath hitched. A pocketknife? Was he, was he referring to *Derry's* pocketknife? Surely the man was not going to suggest Derry used his pocketknife against Miss Weibel.

She cleared her throat. "It was dusk, sir, and Miss Weibel was fully clothed. I would not be able to answer that without having given the body a proper exam."

"I see." He slipped his hands into his pockets. "Did you see any knives cast down in the dirt?"

"I did not."

"Were any of the defendants holding knives?"

"I wasn't looking at them. I was looking at the patient."

"Were you aware a pocketknife was found on Derry Molinari?"

"Course she knows that," Derry said, rolling his eyes. "She's the one what gave it to me."

A groundswell of exclamations filled the courtroom. Her hands became clammy.

The judge pounded the gavel. "Defense counsel, you will control your defendant, please."

Derry's attorney pinched the boy's ear.

Hood eyed her speculatively. "Is that true, Miss Doctor? Did you give Derry Molinari the murder weapon?"

"Objection." Derry's attorney stood. "No murder weapon has yet been established."

Hood immediately retrieved the pocketknife and handed it to Billy. "Did you give this pocketknife to Derry Molinari?"

She turned it over in her hands. Bloodstains had seeped into its pine handle. Initials she didn't recognize had been carved into its side. "There are someone else's initials on it."

He peered at the markings she indicated. "The arresting officer carved his initials into it once he'd confiscated it from Mr. Molinari. Then he gave it to his corporal, who also engraved his initials into it before turning it over to his commanding officer. That way we know this is the actual weapon that was seized."

"I see."

"So is this the pocketknife you gave to Mr. Molinari?"

"I don't know if it is this exact one or not."

"But it looked like this one?"

She rubbed her gloved fingers along its edge. "Yes."

"Exactly like that?"

Of a sudden, she realized this pocketknife, the one in her very hands, that she was stroking with her fingers, no matter who it belonged to, had been used to murder Miss Weibel. Sweet, dear, much-loved Miss Weibel.

Before she could stop them, images of Miss Weibel's brutalized body merged with the woman herself. The professional distance Billy had maintained up to now collapsed as she stared at the knife and thought of the pain her friend had suffered. The terror. Terror so much worse than what Billy had experienced at those same boys' hands.

Nausea settled in her stomach. The room tilted. Opening her hand, she watched the knife clatter down the steps of the witness box and to the floor. The sound loud in the quiet of the room.

Reaching down, Mr. Hood picked up the knife, then held it aloft. "Did the pocketknife you gave to Derry Molinari look exactly like this one?"

The man appeared double, his voice coming from far away. Sweet heavens, she was going into shock. And though she recognized the symptoms, she could do nothing to slow them.

She forced herself to focus on the question. What was it again? Oh, yes. Did this pocketknife look like Derry's? "Yes," she breathed.

She needed out. She needed out from behind this box. Out of this room. Out to where she could get some air.

"What would you say killed Miss Weibel? The knife wounds or the gunshot wounds?"

Mr. Hood's features blurred, morphing into one of her professors from medical school. She answered as if she'd been called on in class. "I'd have to do an autopsy."

"You can't hazard a guess?"

"Objection."

"Sustained."

Mr. Hood lowered the knife. "I have nothing further, Your Honor."

"Mr. Seacoat?" the judge asked the defense.

"No questions, Your Honor."

The judge furrowed his brows, then turned to her. "You may step down, Dr. Tate."

Without conscious thought, she took the hand the clerk offered, then walked past Derry, past Hunter, past the gallery, and straight out the door. She was going to be sick.

CHAPTER 44

Hunter remained in his seat, his expression neutral. He wanted to go after her, but someone needed to stay in here with Derry. Still, she hadn't looked good. She'd lost all her color and acted as jumpy as a bit-up bull in fly time.

He knew the D.A. was trying to establish the murder weapon was owned by Derry. And if Hunter hadn't known Billy, the lawman in him would have been convinced she had, at the very least, something to hide. And he'd have been on her like the first rattle out of the box. It gave him a great deal of pause to realize just how quick he'd been in the past to make snap judgments.

The police officer who made the arrests was called to the stand. He described the scene and verified the pocketknife had been found on Derry, but the gun had been in the possession of Kruse's brother, Ewald.

Men from the West Side who'd first arrived on the scene took the witness box one after the other. Their stories were all the same. They heard the gunfire. They raced to the playground. They grabbed the boys who were fleeing the scene and held them until the police arrived. But none had witnessed the murder.

"What about Mr. Molinari?" Derry's attorney asked. "Was he running away?"

On the stand, an unkempt man's stooped spine and cramped hands were evidence of the many hours he spent in a clothing sweatshop. "No, sir. He beside missy. Hands bloody. Knife . . ." He made a clutching motion with his hands.

Hunter had interviewed this man, and all the others. He waited for the defense to ask about Derry's demeanor while he was next to Miss Weibel. Waited for the moment when the jury would learn of the boy's distress and sobs and anger at those who'd killed her.

But he waited in vain. Attorney Seacoat asked a few clarifying questions, but nothing to highlight Derry's innocence. And between the language barrier of the men on the stand and their fear of being in a court of law, Derry's actions were never brought to light.

Frustration gnawed at Hunter. He almost wished Derry would come to his own defense, even if the judge threw him out. But the boy had curled up in his chair and fallen asleep. Considering the conditions of the jail, Hunter could hardly blame him for taking advantage of a clean surface to rest his head.

The final witness of the day was the doctor who did the autopsy. The man testified the knife wounds could have been caused by a pocket-knife and that both the gunshot and knife wounds were equally responsible for Miss Weibel's death. Hunter frowned. He'd have to ask Billy, but it seemed to him as if there was only supposed to be one cause of death. But the defense didn't challenge the doctor's testimony, so perhaps he was mistaken.

"No further questions, Your Honor."

The doctor was excused from the witness box and the court recessed for the day. All in the gallery were instructed to keep their seats. Judge Phinney and the jurors filed out, followed by the tipstaff and boys.

Rubbing his eye with one fist, Derry waved and Hunter gave him a nod of acknowledgment. After all had cleared the court, the gallery rose, their voices loud as they rehashed all they'd seen and heard.

CHAPTER 45

Billy wasn't in the courthouse, at least not that he could find, so he went to the Women's Dormitory and sent the matron to fetch her. She came out onto the landing in her calico, her face pasty.

"You all right?" he asked.

"No."

He stuffed his hands in his pockets. "Where'd you go?"

"Home."

"So you didn't come back to the courtroom?"

She shook her head.

He'd wondered. He thought she might have sneaked back in to hear the rest of the testimony. "Are you planning to go tomorrow?" he asked.

"I don't think so."

"You should, Billy."

She scrunched up her face. "Why?"

"Because Derry needs us."

A long tendril fell across her shoulder. "I can't even remember those last few minutes on the stand. Was I coherent?"

Of its own volition, his hand came out of his pocket and hooked the tendril behind her ear. "You were fine."

Her lower lip quivered. "Are they going to find him guilty, Hunter?"

"I don't know." As much as he wanted to soothe her, he wasn't going to lie. Anything could happen in that courtroom.

"I feel so helpless. Like I should be doing something. But I have no idea what. I can't call any witnesses. I can't tell the lawyers what questions to ask. I can't tell the jury the things they need to know."

"We can pray, Billy. We always pray. Now, get on back in there and get some rest. I'll pick you up in the morning."

Swallowing, she crossed the landing, then stopped at the door. "Hunter?"

He waited.

"Thank you."

And then she disappeared inside, leaving him to wonder exactly what she'd thanked him for.

CHAPTER 46

Eighteen-year-old Rody Lonborg could not sit still in the witness box. He crossed and uncrossed his arms. He jiggled his legs. He thumped his thumbs. His wide face and thick neck hinted at the power behind his tall frame.

"I never meant to do nothing. We just wanted Miss Weibel to leave so we could have the playground to ourselves. But there were babies in there and she wouldn't leave 'em."

"So you killed her?" Attorney Hood asked.

"Not on purpose. I mean, we pushed her around, but instead of leaving, she pushed us back, then Derry comes running over and pulls a knife on us, telling us to get back."

"What happened then?"

"Miss Weibel told him to put it away. That's when Fred grabbed it."

"Fredrick Kruse? He grabbed Mr. Molinari's knife?"

"Yeah. Then everything went crazy. Fred started waving it at Miss Weibel. Derry tried to get it back. I grabbed Derry. Ewald put a hand over Miss Weibel's mouth and held her back against him." He ran a hand through his hair. "It all happened so fast."

Hood gave the boy a minute to collect himself.

"Well, there's no need to rush now. Just go slow. Think back. What was Mr. Shiblawski doing?"

"Olsen? Nothing, I don't think. Just standing there. I don't really know. But then I seen Fred grab Miss Weibel's, you know, grab her." He looked at Hood and gave a shrug. "Well, we all wanted to take a turn at that, but I still had Derry, so I couldn't. But Olsen could and Fred could. She kicked and fought and scratched and elbowed and bit and . . ." Lifting his brows, he shook his head. "None of the other gals had ever fought like that before."

Billy slid her eyes shut.

"There were other women?" Hood asked. "You've done this to other women?"

"Not killed them. Just, you know . . ."

Looking down, Hood composed himself, then took a deep breath. "What happened when you boys weren't able to subdue Miss Weibel?"

His shoulders slumped. "Fred got tired of it and sliced her with the knife. After that, he said if any of us wanted to have our turn, we'd have to slice her, too. So we did, but we never got nothing 'cause Ewald decided he wanted to shoot her instead. Four times. Then everybody came running."

The scratching of reporters' pencils offered the only break in the sudden silence. Billy hugged herself, trying again to block out what had happened to Miss Weibel. And what could have happened to her when Kruse and his friends had cornered her at the water pump. Thank goodness Hunter had come.

She looked at him. His face was stoic, but not shocked. She thought of the outlaws he dealt with as a Ranger and wondered how a man could do that day after day after day and not become jaded. It wasn't a job she envied.

"What was Derry Molinari's part in this?" Hood asked.

Lonborg glanced at Derry. "After the shooting, Fred dropped the knife and cuffed Ewald pretty good. I was so surprised, I forgot to hold on like I should. Derry broke away and grabbed the knife. Then he turned it on us and threatened to use it if we didn't leave." He looked at the attorney. "All of us. He was thinking him and that puny knife of his would make all of us run scared. And Ewald still with his gun, though he didn't have any bullets left. But Derry didn't know that." He gave a huff. "Molinari's become a regular little tough."

Mr. Hood looked at the judge. "I have no further questions."

Rising, Mr. Seacoat came forward for cross-examination. His back-combed blond hair puffed up over his forehead, adding a couple of inches to his height. "Are you sorry it happened, Rody?"

The boy looked down. "It's an awful feeling to know you killed somebody. You don't feel the same after killing them. You're not the same person you were after you do something like that." He raised his head, sorrow etched on his face. "I wish I was my same person again."

The youthful arrogance Seacoat had entered the courtroom with dissipated. He turned to the judge. "I have no further questions."

When seventeen-year-old Olsen Shiblawski took the stand, the story changed some, but not dramatically. The court had already heard testimony from the doctor who'd performed the autopsy, so Billy knew the location of the knife wounds involved vital organs. Neither attorney attempted to establish who was responsible for which specific wound.

Shiblawski said he'd wished he'd had something to do other than spend his free time in the saloons and with the Kruse brothers. Unfortunately, he didn't substantiate Lonborg in saying Derry didn't have anything to do with the murder.

"He was one of us."

"I am not!" Derry exclaimed.

The tipstaff grabbed Derry's arm, yanked him close, and whispered fiercely to him while tapping the club on his belt. Billy stiffened. Hunter started to rise, then caught himself and settled back onto the bench.

"Mr. Molinari was part of your ring?" Mr. Hood lifted his brows. "That's not what Mr. Lonborg said."

"Rody likes Molinari's sister. He's just saying that because of her. But Derry's been following us and watching us and just waiting for a chance to be part of the fun. That's why he pulled a knife on us. He was trying to show Kruse he could be one of us."

"Did he use the knife on Miss Weibel?"

Shiblawski shrugged. "Sure. That's what I'm telling you. He was just as much a part of it as we were."

Derry opened his mouth. The tipstaff whacked him on the back of the head. Finally, Hood took a seat. To Billy's horror, Seacoat made no cross-examination and Shiblawski was excused from the witness box.

Ewald and Fredrick Kruse confirmed Shiblawski's story.

Fredrick slumped in the witness box, his elbow hooked over the back of the chair.

"Sit up, Mr. Kruse," the judge snapped.

The boy gave his brother a smirk, then pushed himself up. "Derry spends just as much time at the saloon as the rest of us. He drinks, he smokes, and, like Olsen said, he's been spying on us." Fredrick gave Attorney Hood a knowing look. "He's been getting an eyeful, too. Decided he was interested in a closer look. So we let him have his chance with Miss Weibel. I have to say, the little tough did all right."

"Did you kill Miss Weibel, Mr. Kruse?"

"I sure did. Me and the boys all did."

"Why?"

"We had nothing against Miss Weibel. It was the playground we were after. Not her. All she had to do was leave—after we were finished with her, anyway."

Mr. Hood's jaw tensed. "No more questions."

Seacoat took his time approaching the witness box. When he arrived, he studied Kruse for a minute. "Your testimony is different from Mr. Lonborg's. He claims Mr. Molinari wasn't part of your gang and that he did no harm to Miss Weibel. Why should we believe you instead of him?"

"I put my hand on the Bible, didn't I?"

"So did he."

Kruse wobbled his eyebrows. "Looks like somebody's lying."

"It most certainly does." Crossing his arms, he tapped his elbow. "You've admitted, Mr. Kruse, that you took a life because you wanted the playground to yourself. I'm having trouble comprehending why. Just what was so important about that playground?"

"It was my place first." He straightened in his seat. His tone became fierce. "In order to build that playground, those do-gooders had to knock down our apartment. The apartment I lived in with my family and played in with the girls upstairs." He pointed toward Billy. "When Dr. Tate there had it razed, my whole family had to sleep on

458

the street. By the time my father found a new place, he said there wasn't enough room for me and Ewald. That we'd have to find us our own place to sleep." Kruse gave Billy a look of loathing.

A shudder went down her spine. Hunter slipped his hand into hers. She squeezed him back, drawing comfort and reassurance.

"And did you find some lodging?" Mr. Seacoat asked.

"No, we didn't. So, me and Ewald decided we'd sleep on the playground, eat on the playground, drink on the playground, smoke on the playground, and have our fun on the playground. And if Dr. Tate didn't like that, then she could take the playground and—"

"Mind your tongue, Mr. Kruse," the attorney warned.

Fredrick pulled back, then lurched to the edge of his chair and squared his shoulders. "Look, mister. Me and the boys killed Miss Weibel. I'm not at all sorry I did my part. I'm only sorry I did it before I had time to enjoy her."

Billy's stomach turned. Murmurs of shock and revulsion could be heard throughout the gallery. Hunter covered their hands with his other one.

Mr. Seacoat turned his back to Kruse. "I have no further questions, Your Honor."

CHAPTER 47

The clerk put two legal tomes in Derry's chair so he could see over the witness box. He was the last of the accused to be called and the sun had passed into the western side of the sky, sending long stretches of light onto the courthouse floor. Bits of dust floated in its rays.

"How old are you, Mr. Molinari?" the prosecutor asked.

"Nine and three-quarters."

Billy glanced at the jury, but the men looked tired and frazzled, not at all touched by Derry's obvious youth.

"What happened in the early evening of September twenty-fourth?"

"I don't know. When was that?"

"What happened the night Miss Weibel was murdered?"

"Rody told it best. Him and the others charged into the playground after everybody had left but the babies."

"Why were you still there, then?"

"Doc Tate had a 'mergency, but she didn't want to leave Miss Weibel by herself. So I told her I'd stay with Miss Weibel."

"Why?"

Derry shrugged. "Kruse and them were acrost

the street and they're always bullying the girls. Miss Weibel was my teacher." He puffed out his chest. "I'm in the Young Heroes Club and she was reading to us about King Arthur. So, her and me were friends. I didn't want Fred to make her play a game with them. My sister said the games they make the girls play aren't nice ones. She said none of the girls like 'em."

"And what happened when Misters Kruse, Lonborg, and Shiblawski arrived?"

"They started pushing Miss Weibel and she pushed 'em right back. I wanted to be like King Arthur, but I don't have a sword. All I have is a pocketknife. So I held that out instead."

Mr. Hood nodded. "What happened then?"

"Miss Weibel told me not to wave my knife like that. Told me to put it away. I was just about to close it when Fred grabbed it and Rody grabbed me. The rest is just like Rody said it was."

"Did you stab or cut Miss Weibel with your knife?"

"No, sir. I'd never do that. Her and me were friends."

"Mr. Shiblawski and the Kruse brothers said you did."

"They aren't telling the truth, mister. I know they swore on the Bible, but they're telling stories." He leaned forward. "You ought not to go out in a thunderstorm with them. One of the fellows in the jail with me said you get hit by lightning if you swear on a Bible, then tell a story."

"Did you spy on Mr. Kruse and his friends?"

"Sometimes. I'm going to be a Texas Ranger when I grow up. So I've been eating a lot of beans and shootin' things with my slingshot. Mr. Scott is always watching out for Doc Tate. I got to practicing doin' that, too, since I got lots of sisters and lots of lady friends at Hull House."

"And what did you see when you spied on them?"

"Objection."

"I'll allow it."

Derry scratched his ear. "Well, I work ever'day but Sunday, so I don't see 'em all that much. But mostly they drink. A lot. And smoke. They like to smoke."

"And have you ever seen them detain other women?"

"Objection. Speculation."

"I'll allow it."

Hood repeated the question.

"What's de-dain?"

"Did you ever see them keep a woman from walking away if she wanted to?"

"No, sir. I saw 'em bullying Doc Tate once."

"Objection. Speculation."

The judge nodded. "Move along, counselor."

Hood slipped a hand in his pocket. "What about

saloons, Mr. Molinari? Do you frequent those?"

"Do I go to 'em, you mean? I used to. But Mr. Scott saw me once and he got really mad. He told me to get out of there, but Mr. Abertelli grabbed my collar right here and told me to stay. See, Mr. Abertelli only lets Italians drink in his saloon. And Mr. Scott's Texan."

Eyes widening, Derry wriggled upright in his seat. "You should have seen what happened then. It was all those fellows in the saloon and only one of Mr. Scott. Usually when that happens the fellow by himself runs out or gets a beating. But Mr. Scott, he walks right up in the middle of the place and *wham-wham-wham.*"

Derry punched the air. "Then this other fella smashes a whiskey bottle on the counter. He was thinking to cut up Mr. Scott good. But Mr. Scott picked up a chair, tore it apart and used one of the legs for a sword and the rest of the chair for a shield."

Again, Derry demonstrated with invisible props. "By the time it was all over, there were only three fellows left. Mr. Scott let them stay standing, though, 'cause I'd gotten out the door by then. I haven't been drinking or smoking or salooning since. Mr. Scott made me promise." He turned to Hunter. "Isn't that right, Mr. Scott?"

"It certainly is, Derry." Hunter's voice startled the judge and everyone else in the courtroom who'd been absorbed in Derry's tale.

She glanced up at Hunter. When in the world had all that happened?

The judge gave Hunter a stern look.

He held up both palms in a gesture of acquiescence, then put them back down.

Mr. Hood blew out a puff of air. "I've no more questions, Your Honor."

Seacoat rose, but didn't even bother coming around from behind the table.

"Did you stab Miss Weibel, Mr. Molinari?"

He gave the man an exasperated look. "Like I jus' told that fellow, I was King Arthur and she was Gwen-Veer." He glanced down at his hands. " 'Cept I didn't save her. I tried, but Rody held me something fierce."

Billy's heart squeezed.

"I've no further questions."

Her lips parted. That was it? That was all he was going to ask the boy? Eyes wide, she turned to Hunter. He impaled the man with his gaze, but Seacoat had his back to them and resumed his seat, oblivious to her distress and Hunter's fury.

The clerk lifted Derry from the witness box. He ran back to his chair and jumped into it, making it rock precariously before settling.

CHAPTER 48

"Prosecution calls Mr. Hunter Scott."

After taking his oath, Hunter settled into the witness box.

Smiling with his mouth but not his eyes, Attorney Hood stood in front of Hunter. "I understand, Mr. Scott, that Colonel Rice discharged you from duty as a Columbian Guard at the World's Columbian Exposition. Can you tell the court why you were given the sack?"

Billy sucked in her breath.

Though Hunter sat tall in his chair, his posture remained relaxed. "I found out that nine-year-old Derry Molinari, who I'd come to know quite well, was crowded into a jail with the most depraved and vicious criminals. Those cells were meant for two men, Mr. Hood, yet as many as eight were crammed into them. On Saturday nights it became so crowded the prisoners couldn't even sit down and had to stand all night. When there was room to sit, Derry was forced to do so on a floor smeared with human waste that had come from an open trough that substituted as a chamber pot. When night approached, Derry could either sleep on that rank floor with nothing underneath him, or he could take turns sleeping on a plank twenty inches wide with no covering and no pillow. His choices for companions were rats or inmates with syphilis."

Hunter took a quick breath, then plowed ahead. "I decided that doing everything in my power to rescue little Derry from that putrid mire was more important than the assignment I had at the Exposition—which was to escort some duke and duchess through the fair. When I told Colonel Rice I needed a day off, he denied my request. I chose to give up my position rather than my integrity. And that, Mr. Hood, is why I left the Columbian Guards."

Not a sound issued forth. Admiration for him filled her.

Mr. Hood stood flat-footed for a few seconds, then walked to his table, and checked his notes. "What is the nature of your relationship with the accused Derry Molinari?"

"He sells catalogs outside the Woman's Building where I was once stationed and he lives in the Nineteenth Ward, where I helped build a playground."

"Have you ever seen a pocketknife in Mr. Molinari's possession?"

"Yes, sir."

Hood held up the knife in question. "This one?"

"I never handled his knife. I couldn't testify for certain one way or the other."

"Did you see what color it was?"

"Yes, sir."

"What color?"

"Brown."

"Like this one?"

"It was brown, sir."

"You mentioned a few minutes ago that you've come to know Mr. Molinari quite well. Is that statement true?"

"All my statements are true."

Billy bit her cheek.

Hood gave him a quelling look. "How would you describe Mr. Molinari's moral rectitude?"

"Of the highest caliber."

"The highest caliber." Hood looked down at his shoes. A gesture Billy had come to recognize as trouble. "Have you ever seen Mr. Molinari in a saloon?"

Hunter took a deep breath. "Once, but ever since—"

"Have you ever seen him with any alcohol?"

"I've never seen him drink."

"But have you seen him with a drink in front him, say, in a bar?"

His jaw began to tick. "I have."

"Have you ever seen him with a cigarette?"

"I've never seen him smoke."

"But have you seen him with a cigarette?"

He clenched his teeth. "Once, but not ever—"

"Have you ever visited Mr. Molinari's home?"

"Yes, sir."

"Can you describe it to us?"

Billy bit her lip.

"I only saw the living area. I didn't go into any bedrooms."

"Then tell us what the living area looked like."

He glanced at her. She didn't know what to do, how to help him. So she let loose the feelings she had for him, the love she'd been holding deep inside, praying it would shine through. Praying he would see it.

His shoulders relaxed. "It had a table, a cabinet, and a bed in the corner."

"Was the room clean or dirty?"

He looked at the prosecutor. "I've seen cleaner."

"Then it was dirty."

"Objection."

"Sustained. Refrain from putting words in the witness's mouth, counselor."

"Did you meet his parents?" Hood asked.

"I did."

"Do his parents work?"

"Yes, sir."

"Both of them?"

"Yes, sir."

A stirring in the gallery. She tried to suppress her irritation. It was people like Derry's parents and siblings who toiled for hours on end to provide so much of what this crowd took for granted every day. Not to mention Derry's family would most likely starve if the mother and all the children didn't work.

"What's the father's occupation?" Hood asked.

"He's a ragpicker."

Another murmur, for the son of a ragpicker received just about as much respect as the son of the town drunk. Again, Billy's ire began to grow.

"Does the father drink spirits?"

"I never saw him drink."

"Do you happen to know how many siblings Derry has?"

"Eight."

Mr. Hood raised his brows, though Billy was certain the attorney already knew how many brothers and sisters Derry had. "Sounds like his mother has quite a handful, yet you said both parents work. Do you know where she works?"

"Yes, sir."

"Where?"

"In a pickle factory."

"Have you ever seen her drink?"

Billy slid her eyes closed.

He swallowed. "Yes, sir."

"Have you ever seen her intoxicated?"

"Yes, sir."

Whispers ricocheted through the room. A swishing of fans followed as women whisked them open and put them to work. Billy glanced at the jurors. Many looked at Derry. All of them frowned.

She wanted to jump up and rail at them. It wasn't his fault. He wasn't responsible for the behavior of his mother, or anyone else, for that matter.

"How old is the youngest Molinari?"

"I don't know."

"Would it be younger or older than Derry?"

"She's younger." To Hunter's credit, he didn't fidget or rub his legs or even flicker an eyelash. She marveled at his calm, for she feared what was coming and was certain he did, too.

"Is she walking?"

"I never saw her walk."

"So, she crawls."

"Yes, sir."

"When did you first meet her?"

Hunter thought a moment. "The beginning of July."

"What was she doing when you met her?"

"Waiting for her brother to bring her some lunch."

Hood nodded. "Her mother doesn't bring her lunch?"

"I don't know."

She wished the attorney would ask about the deplorable working conditions in the pickle factory, the grueling hours, the lack of breaks. But perhaps it was better he didn't, for it wouldn't help Derry and might even harm him.

Hood crossed to the jury, but addressed his question to Hunter. "So his sister, who is unable to walk yet, is left alone?"

"Yes, sir."

"Isn't there some danger she can wander out and get lost or crawl into the streets?"

"Objection. Relevance."

Hood glanced at the judge. "I'm trying to establish Mr. Molinari's moral rectitude and the type of family upbringing he has, Your Honor."

"I'll allow it."

Billy tucked her arms against her waist.

Attorney Hood returned his attention to Hunter. "What keeps Mr. Molinari's baby sister from leaving the premises while she's home alone all day?"

Billy held her breath. There was only one way to answer.

"She's chained to a table."

Ripples of shock skittered through the crowd. The judge banged on his gavel. Billy's breathing grew fractured.

Mr. Hood slid his hands into his pockets. "So you are telling us, Mr. Scott, that young Molinari, who has frequented a saloon, who has been known to have both a beer and a smoke in his possession, who lives in an apartment with a rag-picking father and a drunk mother who are absent all day, and who chains his sister to the table until lunchtime is of 'high moral rectitude'?" He curled his fingers, making quotation marks in the air.

Hunter face grew stony. "In spite of his conditions at home, Derry Molinari is a hard worker, gives all his earnings to his parents, and holds women and his elders in great respect. He's a very good boy and he'd never do anything to harm—"

"No more questions, Your Honor."

She could see Hunter's frustration. Feel his anger.

Mr. Seacoat stood.

Perhaps this had been his plan all along—to use Hunter to clear Derry's name. She drew a hopeful breath.

Tugging on the hem of his jacket, the attorney approached the witness box. "Can you state for the court what your occupation is, Mr. Scott?"

"I'm a Texas Ranger."

"And as a Texas Ranger, you come into contact with a great many undesirables. Is that correct?"

"Yes, sir."

"With as much exposure as you've had to the criminal class, would you say you're a good judge of character?"

"Objection."

"Sustained."

Seacoat moved on. "The prosecution has uncovered some rather appalling habits of Mr. Molinari's, yet you insist the boy is of high moral rectitude. Why is that?"

"The boy's reliable, hardworking, and hadn't missed a day of work until his arrest. He has never once lied to me. He's been concerned about the bullying Kruse and his cohorts have been engaged in since before the playground was built. And he idolizes the 'good guys,' whether it is in the literature he's exposed to—such as *Idylls of the King*—or in the people he meets, such as officers of the law. He simply needs a bit of direction. When I found him in that saloon, I let him know he wasn't to ever set foot in one again and he was not to touch any alcohol or tobacco. He has heeded my instructions to the letter."

"Is he violent?"

Hunter shook his head. "He might enjoy a tale or two about battles fought and won. But in each instance, it's the good guys he sides with."

Mr. Seacoat paused, letting that sink into the minds of the jury members. "Just one more question, Mr. Scott. Why should we put any weight on your opinion of the boy? What makes your opinion so special?"

Hunter slowly straightened. "I'm a Texas Ranger, Mr. Seacoat."

Billy waited for him to say more, but that was it. As if that were explanation enough. And it might have been if they were in Texas. But not up here. Up here, they wouldn't understand.

Seacoat pursed his lips. "For the sake of any in the court who might not be aware, can you please tell us what Texas Rangers are?"

She let out a breath of relief.

With back still straight, he readjusted himself in the chair. "Texas Rangers are men who cannot be stampeded. We walk into any situation and handle it without instruction from our commander. Sometimes we work as a unit, sometimes we work alone." He turned his attention to the jurors. "We preserve the law. We track down train and bank robbers. We subdue riots. We guard our borders. We'll follow an outlaw clear across the country if we need to. In my four years of service, I've traveled eighty-six thousand miles on horse, nineteen hundred on train, gone on two hundred thirty scouts, made two hundred seventeen arrests, returned five hundred six head of stolen cattle, assisted forty-three local sheriffs, guarded a half dozen jails, and spent more time on the trail than I have in my own bed. We've been around since before the Alamo, and"—he turned to Hood, impaling him with his stare—"we're touchy as a teased snake when riled, so I wouldn't recommend it."

Complete stillness fell onto the room. The judge, jury, and gallery stared at him in shock—Billy not the least of them. All color receded from Hood's face.

Seacoat returned to his table. "No more questions, Your Honor."

CHAPTER 49

Hunter's testimony signaled the end of the trial. After each attorney gave his summation, the judge charged the jury with deliberating the guilt or innocence of the boys.

The court filed out, but no one in the gallery left their seats. A quiet hum of conversation ebbed and flowed. Billy wanted to ask Hunter what he thought. If he felt like Derry had a good chance of being freed. But more than a few eyes were cast their way and she didn't want to be overheard.

She wished he'd take her hand again. He'd been her rock throughout the entire affair. He'd offered sympathy at the loss of Miss Weibel. He'd quit his job in an effort to rescue Derry. He'd conducted an investigation to see if he could round up evidence that would point to the boy's innocence. He'd sat beside her, sharing his strength with her, throughout the trial. He'd hired a carriage to take them to and from the courthouse so she'd be shielded from curious eyes. And he'd found Joey. Their sweet, precious Joey.

She couldn't even imagine going through this ordeal without his support. And receiving it was not a show of weakness, she realized. Quite the opposite. She wasn't impregnable. No one was.

She needed help sometimes, and so did he. There was no shame in receiving it any more than there was in giving it.

Opening her fan, she waved it, stirring the tendrils of hair around her face. Now that she'd conceded the fact, she found she didn't ever want to go through another crisis without him. If she were honest, she didn't want to go through another day without him. And if that meant going to Texas and being a country doctor, it was a small price to pay for the friendship, the laughter, the support, the protection, and the love she'd receive in exchange.

Leaning slightly to her left, she bumped him with her shoulder.

He looked down.

She gave him a private smile. And though his lips lifted slightly at the corners, the worry in his eyes overshadowed it. And it scared her.

Within the hour, the court, the boys, and the jury returned.

Derry slumped in his chair, his energy sapped. She didn't know whether it was good or bad that he had no idea how much was riding on what was about to occur.

The jury took their seats, their backs straight, their bodies stiff.

Stomach bouncing, she reached over and slid a hand into Hunter's. Gripping it, he covered it with his other.

The clerk positioned himself in the center of

the arena. "Gentlemen of the jury, have you agreed upon a verdict?"

The foreman, an older man with a long white beard and black sack suit, stood and answered in a strong voice, "We have."

The clerk turned to the boys. "The defendants will rise and face the jury."

Looking at the lawyers and other boys, Derry perked up, his attention captured by the disruption of routine.

"How do you find the defendants?" the clerk asked.

The foreman pulled a pair of glasses from his pocket, hooked them on one ear at a time, then unfolded a crinkled piece of paper.

The people in the gallery held their collective breath.

"We, the jury," he began "find the defendants Fredrick Kruse, Ewald Kruse, Olsen Shiblawski, and Rody Lonborg guilty of murder in the first degree in manner and form as charged in the indictment and fix the penalty at death."

Gasps and chatter broke out. For the first time, Billy saw a look of vulnerability pass over Kruse's face.

The judge pounded his gavel. "Order!"

The noise settled. She pressed a fist against her waist. Hunter squeezed her hand.

The foreman cleared his throat. "We, the jury, find the defendant Derry Molinari guilty of murder in the first degree in manner and form as charged in the indictment and fix the penalty at imprisonment in the penitentiary for life."

"No!" she screamed, jumping to her feet. "He's innocent! He's *innocent!*"

The courtroom erupted.

The judge pounded the gavel. "The people in this room will remain absolutely quiet. Those who are unwilling to do so will retire from the room immediately."

Standing, Hunter slipped a hand about her waist and urged her back down beside him.

Derry frowned, uncertain of what was happening.

Her entire body began to tremble. She stared at the men on the jury. The plumber, the farmer, the grocery man, and the shoe dealer. The blacksmith, the bank cashier, the railroad clerk, and the carpenter. They were men with traditional lives and traditional jobs and traditional families. How could they convict an innocent boy? A *nine*-year-old innocent boy?

The clerk cleared his throat. "Gentlemen, listen to your verdict as the court has recorded it. You say you find the defendants guilty of murder in the first degree. So say you all?"

In chorus, the men of the jury responded, "We do."

The judge nodded. "That ends your services, gentlemen of the jury, in connection with this case. You are excused."

CARTER H. HARRISON, MAYOR OF CHICAGO[39]

"As a man of great popularity and one who'd been instrumental in the fair's success, Harrison made a point of being available to his people."

CHAPTER 50

Billy walked outside the criminal court building wishing she had a parasol or something to shield her face and eyes from the curious. She made do with a fan and clung to Hunter's arm as he escorted her to their carriage.

Even within the relative privacy of the buggy, she forced herself to contain her emotions until they'd put a bit of distance between them and the courthouse. Then her lips began to tremble, her chin quivered, and tears gushed from her eyes. Covering her face, she sobbed.

Hunter pulled her against his side, tucked her under his arm, and held her. *"Shhhhh."*

She continued to weep. She didn't understand how this could have happened. Hadn't the jury heard what she'd heard? How could they not have seen his innocence? After all the testimony, she'd been confident there'd have been at the very least a reasonable doubt. So confident, she'd expected to have Derry in the carriage with them today. Right now. This minute.

She'd planned to have Hunter take him to the Hull House bathhouse, then she'd wanted to examine him and make sure he hadn't picked up any infections or diseases. She'd wanted to use the Hull House kitchen to cook him a good meal that would help make up for all the ones he'd missed. She'd wanted to take him to Marshall Field's and buy him some new clothes. She'd wanted to talk to his employer and make sure he got his job back. She'd wanted to tuck him into clean sheets at her dormitory, just for a few nights so she could make sure no signs of illness popped up. She'd wanted to let him know everything was going to be all right. She'd wanted to . . . mother him.

But instead, he'd been convicted of murder and sentenced to life imprisonment. And the other boys, all of them youths, had been condemned to die by hanging. Hanging.

The crime was horrific, but they were so young. So very young.

She crinkled her fist around Hunter's lapel. "Is there anything we can do? Anything anyone can do?"

"I don't know." He pressed a handkerchief into her hand. "I'll find out, though."

She pushed herself up. "Mr. Seacoat's summation was awful. His entire case was awful. He hardly cross-examined anyone and didn't call one single witness. He could have done so much more."

"I know."

"What's going to happen now? Where will they take him?"

"I'll find out, Billy girl. I'll find out."

The outcry of Chicagoans who objected to such harsh sentencing for youths, particularly Derry, was not as strong as Hunter had hoped. Some warned such "wholesale execution," as the newspapers called it, would have a hardening effect on the city and its citizens. Some suggested a separate justice system should be set up for juveniles, one that would focus on rehabilitation rather than punishment. But the voices who upheld the jury's decision were in the overwhelming majority.

The judge was not in his quarters, nor would he be anytime soon. He'd left on holiday for an indefinite amount of time.

Mayor Carter Harrison, however, was home. As a man of great popularity and one who'd been instrumental in the fair's success, he made a point of being available to his people. Stepping onto his front porch, Hunter knocked on the door of the man's steep-roofed Queen Anne residence.

Harrison himself answered the door. The rotund, bearded man with a wiry brown mustache and gray beard wore no jacket and made no apology for it.

Hunter tugged on his hat. "I'm Texas Ranger Hunter Scott of Company A."

Harrison's eyes lit in recognition. "Scott, I've been reading about you and your Rangers in the papers. Quite impressive." He widened the door. "Come in. Come in."

Rather than taking him into the front parlor, Harrison led him to a library that doubled as a smoking room. It was a man's room and Hunter immediately felt at ease in it.

A square gaming table along with armchairs and animal trophies populated one corner. Across from them a fire warmed the grate. Clearly the mayor had been enjoying a cigar when Hunter had interrupted him, for a lit one lay abandoned on a tray.

Passing by Hunter, Harrison crossed to a credenza and picked up a brandy decanter.

Hunter rotated his Stetson and glanced at the volumes of books, some classics, some scientific, some of which would be inappropriate for a room ladies were allowed in.

Harrison splashed brandy into two glasses and handed one to Hunter. "So, what can I do for you?"

"I'm here about the nine-year-old who's been sentenced to life imprisonment."

Harrison offered Hunter a chair. "A bit young for that kind of sentence, though the crime was certainly heinous."

Settling into the soft leather, Hunter took a moment to luxuriate in his surroundings. He'd not been in anything close to it since leaving Texas. Then he thought of where Derry was, and where he'd be taken, and where he'd be spending the rest of his life. "He's innocent."

Tugging on his trouser legs, Harrison sat in the chair opposite him. "Who? The boy? Molinari?"

"Yes. Derry Molinari. I know him. He was trying to protect the victim, not harm her."

"You're sure?" Harrison frowned. "A jury seemed to think otherwise."

"The defense attorney was young, arrogant, inexperienced, and he didn't care about looking for the truth."

"What about the others? Surely you don't think they're innocent as well?"

"No, they all confessed, except Derry, of course."

Harrison offered a box of Upmanns. "Cigar?"

Hunter held up his palm.

Picking up the cigar he'd left on a tray, Harrison rolled it back and forth between his fingers. "You realize, of course, I can't do anything. The boy was tried, found guilty, and sentenced."

"I'd like to work out a deal."

Harrison gave him a speculative look. Hunter knew the man was not opposed to bending the law and also knew that people loved him. Not just the common ones, but the influential ones.

Hunter qualified it. "Nothing illegal."

"Of course not. Of course not." Harrison took a sip of brandy. "What did you have in mind?"

"I'd like to have Derry put into my custody.

I'd be his jailer, for lack of a better word. I'd take him back to Texas with me, and I'd take full responsibility for any illegal actions or crimes he committed."

Harrison bit down on his cigar. "The only way something like that would work is if he received a pardon. And I don't have the authority to do that."

"It's the governor I need to talk to, then?"

"It is."

"Will you arrange a meeting? Put in a good word?"

After the enormous success of Chicago Day, with attendance that broke the record of any exposition anywhere in the world, Chicago's fair had now completely paid for itself. Harrison was riding high in the aftermath of that achievement.

The man blew a smoke ring, then another inside it. "I'll talk to him, but I can't guarantee anything."

Picking up his hat, Hunter stood. "That's all I ask. How soon can it be arranged?"

"He's in Springfield for a few days, but will be back in town by the middle of next week." Standing, Harrison held out a hand. "I'll talk to him then and see what I can set up."

Hunter gave him a firm shake. "Thank you, sir. I really do appreciate it."

CHAPTER 51

Making her final notes for the day in the infirmary's medical log, Billy yawned. She'd lain awake all night, finally falling asleep about an hour before she had to get up. She hated that.

Scraping back her chair, she gathered up her coat, turned off the electric lights, and stepped into the parlor. Her spirits immediately lifted.

Hunter sat in his usual spot on the couch, feet stretched out, ankles crossed, hat over his face. The only difference was he wasn't in his uniform, of course, but in his denims.

"Howdy, Billy girl." He'd known she was there without looking.

Hugging her coat against her torso, she walked over and stood at his feet. "Hello, back. What brings you here at this hour?"

"Same thing as always. Waiting for you to finish up." He lifted the hat, his brown eyes making her heart warm. "You okay?"

"It's been an awful day."

He patted the spot beside him.

She glanced at the fireplace. "You want to light a fire?"

"We can't. After the Cold Storage Building burned down, the colonel said no fires anywhere. Not even in the fireplaces."

Disappointment piled on top of her fatigue and grief.

"You cold?" he asked.

She shrugged. "It's always cold in here, but mostly I just like the sound and smell of a fire. That's all."

"If I could order one up for you, I would."

She took in his familiar brown hair, angular jaw, broad chest, and long lean body. "I've been thinking."

Tapping his booted toes together, he tilted his head on the cushion. "Thinking what?"

Looking to the side, she clutched her coat a little tighter. "I've been thinking that being a country doctor might be a rather nice change of pace."

The tapping stopped. His body stilled. "What are you saying?"

She looked at him. "That I'd go to Texas with you if the offer is still good."

Pulling in his feet, he sat up and put his hat aside. "What about me working?"

She waved her hand in a dismissive gesture. "Of course you can work. I can't believe I was so arrogant. I'm sorry. Forgive me?"

He nodded, if a bit cautiously. "What about male patients?"

She gave him a pointed look. "I'm a doctor, Hunter. I'm going to treat male patients. You're being silly about that. You really are."

Groaning, he propped his elbows on his knees and rested his forehead on his fists. "I don't like that, Billy. I don't like that at all."

She smiled, then reached out and combed his hair back with her fingernails. "When at all possible, I've started having the wives and mothers of my male patients stay in the room with me during the men's examinations."

He looked up. "You have?"

"I have."

"Even before today?"

"Long before today."

"What if the wife or mother aren't available?"

"Then I go ahead and do my examination without them."

He pulled his lips down the tiniest of bits, then sighed. "What about babies?"

"Yes, please."

"Yes, please?"

She shrugged. "I'd like some babies. Lots of them, actually."

"Who's going to raise them?"

"We both are, I guess. We'll definitely need to bring in some help. Maybe your mother?"

He made a horrible face. "Bite your tongue, woman. My ma's a great gal, but I don't want to live with her. How about a nanny?"

"A nanny would be fine. But no boarding schools."

"Agreed. No boarding schools."

"So is it a deal?" she asked.

He rubbed his mouth. "You sure you won't change your mind about doctoring fellas?"

"I'm not going to change my mind."

"What about my Rangering and being away from home?"

She scrunched up her nose. "I'm not going to like it. But I'll try not to resent it."

"Then I guess I'll try not to resent you doctoring men." He frowned. "But I still don't like it. I really, really, really don't like it."

She smiled. "But you'll manage it, won't you?"

"I suppose I'll have to." After a second or two, a light began to grow within his eyes. "You gonna stand there all day or are you gonna come here and seal the deal?"

"Guess I'll seal the deal, that is if the Lord's willing and the creek don't rise."

He barked out a short laugh. "You poking fun at me, missy?"

"No, I'm just practicing my Texan."

Chuckling, he grabbed her hand and pulled her down beside him. "Come here, woman, and let's practice something else."

After he'd thoroughly kissed her and she'd gone all jelly-like, he rested his forehead against hers. "There's something I forgot to tell you."

She rubbed her nose against his. "What's that?"

"It's about Derry."

Sobering, she pulled back. "What about him?"

"I don't want to get your hopes up and it probably won't work out."

She pushed out of his arms and sat straighter. "What won't work out?"

"I'm asking if I can have custody of him, on account of his age. I've asked if I can take him to Texas with me under the condition that I'd be responsible for any crimes he were to commit, if he committed any, that is."

Her lips parted. "Will his parents allow that?"

"They're more than willing to let me have him. As you know, they've no great attachment to him other than for the money he can bring in. Still, they said they'd rather let me have him than leave him in jail."

"Well, that's something, anyway. Who did you talk to about his release?"

"I talked to the mayor, but he doesn't have the authority to do that. It'll have to come from the governor."

"Do you think he'll agree to it?"

He shrugged. "I don't know. Probably not. But my captain knows him and met with him about something while he was up here. So I've cabled him, told him what's going on, and asked him to cable the governor and see if he can vouch for me."

Bringing her hands together with a clap, she rested them against her lips in a prayer-like fashion. "Do you think he will?"

"My captain? I don't see why not. But I haven't heard back from him."

She launched herself into his arms, knocking him backward.

He immediately took advantage of their position and kissed her again with a great deal of gusto. When she could see he was at his breaking point, she pulled back before she reached hers.

"Where you going?" His voice was husky, full of promise.

"No more. We have to stop."

"Just one more."

She untangled herself from his embrace. "Come on, cowboy. Time to walk this cowgirl home."

"Cowgirl? Heaven help me. You're already a lady doctor. The last thing I need is for you to be a lady cowboy, too."

Grabbing his hand, she pulled him to his feet. "Come on. You sound like a hog in a woodpile."

He gave her backside a playful swat with his hat. "Sweet Mackinaw, it's hog in a coal pile, not hog in a woodpile."

She lifted a brow. "Then let me say it in Chicago style: Come on and quit your whining."

With a quick shuffle to the side, she skirted out of range, then hurried to the door before he had another hankering to paint her back porch red.

CHAPTER 52

GOVERNOR ALTGELD GOOD MAN STOP
ADVOCATE OF CHILDREN AND WOMEN
STOP HAVE SENT WORD STOP CAPT
HEYWOOD STOP

Hunter tucked the telegram in his pocket, then stepped inside Chicago's tallest building. Just months prior to entering office, Governor Altgeld had finished this building, the crown jewel of his real estate career. Marble floors sparkled beneath Hunter's boots. Tile ceilings gleamed overhead.

Approaching the elevators, he sighed. He didn't like those newfangled things. He didn't see why any fellow felt the need to go two hundred feet in the air. The folks in Babel had tried that and it hadn't worked out too well for them.

But you couldn't tell Chicagoans that. To them, the higher the building the better. The doors opened and folks spilled out like cattle from a chute.

As soon as it emptied, that many more pushed and shoved their way inside. Caught in the vortex of the stampede, he was herded to the center of the box, pressed tight from every angle. All the way up, he kept reminding himself that Billy would be done with the fair in another week. Then he could leave this godforsaken city.

He decided they would head out the day the fair ended. That very night. He'd take her to the preacher the minute the exposition's closing ceremonies were over, then go straight to one of those fancy sleeper cars and have himself the most pleasurable ride to Texas a fellow could ever dream of.

He couldn't quite believe she'd agreed to go. But now that she had, he'd found that his impatience to make her his had increased a hundredfold. Still, at moments like these, he wasn't sure if he was more excited about leaving Chicago or about getting her into his bed.

He shook his head. That was all hat and no cattle, and he knew it, but he was looking forward to being home just the same.

Little by little the crowd eased as folks exited the box. By the time he got to the sixteenth floor, it was just him and two other fellows.

The doors opened. Hunter started walking up and down corridors looking for Altgeld's office. If the man said yes, Hunter would have to figure out what to do about Derry during the honeymoon. Maybe one of the Rangers from home would come up and escort Derry back. That'd be the only viable solution. There wasn't anybody else he'd trust to see after the boy, and Derry would love the chance to meet another Ranger.

In the northeast corner, a plaque announced

Altgeld and his Unity Company. He knocked.

A pretty little typewriter gal opened the door. "He's expecting you, Mr. Scott. Right this way."

He shook his head at all the fancy carpets and wallpaper and scrollwork. Was there something wrong with just plain and simple?

Stepping inside a corner office, the gal held the door open with her back and waved Hunter in.

Reaching above her, he steadied the door with his hand. "I think you have that backward, miss. I'm supposed to be holding the door for you."

She smiled, a pretty blush of pink touching her cheeks. "Thank you."

She dipped under his arm and went back the way she'd come.

He stuck his head in the office.

A man with a respectable black beard and black hair cropped short smiled and came around his desk. "You must be Ranger Scott. Come in."

Letting the door close, Hunter shook the man's hand. "Thanks for seeing me."

"Certainly. I know your captain very well. We've had meetings in D.C., and he was just up to see me late this summer. But I suppose you know that already. Please, have a seat."

Hunter settled into a brown leather chair. "Did the mayor tell you why I wanted to meet with you?"

Altgeld pulled up to his desk. "He did, and so did your captain. So, I've been poring over the records the stenographer took of the trial." He shook his head. "Quite a nasty business."

"Yes, sir, it is."

"And you think Derry Molinari is innocent?"

"I know he is. I've seen him on a daily basis all summer long. The boy's a hard worker and anxious to do right by his family and right by women. Have you read his testimony and that of the other boys?"

"I've read the whole thing. And I have to say, I'm inclined to agree with you. Molinari's testimony was consistent and convincing. Between that, the Lonborg boy's testimony, and your endorsement, I think there was definitely a case for reasonable doubt. The way the defense handled the case was disappointing, to say the least."

Hunter's hopes soared. "So what do you say? Will you pardon him? I'm willing to be his 'jailer,' if you will. And I'll take all responsibility for any mischief he gets into—no matter how serious—until he's old enough to go out on his own."

Altgeld leaned back in his chair. "Ordinarily, given his age and your reputation, I wouldn't even hesitate. The problem is, this case is being watched very closely. Not only by the citizens of Illinois, but by the higher-ups in Washington. And everyone has an opinion—a strong opinion. I'm just not sure what the reaction would be if I released him to you."

"Listen, sir. I know this boy. All he needs is guidance. An example. A father who can give him some extra attention. He simply needs someone to show him how to be a man."

"And you're going to show him how to be a man?"

"I am."

"In Texas, I assume? Where you'll be a Ranger?"

"That's right."

"Don't you think it's going to be hard to give him all this fatherly instruction if you're always away on assignment?"

The click of a fan competed with the ticking of a wall clock.

"I wouldn't always be away."

"I'm no stranger to Rangering, Mr. Scott. As I said, I know your captain quite well. And even if I didn't . . ." Sitting up, Altgeld sifted through several papers, then stopped and laid a finger on one of the lines. "According to your testimony, it says here, 'I've spent more time on the trail than I have in my own bed.' "

Hunter swallowed. "I could settle in the same town as my mother. Then he'd have the influence of not just the woman I'm marrying, but of my ma as well."

"What about your father?"

"He's passed."

Altgeld shook his head. "I'm sorry. Like I said, if the case wasn't receiving so much attention, it wouldn't be a problem. But if I did do this and my justification was that you'd offered to be Molinari's jailer, as you called it, how would I respond when the higher-ups pointed out you'd never be around to do the job?"

Chest tightening, Hunter sat forward. "Sir, the boy's only nine. We can't leave him locked up with vicious, hardened criminals for the rest of his days, especially when he didn't do anything but try to protect the victim. There's got to be a way we can work this out."

Resting his arms on the desk, Altgeld clasped his hands. "Calm down, son. There's a way. I never said there wasn't a way. I just said I couldn't release him to you under the conditions you've described."

"All right. Then what conditions would you pardon him under?"

"I have two."

"Okay."

"One." He held up a finger. "You have to be married. The boy needs a mother."

Hunter's hopes rose. "That's already been arranged."

"Good. Two." He held up the second finger. "You'll have to have a job that allows you to be home every night."

His pulse began to race. His lungs completely quit working. Gripping the armrests of the chair, he forced air through his nose and out through his mouth. Finally, he managed to speak. "You're telling me I have to give up being a Ranger."

"I'm not saying you can't be a Ranger. Being a Ranger is a fine and noble profession. I'm just saying that you need to make sure you're home every night."

"You're talking about sitting behind a desk. Rangers don't sit behind desks. We roam the range. I'd have no choice but to give it up. And I can't do that, sir. It would kill me. I need, I need to be able to move around. To spend time out-doors. To go from one county to the next. I need be able to push my horse to a full gallop and sleep out under the stars. It's too much. It would—"

The room started spinning. His head became light. Spots appeared over his vision.

Sweet mother of all that is holy, he was going to black out. He ordered his blood to go back to his brain, but it had long since gone south and had no intention of returning.

Spreading his knees, he bent over and hung his head between them, forcing the blood to flow back into his head.

"Scott?" The governor's voice rose in concern. "Are you all right?"

He didn't answer.

"It doesn't have to be a desk job," the governor said. "There's plenty of jobs besides Rangering that you could do outdoors. Like farming. You could farm. Or ranch. What about ranching? That involves horses."

"It's not the same, sir." The blood was slow in returning, so he stayed bent over. "There's no chase involved. No tracking. No danger. No sense of adventure. And you have to have a lot of money to be a rancher. You can't just one day say, 'I think I'll be a rancher.' You may as well ask a chicken to fly. It may have wings, but there's just some things it can't do."

Altgeld made no response.

Finally, Hunter felt it safe to raise his head.

Altgeld's expression was incredulous. "I thought you were supposed to be tough?"

"If you want a powder burning contest, I could have you winging it to Saint Peter before you even reached for your gun. If you'd rather use fists, I could knock your ears down so they'd do you for wings. But I could never sit at a desk for years on end or gamble my family's well-being on the whims of a crop or chase cows my whole life. I'm not that tough. I'm just not."

Altgeld shook his head. "Then I can't release Derry to you. I'm sorry."

He scrubbed his face with his hands. "You're positive? There's no changing your mind?"

"He needs a jailer and he needs someone to teach him how to be a man. You can't do those things unless you're home."

Propping his elbow on the armrest, Hunter

pressed his palm against his forehead. He needed to talk to Billy. Maybe she could figure something out. "Can I get back to you tomorrow, sir?"

"That would be fine."

With a deep breath, he picked up his Stetson and pushed himself up. "Thank you. I'll see you tomorrow, then."

HULL HOUSE PARLOR[40]

"The parlor was full of women and children,
along with one man, waiting to see her."

CHAPTER 53

He needed someplace private to talk to Billy, but there was no place. It was still daytime, so the Woman's Building parlor would be open to anybody who wanted to walk in. Crockett's island would have folks coming and going. Her dormitory didn't have a sitting room. And Hull House was always busy.

Still, that was where she was, so that's where he headed. And once he arrived, he discovered Hull House had temporarily given her a private room on the second floor where she could conduct her examinations. The parlor was full of women and children, along with one man, waiting to see her.

He sized the fellow up. Somewhere in his fifties. Hadn't shaved for several days. Hadn't bathed for several months. And he looked kind of green. Hunter decided he'd let the man see her, but he didn't like it. Not one single bit.

It was a good three hours before she finished.

After the last patient left, he knocked on the door and stepped into the room. Several instruments were laid out on a dresser, along with bandages, rags, vials, and her doctor's bag.

Pulling linen off a chaise longue, she glanced up, then froze. "You're back. What'd he say?"

She wore a plain brown skirt and a simple white

shirtwaist, just the way he liked it. She'd pinned her hair in a twist, her cheeks held a breath of pink, and her eyes had a bit of a glow.

"You really like your doctoring, don't you?" he asked.

She nodded. "I love it. Now, what did the governor say?"

"He didn't say yes, but he didn't say no." He took a deep breath. "He, um, had some conditions."

Furling up the linen, she studied him. "You didn't like the conditions."

"I didn't."

"What were they?"

He eyed the chaise longue. "Is it safe to sit on that?"

She glanced at it. "You mean because of the germ theory?"

He nodded.

"Yes. I cover it with multiple linens."

"Well, let's sit then."

She shook her head. "You sit. I'm going to clean up."

"I'd really like you to sit."

Tossing the linen by the door, she crossed to the ewer and began to soap her hands and arms. "You'll want to kiss me and we can't kiss in here. It would be disrespectful to Miss Addams."

"I won't kiss you, then."

Picking up a huck towel, she dried her hands. "No hugging. No nuzzling. No nothing."

"You sure are bossy."

"I mean it."

He sighed. "You might as well keep doing what you're doing, then."

Shaking her head, she started soaping and washing her instruments. "So what are the conditions?"

He admired the view, mesmerized by the jiggling that occurred while she scrubbed.

She looked over her shoulder, then rested her wrists against the side of the bowl, suds dripping from her hands. "Hunter." A warning.

He gave himself a shake, then ran a hand through his hair. "There were two conditions. One of which was pretty dismal."

She turned back to her washing. "What are they?"

"I have to give up Rangering."

She whirled around, soap and water flying, a knife of some sort in her hands. "What?"

"He thinks Derry needs me to be home every night. So, whatever I decide to do, it has to be something I walk away from come suppertime."

Water ran in rivulets from the scalpel to the floor. Crossing to the dresser, he grabbed a rag from her pile and wiped it up.

She dropped the instrument back in the bowl, dried her hands, led him to the chaise, then sat down beside him. "This is horrible news. Tragic. What are you going to?"

"He suggested I farm, ranch, or get behind a desk."

"Do any of those things appeal you?"

"Not even a little. I grew up on a farm and couldn't get out of there fast enough. Ranching wouldn't be awful, but it takes a lot of money and land—neither of which I have."

"And a desk job?"

He gave a shrug. "I figured I'd be behind a desk at some point. Like if I was chief of the Rangers or something. But not now. Not yet. I . . ." He gave her a bleak look. "I can't even fathom sitting behind a desk for the next thirty-something years."

"I thought you were up for the captain's job. Doesn't he sit behind a desk?"

"Sometimes. But mostly he rides around and checks on all of us."

"I see. I wonder if there's a way to compromise." She froze, her eyes widening. "Is the second condition that I have to quit practicing?"

"No, no. The second condition is that I have a wife." He figured the governor didn't realize Billy still planned to work after they wed. And Hunter certainly wasn't going to enlighten him. Besides, she'd office right out of their home just like all the other docs. So between her and a nanny, Derry'd get plenty of mothering. "So, that was the good part. Now you can't back out."

She gave him a soft smile. "I'm not going to back out."

Despite his distress, desire surged through him. "Go sit on the other end of the couch."

"What?"

"Go."

Biting back her smile, she moved to the opposite end of the chaise longue. "Better?"

"No. Nothing's going to be better till we're married and can consummate this thing."

Her eyes warmed. It was one of the best parts of her being a doctor. She wasn't shocked at the same things as other gals. Still, if she didn't stop looking at him like that, he'd never make it.

He faced forward.

"What are we going to do?" she asked.

Propping his hands on his knees, he looked down. "I don't know."

"We can't leave him in jail."

He slid his eyes closed. "I know."

"What about being a sheriff?"

"I thought of that." Leaning over, he picked up a dried piece of mud that had fallen off of someone's shoe.

"You'd thought of that . . . but?"

He swallowed. "It's a pretty big step down."

A set of lacy curtains billowed around a window on the north wall.

"Is there nothing you could do for the Rangers? Nothing that would keep you home?"

He nodded. "We have a quartermaster. He maintains the inventory and issues the equipment. But I don't know, Billy. It'd be just awful to see the boys coming in and going out. Telling tales of what they did and what they saw. All the while me knowing I could do it, too, and perhaps even better." He sighed. "I think I'd rather sheriff than do that. At least I'd be a lawman and I'd be able to get out from behind my desk fairly often."

Moistening her lips, she picked at her fingernails. "You don't have to work, you know."

His gut clenched. "Don't. Don't even start down that road."

Crumbling the dried piece of mud, he sifted the grains through his fingers. No matter what job he ended up with, life as he knew it was over. He would never be chief. He'd never be captain. Shoot, he wouldn't even be a Ranger. He was going to have to put away his badge and walk away from his dreams, his hopes, and his ambitions. Everything. Pitched right out a window sixteen stories off the ground.

He rubbed his face. He wished he'd never come. He wished he'd just stayed home and been happy with his job the way it was instead of always trying to grasp more, more, more.

Rising, Billy returned to the washstand. He watched her. Admired her. If he'd not come up here, he'd have never met her. And that, he realized, was worth it all.

Splashes and plops ensued as she finished cleaning and shining her instruments. A lady doctor. He was going to be married to a bloomer-wearing, freethinking, cum laude lady doctor. His mother was going to have a real corker of a fit.

Squinting, he looked at the neighborhood outside. "We're gonna be as poor as those folks out there for a while. At least until I figure out what to do."

The splashing stopped. Picking up a towel, she began to dry each item. "Not quite. I'll be bringing in some extra, assuming I can find paying customers in Texas."

"You'll find some paying customers." But he didn't think it would happen right away. The folks back home had definite ideas about what a gal should and shouldn't do. It would be a while before she won their trust and respect.

She tucked a sharp, dangerous-looking knife in her bag. "What if you were sheriff in one of those lawless towns? The ones that are out in the middle of nowhere? You know, where bad guys hide in?"

He studied her. "You'd do that for me? You'd live someplace that remote?"

"I would." She pulled up one corner of her mouth. "Just think of all the bullet wounds I'd get to fix."

He felt the first smile of the day begin to tug. "I think somebody's been reading too many pulp fiction novels. We don't have towns like that anymore, remember? The frontier is disappearing. And with it, all the outlaws. That's why those politicians tried to shut us down."

"Tried? Has something been resolved?"

"Nothing's final yet, but it definitely looks like that's not gonna happen."

She blew out a breath. "Thank goodness for that, anyway."

"Even still, there is no Wild West. Just normal towns with normal people who put down their stakes and call a place home."

He shook his head. Even if there were any lawless towns left, he'd never bring his bride to one. No, the three of them would settle someplace quiet and peaceful. A place that would be good to raise a family in.

Holding her bag closed, she latched the buckle. "Well, let's pick the rowdiest one. You can be the sheriff, establish some law and order, then keep the peace. And I can do the doctoring and patch everybody up. It'll be our slice of paradise right in the middle of the great state of Texas."

He knew she wanted to stay in Chicago just as much as he wanted to be a Ranger. Yet she was giving that up. For him. A man with no prospects and no job. Love for her swelled. "I think I have me a slice of paradise right here in this room."

She ducked her head, her smile shy.

The desire that simmered just below the surface sprang to life. "I sure am looking forward to our wedding day, Billy girl."

She looked at him. "Me, too."

Standing, he opened the door. "Come on. We'd best get on out of here."

DRAWING ROOM OF HULL HOUSE[41]

"Across town in the drawing room of Hull House, Billy Jack Tate wore a blue-and-eyelet striped gown with one feminine bow at her collar and another just above the curve of her chest."

CHAPTER 54

News of Derry's pardon was buried in the back of the paper. Instead, the focus of all Chicago was on the murder of their beloved mayor, Carter Harrison, just two days before the World's Columbian Exposition was scheduled to close. Just like he had with Hunter, the mayor had opened his own door to a young stranger. Only this time, he'd invited in his murderer.

The grand celebration planned for the final day of the Exposition metamorphosed into a funeral dirge. And the fair that had hosted twenty-seven million visitors and celebrated the great advance of America quietly closed her gates on October 30, 1893, never to open them again.

Across town in the drawing room of Hull House, Billy Jack Tate wore a bride-like, blue-and-eyelet striped gown with one feminine bow at her collar and another just above the curve of her chest. Beside her, Hunter Joseph Scott slipped his grandmother's ring onto her fourth finger and pledged his troth.

The reverend closed his Bible. "You may now kiss the bride."

Hooking his finger beneath her chin, Hunter gave her a tender kiss, causing an eruption of whistles, hoots, and hollers from half a dozen

Texas Rangers of Company A. The men had traveled up by order of their captain to make sure Hunter received a proper send-off and to escort one Derry Maximo Molinari safely back to Texas.

Eyes bright, Derry stuck two fingers in his mouth, but only air and slobber came out. "Can you teach me to whistle like that?" he asked the large man beside him.

Reaching down, Ranger Lucious Landrum picked up the boy and tossed him across his shoulder. "You bet."

Squealing, Derry swung his head up. "Look at me, Doc Tate! I'm taller than you."

Hunter grabbed the boy's nose. "The name's Dr. Scott, son."

Raising an arm like a conductor, Miss Addams invited everyone to the coffeehouse for refreshments. And though the bride and groom wanted to participate, they had a train to catch.

Hunter shook hands with all his comrades, thanking them for coming. "Don't drink the coffee," he warned under his breath. "They don't make nothing but stump water up here."

Billy, meanwhile, hugged the women of Hull House.

Still balancing Derry across his shoulder, Lucious rounded up the newlyweds. "You better get goin', Fox, or you're gonna miss your train."

"Fox?" Billy looked at Hunter. "Why do they call you Fox?"

"Cause he's a regular chaparral fox for smart," Lucious said. "Graduated cum laude and everything."

Her lips parted. *"Cum laude*?"

"Why sure. Didn't he tell you? He was number one in his class at the A&M College of Texas."

Putting her hands on her hips, she slowly faced Hunter. " 'Praise the laude'?"

Grinning, he gave her a wink. "Tell Derry goodbye, darlin'. We've gotta go."

After a moment of exasperation, she walked behind Lucious and placed her hands on either side of Derry's cheeks. "You be good and do what these men tell you, all right?"

"I will."

"Yes, ma'am," Hunter corrected.

"Yes, ma'am," Derry repeated.

Lifting up on tiptoe, she kissed him on the forehead. "We'll see you in a couple of weeks."

"High above the chairs, a large panel rested against one wall. She knew it was the berth, for there'd been a sample sleeping car in the Transportation Building at the fair."

CHAPTER 55

Billy stood in the plush Pullman sleeping car, the easy, swaying motion of the train indicating they'd left the city behind and had crossed into the Illinois prairies. Hunter had stepped out of their room to "canvass" the train, as he called it, not wanting to retire until he'd made sure all was well.

As a wedding present, the Rangers had secured them a private room on the luxurious train. Intricate carpeting, brocade draperies, and stationary upholstered chairs graced their quarters. A gas chandelier hung from the carved ceiling, and she couldn't help but marvel at the lavishness of the wood, the colors, and the design.

High above the chairs, a large panel rested against one wall. She knew it was the berth, for there'd been a sample sleeping car in the Transportation Building at the fair and she'd watched a Pullman representative lower the bed. It had looked so easy. She felt sure she could do it.

Lifting her skirt, she stepped up onto the seat of one of the chairs and reached for a handle at the top of the panel. As she cranked it, the berth began to open up as if it were an extra-wide drawbridge. The only things suspending it at the moment were two chains on either end that ran on spring pulleys.

Lying atop the berth were two pieces of mahogany that were to serve as the bed's ground support. Dragging one off, she teetered for a moment, then propped it up and wedged it beneath the head of the bed, sliding it in a preformed groove. Blowing a swath of hair from her face, she pulled the other piece of mahogany from the berth and repeated the steps, but at the foot of the bed.

Brushing her hands together, she studied the stationary chairs. In the demonstration, the bed linens had been behind a seat cushion. After some wiggling and a bit of manhandling, she managed to force a cushion to the side, and there they were.

Now, this she could do without difficulty.

Whipping out the sheet, she tossed it up onto the berth. It settled off center. She did it again. And again.

Botheration. She was going to have to get up there to tuck it in properly. But there was no ladder. No stool. No nothing. At least, not that she could find.

She couldn't step on the chair cushion again because the chairs were now underneath the berth, their backs flush with the mahogany pieces she'd stuck in. Mumbling, she tossed the linen onto the bed and removed her boots.

Finally, she hiked her skirt clear up above her knee, then set her foot on the armrest of one of the chairs. Holding tightly to the edge of the berth, she pulled herself up and onto the bed.

Working quickly, she tucked the linen in against the wall, the head, and the foot. She'd tuck in the last side once she was back on the floor. She looked over the edge. It was too far to jump.

Rolling onto her stomach, she inched backward like a worm, her body making progress, her skirts and petticoats staying where they'd started. Her stocking-clad legs made it over the edge and dangled in midair. But her skirts were inside out, cocooning her upper body within their folds. Her pantalets had bunched at her thighs.

In an effort to see where the armrest was, she wiggled her feet. Nothing but open air.

She pushed herself a little lower. Still no armrest. Where was the blasted thing? Had she missed it completely?

She must have. Sighing, she closed her eyes, took a breath, and counted silently in her head.

One . . . two . . . *three.*

She pushed herself off and hit ground almost immediately, then her knees gave. Between her tangled skirts and the unforgiving floor, it took her a moment to orient herself.

A draft she hadn't noticed before swirled around her. The hairs on the back of her neck prickled. Pulling her legs beneath her, she rocked slowly to her feet. Then turned.

Hunter stood inside the closed door, the fabric

of his cassimere suit outlining his broad shoulders, trim waist, and muscular legs. He leaned with one shoulder against the wall and one ankle crossed in front of the other, show-casing his armadillo boots.

He gave her a wicked grin. "Goin' somewhere?"

CHAPTER 56

The hiss of the gas lantern reminded her he could see everything clearly. Very clearly.

Images flashed through her mind. Her body wriggling as she inchwormed over the edge. Her skirts not following as they should. Her pantalets bunching about her thighs. Her back end clearly delineated by her position. Her lower half swinging from the berth as her toes sought out the armrest.

Heat rushed through her body. She wanted to drop through the floor. Following that urge was an overwhelming one to throw caution to the wind and launch herself into his arms.

She couldn't decide which to do. She'd long since lost her ability to reason when he looked at her like that. She cast about for something to say. "How long have you been there?"

"Pretty much the whole time."

She twirled her finger in her skirt, wrapping it round and round. "Why didn't you help me?"

Lifting his chin, he scratched his jaw. "I wasn't exactly sure what to grab."

She bit her lip.

He surveyed her skirt as if he could see right through it. "Those weren't the pantalets-trousers you were wearing last time. Those were . . . I like those. Not that I didn't like the other ones. I did. But these . . . are they new?"

She blushed. "I bought them back in May. I sort of ruined my other ones when I went through that cellar window."

He pushed himself away from the wall. "You've been wearing those see-through things this whole time? Throughout the whole fair?"

She nodded.

He groaned. "Good thing I didn't know that."

Walking to the foot of the bed, he fastened two strong wire ropes from the upper berth to the bottom of the chair.

Leaning over, she watched him. "What are those for?"

"It keeps the berth from snapping closed and smashing us flat."

Us. She glanced at the wide, two-person berth. He was going to be in that with her. She crossed her arms against her stomach.

He fastened the wires at the head of the bed. "The porters will make the bed for us. They also remove the linens and clean them. Every day. So, much as I enjoyed watching you, it's really not necessary for you to do all that."

She tucked a piece of hair up into her coif. Good heavens. She must look a fright. "I need to freshen up."

He straightened. "Freshen up?"

"My hair's a mess. It came all undone while I

was, um . . ." She waved her hand toward the bed.

"And you need to put it back up?"

"Yes."

"Why?"

She blinked. "Why?"

His eyes darkened.

She backed up. The berth skimmed the very top of her head. Before she could sneak underneath it, he slipped his arm around her and pulled her to him.

"You don't need to put up your hair," he said.

"I don't?"

"No."

"Because you're going to take it down?"

He kissed the pulse at her neck. "Because I'm going to take it down."

But instead of reaching for her hairpins, he tugged a streamer at her collar loose, unraveling her bow. His lips moved up her neck to her ear.

Oh, my. She shifted her weight from one foot to the other. She grabbed two fistfuls of her skirt.

He pulled back, looking at her with a touch of surprise. "Are you nervous?"

She spun her skirt around her fists. "No."

He took a step back, his hands resting against her waist. "You are nervous."

"No, no. I'm not." She lifted her shoulders. "I'm just, um . . ." She bit her lip. "Nervous."

Chuckling, he wrapped his arms around her and tucked her head beneath his chin. "Ah, Billy girl. There's nothing to be nervous about. This is the most natural thing in the world."

Humming some song she'd never heard before, he took her right hand in his and held it out to the side, but kept his other around her waist. Then, he turned her about their itty-bitty room in tiny, slow dance steps.

She didn't know he could dance. She didn't know he could sing. Little by little, she began to relax against him.

He nuzzled her head. Kissed her hair. And continued to hum. By the end of the song, he'd backed her up against the wall opposite the berth and bracketed her with both arms.

She slid her hands up and down his jacket, then slipped the buttons free and pushed it from his shoulders.

Keeping his body close to hers, he lowered his arms, caught his jacket as it slid off, tossed it on a chair, then bracketed her again.

Returning her hands to his chest, she undid his waistcoat. It went the same way as his jacket.

He bracketed her again.

She removed his collar and dropped it on the chair. Resting her hands against his shirt, she familiarized herself with the landscape of his shoulders and chest. His sides and the area just beneath his upraised arms. But it wasn't enough. She wanted no barrier between her palms and his skin.

She pushed buttons through the holes of his shirt until she reached the band of his trousers. She tried to pull the rest of his shirt out, but it wouldn't come.

Reaching down, he released his buckle and the fly of his trousers, then returned his arm to the wall.

Her movements became more frantic. More hurried. Pulling the shirttail, she undid the rest of the buttons and shoved the shirt over his shoulders. He'd barely freed his arms when she grabbed his undershirt and slid it up, but the sight of him was too much of a temptation. She placed her hands against his chest, running them across it, down his torso, then back up again.

He whipped off the undershirt, then spun her around.

Resting her forehead against the wall, she reveled in the feel of his large hands working her buttons. When they were free, she pushed away from the wall and rested her body against his while he whisked the bodice down her arms, exposing her blouse.

Those buttons ran down the front, but instead of turning her around, he undid them while she rested against him. When her waistband stopped him, he propped her up, untied it and her petticoats, then held her arms while they dropped to the floor revealing corset, chemise, and pantalets.

Groaning, he whirled her around and kissed her. She wrapped her arms around him, trying to get closer, closer.

His hands were everywhere. Her hairpins fell to the floor, releasing an avalanche of curls.

Tunneling her fingers into his thick, gorgeous hair, she pushed his head back.

His eyes were dark. His breathing as labored as hers.

"I'm not nervous anymore," she whispered.

Scooping her up, he bent his legs, then lifted her above him with his powerful arms and tossed her onto the berth. She gave a squeal of surprise, then scooted out of the way as he yanked off his boots, doused the light, shucked his trousers, and swung himself onto the bed.

Good heavens.

It was her last cognizant thought, for the wonders of the marriage bed began their song of glory.

CHILDREN SWINGING IN PARK[43]

"Designed and landscaped by the same men
who did the World's Fair, the park's
sixty acres burst with June foliage
and sweeping lawns."

EPILOGUE

Chicago
Fourteen Years Later

To the accompaniment of a stirring brass band, hundreds of kindergarten children from Chicago's tenement districts entered Ogden Park in grand march order. Irish kept time with Italians. Swedes partnered with Russians. Whites held hands with blacks. Delegates from all across the country cheered and waved their flags. The closing ceremonies for the first annual convention of the Playground Association of America were well under way.

Designed and landscaped by the same men who did the World's Fair, the park's sixty acres burst with June foliage and sweeping lawns. Hunter stood beside a sparkling lagoon and waved as Derry approached.

A few months after moving to Texas back in '93, they'd received word from Miss Addams that Derry's entire family had been lost to cholera. That week Billy and Hunter made it official. Derry Maximo Molinari became Derry Joseph Scott. He'd been calling them Mother and Pa ever since.

Lacking only an inch to catch up with Hunter's

six-two frame, Derry wore denims, a Stetson, and a pair of armadillo boots. "Mother and the others are waiting inside. They said they're ready for some lunch."

"We'd better hop-to, then."

The two of them headed toward a redbrick recreation building on the opposite end of the park that housed gymnasiums, bathrooms, reading rooms, club rooms, a library, and a restaurant.

A Toronto delegate hailed Derry. "A great festival you and the association have put together, Scott, eh? Now that I know how to go about it, I plan to get to work straightaway. You just wait. At next year's convention I'll be telling you about a half dozen new playgrounds we'll have opened."

Clapping him on the shoulder, Derry encouraged the man, then continued on. They walked around a heated baseball game between boys from two different wards. Onlookers stood on opposite sides of the diamond cheering their teams.

Reaching over, Hunter gave Derry's neck a quick squeeze of affection. "How was work this week?"

Derry filled him in on the case he was researching for the downtown law firm he was with. The boy had long since given up his aspirations to be a Ranger. And it was no wonder. Having experienced the impact a bad attorney could have on someone's life, he'd enrolled in the University of Chicago to study law.

A swelling of pride filled Hunter. In addition to the degree, Derry had had a longing to have a playground within a mile of every child in Chicago's slums. So he joined up with like-minded men from Chicago, Boston, New York, and Washington, D.C., and became a member of the Playground Association of America.

"Scott!"

Hunter glanced at the swimming pool. Men and boys of all sizes and shapes wearing municipal free bathing costumes splashed in the clear, clean water.

"Scott!" someone shouted again. Then he realized they were calling for Derry.

Scanning the frolickers, Derry spotted one of Harvard's professors and tugged the rim of his Stetson. "Dr. Sargent."

The man waded to the edge of the pool; his startlingly white shoulders and arms held a reddish tint. "I think we ought to start considering not how to increase the number of playgrounds, but how to hold the ground we've already gained and develop a plan that will ensure their longevity."

"Let's bring that up at the next meeting."

"Come on, son." Giving the Harvard man a polite smile, Hunter commandeered Derry's arm. "Your mother's waiting."

They skirted girls from Hamilton Park who'd

strapped wooden shoes to their feet and circled in a thunderous dance. They chuckled at the screams from boys flying down a tall slide. Then they gave up any attempt at conversation while Scots in colorful kilts blew into bagpipes as eighty girls did the Inverness reel.

After a satisfying lunch and several hours of play, the Scotts joined the assembly inside the field house's auditorium for the final addresses. Placing an arm on Billy's seatback, Hunter ran a finger up and down her sleeve. Fourteen years and five babies had made some changes, but his love and passion for her had grown to even greater heights. He ran an appreciative gaze over her form. She was all frocked up in one of her city dresses. This one had blue polka dots with a row of blue bows along the hem.

"You look mighty pretty today," he whispered.

Smiling softly, she leaned into him.

With a thumb in his mouth, little Joey slid off his seat, pushed Derry's long legs aside, and crawled up onto Billy's lap. Tucking him against her, she combed her hands through his hair.

Their other Joey would have celebrated his fourteenth birthday last month. Not a day went by that he didn't think of the little fellow. Wondering what he looked like. What he did for fun. What kind of foods he hated to eat. What kind of things he did with his dad.

Hunter and Billy had subscribed to the *Chicago*

Tribune, keeping a close eye on the paper for any mention of the Yorks. And though the real estate magnate was one of the richest men in Chicago, nothing had been written about his son. At least, not yet. But when he came of age, Hunter figured they'd be able to follow Robert Jr.'s successes and failures and cheer him on from afar.

Bending his head forward, he took a gander at the rest of the kids taking up the seats beside Derry. Josie and Jacqueline played scratch cradle with a loop of string. Bessie had curled up on her seat and was using Derry's leg as a cushion. Heywood's eyes drooped and his head bobbed once. He immediately lifted it, only to start the whole process over a few seconds later.

Hunter placed a soft kiss on Billy's temple. "You sure do make good-looking babies, Dr. Scott."

She made a shushing expression with her mouth.

He winked, then looked at the printed program. Once Mr. Joseph Lee of Boston—the undisputed leader of the Playground Movement—wound up his speech, then Hunter would close things out. At the bottom of the page, an acknowledgment had been made to him and Billy, defining them as the creators of Chicago's very first playground. It credited them for providing the spark that ignited citizens to establish the Chicago Playground Association. He shook his head.

"What?" she whispered, looking on the program to see what had caused his consternation.

He pointed to her name. "Never in all my days have I seen a girl with so many boy names."

She glanced at the neatly typeset *Dr. Billy Jack Scott* and smiled.

"I think it quite significant," Mr. Lee said from the lectern, "that President Roosevelt urged all of us to come to this first annual convention of the Playground Association of America so we could, and I quote, 'gain inspiration and see the magnificent system that Chicago has erected—one of the most notable civic achievements of any American city.' So it is with great honor that I introduce you to the man responsible for starting this whole thing by building Chicago's very first playground. Please welcome Mr. Hunter Scott."

A round of applause became a standing ovation. Mr. Lee signaled for Hunter to come up.

Joining the man onstage, Hunter thanked him, and took a place behind the lectern. "Thank you, Mr. Lee. I believe that was the easiest Boston speech I ever listened to. As a man born and bred in Texas, I'm proud to say that I could spell nearly every word."

A rumble of laughter passed among the assembly.

He thanked Hull House and those who had picked up the torch after he and Billy had left.

He praised those who'd gone above and beyond everyone's expectations. Then he reminded the assembly of why they were here. "If you come from a place without a single playground or a single donation, I want to remind you that the playground movement in the great city of Chicago dates only from the nineties. We started with a vacant lot, a pile of paving blocks, and a very special swing."

Smiling, Billy nuzzled Joey's head.

"But my pa always told me, 'Son, there's never a horse that couldn't be rode. Never a cowboy that couldn't be throwed.' So I say to you, if you work hard and keep climbing back up on that bronco, you, too, can have a playground within a mile's walk of every city dweller."

Applause accompanied hundreds of waving handkerchiefs.

"In closing, I encourage you to pin to your walls at home the words my wife has pinned to ours: *Venimus, vidimus, vicimus*!" He raised his fist in the air. "We came. We saw. We conquered!"

All in attendance, from the smallest child to the leader of the brass band, came to their feet. After the fervor died down, the crowd began to gather their belongings and head back from whence they came.

An hour later the playground was devoid of all festival participants. Derry and his brothers and sisters helped gather up the last of the sacks, ropes, potatoes, and balls. A dark cloud rolled in offering welcome relief from the heat.

"We're going to put this stuff in the recreation hall," Derry said. "Then I'll swap the ribbons on the maypole for ropes. After that, I thought I'd take you and the kids over to the soda fountain across the street."

The tired expressions of before vanished. Jumping up and down, the children begged Hunter to agree.

"That sounds good." He glanced at the streamers fluttering from the maypole, then handed Derry a few bills from his pocket. "Why don't y'all go on ahead. I'll do the ribbons and ropes for you."

Derry glanced at him. "You sure you can climb all the way up there?"

Hunter lifted a brow.

Derry grinned. "Never mind. All right. That'd be great, Pa. Thanks. You coming with us, Mother?"

"No, I'll stay here with your pa and meet up with you when he's done."

"Okay, then. Let's go, everybody." Derry headed to the rec center, the little ones crowding about him, all talking at once.

With little effort, Hunter shimmied up the maypole and replaced the ribbons with ropes, loosened a spinning mechanism, and turned the maypole into a giant stride.

Rolling the ribbons into one big ball, Billy looked around. "I really enjoyed myself this week. It sure brings back some memories, doesn't it?"

The breeze took on a cooling edge and the smell of rain. A tendril curling down her back lifted and swirled.

"It sure does." He took the streamers from her arms and wrapped them about the bottom of the pole. "I don't know about you, Mrs. Scott, but I haven't been on a swing in a mighty long time." He held out his hand. "What do you say?"

Eyes brightening, she took his hand. "I've been secretly wanting to all day."

As soon as she settled in, he began to push her, generating a breeze in the late afternoon air. The scent of cut wood clung to the swings. The creak of the rope kept time like a slow-ticking clock.

She gave herself over to the ride, her head back, her feet out, laughter trickling over her shoulder. The wind whipped her blue polka-dot skirt, teasing him with glimpses of petticoat and booted ankles. For the first time in years he thought about the day he'd caught her crawling through that cellar window. He couldn't help but smile at the pleasure she'd brought him then and all the days since.

When he had her going pretty good, he grabbed the ropes and jumped on, his feet straddling her hips.

She squealed, then laughed. He swiveled the seat with the force of his legs, propelling the swing higher. When he'd gone as high as he dared, he stopped driving and simply enjoyed the feel of her and the freedom of flying through the air.

Finally, they slowed. She dragged her feet on the ground. When the swing came to a stop, she slid off and turned to look at him. "That was fun. I haven't ridden double since we were at the Hull House Playground."

A jagged streak of lightning tore across the sky behind her, followed by a distant bark of thunder. Their ride had mussed her hair, leaving a dark blond lock trailing over her shoulder and down her back.

He slid down to the seat and planted his feet on the ground. "Come here."

After a quick glance around, she took his proffered hand, sat on his knee, then straightened the collar on his shirt. "Do you ever regret giving up your Rangering, Hunter?"

The question surprised him and he had to think a moment before answering. "I really don't. I love being sheriff and knowing all the folks in town. Which kids belong to which parents. What their lives at home are like. Who's running with what crowd. As a Ranger, I would have only known that Bobby Wyatt had gone on a drunken spree and shot up the Magruders' prize hog. I wouldn't have known his dad beat his ma, or that he'd lost his brother in a drowning accident two months before his gal left town with Magruder's son. I'm not excusing Bobby, I'm just saying it helps to know that stuff. And I, of course, enjoy being home so much."

"Do you?"

"You know I do. If I'd been a Ranger, I would have missed all those evenings with you and the kids. Watching them grow. Teaching them to ride. Teaching them to shoot. Picking them up when they fell." He sighed. "So many memories we've had and so many still to come. But most of all, we wouldn't have had Derry, and I can't imagine our life without him. He's so, so . . ." He shook his head, unable to put into words the feelings he had for that boy. "I don't regret it at all. Not even for a minute. What about you? And, be honest now, do you ever regret leaving the city behind and becoming a country doctor?"

She tilted her head to the side. "I really thought I would. At the time we left, the knowledge and understanding of the medical field were exploding —still are. And my favorite place to be was right in the middle of it."

He picked up a curl and held it to his nose. Apples, peaches, and summer berries.

She smoothed a wrinkle in her skirt. "Those first few years were hard. The women were much worse than the men. So belittling and judgmental."

"Until you saved the life of the preacher's wife and their unborn baby. You've certainly never had a shortage of patients since then."

"No." She smiled. "I still can't believe she visited every home in the county. I wish I could have been a fly on the wall. I don't know what she said to them to change their minds, but whatever it was, I'm very grateful to her."

He smoothed her hair over her shoulder. "Even if she hadn't done that, the rest of 'em would have come around."

"Maybe. In any event, I love being a country doctor and, like you said, knowing everybody. The slower pace is really nice, too. So, I have no regrets. None at all. And I've come to particularly love Texas."

He lifted his brows. "Well, that was never in question. I mean, what's not to love?"

With a quiet chuckle, she put a hand behind his neck. "Come here, cowboy, and give your lady doctor a kiss."

He didn't have to be asked twice. Scooping up her legs, he draped her over both of his and slid her closer. She hooked her arms around his neck. He tightened his around her waist. Sweet Mackinaw, but he loved this woman.

A droplet of rain fell on his shirt, penetrating the fabric.

He ignored it and ran a hand down her hip to the bend in her knees, then drew her close. She made a tiny sound of pleasure in the back of her throat. Her fingers drove into the hair at his nape, knocking his hat askew.

Another raindrop. And another.

She rocked back, straightening her legs. "It's starting to—"

"I know. I don't care." He captured her lips again.

A flash of light, immediately followed by a shattering clap.

She pushed away and jumped to her feet. The skies opened up. Plucking his Stetson from his head, he jammed it onto hers, grabbed her hand, and they ran toward the field house.

"The ribbons!" she shouted.

"Leave them!"

They continued to run, his feet splattering water with each footfall. When they reached the back steps, they were soaked, laughing, and out of breath.

Tipping her head back, he bracketed her face. "Death and the deuce, but I love you, Billy girl."

He kissed her again. She pressed herself against him. Neither noticed the rain, only the love that comes once in a lifetime and lasts forevermore.

CHILDREN OF WEST SIDE CHICAGO[44]

"The challenges of tenement living, the filth in the
West Side's streets, the children who played there,
the sweatshops, and the little tot who was chained up,
sadly, were true accountings. The names
were changed, of course."

AUTHOR'S NOTE

As with all my novels, I try really hard to be as accurate as I can with the historical facts, but sometimes I have to bend them a little in order to make my story work. There were two major places where I deviated from how Chicago's first playground was established. First, Billy and Hunter are fictional. So all the things they did to make the playground come about were really done by Jane Addams and the volunteers at Hull House.

Second, there was never a murder of any kind on Hull House Playground (or any other playground that I could find). However, there were records of "delinquents" taking over playgrounds in general—nothing about Hull House's specifically. Miss Weibel's murder was loosely based on another murder done by juveniles in Chicago before there was a juvenile court system. Three boys were sentenced to death, two others to life in prison. None were pardoned.

The conditions of Chicago's jail were, I'm sorry to say, historically accurate and representative of jails all throughout our country during that time. The stories I read while researching this were appalling. And I'll just leave it at that.

The major difference between our public playgrounds today and the ones at the turn of the century is that theirs were all supervised. Hull House's playground was supervised from the day it opened. I fudged on that in order to set up the conflict with Kruse. Those kinds of conflicts did sweep the beginning of the playground movement, though, and then spurred organizers to make supervision the norm rather than the exception.

Hull House Playground was supervised by a "paternal and deeply interested" policeman so the boys would have a "big brother" and a man to guide and imitate. Experienced women kindergarten teachers provided "sentimentalism." (Ha.) The philosophy behind the supervision was not only to cut down on crime and dissention, but to break down racial, religious, and class prejudices. An important part of the female supervisor's role was to teach American games and customs—thus Americanizing the immigrant children.

The land for Hull House Playground was donated by a man named William Kent. But it was in 1894. I changed it to 1893 so I could include the World's Fair.

Kent found out about the deplorable conditions of the buildings on his lots through an editorial written by Florence Kelley—a longtime and influential resident of Hull House. She, however, knew whose property it was and mentioned him by name in the article. He immediately contacted her and went out to see it for himself.

The upper level of one of the tenements on the property was, in fact, operating as a brothel (unbeknownst to him). What I couldn't discover was how the playground was funded. Jane Addams had a collection of benevolent contacts who gave toward her causes. I can only assume she called upon them. I have no idea if the Chicago Women's Club donated anything, but it's certainly feasible. I included the club as a way to show that Billy had to work for the funds (as I'm sure Miss Addams did). I also don't know who graded the land, built the equipment, etc. So, I let that fall on Hunter and the boys.

I reconstructed the Opening Day of Hull House Playground—Chicago's first playground ever— as close as I could to the way it really happened. There really were boys who scaled the fence and others who shimmied under it. The races, the maypole dance, the five-man brass band, the military drill, the cheating at tug-of-war, the flower prizes (and the importance the children placed on them), the retired sailor, and even the rain were all just as they happened back in the day. And, believe it or not, once the playground held regular hours, the mothers would roll their baby carriages to it and leave the babies there until "feeding time."

The diagram of the playground was drawn by my daughter, Tennessee Gist, who is a designer. I know the dimensions are correct, but we had to hazard a guess as to where the equipment was. She placed everything based on photographs and interpretation. In some cases, though, I had her move things around to fit the way I'd written the book. For instance, I'm not sure if the Log Mountain was permanent or if it was simply a structure the kids build one day for fun with the pavers. I'm also fairly certain the sandbox wasn't underneath the awning. But I wanted the little ones to be protected from the sun, so I made her put it there. What can I say?

As for Joey, there really was an abandoned baby found at the World's Fair by a Columbian Guard. But it was in the northeast corner of the Manufactures Building inside a French perfumer's exhibit. The guard called together the "scrub-women" working nearby and after a "whispered conversation" they gave the child to a woman who worked with them and whose infant had just passed away. All the guards in the building raised a purse of several dollars on the spot and gave it to the new mother. The baby was a little girl and there was "nothing to lead to identification."

When I read about this, I was so swept up that I was determined to include it somehow. Never did I realize what a big part the child would play in my novel! I changed it to a little boy. I can't remember why, but I know I had a very good reason. (I'm super forgetful. My children used to go to the bus stop and say, "We have a really forgetful tooth fairy." Then all the other moms would look at me. So embarrassing!)

Before we go any further, let me say to the Chicagoans: the Marshall Field's Billy went to was brand-new in 1893. It was an annex building, not the one that is now Macy's. It didn't have the clock nor the beautiful mosaic ceiling. I'm not even sure it had ready-made clothing. But I needed it to, so I decided to use my creative license and stock some shelves. The greeter, the cash boys, the young attendants, the plethora of goods were all accurate—although I don't know what floor everything was displayed on.

The cable car route Hunter and Billy took to Hull House started out accurately, but in real life they would have had to switch back and forth between it and horsecar lines. Getting them on and off at the right stops became too cumbersome to handle within the prose, so I just stuck them on a cable car and had it go wherever I wanted it to. So, for the cable car aficionados out there—forgive me?

As for the Woman's Congress, it really did take place in conjunction with the fair and that huge building really did fill to capacity. Hordes of women were turned away. I depicted that first scene as accurately as possible. There was even a speaker who had to sneak in through the cellar, though I have no idea if she went feetfirst. I do know she didn't run into any guards. The

Memorial Art Palace is today's Art Institute. Even though it is north of Jackson Park, it was still considered part of the fair. If you ever find yourself in Chicago, it still stands, and I got such a thrill when I walked where those women had walked. (They wouldn't let me in the cellar, however.)

Throughout the novel, Billy and Hunter face and discuss hot topics of their era—a woman's place in society, the rights of children, the rights of the underprivileged, the drinking age, working hours, housing conditions, immigrant workers, prejudices, juvenile delinquency, etc. I worked extremely hard to keep my own personal views out of it and depict only what society believed at that time. So any episodes, speeches, presentations, or arguments among the characters were well researched and presented from an 1893 viewpoint (as best I could).

The challenges of tenement living, the filth in the West Side's streets, the children who played there, the sweatshops, and the little tot who was chained up, sadly, were true accounts. The names were changed, of course.

Now let's jump to the fair. I had some great scenes that involved Hunter, Billy, and the fair, but my word count was becoming cumbersome, so we had to trim those out. (So sad.) There was this one scene where a ticket taker won't let Billy into the fair. He says she can work off her entrance if she'd like. But I never saw any indication that this was actually done. I only did that as a shout-out to my video adventure *A Romp at the 1893 Chicago World's Fair: The Invitation.*

It's an interactive video starring Cullen and Della (from *It Happened at the Fair*) and there's a scene about working off your entrance fee by manning the ticket counter. If you haven't seen the video, it's a fun four-minute adventure (RompThrough1893.com) where you get to decide what happens to the couple. And in one of the scenes, Hunter, Billy, and Derry make an appearance. E-mail me if you think you've found them!

I looked and looked, but could never find any information about where the Columbian Guards stayed. I can't imagine them staying anywhere other than on fair property, but I have no idea where. So, I simply invented some barracks. They are totally a figment of my imagination and are not based on any historical findings.

Numerous boys sold catalogs throughout the fairgrounds, but, again, I could not find any mention of their wages. I made a guess of a penny per catalog, but I truly have no idea.

I confess: I just love the Texas Rangers. Hunter is my second hero to be a Ranger, but I wouldn't be surprised if another one finds his way into some future novel. The threat of dissolving them due to the fading frontier was very much a real one, but it happened closer to 1900 than 1893. In 1901 a new law was passed giving the Rangers a new mission—which was basically to suppress lawlessness and crime throughout the state. Their existence was threatened once again early in the 1930s when Texas's governor handed out commissions to men whose character was questionable. But on their 100th anniversary, things were cleaned up and they were incorporated into the Department of Public Safety. They've been there ever since and are alive and well today.

Those of you who have been my readers for a while might have noticed a cameo appearance by Texas Ranger Lucious Landrum from *Love on the Line*. If you were really observant, you might have remembered that Lucious didn't become a Ranger until 1900. So, by all rights, he shouldn't have been at Hunter's wedding. But what can I say? I couldn't possibly have a gathering of Company A and not include Lucious. So, see? I even bend my own fictitious time lines to suit my stories!

Speaking of bending the facts, I wanted to let you know I fudged on three of the images included in the book. The photo of the "Sitting Room in the Woman's Building" was not of the Bureau of Public Comfort, it was of the New York Room in the Woman's Building. I used it because I couldn't find one of the bureau, and the New York Room was fairly representative of what the Bureau of Public Comfort would have looked like.

I couldn't find any images of any upstairs bedrooms in Hull House during the 1890s. So, the "Upstairs Bedroom" photograph was from a different house, but was true to the times and would give the flavor of what those rooms might have looked like.

The final photograph I cheated on was in the Epilogue. I couldn't find an actual image of the first annual convention of the Playground Association of America, so I used one that was representative of what Ogden Park might have looked like at that time. All other photos are authentic and exactly as described.

In some areas of the book—particularly during the court trial—you might have noticed Billy being addressed as "Miss Doctor Tate" instead of simply "Dr. Tate." Well, that was because I found references to women doctors of the time and that's how the men addressed them. Those boys just couldn't bring themselves to out-and-out call a woman "Dr. So-and-So" the way they did the men. Made me chuckle.

Last, I wanted to let you know that Hull House was just up the street from the home where the Great Chicago Fire of '71 started. But the fire moved north and east, just missing Hull House. The mansion had been built in 1856 by Charles Hull and still stands today. Jane Addams moved into it in 1889 for the sole purpose of establishing a settlement for the underprivileged.

As it happens, I went to tour Hull House Museum while I was doing my research and found out that it was planning to do an exhibit about the Hull House Playground the same month that *Fair Play* was to be released. How serendipitous is that! So, if you are in the Chicago area, be sure to stop by and walk not only where Jane Addams walked, but where our fictitious Billy and Hunter walked. ☺

As always, thanks for coming along on this ride with me. It's been a joy!

Deeanne Gist ♥

ILLUSTRATION NOTES
AND CREDITS

1. Hubert Howe Bancroft, *The Book of the Fair* (Chicago: The Bancroft Co., 1893), 922.
2. Moses P. Handy, *The Official Directory of the World's Columbian Exposition* (Chicago: W. B. Conkey, 1893), opp. 182.
3. *Pictorial Chicago and Illustrated World's Columbian Exposition* (Chicago: Rand, McNally & Co., 1893), 21.
4. *A Week at the Fair* (Chicago: Rand, McNally & Co., 1893), 178.
5. Bancroft, 294.
6. *The Photographic World's Fair and Midway Plaisance* (Chicago: Monarch Book Co., 1894), 208.
7. Bancroft, 269.
8. *Shepp's World's Fair Photographed* (Chicago: Globe Bible Publishing Co., 1893), 445.
9. *Week*, 103.
10. Courtesy of the Chicago Transit Authority.
11. JAMC_0000_0193_0295, Jane Addams Hull-House Photographic Collection, University of Illinois at Chicago Library, Special Collections.
12. JAMC_0000_0003_2778, Jane Addams Hull-

House Photographic Collection, University of
Illinois at Chicago Library, Special
Collections.

13. JAMC_0000_0223_0376, Jane Addams Hull-
House Photographic Collection, University of
Illinois at Chicago Library, Special
Collections.

14. JAMC_0000_0221_0370, Jane Addams Hull-
House Photographic Collection, University of
Illinois at Chicago Library, Special
Collections.

15. JAMC_0000_0000_1054b, Jane Addams
Hull-House Photographic Collection,
University of Illinois at Chicago Library,
Special Collections.

16. JAMC_0000_0198_0316, Jane Addams Hull-
House Photographic Collection, University of
Illinois at Chicago Library, Special
Collections.

17. Bancroft, 283.

18. *Shepp's*, 241.

19. Library of Congress, Prints & Photographs
Division, National Child Labor Committee
Collection, LC-DIG-nclc-04305.

20. JAMC_0000_0132_2603, Jane Addams Hull-
House Photographic Collection, University of
Illinois at Chicago Library, Special
Collections.

21. *Photographic*, 191.

22. JAMC_0000_0219_0364, Jane Addams Hull-

House Photographic Collection, University of Illinois at Chicago Library, Special Collections.

23. Handy, opp. 174.
24. Library of Congress, Prints & Photographs Division, Detroit Publishing Company Collection, LC-D4-19539.
25. JAMC_0000_0000_1506, Jane Addams Hull-House Photographic Collection, University of Illinois at Chicago Library, Special Collections.
26. *Week*, 186.
27. JAMC_0000_0296_0437, Jane Addams Hull-House Photographic Collection, University of Illinois at Chicago Library, Special Collections.
28. *The Boy Mechanic, Book 2* (Chicago: Popular Mechanics Co., 1915), 162.
29. *Week*, 81.
30. JAMC_0000_0192_0286, Jane Addams Hull-House Photographic Collection, University of Illinois at Chicago Library, Special Collections.
31. Bancroft, 271.
32. JAMC_0000_0296_0436, Jane Addams Hull-House Photographic Collection, University of Illinois at Chicago Library, Special Collections.
33. JAMC_0000_0193_0293, Jane Addams Hull-House Photographic Collection, University of

Illinois at Chicago Library, Special Collections.
34. JAMC_0000_0003_0020, Jane Addams Hull-House Photographic Collection, University of Illinois at Chicago Library, Special Collections.
35. JAMC_0000_0192_1001, Jane Addams Hull-House Photographic Collection, University of Illinois at Chicago Library, Special Collections.
36. JAMC_0000_0198_3117, Jane Addams Hull-House Photographic Collection, University of Illinois at Chicago Library, Special Collections.
37. J. Chapuis, "French Walking Costume," *Harper's Bazaar*, November 16, 1895, vol. 28, no. 46, 929.
38. Courtesy of Tennessee Gist, Designer. This is an interpretation based on the dimensions recorded, equipment mentioned in resources, and equipment portrayed in photographs. Adjustments have also been made to better match the prose in *Fair Play*. (For instance, the sandbox was, most likely, not underneath the awning. But the author wanted it there, so the designer put it there.)
39. Handy, opp. 42.
40. JAMC_0000_0158_0202, Jane Addams Hull-House Photographic Collection, University of Illinois at Chicago Library, Special Collections.

41. JAMC_0000_0159_0212, Jane Addams Hull-House Photographic Collection, University of Illinois at Chicago Library, Special Collections.
42. Bancroft, 552.
43. Library of Congress, Prints & Photographs Division, Detroit Publishing Company Collection, LC-D4-33401.
44. JAMC_0000_0197_3111, Jane Addams Hull-House Photographic Collection, University of Illinois at Chicago Library, Special Collections.

READING GROUP GUIDE

INTRODUCTION

The only "mannish" thing about Dr. Billy Jack Tate is her name. A female doctor in the 1890s, Billy graduated at the top of her class and won't let anything—or anyone—stand in her way. When Billy lands a job as a doctor at the 1893 Chicago World's Fair, she is already a successful surgeon and finds herself one step closer to her own medical practice. But after her chance (and revealing) meeting with the rugged and very traditional Texas Ranger Hunter Scott, a reluctant romance blossoms, and Billy is forced to consider a future without medicine—or without Hunter.

When Hunter discovers an abandoned infant in the White City exhibit, his and Billy's search to find its parents leads them down a path of discovery, hope, and loss as they help erect a playground for underprivileged children on the West Side of Chicago. As Billy and Hunter pursue their common goal, their passion and respect for each other grow, and the two must decide whether love is more important than having it all.

DISCUSSION QUESTIONS

1. Dr. Billy Jack Tate, a female doctor in the 1890s, firmly believes women are just as capable as (if not more than) men. What events or circumstances may have shaped her beliefs? What kind of challenges would a woman with these attitudes face in the late 1800s?

2. One of Billy's strategies for being successful in a male-dominated profession is to make men forget she's a woman. Is this a good long-term strategy? Why or why not?

3. What are your first impressions of Hunter Scott?

4. Describe Billy and Hunter's relationship at the beginning of *Fair Play*. How does discovering and spending time with Joey change the dynamic between them?

5. Would you describe Billy as a feminist? Why or why not?

6. How does Hunter perpetuate female stereotypes? What about male stereotypes?

7. In *Fair Play*, Billy often defies gender stereotypes and expectations for her generation. Can you think of any examples in which Hunter does not meet similar cultural expectations of how a man should act?

8. Do you think Billy was fair in her terms for her marriage to Hunter? Do you think her terms would be perceived differently if she were the man in the relationship?

9. Hunter and Billy's mutual interest in creating a safe space for children to play on the West Side nurtured their burgeoning romance. Why do you think both were willing to sacrifice their jobs to make this happen?

10. Ownership is a significant theme in *Fair Play*. What are some examples of characters who believed they owned something or someone? How do those examples differ, and why were they important to the characters' development?

11. Billy's encounter with Kruse and his friends reminded her of how physically weak she was compared to some men. What do you think ultimately made her decide not to report them to the police? How do you think this changed her views on women's capabilities compared to men's?

12. In *Fair Play*, we are introduced to people of many nationalities, professions, income levels, and circumstances. Why was diversity so important in the plot? How was it a driving force behind Billy and Hunter's relationship?

13. Billy and Hunter's romance demonstrated that compromise is an essential element of a successful, loving relationship. Do you think their compromises for each other in the end were balanced? Why or why not?